To my Markie and to my girls. I adore you.
Dream big. Love big.
To the voice in my head, screw you. I did it anyway.

"It isn't what we say or think that defines us, but what we do."—*Sense & Sensibility*, Jane Austen.

Rules in Love

Edited by (https://www.theevansediting.com/)

Copyeditor by (https://jennlockwoodediting.com/)

Proofread by Roxana Coumans (booksfreelance@gmail.com/)

Cover design and formatting by Bindi Kennedy

Couple illustration by Kristina (@irdeinfierno)

Published by Bindi K Publishing.

This novel's story and characters are wholly fictitious creations of my imagination. Details of the cities mentioned are not geographically accurate. Certain long-standing institutions, public offices & agencies, celebrities, works of literature, film, T.V. & songs are mentioned.

Author's Note
In the interests of a good tale, the locations in, and geographical
features of Byron Bay, London, New York City and State, have
been fictionalised.

The Romantic ~~Rules~~ Ideologies of
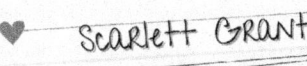
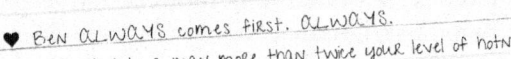 Scarlett Grant ♥

1. ♥ Ben ALWAYS comes first. ALWAYS.
2. ♥ NEVER date a man more than twice your level of hotness.
3. ♥ DO NOT date men you work with. It's just asking for trouble.
4. ♥ DO NOT discuss male 'friends' in front of Ben, and ABSOLUTELY N
'friends' are to sleep over. This is made easier by #7.
5. ♥ Sweet words and empty promises are just that. Empty.
6. ♥ Never, no matter how desperate you become, sleep with Brett.
7. ♥ NEVER settle. Like Lizzie Bennett, "Only the deepest of love will
induce me into matrimony." Morally, the same goes for sex, but that's flexible.
8. ♥ NEVER, no matter how hot or sweet or fuckable, or how intensely he
may stare at me across a room as I play piano, will I become any man
fool. Jane Austen quote for reference: "I may have lost my heart,
but not my self-control."
9. ♥ Purposely left blank, allowing me to make rash decisions
justifiable on the spot.
10. ♥ ALWAYS REMEMBER, these are ideals, not rules. Rules are
made to be broken. Ideals are made to make you a better person.

PS... Note to self..... ~~NEVER LET TEDDY SEE THIS~~

PPS... TOO LATE BIATCH HAHAHAHA

Rules in love

1

Finn

A T SEVENTEEN, THE HANDS of fate redesigned my world, delivering lessons I would never forget, and wounds that may never heal.

I became a dad. I lost my parents and my girlfriend, and some days, when the hole was so deep and dark that I could see no light at the end, I feared my mind too. I became a dad. I lost my parents and my girlfriend, and some days, when the hole was so deep and dark that I could see no light at the end, I feared my mind too.

One thing saved me.

My daughter.

At twenty-four, life changed again. Though, thankfully, it was by choice. My seven-year-old daughter, Iris; my sister, Evie; my Aunt Jocelyn, and I had recently left our home in Australia and taken a twenty-two-hour flight to New York City to begin a fresh life.

That was how I found myself in Manhattan, on Sixth Avenue, walking into the intimidating office of Wise, Bernstein, and Wright. It was my first day on the job as a junior architect. It had been a shit morning, and I felt like I was about to chuck.

Iris had given me hell because I couldn't braid her hair like a twenty-two-year-old influencer named Tatiana. Then, I almost killed myself by turning onto the wrong side of the road when leaving the daycare. Apologies had been issued to the 6,785 people I bumped into on the sidewalk, and I only made it to my office with one minute and thirty-nine seconds to spare. I was a fucking mess. And not just today. There were too many moving pieces in my life recently, and I was not a fan.

My dislike—almost distrust—of change could not be underestimated. I was a routine man, and over the last few years, that routine had been set in concrete. My life consisted of monotonous days alone in Sydney, at university, my first job, and road trips to and from my family's farm in Byron Bay. When at home, my days were filled with doing what I could to ensure my family's happiness, regular dad stuff, and, if I could swing it, a bit of time on the waves with my best mate, Nate.

Suddenly, I was waiting for an elevator, sweating in a suit that felt like a straitjacket, while being sneezed and coughed on by some weird lady who smelled like pizza.

"You look nervous. Let me guess, job interview or first day?" My apprehension must have stuck out like a sore thumb for her to guess on the first go.

"First day. It's that obvious, huh?" Pizza Lady and I entered the elevator. She tried to console me with a tale of her sister and how she was fired five minutes into her last job. For whatever reason, that failed, and the stupid breathing techniques Evie had taught me after a meltdown on the flight from Sydney came to mind.

"Close your mouth. Inhale through your nose for seven counts. Hold your breath for a count of four. Exhale through your mouth, making a whoosh sound for eight."

I only realized I was reciting it aloud when the guy next to me, who was dressed like a member of The Village People, elbowed me in the ribs. "Hey, you got that all wrong, buddy. It's in for eight, hold for eight, out for four."

"You're an idiot! What, are you trying to get him to pass out? It's in for eight, hold for four, out for seven," inserted Pizza Lady.

"You're both idiots," added a hot blonde with a lovely set of, uh...teeth. "It's definitely hold for seven and out for eight." As things got heated, it struck me that New Yorkers were weird. They went out of their way to be nice and help you while speaking to you in the rudest possible way.

When we reached my floor, the elevator was in an uproar with several people Googling simultaneously to confirm that theirs was the correct method.

"Hey, good luck on your first day, buddy," the construction guy yelled as the doors closed behind me.

"You got this," I mumbled, slapping my thigh as I entered my new nine-to-five home. High-end, swanky, and architecturally stunning—pick a descriptor, and this place would be it. High ceilings, exposed brick, floor-to-ceiling windows, and finishes so crisp that I didn't want to touch a damn thing. With each hollow footstep on shiny marble, a twinge of homesickness hit. I missed the feel of sand between my toes and dirt under my nails. I was desperate for something familiar. I told myself, '*You're doing this for them. To give us a better life. The life you promised Shelby.*' I again practiced the breathing exercises, and whether it was my thought, my breathing, or the warm smile on the Martha Stewart look-alike approaching me, I finally calmed.

"Finn Austen, I presume," she chuckled. "I'm Jan from HR. We've spoken on the phone a few times, but it's nice to see you in person. Let me take you through to the partners."

"Thanks, HR Jan. I mean, Jan. Sorry. I'm a touch nervous."

"I expect you are. It's a big step you've taken, not just changing jobs but continents too. I promise you'll be safe, though. We don't bite."

Jan led me to the first of the partners' offices belonging to the youngest of the trio, Jason Wright. "It's great to have you here rather than on a video call, Finn. By God, you are a giant of a man, aren't you? All the singles in the office will be thrilled to meet you."

"Not just the singles," Jan quipped as she twisted her pearls around her finger.

A flush of heat tickled my cheeks. Even though it struck me as an odd joke for someone in her role to make, her humour was appreciated, and I huffed out a much-needed chuckle. As the procession of new names and faces rolled on, not everyone was as engaging.

"Fill these in...please," sighed a beautiful but icy chick named Victoria as she handed me a stack of paperwork, then eyeballed and tutted me as I filled them out. Victoria's role was left a mystery, but the way she protectively hovered over Jason, I guessed she was either his biggest fan, bodyguard, or merely a heavily invested assistant. Next, I was given a business rundown with the other partners, Joseph Bernstein and Herman Wright, the latter suffering the severest case of old-people stank I'd ever come across. Once that was completed, the circus hit the road, and Jan led me on a grand tour. First up was the thrilling copy, board, and conference rooms, then the emergency exits. Jan talked non-stop while I hyper-fixated on smoothing out my accent in reply, aiming more for Sam Worthington, less like Crocodile Dundee.

"Our offices here may be a little bigger and bolder than you're used to in Sydney. And a little more extravagant too."

"It's certainly bigger, but Sydney is bloody—uh...I mean, very extravagant too. We have some of the priciest real estate in the world."

"Well, you should feel at home here in New York, then. I thought I would have to sell a kidney to afford my first apartment." With a silent chuckle, I followed my guide into the kitchen. "This is the single most important item in the office." Jan's hand slapped the coffee maker. "Can I get you one?"

"Caffeine probably won't help the jitters much, but sure, that would be great."

Two cups were poured, and something labeled half and half, which I presumed was milk, was added to the *I heart NYC* mug. "I'm sure you're going to fit in just fine. We have a lovely group of people here. Why don't you tell me about your family? You've moved here altogether, right?"

Too focused on the murkiness I'd been handed and was about to taste, I agreed with a nod and forced a smile.

"Oh, how lovely. You're a close family, then?"

"Super close." I coughed, struggling to swallow what proved to be a terrible coffee. "I don't know what I would do without them. Iris's mum passed away when she was born, and my parents only a year or so before that."

"Good heavens. I'm so sorry, Finn. That's an awful lot of loss for such young shoulders to carry. I hope this big change is the new beginning you deserve."

"So do I, Jan. So do I."

The door at the rear of the kitchen opened, and a gust of New York humidity blew between us. "Oh, that breeze is coming from the garden. I might get Joseph to show you that later. He loves the little tree we have out there. He planted it when we first arrived, and it's his pride and joy."

Jan continued her well-rehearsed newcomer speech as a flash of color caught my eye. I heard the words "essential" and "code" and saw something on a lanyard being waved before my eyes, but honestly, she could have been tap-dancing naked while piggybacking a crocodile, and I wouldn't have noticed. Because my attention had been stolen and my heart besieged by a mop of red curls, a pair of long legs, and a short pink skirt. Wide and fluttering eyes of glimmering green with tiny flecks of hazel I could spot across the room caught mine. Plump, pillowy lips curved ever so slightly into something that was not quite a smile but more than a smirk.

Her breath caught. The rise and fall of her breasts captured my imagination, and I had to hold in the deep-chested groan that was dying to come out.

It was just a moment in time. A shared glance held just that bit too long to be fleeting, but not long enough to be creepy. But with that one glance, that one smirk, I was wiped out. Gone. Done.

That was the very first time I saw Scarlett Grant.

As the bathrooms were pointed out to me, I again caught the mystery girl's gaze and gripped the closest table in a feeble attempt to gather my bearings. But it was useless, and she was no girl. She was all woman, a goddess. One who'd blown my freaking mind and sent blood pumping to an organ not fit to mention in polite conversation.

"Jan... Jan, who is that?" I asked, my voice hoarse, dry like I hadn't just drunk the world's worst coffee.

"That's Scarlett. She's another one of our junior architects. She and Theodore over there joined us from England a year or so ago. They're both your age, you know. Would you like me to introduce you? I'm sure you would have a lot to talk about."

I was about to scream, *YES, DO IT NOW!* But my brain foresaw the danger of a lonely, possibly pent-up young man such as myself meeting such a woman. *Do not talk to her! Do not touch her! YOU WILL BE WEIRD!*

"Hmm. Uh, I'm sure we would, but you know, I might take a rain check. I can make my own introductions once I've settled in. No one else needs to shake my sweaty paws this morning."

"Oh, nonsense. I'm sure they would love to meet you, but you're right. You have all the time in the world to make friends." Jan stopped abruptly and pulled a diagram of the office layout from her pocket. "Okay, that's about it for now. Let's see where they've put you." Clicking her tongue, she studied the sheet of paper, looked up, and then pointed to two empty desks. "Ah, there you are. Your new home away from home."

On the move again, my heart began to race. We were walking right to Scarlett. *This is bad. This is very, very bad. My-ears-are-sweating bad.* I had never had that happen before and hoped to never experience it again. One of the desks was right next to her, the other directly behind her, and thank God, that was the one we stopped at. It was still close. Possibly too close. But I found some consolation in the fact that my back would be facing hers. God help me if we were face to face.

"You have a lovely view from your window," Jan said as she peered down to the neon-light-filled alley and winced. "Well, it's not that lovely, but it is a view. We're so happy to have you, Finn. Just yell out if you need anything." I knew what I needed, alright. But asking to be hooked up with the hot chick in pink probably wasn't what she meant.

With lust and a sense of knowing dread coursing through my body, I took a seat and began to unpack my things.

The urge to keep looking her way, to drop at her feet and beg her to be mine without a word spoken between us, was most inconvenient. I had a plan for success. From the get-go, I was to walk in here focused and determined. The next couple of years would be all work and no play. I would craft my skills and build my expertise, reputation, and wealth. Then, when the time was right, I would pack it all up, take my family back home, and start my own firm in Byron. An instant, heart-swelling attraction was most definitely not on the agenda. Nor were shaking hands and a twitching cock each time I caught a flash of those wild curls.

Deep in my soul, I knew I was fucked.

2

Scarlett

JUST HOW MUCH INFLUENCE should Jane Austen have over a 21st-century woman's love life? It was a question I had pondered frequently for years, but recently, it had rarely left my mind.

Because...

Something of a most alarming nature had happened. I had fallen stupidly, madly, deeply in love with a man I had barely spoken a word to, but to whom my ovaries swore allegiance the first time I saw him—which was yesterday.

To quote my darling Jane from *Love and Friendship*, "The very first moment I beheld him, my heart was irrevocably gone."

My very own heart-beholder was gorgeous, tall, and dashing, which a young man ought to be if he possibly can, but the best thing about him had nothing at all to do with his surfer-boy curls, tall, muscular frame, and a jawline I wanted to cut my tongue on. Though, those points all helped. It was his name. If I were ever so lucky to marry the man of my wet dreams like Emma, Lizzy, or Fanny did, I, myself, would become an Austen. Scarlett Elizabeth Austen.

I'd even started practicing my new signature. Not as soon as I saw him, obviously. That would be weird. I waited a good twelve hours.

Longing for a man I knew nothing about, other than the fact that he was my new co-worker, was not healthy or realistic. Though, in all honesty, reality had very little involvement for a good portion of my life.

Jane did, though. And that was why, years ago, after the first date I'd had since my son was born ended with the words, *"Look, you're hot and all, but I'm not after no baby-mamma drama,"* Jane and her sassy, before-their-time heroines came to my rescue. They, alongside a worrying number of rom-coms and a bottle or two of rosé, helped to create...drumroll...*The Romantic Ideologies of Scarlett Grant.* A set of rules for love that I hoped would steer my future happiness in the right direction. But I decided to refer to them as ideologies, not rules, 'cause I was classy like that.

Abiding by these ideologies was relatively simple. My son and career were my focus, and they became even more so almost two years ago—five or so years after my ideological epiphany. The fact that I was a dateless wonder who made Mother Teresa look like a skank may have helped too.

My best friend and fellow architect, Theodore, and I were approached by a swanky New York architectural firm looking to inject some young blood and international concepts into their designer pool. They had trawled the globe for hot new talent and somehow found us. Becoming their first recruits meant leaving London, warm beer, and our complicated pasts behind to take the big leap across the pond. Whether fate or fortune, it was an almost unheard-of career prospect for two designers with such little experience. But just as Teddy had done years earlier with me, they saw something in us, in our work, and were willing to take a chance. Their faith also delivered my son the opportunity to grow up closer to his dad, a New York native.

Things were going great. Sexless, but great. I was smashing goals, living my best WWJD—What Would Jane Do—life. But then Finn showed up and ruined/sexified everything.

If only he weren't so gorgeous. If you took the most lickable attributes of Sam Heughan, Chris Hemsworth, and the hot model Selena Gomez was obsessed with and was arrested over in that film clip, you have my Finn.

Not that he was mine. But he could be one day. If I ever worked up the nerve to speak to him—and had a complete face, body, and personality overhaul.

Sigh. It really was a conundrum. A sexy, blond, focus-shifting, concentration-diverting, ideology-ruining conundrum.

Two weeks later

"Just one more drink, Scar. After that, I promise to have you home and watching some depressing period piece before you can say Colin Firth is the best Darcy."

"You said that two glasses ago, *Theo*." I earned a scowl for that, which was exactly why I did it. Teddy hated being called Theo. "Your mention of The Firth gets you a pass, but it's Sunday, and I'm fading fast. I need pajamas covering my body in under thirty minutes."

Theodore sighed and rubbed his eye with his index finger. "I find it so depressing that you're in a bar this gorgeous, with these killer views of the city, *and* the greenery, *and* the extravagant chandeliers, *and* the beautiful guys checking you out cause you look like this"—he scanned me up and down and cast a chef's kiss to the air—"and you're pretending all you want sliding over your body when you get home is pajamas."

"I'm not pretending. You know I'm not the type to take some random guy home."

"I wasn't thinking about a random guy. I was thinking of a certain tall, blond beefcake you can't stop drooling over."

"I do not drool over him." *I sniff him. Stare at him. Maybe take an odd sneaky photo. But I do not drool.*

"Please, I can find you anywhere in the building now. You leave a silvery trail like a snail. And I can't blame you. The man is a dish. As much as I love you, you should be here with him, not me."

He made a good point. Just like he always did.

Theodore William Henry Digby III was my best friend, and thanks to his loaded family and their global property portfolio, he was my forgiving and generous landlord. We met as nervous architecture students on our first day at university. He was gorgeous, reminding me of a young Hugh Grant, with soft, fluffy hair that constantly flopped into his big, brown, puppy-dog eyes, and a smile that melted my heart. I was instantly attracted to him, which, with my history, guaranteed he was either taken, gay, or a complete asshole. It turned out he was gay, but our instant, mutual obsession blossomed into one of history's greatest friendships.

I didn't know where I would be without that man or my daily dose of vitamin D—his appallingly inappropriate name for our morning kiss. Showering me with kind words of reassurance and ego boosts was his favorite thing—or was when he wasn't trying to prove a point like a bitch.

We were at M.I.X., our most beloved bar in The Village. Despite wanting to leave thirty minutes early, I'd had an okay night till that point. But Teddy spinning facts about hot Australian colleagues, I maybe had fluid-control issues around, brought it all too a screaming halt.

"There's a chance he knows. I'm pretty sure he knows. Do you think he knows?"

"He knows, I know, even the guy in the office next door with no idea who you are knows. We all know."

"Is it really that obvious?"

"Yes, Scar. Yes. It is that obvious. And all I can say is, thank God you don't have a penis. Your constant, massive erection would be very off-putting." Unable to stop my giggles, I gave Teddy a lazy nudge in the arm then laid my head on his shoulder. He kissed my mess of curls, then handed over an ungodly amount of cash for his drink. "Why don't you just go up to him, introduce yourself, and then climb onto his lap."

"As tempting as that sounds, Ideology Three, Teddy. Number three forbids it."

Promised last beverage in hand, we returned to what had become our regular table. Thanks to Teddy's ongoing flirtation with the staff, we'd secured a prime location. It sat just a few paces from the bar in a quiet-ish little nook overlooking the balcony. It was an ideal spot, letting us feel like part of the action without engaging with anyone, people-watch with ease, *and* still hear each other bitch about what we saw. It also sat directly beneath a cooling vent, which was greatly appreciated by our still-acclimating English constitutions.

With all the vigor of damp linguine, I collapsed into my chair and buried my face in my hands. I could see the pity on Teddy's face through my fingers and watched as he took a deliberate sip of his margarita, then cupped his hands over mine. "You and your bloody rules. They will have you dying a revirginized spinster like your bloody friend Jane. You do know that, don't you?"

"Most likely, yes," I huffed, "but I'm serious about this. I am. *Don't date men from work* is an ideology for a good reason. Young women are held to a different standard than men. I would be judged way harsher for dating a co-worker than you or anyone else would."

"I don't know, Scar. I think it's an easy excuse to hide from the world, which needs to cease immediately. It's time to get back out there, Sweet Cheeks."

Ouch. That hit a little close to the bone, so I ignored it, stole Teddy's drink, and focused on the tequila, rum, and chill E. D.M. infusing into my blood. With each sip, I sighed, breathed in the saffron, garlic, and paprika wafting from the kitchen, and resigned myself to the fact that we weren't leaving anytime soon. Teddy seemed to lose interest in my love life, instead becoming obsessed with the hair of the lady sitting beside us. But chasing the day's lingering warmth, she and her beehive moved to an outdoor table, and his attention returned to me.

"Lonely death jokes aside, Scarlett. You deserve to be happy, and Finn McHunk seems like a nice, massive guy...which, ipso facto, you could confirm if you actually spoke to him."

"Christ on a bike! I have spoken to him!" I hadn't. But I still protested and sprayed Teddy's face in the process.

"Asking him where the loo is, then running away faster than Usain Bolt is hardly talking. I've shared more substantive conversations with that weird cat lady that lives next door."

"Damn it, Digby! I've told you a hundred times. Mrs. Horowitz is adorable."

"And...?"

"Aaand..." I shrugged, looking out the window for beehive lady. "I will converse with Finn at some point. But I must build up my nerve...and vocabulary."

"Pfft. Please."

My eyes snapped back to the warranted disbeliever. "Don't scoff at me, Teddy. Any thought that's ever existed within my scatterbrain dies the minute I look at him. I have no idea what to say or do. It's horrible." I finished my drink, pictured Finn opening his blinds, and continued complaining without waiting for a reply. "He's just so...so...intimidatingly gorgeous and totally out of my league. Why would he be interested in someone like me?" **Ideology #2: NEVER date a man more than twice your level of hotness. It's inequitable, unsustainable, and undeniably doomed.**

"Someone like you?" Teddy choked, "Excuse me, Adele, I adore you. You're fucking gorgeous, utterly brilliant, and the sweetest, strongest person I have ever met. You are totally in his league. If anything, Finn should be intimidated by you. I have said it before, and I will say it again: Scarlett Grant, if I had the slightest interest in people with breasts, I'd be all over you like a rash."

I bit my lip and giggled, "I thought you liked breasts. What about your boy Quincy?"

Teddy tutted, clumsily dipped his fingers into the empty glass, and reclaimed the lime wedge. "Ha ha, very funny. You know I'm a sucker for a bear. And as fun as it is to talk about hairy men and their moobs, this is about you." He sucked the lime with a smirk bordering on evil, then swept my hand into his and kissed it ever so softly. "The fact that my lips are the only ones kissing you regularly is a crime to humanity. One I will never understand."

There it is! That was the hit I was looking for. I knew Teddy and his loving barbs would soothe my soul. Biased affection and brutally honest support had been a constant in our friendship from the start.

Within weeks of our meeting, life threw me a massive curve-ball. I discovered I was pregnant, and the father was a cute, six-foot-two, greasy-haired brunette I barely knew named Brett. Hot, bad, and soon to be leaving the country, Brett was every-thing the shy, eighteen-year-old me craved. He'd recently grad-uated from our university, Cambridge, and was helping as a tour guide during orientation week. The private tour Bret-ty-boy gave me later that night was a tad more personal than the brochures specified and mainly centered around the backseat of his Mini Cooper.

My unexpected news didn't sit well with my new roomie, Alisha, or her parents, who owned the off-campus house we shared. Unimpressed by the influence I may have had on their darling daughter, and my vomiting on their Persian rug three mornings in a row, they politely asked me to leave. With no family to turn to, Teddy took me into his home and made it ours. His generosity, heartfelt commitment, and mercy were overwhelming and only increased my already unhealthy adora-tion and dependency.

As for Brett, he had already returned to the States by this point. I had no idea where he lived or how to contact him. But aided by the sympathetic and rule-breaking women of the university well-being services, I tracked him down in New York. He wasn't such a bad guy after all, and he supported me in what felt like an impossible decision—to keep or not to keep the baby.

Benjamin Grant was born seven and a bit months later, and Brett and his family became as involved as they could be in our odd transatlantic scenario, even coming to visit him several times. But as grateful as I was to have Brett be a part of Ben-jamin's life, it couldn't compare to my gratitude for Teddy. He could be an interfering sass-pot, but not a single shred of my success or good fortune would have been possible without him. He saved me from me, and for that, the family we created, my home, and the daily vitamin D, I would be forever indebted.

Way too much natural light and semi-controlled chaos greeted me at the office the next morning. I still felt unworthy of the place after a year and a half. It was everything I was not. So expensive, fancy, and cultured. And no matter the state of the New York air, trash day or not, it always smelled like lilies or roses and was so clean you could eat off the floors.

The first and only other firm I had worked for was in England, and it was more my pace. But it was also filled to the brim with balding, middle-aged men in tweed and brown corduroy, who constantly regurgitated age-old sex-etary and mother-in-law jokes. Their notion of finery was, coincidentally, their and the building's scent—boiled eggs and kippers. Here in my New York office, it was Prada, Chanel, Jimmy Choo, or nothing. Lunch was a bike-courier-delivered Bento box, or poke bowl, and maybe a gourmet sandwich if you dared bread.

Despite the lack of complex carbohydrates, my newish firm was generally a place of calm. Just not today.

"What the hell's going on?" I asked Jan, our HR rep, who happened to be scooting past me as I entered the kitchen.

"I'll tell you what's going on," inserted the grouchy voice of Arthur, our surly, long-haired IT guy. "While you architect and HR ladies slept, our computer system up and crashed. Everything's dead. No doubt because someone downloaded virus-ridden porn again."

"Don't look at me," Jan said as she continued on her way, blushing.

In a modern-day architecture firm, an outage like that spelled disaster. With two pitches for high-profile clients scheduled for that day and three later in the week, it was all hands on deck. While I knew my design program inside out, it was one of the few computer literacy claims I could make. Luckily, another was how to run a backup.

I rushed to my desk, dropped my laptop amongst the mess of papers and stolen pens, and checked. "Thank fuck." All my work was safe, and because it wasn't connected to our office server, everything was accessible. Daring to approach Arthur again, I offered my useless services. "Ready and willing to pitch in, Arthur. What do you need?"

His expression read: *I need you to go away*. His mouth said, "Can you access anything remotely finished on that prehistoric brick of a laptop you refuse to upgrade?"

"Yes. I think so, anyway. My Hudson River House pitch is pretty much done and backed up on the brick...I mean laptop."

"Congratulations. You're brilliant," he quipped with a distinct pitch of sarcasm. He began to speak again, then paused and smiled menacingly. "The Hudson River project, hey. Fancy that." Leaning back in his chair, he cracked his knuckles and took the evilness up a notch. "As of this moment, only you and one other brainiac can retrieve anything. Get a presentation together amidst this shitshow, and you'll be the hero of the day and running the place in a week." He nodded in the direction of my desk and whistled in a way not dissimilar to a farmer directing a sheepdog.

Slinking away, I was suddenly overcome with the scent of mothballs. *Here we go.* "Good morning, Mr. Wise," I chimed before I'd even seen his face. Herman Wise was our senior partner in both age and rank. He was also a sexist creep, who thankfully came with a built-in stench that alerted you to his presence. It was a lifesaver, often giving you enough time to hide or at least cover your boobs. Wise was the only thing I hated about this firm.

"Miss Scarlett. I couldn't help but overhear. Arthur is right. Get your work ready ASAP, and I'll do my best to get the client in today." He began to shuffle away but stopped. "By the way, in case you were unaware, ASAP means as soon as possible. And if you need any help with the technical side of things, have one of the men help you."

Hmmm. His man-splaining and the office-wide pandemonium were unnerving, but this was my chance. I blocked it all out, sat slowly, breathed deeply, and began. Everything on those plans, every line, measurement, and angle was triple-checked. When comfortable in my readiness, I alerted the team. "I'm ready."

I sighed in relief, reclined in my chair, and took a gulp of my disappointingly cold latte, half of which dribbled onto my dress as the world slowed to a halt.

Why did time—and the very significance of the universe—cease to matter? Because I saw him. Finn Austen glided through the room, cutting through the chaos like Moses parting the sea. Smiling gorgeously while greeting those of inferior beauty around him, he sat at his desk, leaned forward, and adjusted his plantation blinds, flooding his workstation with light. "So beautiful," I sighed as sunshine bounced off the enviable dirty-blond curls God endowed him with. The ones I wanted to glide my fingers through, discovering each ringlet and naming them as you do with stars. The sexy bastard then rubbed his neck and twisted his head from side to side. I almost began to drool.

Dammit, Teddy was right.

My unblinking eyes watched him set to work, and I quickly became lost in the hypnotic movement of muscle beneath cotton. As I stared at him like a hungry kid would at a chocolate cake, he looked my way. His perfectly kissable lips rose on one corner, and he nodded, then mouthed, "Hi."

To me. Me. The cake-kid.

Only unquestionable humiliation would come if I continued to face him, so I spun away and came nose to chest with a smug, headshaking Teddy.

"That...was embarrassing." He plopped his ass on my desk and elbowed my ribs. "So, you know how there's only two of you super-geniuses that have access to their work, and everyone is shitting themselves?"

"Yup. I'm aware."

"Well, last night, you said you wanted to talk to Finn, and now the whole office is distracted. It's fate, Scar. Go. Now. Talk. Ooh! Or even better, snog him." He then gave me a peck on the lips, grabbed the arms of my chair, and tried to spin me around to face Finn.

Fear took hold. "I'm not leaving, and you can't make me." I grabbed the edge of my desk with one hand and clung to it for dear life. The other became a weapon, slapping the shit out of Teddy as he tried to pry me away from safety. After a few moments of returning fire, Teddy gave up, calling me freakishly strong, then maturely landed one last whack on my arm.

Much to my horror, he walked straight toward Finn, smirking at me over his shoulder every few steps, before pulling up a seat beside him and chatting away.

With my stomach dropping like a stone, I watched my worst nightmare unfold in the reflection of a mirrored photo frame—one that I may or may not have positioned in such a way as to allow me undetected and unlimited Finn observation. Yes, it was majorly creepy, and still showed the random woman's picture it held when I bought it. But desperate times called for desperate measures. And clearly, I was desperate.

Almost immediately, they looked way too cozy for my liking. Teddy was tossing his head back in laughter, and after a minute or two of apparent hilarity, he pointed toward me, and Finn's head turned to follow. My spying method meant any reaction could give up my pervy secret, and I was unprepared to do that. It was a lifeline—one I used way too much to let go of. So, I sat with bated breath, hoping they were talking about the Frank Gehry and Ludwig Mies Van der Rohe prints hanging above my desk and not me.

An email notification dragged my eyes from the fire.

Scarlett. Mrs. Crane of Hudson River House will be here by three. Mr. Wise says you need to have that presentation ready, and you better sell it. If you somehow manage not to fail, you've all but sealed a promotion to senior designer. What a surprise.
Victoria
Wise, Bernstein, & Wright.

What a surprise? What does she mean by that?

I had little time to ponder Victoria's shade. After one last peek at Finn, I placed the photo frame face-down on the desk. "Breathe, Scarlett. Breathe... And bloody concentrate." I entered the zone, becoming an architectural machine, focused only on blueprints and my blindingly successful future.

Six and a half minutes later, Teddy slid back onto my desk, closed my laptop, and leaned in close. "Okay, a status update on the king of NYC. And no, I did not mention you. And no, he did not ask about you."

"I wasn't even going to ask that." I was totally going to ask that.

"As suspected, Finn is criminally straight, unmarried, has no girlfriend—not one I could sniff out, anyway—and he lives with a sister and an aunt, who they've lived with since his parents died."

"Oh my God. Really? Poor Finn."

"I know. You have a lot in common, Scar. You're both ridiculously good-looking ex-pat orphans, for starters."

"Theodore," I scolded.

"What? It's true. He seems legit. You should lock him down. He won't stay single for long. The good ones never do."

Despite his many protests, I shooed Teddy away, allowing me the time and space to refocus on what should have been my priority: stressing out and waiting. Patience was a virtue I did not hold in spades, and the little held in my five-foot-seven frame was consumed in the space between waiting and arrival, hope and confirmation. Minutes felt like weeks, and I was more coffee and doughnuts than woman by the time Mrs. Crane waltzed into the room.

With an air of nobility and grace, she approached my desk. Fittingly, I stood to greet her, my hand outstretched, ready to shake her diamond-encrusted one. "Mrs. Crane. Thank—Oh." She walked straight by me, and instead, made her way to Finn. I couldn't fault her taste, but still.

"Auntie, you made it." Smiling and hugging her warmly, Finn received multiple kisses on his dimpled cheeks and just as many slack-jawed co-worker stares, as he took her Hermes bag, set it neatly on his desk, then hugged her again.

"No way! Did he say, 'Auntie'?" Arthur had appeared from nowhere and was standing close to my side, fittingly eating popcorn. "The conference room is set up. You just have to plug in your laptop to the display and connect the temporary data." He took two evil, chuckle-filled steps away before pausing. "Oh, by the way, Finn is the other designer presenting. You are so fucked. Good luck."

3

Finn

THE HEAT FROM EVERY set of eyes in the firm boring into the back, side, and somehow top of my head was so intense I could smell my hair burning.

"Can you feel that? Finny?" Jocie whispered into my ear as we embraced. "You're causing quite the stir."

"I'm not doing anything, old lady. They're all watching you."

"Well, I better give them a show, then." Releasing me, she reclaimed her precious Hermes bag, fished inside, and pulled out her lipstick. "I would have brought the coral Chanel had I known I'd have an audience." A thick coat of mauve stained her lips before they were pressed together and released with a pop. "Are they still watching?"

"Yep. Some people are filming," I joked.

"Excellent. Now take me to that little kitchenette I see and make me some tea. All this attention is making me thirsty." I was there, trying to stop my aunt from Irish-ing up her tea, when soft footsteps and the sweet scent of flowers in bloom drew near.

"Pardon me. Sorry to interrupt, but I was wondering if I might be able to present first today?" Her posh little accent was music to my ears, and as I turned to face her, my shaking hands almost dropped the milk. It was the first time Scarlett had addressed me publicly and not run.

"Hi, yeah, yep, yes, absolutely. I'm more than happy to oblige. Take however long you need. I'm yours...it's yours...time is yours. I mean, it'll give me a chance to calm the butterflies." With darting eyes, she nodded politely, chuckled, and made a hasty exit. "Any wonder she doesn't talk to me? Why didn't I just tell her I have the shits."

"What was that, darling?" Jocelyn asked, smirking as I passed her tea.

"Oh, nothing, Auntie. Nothing. Just talking to myself."

When given the all-clear, I escorted my aunt into the conference room. Scarlett stood at the rear, near the wall-mounted screens, with various displays and 3D models waiting. It was impressive, but the thing I appreciated the most, apart from her red lips and distractingly cute yellow dress, was the absence of Teddy.

The guy was her shadow. Everywhere she went, he went. And if their constant giggling, touching, and chatty chats weren't torturous enough, the kissing nearly killed me. Granted, they were pecks on the lips or cheek, but should the two of them be what I suspected they were—*lovers*—they would hardly be porno kissing in the middle of the office. Their affection would have been endearing had I not wanted to switch places with the man. And not that I held myself on some sanctimonious moral high ground, but if she was indeed playing *hide the salami* with Teddy, why had I so often caught her eyes lingering upon me?

There was no doubt she checked me out at every opportunity, and I sure as hell played up to it. I smiled, unashamedly flexed, or played with my hair. I tried old-fashioned talking too. But each time, Scarlett would turn, walk, or even break into a sprint to escape my apparently abhorrent attention. Directly asking her, him, or anyone else in the office what their relationship was could have alleviated my suffering earlier, but weirdly, knowing the truth was scarier than not knowing. New York was a temporary thing for me, but Scarlett Grant was not a temporary kind of girl.

Scarlett cleared her throat and smiled nervously as the room filled. "Thank you for joining me, everyone. Each of you has a copy of my presentation before you, and I brought some cookies. They're vegan, gluten-free, sugar-free...taste free. Enjoy!"

The squeak of my aunt's chair as she leaned into me drew my attention away from where I wanted. "You never told me how beautiful Ms. Grant is, Finnley," she whispered. "Was that a deliberate oversight, or did that detail just slip your mind?"

"Is she? Never noticed, Jocie."

"Hmm. Sure."

After her warm but slightly shaky beginning, Scarlett soared. I watched on in silence and was quickly swept up in a wave of awe, agony, and admiration that bordered on idolization at several points. Step by step, screen by screen, she laid out her vision.

"Incorporating environmentally conscious design, Hudson River House is the best of modern Australian, open-planned living, and classic New England architecture. You'll notice the structure is positioned to capture the stunning landscape and river views, making nature the focal point. This aspect increases the appeal of the interior, but also harnesses the sun, maximizing the effectiveness of the solar panels and reducing the need for artificial lighting."

God, she was talented and stunning too. I thought of the first time I saw her, of how she took my breath away then and every day since. Witnessing her brilliance and watching her do her thing shook me to my bones. So much so that I began to take notes, sketch, scratch at my head, and stroke the scruff on my chin just to keep myself from pulling her onto my lap should she pass by.

"Mrs. Crane, my design gives you not only a functional, practical, beautiful home, but also a landmark piece of art. Now, do we have any questions?"

As she answered, the heavy rain clouds shifted just enough for a single sunbeam to shine upon her through the window. With her hair and skin aglow, she looked like an angel. One I desperately wanted to fuck. My cock jumped and twitched against my fly. It was blissful torture. I could only hope her presentation finished before I did.

Scarlett's pitch lit my world just as that sunbeam had done with her curls. She absolutely deserved the job, but for me, the afternoon's high point was still to come.

With the last question answered, we waited in line by the door, like you see people do when they meet the Queen. All eager to share a moment with royalty. Each posh little farewell, each shuffled step in her cute little shoes brought her closer, and then, she was before me.

This was it. We were about to have our second conversation.

Her feminine, floral scent hit me, and I was done. The woman could have asked me for my liver, and I'd have torn it from my body right then and there.

My hands twitched with need. I wanted to wrap the hem of her dress around my wrist and pull her against me, but I restrained myself and took an all-too-brief, hopefully discreet scan over her curves. I started to sweat around hip height but bravely carried on to the breasts that would fit so perfectly in my hands. It was almost too much, but then I reached it. The Grant oasis. The most beautiful face I had ever seen. I took in her soft, slightly parted lips, wet as though freshly licked by the lovely pink tongue I had the tiniest glimpse of. Then I tried to memorize the tiny smattering of freckles decorating the bridge of her nose and the exact color of the flush on her cheeks.

"Finnley." *Oh. Good. God.* It was the first time I'd heard my name pass those lips and the closest I'd ever come to a religious experience. I looked up and found green eyes disarmingly staring into mine.

"Finn. Please, call me Finn."

"Finn," she whispered and looked away. Those soft lips were licked, and I was sure I heard a sigh escape them. For two, maybe two hundred heartbeats, we stayed that way, connected and alone. It was just us in that room.

Finn and Scarlett. Scarlett and Finn.

I was consumed with fear. She was going to walk from that room, and I would never feel the same way again. All I wanted was for this moment to last forever and to know if she was as affected by my touch as I was by hers. Her eyes would tell me, but I couldn't look. My courage had abandoned me along with my dignity and, apparently, the ability to let go of her hand.

It was perhaps for the best, then, that before things could get any more inappropriate, some inconsiderate asshole behind me dared to breathe, cough, or merely exist. I flinched at the distraction. Scarlett gasped, and my hand fell to my side.

Achingly, she stepped away. My moment in the sun was over.

She left me, and I remained still, looking down at the hand that touched her, bewildered to find it unchanged when everything within me felt so entirely different.

Desperate for an answer to the 'are they, aren't they' question, the minute I was done with my presentation, I ran to Teddy. Tumbling over several indoor plants in the process, I landed face-first at his feet, gasping like a fool.

"Can I help you with something?" He smirked, trying hard to suppress his giggles.

"I bloody hope so. I need to know what the hell is going on with you and Scarlett."

It was like he'd been waiting for the invitation. Teddy immediately dragged me to a pub near my house on Bleecker Street. It was my kind of place. I had a beer in hand, football was playing on one giant screen, and rugby on another. My need to learn all I could about Scarlett and Teddy's relationship may have led us there, but I couldn't seem to find the nerve to ask him anything. Even after loosening up with more drinks than I would normally allow myself, I was sure all I would leave with was a new mate and the promise of a massive hangover. Meanwhile, Teddy was the one asking all the questions, treating the evening like an episode of *Who Wants to be a Millionaire?*.

"Finn, tell me about Australia."

"What's the deal with your family?"

"How do you feel about other orphans?"

"So, you don't have a girlfriend. Why is that?"

"What shoe size are you?"

Eventually, extreme intoxication helped me get to the point, and I wrangled the metaphorical mic from Teddy.

"Theodore...Teddy...Big Ted...I gotta ask because I am dying here. Are you and Scar sleeping together? Like, you know, sleeping together but not just sleeping? Bumping uglies? Rooting? Fucking?"

Hysterical laughter was not the answer I expected. After a solid minute of hilarity, he realized it was one-sided and abruptly stopped. "Shit. You're serious. Oh God, Finn. You are precious." He wiped his eyes dry of tears, then grabbed and kissed the top of my head. "Finny, my darling, I promise, Scarlett and I have never and will never be romantically involved. If I were struck by lightning tomorrow and suddenly rendered straight, she would be my number-one gal. But until that happens, you have nothing to worry about."

"So, you're..."

"Gay? Yes, Finn. I am gay. I love willies, cocks, and dicks of all shapes and sizes. Scarlett's undoubtedly gorgeous vagina holds little to no interest to me."

I should have been relieved. This was what I wanted, after all. But somehow, my bewilderment and anxiousness reached new heights. Moving from beer to whiskey proved less helpful than I predicted, and my rapid mood deterioration was noticed.

"What's up, muchacho?" Teddy asked, rubbing my back.

"Well, now that I know Scar's not your girl, I think I'm safe to tell you. Teddy, I think your mate is hot as fuck."

Teddy slapped his cheek. "No!"

"I know! It's a shock, right? I've kept it pretty tightly under wraps. But, yep, I like her...a lot. But see, the thing is, I cannot figure her out. I thought you were the root of the problem, but now, I dunno. Did I do something to irritate or offend her? Or do I have appallingly bad breath or body odor? Whatever the reason, she can't stand to be around me...but is always around me. Know what I mean?"

He nodded and chuckled while pursing his lips and motioning for me to continue with a roll of his index finger. "So, yeah, as I said, Scar avoids me like the plague, but I catch her glancing at me all the time, which feeds my neediness and insecurity and sends my need for her approval into the stratosphere." I paused to breathe but only briefly. "My brain has created a million worst-case scenarios, each explaining what could be driving her behavior, most of which came to a screaming halt when you told me about your love of cock. That should make me feel better. But it kind of makes it worse. Now that I know she's not your girl, it's going to be even harder to function amidst the conflict. Can you please, please tell me anything that will put me out of my misery? Please."

It was not until my slurred and lengthy monologue was complete that I became aware of my precarious sitting position. I was on the edge of my barstool, my dangling legs intimately wedged between Teddy's knees, my hands holding his. After appearing to appreciate the closeness of our bodies, he freed himself, wiped his hands free of moisture, and took a leisurely sip of his beer. The bastard was enjoying my agony.

"Finny, you do not stink. Your breath is minty fresh, though maybe not right this second, and she doesn't hate you. She may, in fact, feel quite the opposite." He took another pull of his beer, never taking his eyes off mine. "Scar may be covered in coffee stains and awkward as fuck, but she is truly the most gorgeous, incredible, generous person. She's also been single for way too long, and I need it to end. I'm not going to tell you what to do or how to feel—or how she feels, for that matter. But don't give up. Be patient, give her time, and let her get to know you. She's a thousand percent worth the wait."

I nodded and tried to take it all in, but the bloody beer, whiskey, and talk of feelings and shit made it hard. I was embarrassingly emotional and needed a minute alone. After borrowing the words of my heart's desire, "Mate, do you know where the loos are?" I bolted.

The fragrant men's room was not the best place to think, but it was all I had. Hunched over the sink, I stared into the mirror.

You can do this, Finn. You can talk about her. Or not. Maybe just talk about cricket. Or golf. Or maybe just drink some more. Yeah. That sounds like a solid plan.

I washed my face and was in the midst of a final pump-up when my phone buzzed in my pocket. I pulled it out and squinted at the screen. It was my best friend, Nate—or Nathaniel, if you were his mum, or if you were really pissed with him. He was the twin brother of Shelby, Iris's late mum, and we'd been friends for life. Our birthdays were three days apart, we grew up on neighboring farms, and were together in every class throughout school. I knew everything about him, and he *thought* he knew everything about me.

Nate

> Finny. Miss your ugly mug, bro. How's it going? Settling in? You made a move on the redhead yet? You can tell me you're not interested till you're blue in the face, but I don't buy it.

> NO NATE. can't talk new, can't tpey . Drunk.

Nate

> That's what I like to see. Have fun, Finny. Go get some

> Up yours, dckhed. Miss too you.

What a tool.

Now feeling homesick as well as shitfaced, I shoved my phone back in my pocket on the third attempt and left the stench behind. The second Teddy saw me weaving my way through the crowd, he dropped his phone into his lap and smiled. He was up to something cheeky, that was clear, but we dove into a lengthy debate over Australian vs American beers, and I quickly forgot all about it.

"So, tell me, Finn Austen, super hunk from Down Under. What do you think about Budweiser?"

I took a long, slow sip and sighed. "To be honest, not much. Too pale and flat for me. I like a thicker, fuller body." I signaled the waiter to bring us another round. "I mean, I'll drink it, but give me a full-strength Aussie draught or bitter any day."

"A Foster's, right?"

The glass slipped from my hand. A handful of Teddy's shirt replaced it, and I may have shaken him till his phone fell right from his pocket. "No Australian drinks Foster's, Theodore. Not one. It's that bad, that much of a national disgrace, that I don't think they even sell it at home anymore."

"Okay, no Foster's. I get it. Now, unless you're taking me home to bed, you better let go of me. I'm enjoying this way too much."

"Shit, sorry." I relaxed my grip and smoothed the wrinkles. "It's a real sore point for me."

"Yeah, I can see that. Let's stick to wine next time."

4

Scarlett

B Y EIGHT, A BOTTLE of wine, *Mansfield Park*, and my pillow were calling my name. In my favorite, softest t-shirt stolen from Teddy, I snuggled in my four-poster bed, poured a glass, and melted into the sheets. Despite my best intentions, my mind trawled the remnants of my day. Finn and his aunt featured heavily.

I'd been a walking contradiction on my way to pick up Ben. Proud of my work and how well I did in the presentation, frustrated because I knew Finn would most likely get the job despite that, and disturbed that, with even the flagrant favoritism I was likely to witness, my body had utterly betrayed me.

I was horny.

The arousal achieved from a simple touch of Finn's hand was unprecedented. I swore I could still feel him. Smell him too. How, on a humid New York day, he smelled like he'd just stepped from a tropical ocean while sipping from a fresh coconut was beyond me. It was hot. He was hot. God dammit, why did he have to be so hot?

Maybe I shouldn't have harbored such guilt over the attraction. There was a distinct possibility that I was jumping the gun with my Finn-is-a-complete-suck-up theory. Despite everything pointing in that direction and no evidence to back it up, my gut told me he wasn't the type to flex family influence. And Jocelyn certainly didn't seem like the kind of woman to play games. She appeared genuinely impressed by my concept too.

Still, my insecurities lingered and ran deep. I'd been under-estimated and undervalued my whole life, professionally and personally. Sadly, as a foster kid, I'd almost come to expect it.

At the age of four, a fire destroyed our home and stole the lives of my parents. According to witnesses, Dad was woken by the smoke, and after rousing mum, who insisted he save me while she gathered our photo albums, he did just that. But with no sight of Mum, I was left in the arms of our neighbor, and Dad ran back into the flames. Neither made it out.

Orphaned, my childhood became a revolving door of foster and group homes. Some good. Some cruel, violent, horrible. I yearned for love, family, and understanding. A kind and sup-porting hand to guide me into the future. What I got were homes where all that was expected or accepted of me was being quiet, compliant, and inconspicuous. I learned to make myself small. To please.

My tale is not typical of every foster kid. Many of us are raised by loving, caring families. But it was my story, and it formed a belief I carried to this day. No matter how I tried, it was never enough. *I* was never enough. Perhaps broken or unlovable. The judgment I later experienced as a teen mother only compound-ed my belief.

As the shadows of the past darkened my room, I willed myself back into the light. *Stop thinking about things you cannot change. Drink, Scarlett.*

Letting the words of Jane heal me again. I sipped and skipped to Edmund and Fanny's first kiss. Like me, Fanny believed her-self broken, but Edmund saw the beauty of her sharp angles and edges and loved her even more for them. I swooned as he chased her, cupped her face in his hands, then kissed her deeply. Thoughts much more pleasant than those preceding filled my heart, and I began to feel all warm, and giddy, and maybe a little bit hopeful.

Of course, at that exact moment, my phone rang, the vibra-tions tingling against my bare thigh beneath the quilt (sadly, the biggest thrill I'd received in bed in quite some time). I knew it would be Teddy. Ben's bedtime led straight into our evening bitchfest, and I bloody loved it.

"Hello, Teddy. Who are we complaining about tonight?"

"Shut up and listen. Guess who I'm with. Go on. Guess."

"Ummm, Harry Styles?"

"Pffft, I wish. If I was with Harry, do you think I'd be on the phone with you? Stop wasting my time and guess again."

"Geez. Don't get so pissy. Ugh, I don't know. Asher, that waiter from M.I.X.?"

"No! Again, I wouldn't be calling you if it was Asher. Also, he's the owner, not a waiter. It's...Finn Austen. I am at an Aussie pub on Bleecker, drinking beer with Finn bloody Austen!"

"What the hell, Theodore?! I swear to God, if you say anything to embarrass me, I will kill you."

Evil cackles rattled down the phone, but only briefly. He soon began whispering so quietly I could hardly hear him. "Oh, he's coming back. I'll stay on the phone but put you on my lap so you can hear, okay?"

"Teddy! No!" It was too late. I heard a muffled voice with an Australian accent approach, then a few bumps and thumps as he sat back at the table. Why on earth I didn't hang up is anybody's guess, but it may have had something to do with my earlier comment about my phone and its vibrations. Background chatter and music made some things inaudible, but Teddy swooning and flirting his ass off was clear. Then, just as I took a sip or several of my sweet fragrant rosé, I heard, "So, tell me again, Finn Austen, super hunk from Down Under. What do you think about—"

"Mummm!"

"Wait, Ben!" I screamed as panic filled me to my very core. Shit, did Teddy say my name? Did he? "What did you say, Ted? What did you say?"

In my panic, I dropped the phone. It took three fumbled attempts to get the damn thing back up against my ear. When I eventually did, I wished I hadn't.

"To be honest, not much. Too pale and flat for me. I like a thicker, fuller body."

What the actual fuck?

"Really? That's disappointing. I really thought you'd be into—"

"Mummmmmm."

"What? What? What?" Again, my phone tumbled from my grasp. I jumped to my feet to attend to my screaming child. My butter fingers retrieved the phone from the floor, but Teddy was gone. I could hardly go and ring back, so with my phone gripped tightly in my hand, I checked on Ben, assured him there were no flying monkeys in his room or in New York, and then sat on the edge of my bed for an hour, bordering on hurling and waiting for Teddy to call back.

I woke to my shrieking alarm at six am, face-down, sideways, with my head hanging over the edge of the mattress. It must have been the last position I was in when I fell asleep...or suffered a rosé-related collapse. Judging by the empty bottle at my feet and the pounding of my head, I gathered it was the latter.

Damn it. Teddy didn't call me back. I yawned, and stretched, my muscles aching from my awkward sleeping arrangement. Yoga was what I needed, but not what I did. I fell back asleep and was woken an hour and a half later by Ben sticking a wet finger in my ear and screaming, "WET WILLY!"

"An American custom?" I asked as my face screwed up like I'd sucked a lemon.

"I dunno. It's funny, though, isn't it?" His annoyingly cute giggle made me smile when I didn't want to. "Are we late, Mum? We might be because I saw Mrs. Horowitz walking her cats, and I only see her does that when we are late."

Yes, my neighbor walked her cats. Not on leashes or anything. That would be weird. She did it in a pram. "Shit! Yes. If you saw Mrs. Horowitz, we are late. And Ben, we say 'do that'. You saw her do that, not does that."

"I saw her do what?" Ben asked, his head turning from side to side in confusion, much like Mrs. Horowitz's hairless cat, Brutus, did when she talked to him like a person.

"Oh, forget it. Just go get dressed, and I'll make us breakfast."

Knowing my darling son could take ten minutes to put on a sock, I snuck in a thirty-second shower and dressed, then hit the kitchen. *Okay, we have half a red pepper, some leftover Shepherd's pie, a brown thing with a weird odor, and stale Captain Crunch. Cereal it is. Oh, but there's no milk. Hmm. This is bad. I'm failing adulting.*

As the mum guilt kicked in, the doorbell rang three times, and Teddy and his trademark patchouli, cedar, and bergamot scent burst through the door. "My darling, why do you insist on buzzing if you're going to invite yourself in anyway? Also, please tell me you brought food."

"You know I like to make an entrance, Scar. And yes, I did. I have coffee, bagels, salmon, cream cheese, some fruit, and a doughnut for Ben. I figured the banana would balance out the doughnut."

"Ughhh, you could give him a bowl of sugar cubes in battery acid this morning, and I would be okay with it. Well, maybe not the acid." It was then, after the food was in my possession, that I remembered I very much hated Theodore Digby. In the grouchiest voice I could muster, I lethargically slapped his arm repeatedly. "Why the hell didn't you call me back? I waited for hours."

"You did not! I did call you back. Several times. Check your phone, Sleeping Wino—Beauty."

Confident I would find no missed calls, I swiped my screen, saw five, then told Teddy my phone was dead, and put it on the charger before he could see my lies.

All was forgotten as Teddy grabbed me and stood with my hands in his. "Now, before I tell you anything about Finn, you left work yesterday without telling me how the pitch went, so I'm asking now. How did you do, Scar? Did you smash it? You did, didn't you?" Wide-eyed and giddy, he pecked me on the lips and gushed, "You bloody killed it."

The much-needed vitamin D brought a smile to my face. "I think I did, but I don't know if it matters. Obviously, you know about the whole nephew-aunt thing."

"Sure do. Ouch. I should have guessed it the minute she walked in. Blonde, tall, and beautiful runs in the family."

"As does business, it seems. I have a snowflake's chance in hell of getting this job, and the unfairness of it all really pisses me off. I'm not normally this confident about anything, but I thought I did good, maybe even great." The sympathy in Teddy's big brown eyes threatened my stability, so I turned to the food and packed my bagel with cream cheese and salmon.

"Are you going to say anything to the partners, then? You should speak up and fight for this. Finn would probably back you up. He seemed embarrassed by it all and was super impressed by your work. He hardly shut up about you."

I tried to disguise the thrill that gave me and took a bite of pumpernickel bliss. "I thought he was impressed too." I chewed. "He took lots of notes and seemed really into my work."

"Yeah. I'm sure it was the work he was into," Teddy muttered.

"But honestly, when do I ever speak up about anything? It won't get me anywhere other than being labeled a complainer or sore loser." I licked my fingers and blew out a heavy, resigned sigh. "Nope, I am putting my big-girl pants on and chalking this one up to experience."

"I think that's a mistake, but you knew that already. Let's talk about last night."

"Yes, good idea. Tell me everything, including where these bagels are from. They're amazing."

Teddy looked around, no doubt for Ben, then dished. "Okay, so. The bagels are from Max's, but here's the real goss. Austen Powers—that's my new name for him—suits him, don't you think? Anyway, he was so wasted and so cute. We stayed at the bar till one am, and he told me all about his farm and stuff. Oh, but the best thing was, he thought you and I were an item!" Teddy almost doubled over in laughter.

I did not.

Terror seized me. I dropped my breakfast and gripped the closest part of Teddy I could, which happened to be his elbow.

"Why? Why did he think that? What did I do to make him think that? Oh my God. Please tell me you didn't fuck around with him. You told him you were gay and disgusted by me, right? You did, didn't you?"

Teddy wiped a schmear of cream cheese from my cheek and laughed. "Calm the fucking farm, Scarlett. Of course I did. You need to have more faith in me."

"Well, what was flat and pale? My hair? My pasty, English skin? My boobs?"

"American beer. Geez, Scar. Paranoid much?"

I collapsed against his shoulder. "Oh, thank fuck. You're right, darling. I should never have doubted the bestest bestie ever."

"No, you shouldn't have, and yes, I am. Finn could very well be the best boyfriend ever too. He really is quite something. Charming, funny, sweet, a beautifully big personality, and from what I could see up close, an even bigger—"

"Hi, Uncle Teddy!"

"Fuck it!" Teddy and I coughed in chorus as Ben appeared before us, still shoeless but dressed appropriately. Thanks to **Ideology #4 - DO NOT discuss male 'friends' in front of Ben, and ABSOLUTELY NO 'friends' are to sleep over,** no further Finn talk was had.

This strict "no talk, no matter how hot" ethos was easier to disregard when Ben was younger. Then, we could say almost anything without fear. But now that he was old enough to hear, repeat, and ask questions, I felt kind of icky talking about a guy until I was sure where we stood. Not that there was anyone to introduce. I had been a dateless wonder since we arrived...and for a long time before that.

Much to my displeasure, Ben gobbled up his doughnut. I wasn't worried about the healthiness. I just wanted it myself. It was all washed down with a glass of milk, which Teddy also brought, and after finally getting Ben to put his shoes on, we were off.

Running late was nothing new to me. Luckily, one of the many benefits of Teddy's friendship was the location of our homes. Our 6th Ave office sat in one of the most expensive areas in NYC. Sarah Jessica Parker lived around the corner, for Christ's sake. Never in a million years would I be able to afford the shittiest of shit apartments within walking distance—within Manhattan, in reality—without him. At my insistence, and much to Teddy's annoyance, I did pay rent, but I knew it was a tenth of the market value. This added to the already daunting literal and figurative debt I owed Teddy.

Somehow, we all made it to Ben's school on time, and with my head cock-a-block—sorry, chock-a-block full of Finn, I soaked up my precious goodbye kiss from Benny and waved him off for the day. As soon as the kid was out of earshot, I turned to Teddy, grabbed his forearms, pulled his ear to my lips, and whispered, "Tell me now. Exactly what did he say about me? And what else was big?"

5

Scarlett

THANKS TO TEDDY AND our descriptive walk, I'd arrived at work with my mind in the gutter.

"The man rolled his sleeves up, and I almost fell off my stool. He could pick you up and carry you with one arm, Scar. Ooh, and he had a horse on his farm. Can't you imagine those saddle-gripping thighs powering into you from behind?"

Imagining it was easy. Stopping was harder. I tried, but Finn walked up wearing a sharp royal-blue suit, a crisp white shirt, and Converse shoes. He floated through the room as though transported by a cloud—a cloud that slowed as it approached me, giving him time to smile and wink the hottest wink that ever winked. I just gave up at that point.

As the morning progressed, I noticed a definite shift in the energy between us. His attention was appreciably more brazen, while I was significantly more receptive. For instance, when he said, "Excuse me, Scarlett," in the kitchen, I didn't squeal, run, or laugh hysterically. I simply pulled my head from the fridge I had been hiding inside since he'd walked in, moved my ass out of the way, and let him get his lunch out. It was a significant improvement—a real achievement.

Old habits were hard to break, though, so while he ate his chicken salad in the common eating space, I ate my cup of noodles alone at my desk. Peeking up at him intermittently, I told myself that the earlier cheeky wink probably meant nothing. *Looking like he does, he's probably an outrageous flirt. Those winks could be handed out like lollies. I've not really witnessed that, though. Still, I'm sure every woman in this office has been on the receiving end of his dreamy eyes and long eyelashes. Why do hot guys always have nice lashes?*

"SCARLETT ELIZABETH. WHAT ARE YOU STARING AT?"

Two hands braced my shoulders, and Teddy was before me, nose to nose. "Jesus Christ, Teddy! Why are you screaming in my face?"

"Well, I said your name twenty times, and you ignored me. You know how I feel about being ignored, Scar."

"Yes, I know. You may as well be dead."

"That's right. So, what, or whom, were you thinking about? Hmmm. Let... Me... Guess...."

Plopping in the chair at the empty desk beside me, he began to spin with his trigger finger pointed. Naturally, his immaculately polished Louboutin's dropped to the carpet when aimed at Finn, who, thank God, had his face buried in his bowl. I slapped Teddy's finger away, grabbed the back of his chair, and spun him back to me.

"For fuck's sake, Teddy. Stop being such a dick."

"What? I was just guessing."

"Yes, well, stop it. If you must know, I was thinking about...umm...what to do for Ben's birthday. It's coming up, and I need to get organized."

He smelled bullshit, and he was right. "Ben's birthday?"

I casually flicked my hair. "Uh-huh."

"Really? The birthday that's a good ten months away? You're going to use your child like that? Damn, that's my mum's level of cold, Scar."

"Shut up. I was. I swear."

"So, you overlooked Captain Koala and his blue suit? He looks very dapper. I wonder what he's so dressed up for. Maybe he has a date? Hmmm."

"Yes, perhaps he does, but it means nothing to me. I couldn't give two hoots about Finn Austen's dating habits."

A throat cleared. It wasn't Teddy's. And it wasn't mine. "Well, that's disappointing. I would have thought the dating habits of an overworked homebody that lived with his sister would have been fascinating."

FUCK. FINN. "It's you. You're here...I mean, Finn. You're Finn from over there." I pointed to his empty desk. "Hi... Hi, Finn."

I could see Teddy covering his face in shame from the corner of my eye and wished I could do the same.

"Yes. It is I, Finn from over there. How are you, Scarlett from over here?" He smiled his dimpled smile and copied my desk pointing.

"I... Umm... I..."

That was all I could come up with, and Finn kindly moved on. "My aunt just sent me a message. She's decided, and she wants to speak to us. I know it's short notice, but would around three be okay for you? Otherwise, she can only come in later, and I know you leave at four."

Showing every tooth in my mouth, I smiled and tried to bat my lashes. Teddy's snort didn't help my confidence. "Already? That was quick. Umm, yes, that would be fine—wait, you know I leave at four? You noticed that?"

Unruly curls flopped into his eyes as Finn smiled again and stepped closer—too close, but not nearly close enough. "Of course I noticed that. I notice a lot of things about you, Scarlett."

Oh, good God.

My name had never sounded the way it did rolling from *those* lips, in *that* accent. It was easy to imagine him calling it out again and again as he bent me over my desk and railed me. I felt the blush burning from breast to earlobe but was determined to remain calm and professional. Because that was what I was: mature, steady, and professional.

"Yes, I'm free for you anytime... I mean, Mrs. Crane. I'm free to see Mrs. Crane with you and us together." *What an idiot.* "Why does she want to speak to both of us? Clients normally go via the senior partners. Especially in this case, when the outcome was predetermined."

Finn furrowed his brows and made a cute little grunt. "Trust me, nothing is predetermined, Scarlett. This is an open race. As for why she wants to talk to us, I'm as clueless as you. The old girl is a woman of mystery. Obviously, I've known her my whole life, but I still have no idea what she's up to. That's part of her charm and why she's such a success. Best poker face in town."

"Well, if business success and *not* having a glass face are linked, I'm screwed." His eyebrows shot up, and a smile, or more of an amused smirk, teased at the corners of his lips. It was devastatingly hot, and I did my best to remain breathing. "Yes, well, as I said, it's fine. Let your aunt know I look forward to seeing you at three...her at three...I mean, seeing you both at three."

"Ripper. Job done."

I didn't know what ripper meant, and I didn't care because his strong-looking fingers then moved toward my face. Time slowed. My stomach knotted. His eyes flicked to mine, and his cheeks flushed red as his thumb brushed and dragged down the edge of my lip. "You had a noodle on your..." Suddenly, he froze, then the same hand shot through his dreamy curls. He puffed his cheeks, exhaled loudly, and backed away. "Right, three it is."

"Wow. That was hot."

I'd forgotten Teddy was beside me. "Yeah." I sighed. "I really need to use a napkin."

"Why? I'd walk around with a rotisserie chicken on my face if it meant he'd touch me like that."

I had no recollection of anything I did between one and two fifty-two pm.

None. Zero. Zilch.

Actually, that's not true. I panicked, ate three doughnuts and a fucking amazeballs thing called a bear claw, and drank a liter of coffee. My surroundings were only heightening my insecurities. I was in conference room A. It was the big money room with the best tech, the comfiest seats, and the view of our cherry blossom tree.

Until today, my authorized entry to this space was limited to note-taking during meetings and bringing a man in a suit some coffee like a good little girl. Unofficially, though, I'd sneak in here to cry when the restroom was full, and sometimes, I ate my

lunch here too, pretending I belonged while relaxing in the high
wing chairs and gazing out the window. My mood determined
the object my eyes fixed on. When career driven and focused, it
would be what I could see of the city surrounding me and the
endless possibilities that dwelled within it. When feeling more
worried, stressed, or homesick, it was the garden. I pictured myself beneath the cherry tree, watching how its branches would
bend with the breeze, always accepting its fated direction, never
resisting, never questioning, just going with the flow. I yearned
to be like that tree far more than that cold, rigid city. But for
now, those steel giants and the money encased within them were
much more in control of my future than I wanted them to be.

"Miss Scarlett, may I have a word?"

"Hmm, yes. Yes, of course, Mr. Wise."

"Now, we've talked about this before. It's Herman, not Mr.
Wise—he's my father." He chuckled heartily at his joke as I
considered at what age you should stop using that line. I would
hazard a guess and say old Hermie was well past that point.

"Sorry. What can I do for you, Herman?"

He sat beside me and took the world's most indiscreet look
at my breasts. "When Mrs. Crane comes in today, I don't want
you to overreact or become emotional should she choose Finn's
design. You should feel honored that a young designer such as
yourself was asked to prepare something. A wealthy woman like
Mrs. Crane need not be concerned about showing her understandable bias. In this city, it's not what but who you know."
Herman groaned as he stood, patronizingly patted me on the
head, and left. Finn, who I hadn't noticed entering the room,
followed his exit with a scowl, and then gave me a sympathetic
smile.

I refused to acknowledge his gesture. A rash conclusion had
already formed in my mind. Herman's condescension served as
a timely reminder of how the world worked. This firm had the
facade of a modern, equal-opportunity one, but underneath the
thin veneer, the old boys' club reigned supreme—just as it had
in England. As for Finn, perhaps all he cared about was getting
this job, making out to everyone that he was sweet and fair

by giving poor, little Scarlett—the most inexperienced designer here, APART FROM HIM—a shot, when clearly, I had none.

My blood boiled. Finn wandered over, leaned in close, and put his hand on my shoulder. My traitorous body fluttered head to toe at this unprecedented touching, but I was too pissed off to enjoy the rush. "She's here, Scarlett. Are you ready?"

"Definitely. Let's get this over with so I can get back to nothing, eh?" I shrugged his hand away, and that still-furrowed brow of his almost turned itself inside out. But I didn't care. I was too busy trying to breathe through the rotten stench of nepotism.

"Are you alright, mate? Did I do something to upset—"

"Don't call me that. I'm not your mate," I mumbled under my breath, unsure if I wanted him to hear me or not.

"Scarlett? Wait—"

It seemed entrance-making was genetic. Interrupting her beloved nephew, Jocelyn Crane rolled in like she should have theme music pumping through speakers wherever she went. Carrying plans tucked under her Armani-clad arm, her regalness saved me from a conversation I didn't want to have. After greeting her, Finn and I sat opposite each other at the large boardroom table while Jocelyn hovered by a wall-mounted bench beneath the window. There lived an impressive drink and snack station and fancy indoor plants that I would kill in five seconds. Both drumming our fingers on the table, Finn and I watched as she trickled water into a glass so slowly each drop could be counted. Thankfully, I didn't need to go to the loo. It would have been torture. Her eyes flared as she sipped, and every swallow was exaggerated. *The woman loves the limelight as much as Teddy. I should introduce them.*

"Ahhh," she sighed, "that's better." She placed the glass down and began to pace. "Thank you for meeting me on such short notice. I've already spoken to the partners and informed them of my decision. But I wanted to speak with you two personally." She looked at Finn and me, then smirked, much like Cruella De Vil would at the poky little puppy. A chill ran up my spine. "I'm going on holiday but wanted to run this past you before I fly out." I couldn't help but sneak a peek at Finn. He seemed surprised. *Did he not know about her vacation? Maybe they weren't as close as I thought.* "Open those plans, and tell me what you think."

Does she always talk like this? So, demanding and bossy. I didn't much like being on the receiving end of it, but I couldn't help but admire her grit. "I see two designs I love and two designers that could make magic together."

Poor Finn—no, not poor Finn, Poop-head Finn went white as a ghost and rubbed his hand down his face. I was so busy studying his reaction I didn't process the words that inspired it. "I will be in France for one month, and while I do have a favorite, I cannot choose between your designs. Both contain elements of what I want, but neither captures it fully. You two," she said, pointing between Finn and me, "will design my forever home together."

That, I got. The collective thud of our chins hitting the floor garnered attention office wide. Like finned inhabitants of an aquarium, we were ogled at through the glass walls. Fittingly, Finn's mouth flapped like a fish gasping for air while I watched on, wholly bemused and at immediate risk of floating on my back.

I—and Herman, for that matter—had misread the situation and not given Jocelyn enough credit. A collaboration wasn't what I had hoped for, but it was better than what I was expecting. Still, even if he wasn't a massive nepotistic dickwad, there was no way I could work directly with Finn. I was one breathy, whispered word away from orgasm when he touched my hand, for Christ's sake. How could I sit beside him for hours on end, smelling his smell, eyeing his eyes? Protests I hoped would sound more professional than my first thoughts (but I like him, I hate him, he's too hot, do I have to talk to him?) formed in my mind, but I was beaten to the punch.

"Jocie, I... She... I haven't worked on a project with someone else...well, not since uni," Finn stammered, watching me from the corner of his eye while his tapping hit overtime.

"Lucky for you, it's only been a short time since you graduated."

"But—"

"I don't want to hear any buts. You know what I'm like once my mind is made up and made up it is. You want my business, then you do this my way." She began to play on her phone until both of ours buzzed repeatedly. "I've just sent you both a list of everything I want. Study it. Perfect it. When I come back, we will meet again, go over the ideas, and I will choose between the current front-runner or your joint creation. Now, off you go, young people. Hop to it."

I was speechless. And as much as I didn't want to admit it, I'd be damned if I didn't respect the fuck out of that woman and officially wish to become her when I grew up. Then I remembered I was a grown-up, had a son, and my ability to feed him very much depended on my employment. This was a big deal.

In a much less sexy way than I had pictured in many of my dreams, my fate lay in Finn Austen's giant and capable-looking hands.

6

Finn

AFTER WAITING AN APPROPRIATE amount of time to be mildly discreet, I fled the conference room, chased my aunt down, and caught her as she climbed into her town car.

"Jocelyn! What the fu—" She gave me the 'Don't you swear at me, child' look I instantly recognized and adhered to. "What the heck, Jocelyn?"

"I'm sensing some tension, my darling. Do you have a problem with my request? You're not going to cry, are you? Because I can easily choose Miss Grant's design like you wanted. I *would* have to explain my sudden change of mind, though."

"As I *recommended*, I think you mean," I whispered, looking over my shoulder guiltily.

Long before my family and I left Australia, my Aunt Jocelyn had tasked me with designing the very upstate home she was now using as a weapon. I was excited by the opportunity and honored she would entrust it to me.

My initial concept was near completion when we arrived in NYC, and though I loved and was proud of what I had done, after seeing Scarlett's talent, I knew I wasn't the one who should bring Jocelyn's dream to life. I begged her to let my co-worker make a pitch, and her initial hesitation passed the minute she saw Scarlett's talent with her own eyes. Once I had her hooked, two further demands—no, requests—were cautiously made to my aunt, someone unaccustomed to demands or pushback.

One, Scarlett would never find out I was involved in arranging her pitch opportunity. It was between me, my aunt, and the senior partners. Watching her interoffice interactions and how she carried herself, I knew Scarlett was unlikely to appreciate my interfering in her work. She was strong and independent, and I respected that. I respected her.

Two, the best design was to be chosen—with no favoritism. Yes, Jocelyn was my beloved aunt, but she had to go with her gut. If that meant Scarlett's concept bettered mine, then so be it.

Seemed my deal with the devil was biting me in the ass.

"I told you Scarlett deserved this more than me. How does forcing us two to work together accomplish anything? Her design is already perfect."

"I agree, and yet I remain unmoved." Her hand reached for the door to close it, but I grabbed it and ripped it from her hand.

"If it's perfect, why do we have to design something different?"

"Because, apart from being old, rich, and your aunt, I am a woman. One who has twice sat in a room with you both and witnessed whatever the hell is going on. Finn, I don't think I have ever seen more heart eyes or felt such dizzying chemistry. Nor have I seen two bigger idiots who have no idea how to act around each other."

"What? You've lost it, old lady. Scarlett and me? Please. The woman's my complete opposite, and it's possible she hates my guts. You saw her in there. She could barely stand to look at me. Plus, she's disorganized, easily distracted, and disturbingly messy. Did you see her bomb site of a desk? Oh, oh, and she drinks way too much coffee, eats too many doughnuts, and—"

"And you're completely crazy about her."

I huffed out a sigh and scratched the back of my neck. "And I'm completely crazy about her." My ears began to burn. "That's why I can't—"

"Nope, I'm sorry, Finnley. But I refuse to let you waste this. You will work with her, and you will make magic together—hopefully in more places than just that boardroom." Before I could protest, her fingers grabbed and squashed my cheeks together like I was still a fat eight-year-old. "Do as I say. You can thank me later."

Scarlett didn't acknowledge my return. She was staring out the window and jiggling her feet like she did whenever Herman was around. I hope to God I didn't make her feel uncomfortable like that prick.

"Are you ready for this, Scarlett? It's a big job and—

"Why would you presume I'm not ready? God, does no one besides your aunt think I deserve or can do this?"

"No, I didn't mean it like that. Your concept is amazing. You absolutely deserve it. I think we both do. No, what I meant was the working-together part. You don't seem thrilled."

"Neither did you." Absentmindedly shuffling her belongings on the desk, she looked at me through her curls. "You really think my work is amazing?"

"Yes, I do. You know it is, and that's why you've been asked to do this. I know it may be uncomfortable for you to work with me. We haven't spent time together since I've been here, and things have been a little awkward between us. I'm also very aware of how working for my aunt looks. But there is a history behind that, and I hope to be able to explain that at some point. Just know I want to prove myself to everyone as much as you do. Let's do this. Let's show them what we can do and smash this out of the park, as the locals say."

It was hard to summarize the expression on her face. Relieved but stressed. Anxious but happy. Perhaps remorseful. She exhaled loudly, then bit her lip. "You're right. We can do this. I'm sorry, I just... Something Herman said got in my head. I may have made some harsh assumptions about you and—"

"What kind of presumptions?"

"What?" She turned her head to the right like she didn't hear and nervously played with her hair.

"You said you made presumptions about me. What kind of presumptions?"

"Did I? I don't remember that."

"Scarlett, it was two seconds ago. Just tell me."

Her cheeks puffed out as she held her breath, then she winced and released it loudly. "Fine! I thought you were a smug, spoiled, nepotistic, rich kid, skating through life on the tailgate of your aunt's Audi...a bit...maybe."

"Ouch." I sucked in an exaggerated breath.

"Yeah, sorry. But you did ask."

And released it. "That I did."

"And if we're to work closely together, you should know I'm very short-tempered and quick to jump to conclusions. I need to work on that."

It was hard not to laugh. She was so damn cute. "I appreciate your candor, Scarlett."

"And I yours, Finn. Thank you." Nodding, she collected her phone, plans, and bag, then shuffled to my side.

"Sorry again. I'm ready if you are. I'll see you tomorrow. And then, we'll begin."

On the evening of my first day at work, the minute my feet crossed the threshold of my room, a sheet of paper and a piece of charcoal became an extension of my desire. I sketched the face I saw each time I closed my eyes.

As I waited for Iris to get ready for bed, I held that sketch in my hands. It had become a constant in the chaos of change. I don't know how or why Scarlett—someone I barely knew—could smooth my new life's jagged edges, but she could. And seeing the mistrust and vulnerability in her eyes today hurt more than it should have, especially when directed at me. I didn't know her history or what wounds had caused her scars, but I wanted to. I also wanted to be the one to help her overcome them. Just as she was unknowingly helping me.

"Daddy, I'm weady," Iris sang.

"Be there in a sec, bubs." Exhausted from work, my morning workout, and worry, I folded my picture, placed it back under my pillow, and traipsed down the hall. "You know it really would be quicker if you let me help you, Iris."

"I'm a big giwl. I don't need help. My new fwiend Bunny says only babies need help getting dwessed."

"Well, if Bunny says it, I guess it must be true." I had no idea who Bunny was. I tapped the bed and watched my big girl in her Bluey pjs climb into bed, her tongue poking out the side of her mouth as she slipped under the pink polka-dot sheets.

"Daddy, Aunty Jocie said you wowk with a pwetty lady and that pwetty lady was weally nice."

"Hmm, did she now? When did she say this?"

"When I was in the bath, and you wewe cleaning. She said you were stwess-cleaning because of wowk and the pwetty lady."

Jesus Christ. "I was not stress cleaning, Iris. I was cleaning the mess you made after dinner. It had nothing to do with any pretty ladies." It absolutely did. I tucked Iris in extra tight, her blankets extra high, almost high enough to cover her mouth but still allowing her the ability to breathe. It didn't shut her up.

"Oh. But do you think—"

"No, I don't think anything, and neither should you. Sleep-ytime starts...now!"

"But Dad."

"But nothing. Sleep." I brushed gorgeous bubble-gum-shampoo-smelling curls from her forehead and kissed her goodnight.

Not two steps out her door, my phone vibrated in my pocket.

"Nate," I whispered. "Hang on. I'm just sneaking away from Iris."

Every floorboard squealed like a stuck pig as I tiptoed down the hall, entered my room, and slumped on my bed. "How are you doing, mate? How's the farm?"

"Hey, bro. All's good here. It's been bloody cold, though. I haven't even been bothered to go out for a surf. How's Evie? Has she settled in, okay? Oh, and Iris and Jocie?"

Jesus Christ. I closed my eyes and shook my head. Nate had a thing for Evie, and everyone, apart from the two of them, knew it. Hopefully, for him, it stayed that way. If he and Evie ever got together, the shit he gave me over Shelby would be repaid twofold.

"They're all good. Thanks for asking about me, by the way." I reached beneath my head and held Scar's picture in my hand. My fingers caressed the crinkled lines as I spoke. "Are you shearing yet?"

"Yep. We started today, and I am knackered. It went well, though. We've got a good team of boys this year. Not just boys, mind you. I snagged a few chicks—some hotties too."

I held the phone away from my ear as Nate whistled. "Jesus, Nate. Can you try and keep it in your pants for five minutes?" This was yet another reason I wanted him away from Evie. Apart from being my best friend, Nate was also a complete slut.

"Fuck off, bro," he laughed. "Just because you choose to live life as a monk doesn't mean we all have to." I had no comeback for that. One, because he was right, and two, because I didn't want to. The phone fell silent, but I swear I could hear Nate sweating. The backpedaling began. "Shit. Sorry, mate. I didn't think."

"Nah, you never do, do you? I gotta go, Nate. Your niece is calling me."

"Finny—"

I didn't have to go. Iris was silent, but I was done with talking, my family, and thinking. Though, somehow, I knew my brain and its constant churning would be harder to silence than Nate was.

In the restless hours that followed, mental lists of jobs I needed to complete and weekend activities I could do with Iris were made. I read a little and decided I needed more exercise. Maybe that would help with some stressors, aid my sleep, and take my mind off the affairs of the heart.

While I may have chastised Nate for thinking only of sex, as night became morning and I cursed the freaking cats meowing outside my window, there was very little else on my mind.

Visions of Scarlett were inescapable. Palpable. I could feel her skin against my palm and smell sweet peas and violets on every shaken inhale. How could a woman I'd barely spoken to possess such power over me?

The stroking began without conscious thought but continued with my absolute knowledge. Christ, I wanted her to be there. To feel her hand or lips wrap around me. To pin her body beneath me. To trail my tongue down over that stomach, dip between those long fucking legs, and have them wrap around my ears. It was so real I could taste her sweetness.

"Oh, God. Scarlett," I growled as I thought of everything I could do to that body. Of burying myself inside her. Biting down on her breasts and slapping her ass. My hips became frantic, wildly bucking into my imaginary Scarlett as we came, lay together, and drifted off to sleep. These visions continued, almost tormenting me with their realness until I found my own release. One part of my fantasy then came true. I fell asleep. But as always, I was alone.

7

Scarlett

I F YOU LOOKED AT the collective history of Finn and me, one could almost believe we were fated to be together. But not twenty-four hours after I pledged, *I'm ready if you are. Tomorrow, we begin*, fate forced us apart. Ben had chicken pox, and I was stuck at home, trying to video-call Finn on my stupid laptop. Arthur had tried forcing me into a fancy, office-issued upgrade, but I loved mine. I'd had it since uni and knew every quirk and *almost* every trick to get around them. I also knew it was a piece of shit, but it was the first thing I had bought for myself when I left the foster system, and I couldn't bear to part with it.

I could curse at it, though. And I was, all while looking fab in a lovely lemon chiffon shirt, stained red lips, and SpongeBob pajama bottoms. As far as Finn knew, I had a nasty case of strep, so I was talking an octave or two lower as well.

Once connected, there was no hi or hello, just a pair of shining eyes almost as wide as his smile, and the THUMP, THUMP, THUMP of my heart. "Scarlett, I, umm...everyone misses you. Are you feeling better? I hope so because it's day one for Team Finlett. Or should it be Team Scinn? No, that's not right." He looked kind of edgy as he continued mumbling. The idea that *I* could be making *him* so nervous was ridiculous, but also undeniably hot, and full gushing commenced.

He is so bloody cute, and he misses me. Look how his curls sit behind his ear. Oh, and that little one right at his temple. Bouncing with glee. You are bouncing with glee. Stop it! This is business.

Pinching myself beneath the table was the only way to stop my fawning. "I'm getting there, thank you. And both names sound great, but how about we leave the nicknames for now and decide how we're going to do this when we aren't even in the same room."

"Good plan, boss." He fidgeted, tapping his pen against the table. "That's why yours should go first when we do come up with a name. Ooh, what about Scarinn?"

I bit my fist in an attempt not to laugh but failed miserably. "This is serious, Finn. We need a plan. What can we do today and over the weekend to catch up?"

"Right, catch up. Right. Well. Let's think about this. Hmm." Finn adopted the classic thinking-man pose, elbow on the table, the weight of his chin resting on his clenched fist, cute pout. "I know. How about you do nothing other than get better, and I'll continue going over our designs, comparing similar elements and seeing where we can incorporate each other's ideas?"

"That's very sweet, but I can't keep doing nothing."

"You can, and you will. The doctor said to take a week of rest, and a week of rest is what you shall get. I'm confident Team Farlett can come through." He wriggled his eyebrows mischievously, then began to wave. "Goodbye, Scarlett. Go rest now. Talk Monday."

Damn him for being so adorable and optimistic when I possessed so little of both. This really would have been easier if he was a pushy asshole. We'd effectively lost a quarter of our concept time to the application of calamine lotion to an eight-year-old he had no idea existed. I was the asshole. But for a reason.

Scarred by the prejudice I faced as a young single mother, I made the tough, maybe overly cautious decision to reveal Ben's existence to only Jason Wright. People treated me differently when they knew I was a mum. It was something I hated and something that had carved a massive chip into my shoulder. Pregnancy in the first year of university thickened my skin to the slut-shaming barbs and stereotypes young mums faced, but I learned early that, even around a supposedly more mature audience, teenage motherhood carried a stigma. *Unreliable. Unpredictable. Unworthy.*

I'd felt safe telling Jason about Ben, as I learned during my video-call interview process that he himself had been raised by a single, teenage mum. I'd noticed a photo of a beautiful blonde on a sideboard behind him. Attempting to be chill and cool—which I was not—my big mouth said, "Is that your wife or girlfriend, Jason? She's quite the stunner. In England, we'd say you were batting above your average."

He looked at the photo and smiled. "Yeah, um, that's my mom." To this day, I could not believe he still hired me.

Out of necessity, our wonderful, slightly pervy HR lady, Jan, who seemed to be as big of a fan of Finn as me, knew too. As, of course, did Uncle Teddy. But the guilt of keeping Finn in the dark was gnawing away at my soul. Even if, much to Teddy's disgust, I did nothing about my physical feelings for Finn—except continue having them—I liked him and didn't want to lie even if through omission. He was silly and fun, and despite my reservations about the situation at work, I appreciated and respected that he, too, felt a need to prove himself. In all honesty, he could probably have pushed his aunt to get this job all to himself, but he didn't. Something in my gut told me he was a good person. That I could trust him. And it wasn't just that. I'd been hiding a huge part of me for over a year, and I was tired.

As I laughed at Finn, who was still on screen and trying to figure out how to hang up, it was decided. I was going to tell Finn about Ben. I just had to find the courage. And the right time. And make it through chicken pox.

Ben and I survived the weekend, though I was forced to stay at home Monday too, as his pesky pox were still itching away.

While, workwise, the timing of my absence was poor, for my heart and hoo-ha, it may have proved perfect. The recent decision by Finn to cycle to work on sunny mornings had sent

a ripple of hormones through the office. For Teddy, the sight of
Finn strutting past in his biking gear was too much to ignore.

Teddy

> FINN IS SPORTING BIKE SHORTS AND A
> FUCKING MAN BUN. REPEAT. WE HAVE
> SHORT SHORTS AND A BLOND MAN
> BUN.

A blurred, stealth photo was attached as evidence. That damn
sexy hair and peachy ass were the last nail in my denial-laced
coffin. I wanted that man. The buns, too.

Ideology #3 - DO NOT date men you work with was
a major obstacle. Global architectural domination—well, New
York at least—meant adherence to it was essential. A fling with
the hot guy at work wasn't going to get me there. I'd hoped
the time away from his blue eyes and dirty-blond locks would
assist in breaking the back of my crush, but if anything, their
absence, Teddy's photos, and the odd combination of Austen
adaptations and *Magic Mike* only intensified their appeal.

I reminded myself repeatedly, *my sexy dreams are just
that—dreams.* I was not an X-rated Lizzy, and he was not my
chair-riding Darcy. No, I was a sexually frustrated architect and
mother, riding out the final hours of a toasted-sandwich-mak-
ing, *Peter-Rabbit*-watching, scratch-stopping marathon. And at
that stage of my life, that had to be enough.

Later that afternoon, as Ben picked up his toys and I peeled
burnt cheese off the grill, I received what felt like Teddy's thir-
tieth text of the day.

Teddy

> Just saw on Asher's Insta. M.I.X
> . is doing raspberry margaritas tonight.
> Whoop-whoop.

It was the injection of hope and adulthood that I sorely needed. Five days slothing around the house in oily hair and baggy sweats with an itchy, whiny eight-year-old was well and truly enough. I loved him with all my heart and soul, but honestly, I couldn't wait to see the back of the kid's head.

"Ben, are you ready? Let's go!"

This was Brett's week with Ben, but since he was sick, I'd kept him home the extra day. We were a few months into a shared-custody trial. Week on, week off, Sunday to Friday. We were fairly relaxed with the times and days. If one of us had a work thing or an appointment, we were happy to switch things around, and so far, it had been working well. I couldn't have imagined agreeing to it a year ago, but father and son had formed a bond, and all of us—Brett, his parents, and I—wanted to foster that. My child-free week was usually filled with extra work and tinged with loneliness, but to be honest, I also relished those times.

I couldn't say I felt the same enthusiasm for seeing Old Bretty, who had made it clear he wouldn't mind picking up where we had left off in England. Where Brett and I had left off was cherry-popping sex in the back of a Mini Cooper and an unplanned pregnancy. It was not a place I particularly wanted to revisit, hence **Ideology #6 - NEVER sleep with Brett, no matter how desperate you become.** I told him this in no uncertain terms last month, when he slid his hand around my waist and went for my ass, but he was nothing if not persistent.

Arguably, Brett was still hot, and I could easily see how he charmed the pants off a young me, but part of his original charm was the novelty of his accent. But I was now surrounded by Americans, and it, like Brett, had lost its appeal.

It was a short walk through the park to Brett's place, and I could practically taste the tangy raspberry of the margarita awaiting me when I buzzed the doorbell. Sprightly footsteps approached, and through the thick, iron-barred glass door, we heard, "Is that my Benny Boo Boo?"

"Grandma! Of course it's me. You can see me, silly!"

Ben ran toward Hillary as soon as the door opened and was swept up into her lululemon-clad arms.

"Hi, Hillary." I smiled as she kissed my cheek. "Just finished a class?" The woman was a Pilates nut. At fifty-something, she was ten times fitter than me.

"Sure did, kiddo. It was a monster too. You should come and join me one weekend. Class starts at twelve sharp." I nodded politely, but there was no way in hell I was doing Pilates with that woman. She would kick my ass, and my ego didn't need that.

We followed Hillary into the kitchen and were met with the smell of oatmeal cookies and wealth. Both Brett and his father, Bill, were investment bankers, and their success in business was evident. Their home was stunning and utterly intimidating. My childhood couldn't have been more different than Brett's, and I was terrified the first time I had slunk through their doors. Thankfully, Hillary was the warm, all-American, bake-an-apple-pie-a-day-while-ignoring-her-husband's-indiscretions kind of stay-at-home mum that I dreamed of as a kid. As an adult, not so much. As for Bill, in both frequency of sighting and hair color, he was like Moby, the great white whale. I'd met him three times and was not the slightest bit bothered by it.

"Where's Daddy?" Ben asked, stealing a still-warm cookie and sighing with pleasure as he bit into it.

Hillary grabbed some milk from the fridge and poured Ben a glass as she answered, "He's working late tonight, darling. I hope that's okay, Scarlett. He and Bill only called thirty minutes ago. They had a late meeting, and I didn't want to let you down on such short notice." There was a definite shaking in her voice. Was she nervous I wouldn't want Ben here without Brett? In all honesty, I was more comfortable in his absence.

"Of course, Hillary. That's no problem at all."

I left after a few cookies, fifty sloppy kisses, and a hundred whispered promises to be good.

I couldn't say the same for myself. Within minutes of walking through my front door, I was naked and wet. My honey rose bath ball hissed and fizzed in all manner of places. A chilled glass of rosé was within my reach. And Finn Austen was on my mind.

I'd tried to push the image of him out as I lowered my body into the scalding water. I did. Sort of. But my bath-time playlist—specifically Selena Gomez and her talk of being good, messes, dresses on floors, and hands not keeping to themselves—was not helping.

"Finn." A needy moan escaped my lips, as I rhythmically slid back and forth against the smooth porcelain. My fingers, out of sight and busy amidst the bubbles, were between my legs. I pictured us together as I circled, rubbed, and melted deeper and deeper into the water. Finn had drawn the blinds, locked the door and spread me out like the finest set of plans he'd ever laid his hands on. "Scarlett." Over and over, he groaned my name as he tasted me. When fantasy-me reached my peak with his tongue, reality-me fell apart on my fingertips.

My bath exit was timed perfectly. It was a long enough soak to do my thing and enjoy the glow, but also over before I turned into a prune. The temptation to collapse into my soft, pillowy mattress was strong, but I resisted and glammed up for the evening. Nails were painted, toes included, and my hair was straightened and styled. I slipped into the slinkiest, naughtiest dress in my closet, and finished the look off with black peep-toe stilettos and my namesake color staining my lips.

"Grant, stunning as always." Teddy smirked as my shit-hot self skidded into the cab beside him. "Your skin looks amazing. Fuck, you're beautiful." His eyes roamed my body as we pulled away from the curb. "You rubbed it out before you left, didn't you?"

"Teddy!" I squirmed in my seat, trying not to die of shame or laugh like the cab driver. "How the hell would you know?"

"You forget how long we lived together and how thin our walls were? I'd recognize that post-masturbation glow anywhere." Though unable to see my face, I could feel that I was redder than Mars. "God, Scar, don't look so horrified. There's nothing to be ashamed of. I did too."

"Oh, for fuck's sake."

The origins of Margarita Monday laid within my cheapness, sometimes social awkwardness, and the relative quietness of Monday at M.I.X. But thanks to warm summer nights, alcohol, and the promise of refrigerated cooling, the bar was packed.

Luckily, Teddy's friend, Asher Kim, still saved our favorite table by the window.

Exchanging major sex eyes, Asher escorted us to our table, pulled out Teddy's seat, and winked before strutting away. "Don't you ever give me shit about lusting over Finn. You two have it so bad for each other." I laughed, and Teddy choked on air, immediately raising my suspicions. "What? What's going on? Something's going on. You have a secret, Theodore, and I demand to know it."

A grin wider than the Hudson lit Teddy's face, and he leaned closer toward me. "Secret's over. Do you remember last New Year's? How I fell in love with the mysterious, hot asshole who touched my hand, then stole my cab?"

"How could I forget? But what's that got to do with Asher?" Teddy's adorable eyebrows hit his hairline, he shrugged, and the penny dropped, "Oh my God. No way. Asher is the—"

"Yes way! Asher is the hot asshole. I've been seeing him on the sly for weeks, and for various reasons, I couldn't say anything. Please don't look at me like that. It's been tough. Honestly, it nearly killed me not sharing with you, but we're official now and...he...he's really something, Scar. I am in deep."

Secrets between Teddy and I were a rarity, and I would usually scratch his eyes out for this level of deception, but I could see by the smile, not only on his lips but the one shining brightly in his eyes, that he was, as he said, in deep. Pettiness and jealousy had no place here. So, I did what any best friend should. I squeezed the shit out of his hand and squealed with glee. "I am so fucking happy for you!"

We left our coats at the table, hug-walked our way to the bar, and ordered two extra-large, extra-boozy, extra-drinky drinks with an extra wedge of lime for me. "Alright, lover boy, tell me everything and don't leave any horny bits out. I'm a lonely woman, and it's been a loooong time between drinks."

"Scar, he is fucking amazing. Every smile that leaves his lips and comes my way is a gift from God. We love all the same things, he loves kids, and..." Teddy's eyes lit up like a Christmas tree, and I was waiting for the dick-size comments to flow, but instead, I got, "he's sweet, determined, so freaking funny, and has just the right amount of arrogance. Maybe even a secret or two." He sighed and dreamily stared off into the distance. "Shit, he tolerates my 80's English Pop too. Last night we listened to Rick Astley, Mel and Kim, and Kylie records. It was a Stock, Aitken, and Waterman marathon, and he didn't complain once."

"Wow, that sounds great, but I was hoping for latex-related gossip rather than vinyl. Come on, give me the dirt. How is he, you know, between the sheets?" My BFF turning the color of the raspberry margarita on the bar beside us was an unusual sight. Teddy didn't have one shy bone in his body. Inappropriate was his middle name. He looked around us as if inspecting for the all-clear and then whispered, "There has been no between-the-sheets action. I mean, we've fooled around and kissed and stuff, and Lord, can that boy work with his tongue, but... I like him, Scar, and we've decided to wait."

"My baby is growing up!" I grabbed him by the ears and held his cute face to my chest, kissing his head repeatedly. "This is a first. You'd normally have banged his brains out and been done by now. I'm so happy and proud of you." And I was, but honestly, a tiny part of me was jealous. No, not jealous. Envious. And not of Teddy seeing and clearly being besotted with someone, but because he was keen on Asher and dared to do something about it. Unlike me.

"Even though you have me pressed into your heaving bosom, I can tell what that look on your face means. Finny must have asked me a hundred times when you were coming back to work," he said, freeing himself and straightening his boob-tousled hair. He kept one eye on me and one on Asher's ass as he slipped past, carrying a tray of drinks. The DJ kicked in at that moment, the bass dropped, the lights dimmed, and the crowd cheered. "I can read you like a book, Grant," Teddy yelled. "You can do it too. Ask Finn out, I mean. I know things are more complicated for you, but you can't use Ben and work as an excuse forever. You must put that lovely round ass out there." He nodded toward said ass before carrying our drinks toward our table. "I mean it, Scar. He's been here for, what, six months?" It had been three weeks. "You've waited long enough. Your vagina is shriveling up into itself more and more by the day. You need to talk to him, and here's your chance."

Before I could ask him not to reference my vagina in public, the two chilled, salt-rimmed margarita glasses were shoved into my hands. I was most inelegantly spun around on my toes—almost falling sideways—until I stood face to face with none other than Finn Austen. Thank fuck I didn't say vagina.

"Perfect timing, Finn," Teddy said, pushing me closer to the stunning blond standing like a god before me. "We were just about to sit down and have a drink, but I've been called back to work. Why don't you take mine and sit with Scar?"

Called back to work at nine on a Monday night? Yeah, sure.

Teddy's rough handling of me continued. He pushed me back into my chair by the shoulders, grabbed one of the glasses from my hand, and set it on the table in front of the empty chair opposite me.

I watched in mortified silence as Finn blushed but nodded and took a seat. His eyes flicked briefly to mine, and he smiled but mostly still looked at Teddy as they talked. I had no idea what they were saying. He was simply so beautiful that I couldn't concentrate. Coordinating listening, looking, and breathing at the same time seemed impossible.

The different environment brought a new appreciation for his size. He was massive—had to be six foot four or six foot five—with a thick, broad body. He was the owner of the deepest, shimmering, break-your-heart blue eyes I had ever seen. I thought back to my presentation. Of how I felt when he had touched me. I'd stupidly held his gaze and feared I'd end up like the Wicked Witch of the West, just an aroused, bubbling pool of wetness screaming, "I'm melting!"

Even on the video calls we'd shared, I'd actively counted how long I let myself gaze upon his face. Remembering that feeling, I tried hard to focus on his ear, or nose, but I couldn't help myself. I had to take all of him in. He had that cheekiness I loved in men. His crooked, dimpled smile could light up the whole city.

I wonder if he has a hairy chest. He doesn't seem hairy. Even if he is, he's very fair...

"Scar...Scarlett Grant!" yelled Teddy, poking me in the side with his index finger. He was determined to embarrass me, the bastard.

"Yes, yes, what? Why are you poking me?" I whined like a child, slapping his hand away and trying not to notice Finn laughing.

"I said, maybe you and Finn could split a cab home. He lives off Bleecker, only a few blocks away, fancy that." Before I could point out that Bleecker was indeed just a few blocks away but in the wrong direction, Finn and his incredible lips replied.

"I'm showing my new New Yorker-ness here, but I have my car. I needed to drop off my—uhh...needed to drop something off this morning, so I'd be happy to give you a ride, Scarlett."

I'd be happy for you to give me a ride too. That's why I need to say no.

"That would be lovely, Finn. Thank you."

Christ on a bike.

"Brilliant." Teddy slapped my shoulder again to emphasize his joy. He bent down and gave me a kiss on the cheek, leaned across the table, shook Finn's hand, then winked at me and bolted for the door. Before I'd had the chance to move, blink, or dramatically collapse, my bag buzzed and vibrated across the table. *Dear God, I hope that's my phone.*

I slapped my hand over the top, it continued to buzz in my palm, but yes, it was my phone. "Excuse me."

Teddy

> Did you notice the bulge? OMFG.

> I know you are shitting yourself, but you can do this. You deserve to be happy...and fucked senseless.

> Just sit and talk and make him love you. Or fuck you. Either is good.

> I will chop you up into tiny pieces and feed you to Cat Lady's cat.

Teddy

> You said Mrs. Horowitz was nice.

> She is. Her cats may not be.

My attention returned to Finn, who had attracted a blonde waitress to his side by simply existing. Batting her eyelashes and licking her lips, she walked Finn through each variety of wine available in what seemed like the greater Manhattan area while eyeing him like a prized steak. I was highly offended. How did she know I wasn't his girlfriend or wife? What, was I not worthy? Well, I may not have been, but she didn't know that! She didn't know me. She couldn't judge me. It was extremely vexing.

And also, when did this place offer a new service—feeling the bulging biceps of handsome customers as they ordered? Which was precisely what she was doing as my phone beeped again.

Teddy

> Just be yourself. This can't go on. It's painful. As I'm sure Finn's hard-on for you is. Also, don't eat cheese. It reacts badly with your breath.

"Scarlett, would you like another drink?" Finn asked, drawing my eyes from the phone and halting my attempts to smell my breath in my hand.

"No, I'm fine. Thank you."

Blondie McWaitress left, but not before one final brush of Finn's arm while giving me the foulest look I'd ever received. With her gone, it was just the two of us, the prized steak, and the budget rump.

8

Scarlett

M.I.X. WAS PUMPING. CLINKING glasses and drunken laughter surrounded us. But Finn and I sat in a cringe-worthy silence that was broken only by slurping on straws and throat clearing. Oh, and the rattling thump, thump, thump of my leg restlessly bouncing beneath the table. I desperately wanted to say something clever and witty but could think of nothing but funny cat videos Teddy sent me on TikTok. It was ridiculous. I was a highly educated woman working my way up the ladder in a male-dominated industry. Becoming a senior designer in record time was my destiny. But in the presence of this man, I was like a giggling, hormonal, seventeen-year-old girl.

When he scratched nervously at his curls, I sighed out loud. On receiving a compliment on my dress, I broke out in a head-to-toe blush. And when he rolled his sleeves, my mouth fell open like a sideshow clown. I was lucky no one wandered by and shoved a ball down my throat. NONE of it was discreet. NONE within my control.

My body was the victim of a chemical reaction. It was science. Biology. My brain was intoxicated by the sight of him. Pheromones forced my eyes to focus on his hands, to obsess over how his fingers wrapped around the cold, frosted glass. How he stroked, and tapped, and clenched it tightly. It was the sexiest thing I'd seen in months, and my mind wandered to dangerous places—my waist in his grip, his thumb stroking the silk of my dress, slowly gathering it between his fingers...

"Scarlett, should we get some food?" Hearing something other than, *'How was your day? Good, thanks. Yours? Yeah, good, thanks... So, you had a good day?'* almost made me jump. "Apparently, they do great tapas here, and I thought we could eat and talk over some ideas."

I wanted to reply. I really did. But the only thought in my head was how he said 'tapas' and how I could get him to say it again. Tapas, tapas, tap ass, tap my ass... Oh my god, I've lost it. Eventually, I choked out, "Tapas. Good," and nodded. *Well done, Grant. You sound like Borat.*

Finn clicked his fingers to get the waitress's attention, which was a joke as she was standing two feet away, ogling him. "Hi, could you tell me what's good to start with?" he asked, rubbing his fingers back and forth through the scruff of his chin. Blondie and I followed each scratch, but she had much better moves than I did.

She giggled, tossed her hair over her shoulder, and coyly replied, "Apart from me?" *Yep. I'm going to take out the waitress.* "I always recommend first-timers try the Angus Eye Fillet, the chorizo on the grill, and then some Mediterranean salad, mixed green vegetables, and Patatas Bravas. It gives you a little bit of everything."

"Awesome." Finn nodded. "Let's do that, then. And what about wine? What do you think, Scarlett? Red or white?"

"Red," I said, finally finding my voice and narrowing my eyes at the competition—I mean, waitress. "You should always go for red." *Oh, that was a good one. Take that, Blondie.*

Cocking his brow, Finn looked up from the menu. "Red it is." Without taking his eyes off me, he handed it back to the waitress, thanked her, and shifted forward in his seat. "So, Scarlett. That mate of yours, Teddy, is quite something. Did he tell you we went to the pub for a beer or twenty?"

"He most certainly did. I heard it was quite the evening. He's the master of hangover recovery, but even he was a little seedy the next morning. He's quite the storyteller, my Teddy."

"Hmm, I agree. Did he tell you any stories about me?" He wriggled in his seat again, and the vein that ran down his temple bulged. I'd only seen that happen on two occasions. Once when his football team lost the Sydney Derby—whatever that meant—and the other when he witnessed Herman have a discussion with my boobs instead of my face. The poor thing was sweating over what Teddy shared. I decided not to mess with him...much.

"No, not really. All I heard was his beer and whiskey stats. Oh, and that you were a cool guy who became even more Aussie with a few drinks under your belt." Relief spread over Finn's face, he huffed out a sigh, and the vein subsided. "Oh, and that you thought he and I were fucking."

The vein was back. Big time. That thing looked like it was a millimeter away from erupting, and Finn's whole face was as red as the Bloody Mary being consumed at the table behind him. "What! The bastard said he wouldn't say anything. Shit, that's...so embarrassing. God, you must think I'm such a dick."

"It's okay, Finn. I get it. We are weirdly close. He kisses me on the lips each morning before heading to his desk. He's a cute gay—I mean, guy."

An adorable chuckle rumbled from my companion's belly. "I'm never going to live this down, am I?"

"Of course you will...once I've had my fun."

"And exactly how long will that last?"

"Indeterminable." I sucked my lips between my teeth, releasing them with a loud pop. "I'm pretty sure I overheard you two waxing lyrical about Kylie Minogue one day. His squealing admiration of the superest of gay icons didn't give you any hints?"

"Jeez, I just thought it was because she's an Aussie and hot, and I'm Aussie. She's not that well-known over here. I thought he was trying to bond."

"Aww. And he was. He was sharing his love for the Queen of his people, and you thought he was sharing the love of her ass in short shorts. I think it's delightful."

"I just can't stop embarrassing myself, can I?" Finn rolled his eyes and gripped the arms of his seat so hard it groaned. "Alright. Let's get it all out there and give me a chance to redeem or defend myself. What else did Teddy tell you about me?"

Humming, I tapped my finger against my lip and let him hang for a second or two. "Honestly, Finn. You have nothing to worry about. I heard you grew up near the beach, surfed, and lived on a farm with sheep and horses. Oh, and that you are very sensitive about Foster's, and I should never bring it up."

"All true, but there was only one horse, and I did apologize about the Foster's incident. I'd had a few too many by that point."

"Not Foster's, I'm guessing." Finn's nose scrunched as he laughed. I had to hold myself back from brushing my finger across the cute little wrinkle it created. "I had no idea beer could be so controversial Down Under, but I suspect there are lots of things I don't know about Australia."

Never taking his eyes off mine, Finn picked a piece of ice from his empty glass, "I'd be happy to teach you them all, Scarlett." He then popped the lucky cube into his mouth. Crunch. "One by one by one."

Oh, good Lord.

Blondie became my favourite person in New York, returning with our food at the exact moment I needed to put something other than my foot or Finn's tongue in my mouth. "This is delicious," I said, talking around a forkful of spicy potato. "Teddy and I normally stick to a liquid diet when we're here. And look, I'm almost finished, and I haven't spilled a drop. I'm quite proud of myself." I laughed, and a piece of potato rolled down between my cleavage. Finn's eyes followed, his cheeks flushing red briefly before his eyes flicked back to mine. I could easily imagine what a man like Herman Wise would have said in that situation: "Would you like me to fish that out for you, Miss Scarlett?"

What would a man like Finn say?

"You have a beautiful, sexy giggle, Scarlett. It's nice to hear it up close. I'm normally on the other side of the office, looking back at you."

I handled this revelation by blushing and snorting like a pig. It was all very sexy. "You...you look over at me?"

"Uhh, yeah. You know I do. I see you looking at me too."

"What? I... I am just looking out your window... At the—"

"At the red brick wall and blinding neon light that I look out upon?" He smirked. "I'll grant you that, Grant. It is a very nice wall."

"And I am an architect. I appreciate a good erection." *What the fuck?* "Building. I mean, a wall. It's a wall... Oh God."

As the table vibrated with Finn's laughter, I contemplated running away, quitting my job, and leaving America forever. My shame was clear. He controlled himself to the odd hiccup, took my hand, and brushed his thumb across my knuckles. "Please don't be embarrassed. I think you're funny, and you know I say stupid shit all the time. It's okay."

I smiled and blew the hair I was trying to hide behind my face. "Promise you don't think I'm an idiot?"

"Promise. Let's change the subject. Umm, tell me, how long have you been at the firm?"

Swallowing the last of my drink, I signaled the hovering waitress for another. "Okay, that seems safe. Well, I arrived in the States just over a year and a half ago and started almost straight away."

"And you came from London?"

"Yep. It's been a big change, but I've worked hard and had some luck. One of the first houses I did was nominated for a design award, and I think I'm starting to build a solid reputation. Maybe that's why they picked me to work with your aunt. I'm hoping the success of the awarded project, and now Hudson River House, will help me become the next partner."

"I'm impressed." Finn nodded. "You have quite the plan. I'll be calling you boss in no time."

"Boss? God, sorry. Did that sound arrogant?"

He shook his head and chewed his bottom lip. That thing must have tasted as good as it looked. "No, not arrogant at all. Confident. And so you should be. No one would think anything of it if you were a man."

"Yes, Jesus. You're so right." *Stop watching his lips.* "It's nice to hear a guy say that. If only you knew how many people have suggested I slept my way ahead."

"Well, my sister would kick my ass if I thought differently. Then there's Jocelyn, and I'm sure you can imagine what she'd do to me. I admire a strong woman who knows what she wants. It's sexy as hell, Scar."

Two things caught me off guard. Finn calling me Scar was the first. It was a direct hit to the heart and hoo-ha. The second was his intense, dare I say, hungry expression. It was straight-up Darcy watching Lizzy at the piano, but this was real. There were no corsets close by, and no one was dying of consumption.

"Not many men, especially of your age, feel that way. It puts a lot of guys off."

"Only fools that don't know what they're missing out on. A woman with a bit of mongrel fight in her is much more fun. Keeps a man on his toes."

Did he call me a mongrel? Is that an Aussie thing? And why did it turn me on? I needed a distraction before I mounted his leg. "You better tell me more about the spectacular women that have trained you so well."

"Well, Evie is about half my size but twice as loud and can take me down in a tackle faster than you could with one of those smiles... That's the one." He winked when my lips curled at the corners. "And Jocelyn Austen Magarey White Crane is my late dad, Russel's, sister. Here's where it gets interesting. When he was twenty, he fell in love with a broke but beautiful nineteen-year-old Irish backpacker—my mum, Saoirse. My grandparents liked Mum as a person; Nan loved her. She was impossible not to love. But the hippie-surfer-farmer life they fell into wasn't what they expected for their private-boarding-school-educated son."

"Ooh, la dee da!"

"That's right. They were very fancy for farmers. So, yeah, they disapproved. Dad walked. And he and mum bought our little farm. Luckily, they did it before Byron became Byron Bay, home of the Hemsworths. With Dad gone, Jocelyn was left to inherit and run the family farming empire. She did it brilliantly too."

"Sounds like a movie plot. We need to throw in a bit of sex and a car chase, and we could sell it."

"Sex?" Finn's eyebrows twitched with pure cheekiness. "That can be arranged. Just say the word."

"In the movie, smart-ass." *For now.* "And you still haven't told me when Jocelyn came to live with you."

Color drained from Finn's face, and in a heartbeat, his whole demeanor changed. "It was kind of my fault, really. The day before my seventeenth birthday, Mum and Dad—" He took a sip of his drink before continuing. "They were going to pick up a gift for me and died in a car accident. Aunt Jocelyn was our only living relative and gave it all up—the house, the trappings… Just like Dad had done all those years ago, she walked away from Sydney to live with us on our little farm."

"Finn. God, I'm so sorry. For your loss, for the grief and unnecessary guilt I can hear in your voice, and because I shouldn't have pried. "

"Hey, no, it's fine. Please don't feel bad. I think I'll feel guilty about it for the rest of my life, but honestly, I like talking about them with you. It helps keep them alive." He continued to smile and chuckle, his dimple popping and his eyes shimmering as he talked about surfing, camping trips, and his neighbors that were more like family. It may sound weird or selfish, but I was almost envious. I, too, knew the pain of losing my parents, but that was where our similarities ceased. I rarely talked about them. Even to Ben or Teddy. For me, there was no point in dwelling on what I could never change. And even if I wanted to reveal my own childhood loss, I knew I'd say something stupid or spill about Ben. I wasn't ready for that, and besides, I was enjoying getting to know Finn.

To stop myself from talking, I plucked my lime from the side of the glass and placed it between my lips, casually chewing and swallowing the juice that was refreshing and tart and made one eye squint. It was something I did all the time in front of Teddy with no reaction at all, so I didn't give it a second thought.

Until I heard what sounded like a little moan. My eyes lifted from the citrus wedge and found Finn watching my lips and licking his own like he wanted to eat me alive. He shifted in his seat, his hand moved toward me in slow motion, and his thumb began to caress my face.

I almost climaxed right then and there. But I also remembered the last time this happened. I'd had a noodle on my face then. What now?

"Pip." His eyes slowly rose to mine. "From the lime. You had a pip—or do you call it a seed?—on your chin." Teddy was right. I would leave a whole chicken on my face to be touched like that again. Luckily, that pip seemed really stuck as his thumb continued to sweep between my lip and chin for quite some time. It was warm and lovely. The temptation to suck his thumb into my mouth was strong. But then, some clumsy oaf of a waiter—who I wanted to track down later and kill—dropped a tray of glasses. We both jumped, and his thumb fell from my face. "Shit! I...umm. Red. I...umm...let me get you another drink. You want more lime too?"

"Yes. Please. Limes are good." *Limes are good? You're a complete tit.*

"Great. I'll be right back. Don't go anywhere."

He almost ran to the bar and left me kicking myself under the table. I also used the time to scan up and down, side to side, over his body. Especially that peachy ass. Could he feel my gaze burning through him? Did he know I wanted to jump his bones that very second? Was he clenching? I was trying to determine just that when he turned his head, winked, and smiled.

Yup, he knows.

Waiting for Finn to return was like waiting for winter to end. My body craved the warmth of his eyes, the heat from his touch.

The depth of my attraction to this stunning man hit me. So did the fact that apart from the potato boob and bringing up dead parents, things were going well... too well. He was too sweet, his ass too perfect. What the hell would he want from me? He was too good to be true. Could I ever make a man like this happy?

The longer he was gone, the faster my heart raced—and not in a good, this-hot-guy-felt-my-thigh kind of way. This was terror, and I knew I was in trouble when I lost all feeling in my lips and fingertips. Seventh-grade first aid came flying back to me. I pushed myself away from the table and dropped my head between my legs, sucking in several slow, deep breaths.

Finn seemed like a great guy, incredible perhaps, even if he got work via his wealthy aunt. But he would also have to be a freaking saint to hang around for this. Panic attacks on what may or may not be the first date were hardly enticing. *If he's not pointing and laughing at me, he'll be gone by the time I lift my pathetic head. Also, why was he taking so long? Did they have to climb a tree for the limes?*

I was convinced he'd take one look at me and run. So, you could imagine my surprise when he ducked beside me, and I felt a large hand span the small of my back and the other caress my knee. "Scarlett. Are you okay?"

Shite! He was still here. Is that good or bad? "You're still here?" I mumbled, my body compulsively leaning into his.

"So, it seems. As are you. Now we've established we're both here. Can you please tell me what's wrong?"

"Nothing's wrong. Everything's fine. I'm fine. If you could just leave now, I would greatly appreciate it. I can get a cab or just roll home from here."

"Oh, so you are planning on moving from between your legs at some point, then? That's good, because I'd like to keep my job, and I really do think I can't do that without you. I need you, Scarlett."

"You need me?" I squealed, bolting upright and knocking him onto the lovely arse that got me in this position in the first place. "Shit, shit, I'm sorry. I'm such a clumsy idiot," I stuttered and leaned down to help him to his feet.

"Don't worry. I'm sure I'll be fine. I'll let you know tomorrow if I sustained any nasty bruises or scratches. Maybe you can kiss it better for me." He winked. A flash of blue warmed my heart. Something shifted internally, and a sense of calm washed over me. "You may lean into the clumsy side of things, but you are most definitely not an idiot. And yes. I do need you. I mean, the whole firm needs you, but especially me."

"Promise?"

"Promise. Here. Have some more lime.

9

Finn

TEDDY PROMISED ME IT would be a work meeting. We both knew he was lying.

Not a word regarding our project or anything related to the office passed our lips for the rest of the night. Knees, hands, and feet brushed, and each 'accidental' touch led to a maddening set of blue balls. And a big, big problem. One that wasn't attached to the blue balls.

I was very much at risk of falling for Scarlett Grant.

"Number three, number three, number three," she repeated in a whisper barely loud enough to hear.

"What's number three?" I quizzed.

"What? Did I say that out loud?"

I nodded, noting how her ill-behaved curls somehow fell gracefully over her collarbone as she chugged her drink, her green eyes darting up to mine nervously. "Number three...on the cocktail menu. Yes. That's it. I was thinking of ordering number three next."

I don't know what Scarlett was fibbing about, but she was clearly fibbing and pleased with herself too. But only for a second. Regret quickly appeared in her eyes. "I'm not an alcoholic or anything. I don't go around memorizing cocktail lists. Teddy and I come here every other Monday, so I know the menu by heart." She paused and blinked slowly. "That probably doesn't make me sound less like a wino." The blush that radiated from her ample cleavage made her skin glow more than it already did. So, I decided to make it worse.

"What is it?"

She froze. "What is what?"

"Number three on the menu. Let me know what it is, and I can order it for you."

"Oh. No, that's okay. You got the last round. This is on me. I'll go get them." She moved to push out her chair, but as she did, our waitress, Jen, floated by for the fiftieth time. I seized Scarlett's hand to hold her in place and waved over Jen with the other.

"Can I get you anything? Another drink? More tapas? My number?" she asked with a well-practiced hair flip.

"Just some drinks. Thanks, Jen. Scarlett would like a number three on the cocktail menu. I'll get one too, but a virgin, if you have it. And don't tell us what it is. I want a surprise."

Finding the words to explain the look on both Jen's and Scarlett's faces would be difficult. "Sure," Jen said slowly, "coming right up." She then flitted away, looking confused.

Scarlett's lips formed a smile, but every other feature read panic and screamed FUCK. I was the one who was fucked. She was cute as a button. Sexy as hell and mad as a cut snake. I loved it. "I'm just going to go to the bathroom. I'll be right back," she laughed and bolted.

I settled our bill in her absence, fended off Jen one last time, and by the time Scarlett returned, her drink was waiting for her on the table. The relief on her face was precious. "Espresso martini. Good choice, Scar. I hope you enjoy it."

"Oh, I will." She sat, sighed, and took a sip, her eyes closing as she swallowed. Damn, she looked good swallowing. Without my consent, my eyes zoned in on her lips and occasionally lowered to the cleavage I would forever remember as potato valley. She was stunning, even with a tiny espresso moustache. The view made my virgin version—basically a tiny, twenty-dollar iced coffee—taste even better.

It was midnight. The bar staff began vacuuming around our feet, and we took the hint to leave. Keen to act the gentleman, I pulled out her chair as she stood and then undid the deed by being caught in a not-so-subtle, not-so-gentlemanly checkout of her ass.

"Eyes up, Austen."

Thankfully, it was a short trip home, and I didn't say that because of the company. That was awesome. No, my gratitude was born more from the desire to remain alive. My driving was appalling, and we found ourselves on the wrong side of the road several times. Partly because I was distracted by her jokes about me being the last person in New York to drive anywhere, and partly because I was still not accustomed to driving in the States. And a bit because of the way the seatbelt highlighted potato valley.

Facing the wrong direction in a one-way street, I parked a few houses up from Scarlett's. There, we sat in the New York version of the dark, breathing like we'd run, not driven. My hand was resting on her seat, dangerously close to the exposed thigh I wanted to bite into. I could feel the heat emanating from her body as my fingers swept back and forth along the stitching. I wanted her heat on me, her hand caressing me as I did the bloody leather.

"So, what are we gonna do?" I whispered.

"What are we gonna do for what?" she parroted back, mimicking my accent.

"Hmm, you're a cheeky one, aren't you? Terrible at accents, though." I paused, smirked, and eyed her up and down. "Tomorrow night. What would you like to do? Maybe we could get together again, talk more about work, improve your accent..."

Edging closer, I accidentally-on-purpose began to play with the hem of her dress. It was the smallest action I could think of to make while resisting the urge to launch across the center console and pull her atop me.

"Oh, I don't remember agreeing to tomorrow night. I'll check my calendar and have my assistant get back to you. I'm terribly important, you know." She turned and made a move toward the door handle.

"Lemme get that for you!" I bellowed, rushing from my seat, out of the car, and running to hold open her door. Warmth engulfed me again as I took her hand and helped her slide from the seat, watching her long legs the entire time. Her heels hit the road with an elegant clunk, and we stood in silence, face to face on the curb.

"This is a nice street. I like the trees." I smiled, plucking and rubbing the Gingko leaves between my fingers.

"Yes, trees are good."

She looked so cute, shy, but with a kind of naughty twinkle in her green eyes. She looked me up and down and fidgeted, rolling back and forth onto the outer sides of her feet. I hadn't known Scarlett for long, but even I knew that would never be a good thing for her to do in heels *or* flats. Her ankle rolled, and she went hurtling toward the ground, expelling a massive, grunty, "Oof."

In one sweeping action, I grabbed her, bracing the small of her back in one palm, her flat stomach in the other, and pulled her back to her feet. "Scar, are you alright?"

She felt so good in my arms. So natural. She also seemed unable to reply. Her eyes were focused on my hand. On the sweeping of my fingers over the soft fabric of the sexiest dress I'd ever seen. With the hand resting just above her ass, I pulled her tighter against me. She had to have been able to feel my hardness, but I didn't care. I wanted her to feel me. My eyes shifted off hers as my thumb drifted higher and higher towards the breast I wanted to pull into my mouth and bite. The teasing thumb briefly paused at the underside of her rapidly hardening nipple, and when I grazed the pebbled edge, I moaned. She gasped, and I freaked out.

"Shit. Sorry, I didn't mean to feel you, shit. Are you alright? Do you need me to walk you in?"

She nodded, and my heart raced. "I do...I want you to come...inside. I want you to come...to walk me inside my house, but I don't know if you should...do that. If we should do that."

It was a confusing, devastating relief. I wanted to go in but was terrified of doing so. I wanted to kiss her and felt she wanted me too, but I knew It would be a mistake. If I allowed what I wanted to happen to happen, I wouldn't want it to stop. I wasn't ready for that. I didn't think Scarlett was either. Proving me right, she stood on her tippy toes and laid her trembling hand against my chest. With my heart pounding beneath her palm, she gently pressed her lips against my cheek. The scent of sweet peas and violets dizzied my head and stiffened my cock as she softly whispered goodnight, then turned to walk away.

"Bonsoir, Scarlett Grant." My voice came out as a rough scratch I barely recognized. She looked over her shoulder, her beauty almost knocking me flat on my face.

"Bonsoir, Finn Austen." With all the elegance and poise of a baby giraffe, she floated up the stairs, swinging the hips my fingers ached to touch a tad more than proper.

"Lord, give me strength."

"You're home late. I thought you were only going for a beer?" said a voice traveling down the hall from the kitchen. With much reluctance, I walked toward it, knowing my sister would probably follow me upstairs for her answer if she didn't get one.

"I was. But I ended up having fun and stayed. Then I had to drive Scar—a friend home. Is that okay with you?"

"Jeez, calm down, Snappy Tom. I just asked."

"Yeah, I know you, and you don't just ask anything."

"Bloody hell, Finn. I gather whoever you took home didn't put out, or you wouldn't be in such a shit mood."

"You're disgusting. I'm going to bed."

"I knew it. She didn't put out. Probably just as well. You don't have time to chase girls around New York, not when you should be home with your daughter." Evie Austen, my little big sister, could be the most incredible and giving woman. She'd truly been a lifeline for me since my girlfriend, Shelby, had died. She also was a walking, talking pain in my ass. One that loved to antagonize me, and one I normally loved to fight back against. This, though, was bullshit. I knew it. She knew it.

I swallowed the venom stinging the tip of my tongue. Walking away was the only way I could stop myself from getting into something I had no desire to get into. I'd had a great night and felt more alive than I had in God knew how long. I wasn't about to let my sister ruin it. I made it up three steps before I heard her again.

"Finn. Stop. That was uncalled for. I'm sorry."

"Damn right it was. Before last week, I hadn't been out once since we got here, Evie. Not once. Even before we left Byron, I could count on one hand how many times I left Iris, apart from school. You can take your apology and shove it."

After stomping up to my room, grumpily mumbling about assholes through teeth-brushing, aggressively discarding my clothes on the floor, then sighing, stopping, and neatly rearranging them, I made my way to bed. I knew it was futile, but I had to try.

The city that never sleeps. It might have been the most apt nickname ever, as I hadn't had a solid eight hours in weeks. The streets were alive and kicking day and night, and even in the quieter residential areas, it was impossible to escape the pulsing hum.

But tonight, it wasn't noise keeping me awake. It was visions of wild eyes shining up at me through untamed falling strands of red. A round ass, sashaying away from my car. And a devilish grin that beamed over her perfect and bare shoulder. Scarlett had awoken an almost forgotten part of me, and I feared I might never sleep again.

At three a.m., exhausted, and with my sheets wrapped around my sweat-covered body, I gave up hope for slumber. After freeing myself from my Egyptian cotton bindings, reorganizing my desk, and straightening my wardrobe, I went through the last remaining moving boxes in my room. Evie had been nagging me endlessly about them, so she'd be thrilled. Not that I wanted to thrill her. After the shit she pulled, I should have dragged the bloody boxes to her room.

Choosing the higher ground, I grabbed a pair of scissors from my immaculate desk and began hacking away at the cardboard. Houdini himself would have had difficulty getting past the seventy-six layers of tape, but eventually, brute force won the day, and with a cheer of success, I got them all open.

Halfway through the second box, I realized how valid my procrastination had been. Each contained various oddities that could be grouped into two categories—utter crap or utterly heart-breaking. The first box I opened was the crap. Old

Women's Weekly cookbooks, an Australian cooking icon that had a place in every home. A dozen old tablecloths and two of the ugliest vases I've ever seen, haphazardly wrapped in sun-bleached beach towels.

The second box was equal parts crap and items of enough sentiment to cause an unease, while the third, marked "Evie", was jam-packed with pure, tear-provoking heartache. Individually and lovingly wrapped were several of Mum and Dad's old photo albums; my, Evie, and Iris's baby things, and one of my old shoe boxes with 'Shelby' handwritten in the white Nike swoosh.

Sitting on the floor surrounded by piles of stuff, I removed the lid. Its distinct, musty, old-photo smell hit me, and I fell to pieces. The first thing I removed was a photo of Shelby and me from school. We were maybe sixteen, both sunburnt and smiling, with no idea that tragedy was lurking just around the corner. *Christ, she was probably pregnant.*

Tears fell freely and increased with each discovery. There were more photos of her and Nate and some more with me. The next layer revealed an ugly-as-hell shell necklace I'd made for her seventeenth birthday, her final year report card, and then, at the very bottom, something I'd never seen until that moment—an envelope containing more photos and a handwritten letter from Shelby.

Hello, Baby.

My name is Shelby, and I'm your mum, but of course, you'll know that by the time you read this. I wanted to write you a letter to tell you how much I loved you even before I ever saw you. And to tell you how much fun I had with you in my tummy.

It was hard sometimes, baby. Some people were mean and cruel to both your daddy and me, but feeling you grow and move and kick inside me was worth it.

I have taken a photo of my belly each month to see how you grew and how we both changed. I am eight months pregnant now and cannot believe there is only one more photo to go before you arrive. I also can't imagine how I could possibly get any bigger, but your nanna assures me I will.

Your daddy and I are so excited and can't wait to meet you. Speaking of Daddy, you are so lucky and will love him so much. He is so fun and cute, a great surfer, and just the best guy ever. I have loved him my whole life (don't tell him that, though; it will give him a big head) and loving you has brought us closer, so thank you for choosing us to be your parents.

I also wanted to make you some promises.

1. I promise I will read you a story every night.

2. I promise that, even when I'm tired, I will kiss and cuddle you and never yell (unlike your nanna).

3. I promise to look after your daddy and love him as much as I love you.

4. I promise to give you a pretty name (because I know you are a girl despite what Daddy says).

5. Baby, I promise that your daddy and I will always be happy and always love you. We will never leave you alone, and we will always be a family and love each other no matter what. We WILL live happily ever after.

I love you so much.

Mummy. XXOO.

Pain and grief pushed all sense and reason from my brain. With the tear-soaked letter in my hand, I ran to Evie's room, almost slamming the door through her wall as I burst in and shook her awake.

"What's wrong? Is it Iris? Is she okay?" She almost fell from the bed in her rush to rise, and I made no attempt to help her stay upright.

"Where did you get this? How could you keep this from me? Fuck, Evie, you had no right."

"What? What are you talking about, you dickhead?"

"This, Evie. I'm talking about this." Filled with rage, I threw the letter into her face. Sleepily rubbing her eyes with one hand, the paper crinkled between her fingers, and I watched as her face switched from blurry, confused annoyance to a look of *oh shit*.

"Where did you find this?" Her voice was pained, hollow.

"In those damn boxes you left in my room. The one that had your name written in bright-yellow marker. Was that deliberate? Were you trying to have me find it and make me feel like shit about Scarlett?"

"Scarlett? That girl from work that Jocie says you have the hots for? What's this got to do with her?"

"I dunno, you tell me. You're the one giving me grief about coming home late, and now this. You have no right to make me feel guilty for even thinking of having a life."

"Finn! You are acting like an idiot. Number one, I didn't even know you were with Scarlett tonight. And two, those boxes have been collecting dust in your room for weeks. What, you think I foretold all this happening with your stupid Magic 8 Ball and planted the letter?"

Fuck. I hate it when she's right.

"I don't know. No, probably not. But still, why would you not tell me? Don't you think, as Iris's father, I had the right to give it to her myself one day?"

"Yes, I do think that. But if you must know, Nate found it years ago in Shelby's things and only gave it to me before we left. He made me promise that I'd keep it until I thought Iris was ready. He was so sad and said it was the last piece of her he had. I know you are her dad, but I am with her day in and day out, and I wanted to do as Nate asked and give it to her when she was old enough to appreciate it, and I don't think she is yet."

"That's not your decision to make. I'm her dad. I was Shelby's boyfriend. Even if I didn't show Iris, I should have been the one to choose. Congratulations, Evie. I had the first fun night since I can remember, and you've completely fucked it. Hope you're happy."

After quite possibly waking the entire house with my yelling, I then made sure of it by slamming the door as I made my exit and again when I entered my room. I waited for the footsteps to echo down the hall behind me, but they never came.

Neither did sleep. It remained elusive the rest of the night, giving me a horrendous amount of time to worry and ponder the terrible things I was and wasn't doing with my life. By the time my alarm went off at six, I had all but decided again that nothing could happen with Scarlett. There was something there between us that enticed but scared me. And like I'd said to her at the bar, I needed her—truthfully in more ways than one. But I really needed her for my job. Messing around with my heart and dick was one thing, but I needed to remain in control.

I was here for my daughter's future and Evie's too. The future I'd promised Shelby on her deathbed was my responsibility, and that was something I couldn't risk messing up.

10

Scarlett

A S THE SUN ROSE, my spirit soared with it. Waking before my alarm and at least three cycles of the snooze button was unheard of, but I had been blessed with the sleep of the gods last night. Either that or I suffered a hormone-induced coma.

Finn Austen was the last thing I thought of as I closed my eyes, and his sunny, smiling face, eyes, and scent were the first things on my mind come morning.

Delusional grandiosity carried me to the shower for the first time without coffee in possibly ten years. Its sustenance got me through dressing, hair, makeup, and cooking myself French toast for breakfast. A sip of the good stuff hit my lips only as the first golden toasty bite hit my belly. And man, was it good. As was the roasted Colombian goodness I savored rather than guzzled without tasting.

By six forty-five, I was done with breakfast and washing up, so I decided to tidy the house a little—well, a lot. I couldn't say for sure what inspired the sudden burst of domesticity at the crack of dawn on a Tuesday, but I think a certain blond Aussie may have had something to do with it.

Finn was methodical. I was not.

At work, his desk was spotless, bordering on compulsively neat. The four separate pencil/pen holder thingies were a perfect example. There was one for pencils, one for blue pens, one for black, and one for red. The rest of the stationery lived in a cute little caddy that was filled to the brim with Post-its, staplers and refills, erasers, and paper clips. By comparison, my stationery items were either thrown into my top drawer, could be found rolling around in my bag, or were stolen from Teddy's desk when I walked past.

Then there was his morning routine. Studying it as I had, I knew it by heart. Each day when he arrived, first and foremost, his blinds were opened, allowing the morning light to stream in onto his beautiful face. He then sat. His satchel was lifted over his head and seated on his powerful-looking thighs. His phone was removed first and placed on the right of his desk. Plans came out next and went in the center, and pen and pencil were taken from the appropriate holder and positioned above them. Finally, a water bottle and an apple or banana were set on the left. Once, he really shocked me and brought in two kiwi fruits instead. It was a big day. This routine was completed with an adjustment of his iPad, his hot and glorious signature look of concentration, and a satisfied nod.

In all good conscience, I couldn't let that man walk into my house in its natural condition. It wasn't that I was a slob or hoarder or anything, just...chronically laidback in this one area of my life. I was convinced my mess would change how he looked at me, and I couldn't bear that.

I dusted the place from top to bottom, sneezing my ass off while thinking back to last night. The cheeky hopefulness in Finn's eyes when he asked me out and the playful sexiness in his, 'Bonsoir,' served as the perfect motivation. My rugs were vacuumed to within an inch of threadbare. The beds in mine, Ben's, and the guest room were stripped and remade with my fanciest, highest thread count sheets, and a well overdue load of laundry was started. Cinderella herself couldn't have done better.

Once I had done all I could, or was willing to do, I ran one last check over to make sure there was none of Ben's stuff laying around. Because I'd worked up such a bloody sweat, I took another shower and put on my second outfit for the day, a sexy but appropriate black pencil skirt and white ruffled-collar shirt so soft it felt like fingers pressing against my skin each time I moved. It was much cuter than my first ensemble, and I was checking how my ass looked in the mirror when I heard Teddy banging on the front door. "I forgot my keys! Let me in!"

The house filled with light as I swung open the door and puckered up for my morning kiss. I was left hanging, though. Teddy was too busy smirking and inspecting me with an eyebrow raised to his hairline. "Ahoy, Captain."

"Fuck! Really? Do I need to change?"

"No, don't you dare. You look like the sexiest pirate in New York. It's the perfect welcome-back-to-the-office-check-me-out-Finn-Austen outfit. I can just see his dirty mind thinking up all kinds of filthy puns. Plugging your blowhole while his parrot watches, for example."

I was halfway up the stairs by the time he'd finished. "Okay, I'm definitely changing."

"Please, Scar, I'm just kidding. I'm sorry. Please don't. You look adorable, and I'm sure Finn will think nothing of the sort—holy shit!" His jaw dropped. "Someone's been busy. This place looks fantastic. Did you do it all this morning? What time did you get up?" The penny dropped. "Fuck, Scar, is he coming over tonight? And that's why you're wearing the skirt? Easy access?"

"Teddy! No! But also, yes, I have been busy. And yes, I did it this morning. Ben's at Brett's place, so I thought I would make the most of the time and tidy up."

"Andddddd...."

"And Finn asked me to see him again tonight." My arm was almost ripped from the socket as Teddy dragged me into a ferocious hug. "To work on the project, Teddy. I thought I should tidy up a bit in case he needed to come in to use the toilet or something. Fuck, I forgot to clean the upstairs toilet."

"To work on the project? Yeah, sure. There's only one project you two will work on, and it's all about him anchoring to your port."

"Eww, you're gross. Get off!" I pushed my clinging friend off me, grabbed my things, and headed out. Mrs. Horowitz, whose house stood between Teddy's and mine, was standing at the bottom of my steps, calling out to what was likely to be one of her cats.

"Mr. Pickles! Mr. Pickles, breakfast time." She turned when she saw us approaching. Tears were pouring down her face, and the spoon and tin of cat food she held in her trembling hands looked close to dropping.

"Are you okay, Mrs. Horowitz? Can we help you with something?" I gently took the can from her hands and instantly regretted it. The scent of tuna and guts hit me hard, so I immediately gave it to Teddy and took her hands in mine.

"Mr. Pickles didn't come home last night. You haven't seen him, have you, dear?"

"Gosh, I'm sorry. I haven't been outside since last night. Hmm, Mr. Pickles...is he the orange one, the tabby, or the hairless?"

"No, he's my black cat, the one with the white line on his nose shaped like a pickle and two white front paws."

"Oh, right. I think I've seen his little face in the pram when you walk. What about you, Teddy? Did you see him this morning?"

"No, sorry. No black cats crossed my path." He couldn't suppress his smirk. "Does he do this often? Have a night out on the town? Maybe he has a girlfriend and spent the night with her?" For that, Teddy earned a hearty elbow in the ribs. He may have been genuine, but it was hard to take him seriously after all the pirate jokes. Luckily, Mrs. Horowitz failed to pick up on the sarcasm.

"Never. But I had caught a bug in the house and opened the door to throw it out. Unfortunately, Mr. Pickles followed with it. I looked everywhere I could but couldn't find him. It's not like him to miss his breakfast." Her eyes shifted furiously between me and the tin. Teddy saw it, too, and began to tap it as she had been. The nervous darting settled.

"Well, I'm sure he'll be back soon. We'd love to stay and help look, but we really must get to work. I promise, though, we will keep an eye out, and if you haven't found him by the time we come home, we will help you then." The can of food was handed back to its owner, who I gave a gentle and hopefully reassuring rub on the arm. With an unconvincing nod, she tottered off down the street, banging the spoon against the tin.

The clanging was still audible in the distance when Teddy covered his mouth with his hand, screwing his face slightly because it reeked of fish, but giggling beneath it, nonetheless. The man was a child. I knew what he was laughing at, and it wasn't the damn cat.

"Just spit it out."

"Finn wants to ram his schooner into your porthole."

"How many other hole jokes do you have?"

"Ahem, Scarlett, trust me, you don't want to know."

My confidence was as high as ever striding into my office. So much so, that as I entered our building, I decided today was the day to tell Finn about Ben. There was something between Finn and me, and even if it did stay strictly business, I didn't want to lie through omission anymore. We were partners. One needed the other—in a strictly professional sense, of course.

I should have known my certitude would diminish. With three and a half steps to go to my desk, the stench hit me, and I heard, "Why, good morning, Miss Scarlett."

My hungry eyes scanned the room for Finn as I replied, "Good morning, Herman. How are you today? Enjoying your last days as a working man?" His retirement had suddenly been moved forward and was only a few days away. The whole office was thrilled.

"I am. Coincidentally, that's what I wanted to speak to you about. While you and Austen are working exclusively on the Crane project, I wondered if you could find the time to plan one or two small retirement parties for me. Without the fear of being fired, my assistant has gone rogue and refuses to do it, my children hate me, and my wife...well, she just divorced me. An old man like me has no business meddling in these things, but you and Finn are the young blood in this place. I trust you to make it wonderful. Spare no expense." A list of wants and demands was shoved into my hand as he patronizingly tapped it, checked out my boobs, and then walked away before I could argue.

Planning a party and movie night for a pompous old windbag wasn't my ideal way to start the day. When Finn barreled into the office not ten minutes later, disappointingly Lycra-less and looking like he just ate a bag of shit, it seemed it wasn't about to improve. It was the grumpiest I'd ever seen him, but he still looked hot as hell.

"Typical. Your first day back, and he ditches the bike." Teddy plonked beside me and passed me a fresh jam doughnut. "What did Old Man Time want? Apart from checking out your tits, which you need to say something about. You're a bloody full-breasted doormat, Scar."

"Well, that's up for debate. One thing that isn't, is Finn and I being tasked with planning the old prick's retirement party—parties, I should say." I shook my head as I watched Herman sleazing onto Victoria. "Tell me, Teddy, is this guy popular enough to deserve a party and a movie night?" The gooey red jam was licked from my fingers as I passed Mr. Wise's note. "Don't suppose you want to help too?"

"Are you kidding? Who do you think is doing all the crappy jobs now that you and Finn are working only on Crane's house? Besides, this gives you an extra reason to work...alone...in the still of the night...with no other sounds but the combined beating of your hearts and the expansion of his massive coc—"

"Morning."

Fuck. Finn.

"Finn, hi, good morning. How are you?"

Feeling an instant blush from cleavage to eyes, I spun to greet him but was met with a stranger's face. His typical exuberance and light had vanished, replaced by a sullen, stone-eyed expression that left me cold.

"I'm fine, but I wanted to let you know that I can't go out tonight. I have some family commitments that I forgot about. If you can wait around, I could work until six or seven, but that's it."

"Oh, yes, that's fine. We were only going out for work after all."

He replied with his head down, looking toward his shuffling feet. "That's right. It's just work. Speaking of which, if you're ready, we should get to it. Meet in the conference room in ten?"

"Perfect, see you then. Can't wait."

My heart sank as he walked away. *Where was the joy? My morning flirty, winky smirk?*

There was no way I'd imagined how into me he'd been. That was not an Austen-inspired fantasy. The way he looked at me as I left him last night, whispering French in the dark and a lingering lusty gaze could not have been faked. That was real. The feeling in every fiber of my body, what pressed against my stomach as he held me to him, could not have been denied. He was hard as stone. He wanted me as I wanted him.

What the hell happened?

That glass face of mine was obviously as transparent as ever. Teddy rubbed my arm sympathetically, like he would one of the neighbor's cats when he thought no one was looking. Finn's standoffishness appeared to confuse him as much as it did me. "Maybe it's just because we are in the office? Maybe when he has you alone, he'll throw you up against the door and—"

I placed my hand on Teddy's lips to shush him. "Don't, love. Please. No more teasing. Not today."

No air-conditioning was required on this late summer's day. The sudden chilling of Team *Finnlett* had continued all morning and took care of any residual heat between us. Any attempts at communication were instantly shot down with a 'nope', 'yep', or drawled 'dunno', and there was ZERO touching. The only glimpse of flirtation and fun was over lunch when we ordered sushi.

"What is that stuff? Looks dodgy," Finn quizzed with a grossed-out expression as I drizzled yum-yum sauce all over my sashimi.

"Dodgy? It's not dodgy. It's yum-yum sauce. I'd never heard of it before coming to America, and now I refuse to eat Japanese without it. Try some." I handed him one of several little containers of deliciousness. With narrowed, suspicious eyes, he sniffed, dipped his pinky in, and then let the good stuff hit his lips.

A pink tongue darted out to lick his bottom lip as his whole face lit up. "Fuck, that's really good." Like my own, Finn's lunch was soon covered in the stuff, but it was only I who ended up wearing half of it on the sleeves of my pirate shirt. "It should come out. When you get home, run it under the tap for a bit and then leave it to soak. Evie always says a good soak will cure anything."

"Are you sure she wasn't talking about bubble baths?"

"Possibly both. But give it a whirl. It would be a shame to waste such a pretty shirt."

"Oh, you like it? Teddy was making pirate jokes all morning."

"I like it very much. The skirt too. You look beautiful. You always look beautiful, Scarlett." For a second, he smiled at me in a manner that could melt the skin off my face. But he seemed to catch himself, almost grimace, then look down to study his food. "I guess we better hurry up and get back to work.

That was it. The fun—if you could call it that—was over. For the rest of the day, I was forced to make do with the occasional lingering smile, raised brow, and two or three definite glances toward my lips as I spoke. I would even call him snappy, at a few points. The pitifully held-on happy moments were spaced out over a nine-hour day, leaving a lot of time for nothing. Nothing but business, which I reminded myself, is how it should be.

Our initial thinking was to combine some aspects of each design we knew Jocelyn approved of into one—a beautiful Frankenstein if you will. But it wasn't coming together. The flow and openness of both methods worked well together, but Finn's design was more controlled by traditional form and space constructs, whereas mine was modern and informal. We tried numerous ways to meld the two, but none felt right. We both knew it, but neither seemed to want to admit it.

Fatigue began to set in. Noticing the decreased hum from the main office, I looked over to Finn, who was busy working away with his tongue poking from the side of his lips, then at my watch. It was already six, and we were the only two remaining in the building. The dull thud of rain began patting against the window, and heavy thunder rumbled through the heavens. If I'd pictured this situation as I lay in bed last night, I would have considered it a perfect setting for romance. For bending, if not breaking, my ideological stance and my Sahara Desert dry spell.

But it wasn't. Finn's indifference had made that perfectly clear. He regretted last night. Work was work and nothing more. I'd had enough, and I wasn't the only one.

"Scarlett, this isn't working. We need to start from scratch, to design something from the ground up...together. It will mean a lot of time locked away with me, working one on one. Are you up for it?"

Am I up for it? This time yesterday, I would have screamed, 'HELL YEAH,' and tossed my knickers in the air. But now?

"Yes, absolutely. Are you?"

"I don't have much of a bloody choice, do I?" *Exsqueeze me?* "No more for tonight, though. I'm done. I can't spend any more time locked up here with—" Catching his words, Finn looked up at me from beneath his curls guiltily, maybe even apologetically. But it was too late. The intent was clear, and the blow landed.

11

Scarlett

THUNDER AND LIGHTNING DROWNED out my self-pity-ing mumbles. A torrential downpour was unleashed from above, and I was caught smack-bang in the middle of it as I walked home down Sixth Avenue.

It was a perfectly miserable end to a fucking miserable day.

I can't spend any more time locked up here with—

Me. He couldn't wait to get away from me. What the hell was with that?

Why was he acting so differently? So cold, so jerky, so...un-Finn. I wracked my brain, replaying the events of the last twenty-four hours again and again, looking for any clue, but I drew nothing but blanks.

Naively, my hope remained. Maybe tomorrow would bring back the smile that had lit my world. Maybe I would look into his eyes and see that cheeky, flirtatious sparkle that inspired such trust in me. Maybe then I could forget the eagerness he'd displayed to be rid of me.

Maybe, maybe, maybe.

Maybe I should have checked the weather forecast, brought a raincoat or umbrella, and not strutted around in a white shirt and baby-pink bra. But I didn't, so I splashed my way through the puddles in what was essentially a corporate dine-and-dash. Terrified that Finn would feel obligated to drive me home, I waited for him to go to the bathroom and bolted. The fear of being in his car again, of not feeling what I felt last night, was so strong, I'd rather risk death by lightning. At least that would be quick.

Two blocks into my journey, the menacing little toot-toot of a car horn scared the absolute crap out of me, and I almost slipped on the wet sidewalk. It didn't take a genius to figure out who the driver would be.

Do not acknowledge him. I tilted my chin and stared to my right. But my dismissal was rendered useless by the sparkling glass of the Capital One bank branch. It acted as a mirror, reflecting the approaching headlights, a Jeep slowing to a halt on the wrong side of the road, and a familiar, beautifully concerned face. "Scarlett, what are you doing? Why didn't you wait? Let me give you a ride."

Even yelling over a storm, his tone was softer than it had been for ninety percent of the day. It pissed me off. *He treats me like a BO-riddled leper whose finger had dropped into his coffee, ignores me, then chases me down in his stupid, sexy Jeep and beckons me? I don't think so, buddy.* At work, I had to be polite and kind. Here, on the mean streets of New York, I didn't.

"Fuck no." Shit. "I mean...no, thank you. I am fine as I am. Thank you. Have a good night. Thank you." *Way to stick it to him, dipshit. That'll show him.*

I kept walking, and he kept creepily rolling along beside me. It was the stuff slasher flicks were made of. "Don't be stupid, Red. It's pissing down. Get in the car."

"Safety 101. A woman should never accept a ride from a stranger, especially in New York. You could be a mass murderer for all I know. The fact you insist on driving instead of walking like a normal person tells me everything."

"What, I'm a stranger now?"

I stopped and threw my hands to my hips. "Quite frankly, yes. The man I spent today with was not the same one I shared tiny morsels of Spanish food with yesterday. And since I don't know which version of you is the real you, you are, for all intents and purposes, a stranger. Hence, no ride. Thank you."

"What?" The confused bastard laughed. His Jeep stopped, the door opened, and he strode toward me in the rain. "Come on, Scarlett."

"No, you were horrible to me today, Finn. I want to know why, but I don't need to. We work together. Whether or not you're a good guy doesn't matter. Thanks for the offer, but I think it's best if I walk."

"Please, Scarlett. I'm sorry for being such a dick. I am the man who ate your olive and then drove you home, I promise. I just... I forgot about him for a bit today. Forgive me, please."

Pride demanded I tell him and his wriggling eyebrows to fuck off. To flip him the bird and keep on going. But I was quickly discovering I was vain as hell. He looked so freaking good. His loose blond curls turned to ringlets that framed his face, and his blue eyes shone even brighter under the streetlight. And his shirt. His shirt was white and, just like mine, transparent. I could see the defined lines of a *one, two, three*...eight-pack, the curve of his pecs, the shape of his nipples. *Shit, my boobs!* I crossed my arms over my chest, dropped my head to avoid his gaze, and watched the filthy water swirl down the storm drain.

A warm hand reached out to mine and squeezed it gently. "Shit, you're freezing." He shifted his grip from my wrist, snaked his arm around my waist, and pulled me closer to his massive, hard body, warming me instantly. His free hand cradled my chin and raised it till my eyes met his. "Please, Red. I am a good guy, I promise."

I watched night become day in his eyes as a fork of lightning lit the city. I jumped, Finn held me tighter, and my treacherous body molded to his. I swore I could feel his heart beating through his chest. "I'm sorry, Red. Please don't be stubborn. Get in the car and let me take you home."

He did look sorry. Sad, too. And I had the power to make it better, even if only temporarily.

You're a bloody full-breasted doormat, Scar. Teddy's loving barb whistled through one ear but blew straight out the other.

"Well...okay, then. But if I end up chopped to pieces in the back of your Jeep, I will be really pissed."

"I'll try to keep that in mind." Smirking smugly, he rushed to open my door while blatantly checking out my bra and its contents through my see-through shirt. I could hardly point it out as I was doing the same to him.

My ass squelched into the seat, and my hair dripped water all over his lovely leather upholstery. *Good. I hope it ruins it.* I sat quietly, adopting the classic angry-woman car pose—looking out the window my body was turned to, arms crossed around my waist.

While I may have caved and gotten into his car, I was at least proved right by the awkward silence. In my periphery, I watched Finn looking my way and nodding, which was annoyingly cute. "This is fun." He smiled. It wasn't fun. I had run from the office to avoid this very thing and began to consider fleeing at the next red light. Perhaps he sensed it. "Why don't I put on some music?" A song I couldn't quite put a name to started playing, and my fingers absentmindedly tapped along.

"You like INXS?" Finn asked, pumping the volume and singing along. *Of course he has a great voice. What the fuck can't he do?*

"INXS? Is that what this is?" I pointed to the Apple CarPlay screen. "I think Teddy likes the singer. He has long hair, right? Kind of sexy and curly like yours?"

Shit.

"Yeah, he does." He snorted. Again, it was super cute. "Michael Hutchence was his name. The band is INXS. They're Australian, kind of old school, but one of my favorites. My dad's too. He used to play this album in the car or when we worked out."

Aww. He worked out with his dad. Shit. Be angry.

"Hmm. It's okay, I suppose." We continued driving, and despite myself, I continued tapping along.

After a street or two passed us by, I noticed it was the same street, the same stores, and the same signage. He was driving in circles. For a moment, I feared I had manifested the whole serial-killer thing, but then, a more logical conclusion came to mind. The man who couldn't wait to be rid of me wasn't ready to let me go. A giggle of joy slipped from my lips.

"What? What are you laughing at?"

"Nothing. Just enjoying the fun ride. And about that...why drive? The traffic is hideous, there's no parking...ever. I don't get it."

He shrugged his shoulders and smirked annoyingly. "Just like it. Reminds me of home too. I had the same car, you see."

"Well, that sounds reasonable, I suppose. Give it a few weeks, and you'll be bitching about the subway and blisters like the rest of us." I then made the mistake of looking at him and paid the price. His eyes met mine, and he winked. My thighs spontaneously clenched, and I think I sighed out loud. Those winks of his were not only a direct hit to the hoo-ha, but they also seemed to unfreeze my heart and mouth.

"Do you like cricket, Scarlett?"

Random, but okay.

"I do. We English created it, remember. Teddy and I used to go to a test match every summer. There's nothing like a Pimm's at Lord's."

"I'm sure that's true. But never forget, the English may have invented the game, but we Aussies perfected it."

I scoffed and rolled my eyes. "I'm pretty sure a New Zealander would say the same."

He wet his lips and flashed a devilish smile, "You know, some blokes back home would call you a ripper Sheila for going to a test match."

"And that's a good thing? Being a ripper Sheila?"

"It's a very good thing." He nodded, stole a glance toward my still-damp chest, and then licked his lips again. Oddly, when Old Man Time did it, I felt like gagging on my vomit. But with Finn, I wanted to rip my shirt off, grab his head, and shove it between my boobs. I realized then that I was officially un-mad at Finn.

In fact, I thought he was pretty ripper too. I also wouldn't mind him ripper-ing his clothes off whenever it took his fancy.

Okay, enough ripper jokes.

When the endless looping of the same streets became a little too hard to ignore, we took three left turns in a row and ended up on my beautiful tree-lined street. We pulled up to my house, and as I predicted, no parking spots were available. Being forced to double park didn't stop Finn from his gentlemanly duties. He leapt from the car and ran to open my door, but something strange happened as he scooted around the hood. He stopped, dropped, and disappeared.

"Finn?" I climbed out of the Jeep, shielding my eyes from the pouring rain with one hand and the same to my frizz-prone curls with the other. While I couldn't see him, I could hear him.

"Puss, puss, puss. Come here, little matey. I won't hurt you."

Edging closer to the sound, I peered around the hood, and there he was, his ass aglow in the headlights, face-down on the wet asphalt in a full-body stretch with his hands reaching under the car parked in front of his.

"Is this a hobby of yours? Lying on the street in the rain?"

"Oh yeah. Everyone does it in Australia."

"Really?"

Finn's whole body jiggled as he broke into laughter. "No. Not normally, no. God, I can't believe you believed that. A bloody cat ran under the car, and I think he was limping. I can't just leave him."

I gasped. "Mr. Pickles!"

"What? Ohh, fuck!" Finn jumped, his head cracking loudly against the underside of the car. My laughter outweighed any concern I may have felt, rendering me useless to help in any way, shape, or form. So, I just stood there and laughed some more. I may have even pointed. Hearing the commotion, Mrs. Horowitz, who never strays far from her windows, ran outside, massive umbrella in hand.

"Look! We—well, Finn found Mr. Pickles! He's under the bloody car."

Finn was still lying in the filthy street and began to laugh as he resumed his search.

"Oh, thank you, young man. He hates the rain and won't make it easy for you to get him."

The once-pristine shirt, made even more delicious by the rain, rode up his back, exposing his obliques and the tanned dimples at the rise of his peachy ass. Never in my life had I desired to be compacted layers of dirt, gravel, and tar, but there I was, envious of the road scraping against and tasting his skin.

My eyelashes didn't know whether to blink rapidly or glue to my brows, as I stooped to take cover beneath my short neighbor's umbrella. Thankfully, she was holding it as I needed both hands to wipe my drool. Apparently, I wasn't the only one.

"Is that your boyfriend, Scarlett? I hope you don't mind me saying, but he has a lovely bottom."

"Yes. Yes, he does," I replied robotically, mesmerized by his continued writhing. "But no, he's not my boyfriend." Not yet, anyway.

12

Finn

FETCHING THAT DAMN CAT took me twenty minutes and cost me half the skin off my stomach. For a good, tortuous portion of that time, Scarlett was crouched beside me in her short skirt and see-through shirt. The soft, creamy thighs and the teasing hint of pink lace that greeted me each time I turned my head were tattooed on my mind and added another layer to an already complicated day.

Working in a confined space with the hottest woman in New York should have been a pure delight. She was dressed as the sexiest pirate I'd ever seen, after all. Her outfit inspired a bevy of inappropriate puns that would have had me in a sexual harassment lawsuit before I could blink. *I wouldn't mind docking my bow in your port*, for example. But it was a fucking nightmare, led by the ghost of Shelby that I couldn't escape. I had left the house with a plan. I was to distance myself from Scarlett, be the red-hot temptress's antithesis, acting colder than a witch's tit. It was my only hope. I'd also left without saying a word to Evie or eating the suck-up pancakes she made me. The whole Nate-monk thing was still bothering me too.

It would have been so easy to seek comfort in Scarlett's arms. My fingers still buzzed with her touch. But I couldn't. Shelby's face flashed before my eyes every time I even considered it.

At lunch, when Scarlett licked that damn yum-yum sauce from her plump, red-stained lips and sucked it from her fingertips, my cock rebelled and twitched like it had the first time I saw a real booby, but then I heard Shelby's voice...*I have loved him my whole life. We will always be a family.*

The opposing thoughts and feelings drove me to the point of distraction. I was frustrated, a complete ass, and Scarlett was right to flee. But, in all good conscience, I couldn't leave things like that. I wanted to distance myself. I didn't want her to hate me.

My internal conflict waged on as she fished around in her bag for her keys, swearing under her breath and occasionally peeking up at me beneath her long lashes. She was so pretty and sexy. And then there was her scent. Even the stench of a Greenwich Village Street couldn't stop the undeniable lure of her perfume, or was it just her?

Damn, she smelled so good. On every inhale, I was transported back to Byron, to Mum's flower garden that sat below the kitchen window, overflowing with violets, lilacs, and freesias. They all smelled amazing, but ironically, the scarlet-red, white and pink sweet peas were my favorite. Each color carried its own fragrance and would linger on my skin for hours. Every day after school, I would get off the bus, lug my heavy backpack down our dirt drive, and stop to pick Mum a posy. Evie always called me a kiss-ass, but I loved the smell as much as Mum's expression of love and pride when I placed them in her hand. It was a tradition I kept up till the day she died. I missed that scent as much as I missed Mum. Being surrounded by it again gave me a feeling of home.

It was comforting yet confusing.

Scarlett found her keys and celebrated with a hop on her toes and a cute cheer. I really was fucked. "Would you like to come in?" she whispered, keeping her gaze on the door while sliding the key into the lock.

Such a simple question but painfully difficult to answer. I rubbed the back of my neck and managed to eke out, "I don't know." It was a blatant lie. I wanted to go inside, alright. I then wanted to peel that damp, clinging shirt from that body and warm it up as only I could.

"You don't know?" she repeated, almost sounding unsure if she'd heard me right.

"Yes, I don't know. I don't know what to do, Scarlett. I have to be honest. I am terrified of being alone with you."

"Oh. Well, that's something every woman wants to hear when she invites a man in." Chuckling nervously, Scarlett appeared to be having trouble working the lock. For my poor nerves, the jangling keys sounded almost as loud as the thunder, still rolling through the skies. "I promise I won't bite, and maybe you can tell me exactly what it is about me that scares you so."

The door swung open, the keys rattling again as she pulled them free and stepped inside.

It was all up to me.

I knew Scarlett's home would be styled as beautifully as she always was, but I had also expected a bit of a mess. Surprisingly, it was spotless, huge, modern, and—courtesy of open blinds and the lights outside—awash with the muted tones of the large stained-glass window overlooking the street. My hesitancy to enter meant she was a few paces ahead of me, and her stunning silhouette drew me deeper inside.

She looked back playfully, her hair falling into her eyes as she smiled and motioned farther down the hall. "Coffee?"

"Umm, maybe a quick cup of tea if you have some. Otherwise, I'll be up all night, and I have to get up early for a workout. Shit, I'm double-parked too, don't forget."

She giggled. She was giggling at me, and I loved it. "Wow, you are a rule follower, aren't you? And of course I have tea. I am English, don't forget."

My feet squared against the timber floor as I froze at the entry of her kitchen, my mouth agape. The soft-mint, almost white cabinetry, white marble benchtops, stained wood floors, and pops of color in framed prints and rainbow stools, were so perfectly her I could imagine no other person ever living there. "This place is amazing. How—?"

"Teddy. It's a Digby family home. He's practically royalty, if you didn't know. They own this one and the two beside it."

"So, King Theodore is next door?"

"Kind of. Mrs. Horowitz, your new biggest fan, is next door, and then Teddy. It's lovely, like our own little community. Oh, and never call him King Theodore to his face. He would die of a swollen head...and I'd never hear the end of it." As she spoke, she reached behind, lit the flame on the stove, and plopped the old-fashioned kettle—the kind my nanna had—in place without looking. Impressive. She then tried to kill me. "Okay, now take off that shirt."

"Uhh... What?"

"Your shirt. Take it off. It's wet and dirty. I'll get you one of Teddy's from the laundry."

Please say wet and dirty again.

My fingers fiddled with the collar of my shirt, waiting for my brain and cock to battle out the merits of de-robing before her. "Is this your way of asking to see me naked, Red?"

She shrugged, then leaned over the kitchen island. "Can I get you something to eat?" That was an unfair question. I reached for a kitchen chair, covered my shame by standing behind it, then shook my head. "Suit yourself. I'm starving."

A bright-red apple that Snow White would find irresistible was selected from a fruit bowl while I caved and undid the top two buttons of my shirt. A second later, I forgot what I was doing. Those emerald eyes never left mine as she took a large, seductive bite.

That is a lucky piece of fruit.

I abandoned the chair and gravitated toward her, wanting that apple to be replaced by any part of my body but one in particular. My right foot slid over the shining oak boards, and at that very moment, just as my toes clumsily—deliberately—bumped against hers, there was a knock at the door.

Scarlett rolled her eyes, placed the blessed fruit down, and excused herself.

As they tend to do, the apple just sat there staring at me.

I couldn't help myself. My fingertips traced the outline her mouth had left on the red skin and white flesh, and I was tempted to take a bite just to be closer to her lips. I thought of them on my skin, her teeth on my flesh, and died a little inside.

I was rock-hard and jealous of an apple.

Mumbled conversation and intermittent meowing traveled down the hall.

Get your shit together and nude up, Austen. I was still trying to figure out if I should take off my shirt when her footsteps approached. I went for it, and my heightened senses meant I heard each button clunk against the floor just as she reappeared, carrying a cheesy grin and a Tupperware container that looked older than us.

"For you, from you know who." Scarlett's feet skidded as she came to a sudden halt. The grin vanished, and her eyes widened as they took a long and expansive tour over the peaks and valleys of my puffed-out bare chest and sucked-in stomach. Slowly, that grin was reborn—albeit more naughty than cheesy—as she handed the container over like there was nothing unusual in this situation. "I think my neighbor plans on making a move on you, and I have a feeling she'd be all kinds of kink—"

Our fingertips connected. It was a mere brush but one that sent waves of heat through my body. I wanted more. I claimed her hand, pulled her toward me, and once again, Scarlett Grant made time itself stop.

A squeaky, moany kind of sound came from deep within her as her hand landed on my chest. The heat of her breath tickled my cheek as she sighed and smoothed her fingers down my stomach, tracing each line until she found my hip. She looked down, gripped me tighter, and another moan I never wanted to forget left her lips. I knew she could feel me hard against her, and I rolled my body, pressing lower into her belly, right above her pussy so she could feel it even more. "Oh, wow. Is that what you were afraid of?"

"Maybe, yeah. Sorry 'bout that." I wasn't sorry.

I don't think she was either. Her soft body molded around mine. The rolling became mutual grinding, and I traced the lines of her neck with the tip of my nose. Her skin was damp, and smelled of rain, and felt so, so soft. I was desperate to take a bite, just a tiny nibble beneath her ear. Like she knew my thoughts, she rolled her head back and to the side, exposing the exact spot. Just as my lips parted, fate interjected. The cookie lid spontaneously popped open, half tumbled out and crumbled against our feet. The kettle bubbled and whistled, demanding attention, and the almost horizontal rain smashed so hard against the windows I feared the glass would shatter. But we, a bare-chested man and a dirty, wet woman, remained rooted to the ground beneath us like two century-old Elms in Central Park.

"I guess you better get that kettle." I gripped her tighter, my hand dropping to her ass. "I should clean up the cookie mess too."

"No, don't. The dog will get it."

"You have a dog?"

"No. I just don't want to let go of you."

The damn kettle sounded and smelled like it was boiling dry. Scarlett smiled, bit her lip, then looked over her shoulder. "Hmm, maybe I better get it." Feeling her pull away hurt, and it wouldn't do.

I claimed her waist again, ran my hand down over her ass, gathered her skirt in my fingers and caressed her pebbled skin. We were so close I could feel her heat and almost taste her and that bloody apple. She inhaled deeply, held her breath, and then sighed out my name as she rolled against me. "Finn."

Something flicked inside me. Perhaps just hearing my name reminded me of myself...of my promise. "I—I should go," I stammered. But I didn't. I didn't release her. I didn't take my eyes off the fire in hers.

"If you must."

"I feel like I should."

"Yes, you already said that." She stretched and stood on her tiptoes. Her lips ghosted mine. I could feel her shake.

Is she wet for me?

Fuck me. I wanted to find out. My fingers were right there. Just a twist of my wrist and an inch lower and I could slip up the inside of her thigh. All I had to do was give in.

I have loved him my whole life... Your daddy and I will always be happy.

"Fuck. Fuck. I can't... I have to...go...the car." Shaking the voices from my head like water from Scarlett's non-existent dog, I intended to step away, but Scarlett, seeming to sense my retreat, released a breathy no and took a hold of my belt.

I took her hands in mine, raised them to my lips, and pressed a soft kiss against her knuckles. "It's for the best. See you tomorrow, Red."

The first day Scarlett and I were assigned to work together, she'd left for the day on a promise. "*I'm ready if you are. I'll see you tomorrow, and then we begin.*"

I didn't see Scarlett for a week.

Last night, I'd run from her house with the parting words, "See you tomorrow, Red," but I didn't see her the next day or the next, and not because I was a cowardly lion—which I totally was—but because I had fucking chicken pox. I had no idea where I caught them, but I was covered head to toe.

Did you know adults with chicken pox are more likely to be admitted to hospitals than kids? Me neither, but I did after doctor-Googling all afternoon on my third day at home. I felt like shit, was covered head to toe in itchy spots, and was deeply concerned that the headache I was nursing was actually encephalitis. Iris was faring much better than her pitiful dad, and she frequently reminded me of that fact. As did Evie.

"Would you stop Googling your symptoms? I swear to God, you're a bloody hypochondriac, Finn." I was then hit with a tea towel while she looked over my shoulder.

"Evie, you should be nice to me while you can. According to John Hopkins, death is a symptom. DEATH. Fuck, so are infertility and impotence. I dunno which is worse."

That made her laugh but didn't stop her from calling me a pathetic baby and asking if my deadly disease also manifested as male moodiness. Perhaps it was the brain infection kicking in, but I didn't take the insults well. I turned my nose and took myself off to bed to rest and sulk.

My sub-par frame of mind was obviously affected by my possibly fatal condition but also from pining. Visions of rosy, flushed cheeks and red lips. Heaving boobs in pink bras and soft lace knickers had been my constant companion, as was a massive boner should I dwell on either of them for too long. So far, so good with the impotence, I guessed.

Hitting shuffle on the most depressing playlist I could source, I buried my face into my pillow. Three bars into Adele's "Hello", my phone vibrated and grunted at me like Peppa Pig's bloody dad, scaring the absolute bejesus out of me.

"Iris! Stop changing my ringtones."

"I didn't, Daddy."

"My message tone, either!"

"Oh. Okay. Sowwy, Daddy."

I picked up my phone, and all the air was sucked from my lungs.

Scarlett

> Hello, stranger. I hope you're doing okay. I know the itchies are still itching, but I'm immune, and I made you some chicken soup. Can I bring it over?

Holy fucking hell, she made me soup.

Twenty minutes later, I replied. It wasn't a deliberate delay. It just took me that long to pace around my room and decide what to say. It had to be perfect.

> Yes.

Bravo, Shakespeare.

13

Scarlett

Just as it had been all week, Finn's gift of morning tea for the office was delivered at ten-thirty sharp. Weight was gained just by sniffing the sweet air. Cakes, muffins, and protein balls for the health-conscious filled the boardroom table. There was a giant coffee for Teddy and me too, and today, there was an extra addition—a gift just for me. A smiling delivery girl appeared with a brown paper bag filled with tissue paper and handed it to me with a wink.

"This is from Finn. He's very sweet. You're very lucky." She sighed and disappeared.

"What is it? Open it now. The suspense is killing me."

"Teddy, I've had it in my hands for, like, ten seconds. Chill."

I was a damn hypocrite. I wasn't chill. I was close to peeing my pants with excitement. Even in his absence, even when feeling poorly, Finn's thoughtfulness was so sweet it hurt. I grabbed a blueberry muffin, and together, Teddy and I snuck into conference room A, Team Finnlett's base. Damn if that name hadn't stuck.

"For the love of God, woman. Open the bag." I gave him the standard mum 'shut up' through gritted teeth, reached into the bag, and pulled out an umbrella. Bright red with white polka dots. It was cute. Very me.

"What in the Rhianna?" Teddy snatched the card still sitting at the bottom, read it, and clutched at his chest.

"Digby, you have a call on line three. She's English and angry," a voice called from outside.

"That sounds like my mother. I'll be back. Don't you go dying on me when you read that note." Teddy handed me the card and made his exit.

Too scared to read it, I held it in my hand for a disturbingly sad amount of time, wanting it to be romantic but needing it to be platonic. I closed my eyes, held the card in front of my face, and then opened it.

To Miss Grant, to keep you from getting dirty and wet.

Cheeky bugger.

This time, the card was held to my chest as I spun in my chair while kicking my feet in the air. It was very mature. The several people laughing at me through the glass walls seemed to think so. I slowed the spinning and sat facing the garden. The leaves on my cherry blossom were starting to fall to the ground. In no time at all, the changing seasons would strip that tree bare, leaving it naked, exposed. I wanted Finn to do to me what autumn was gonna do to that tree.

I sat in my chair with the umbrella swinging around my wrist. All day I pondered what my response to Finn's gift should be, and by home time, I had procrastinated so long that I feared whatever I said would seem ungrateful.

Just send something. Anything is better than nothing. I caught the umbrella and was about to pick up my phone when I noticed. They weren't polka dots. They were tiny apples, each with one bite missing. A thrill like no other rushed through me. My knickers were soaked in a flash. I had tried so damn hard to bite that apple seductively, and it bloody worked.

Squealing with glee, I grabbed my phone and typed.

Hello, stranger.

> I hope you're doing okay. I know the itchies are still itching, but I made you some chicken soup. I'm immune. Can I bring it over?

Hunched over my desk, I watched the bubbles appear and disappear for maybe twenty minutes. Anticipation built with every second that passed. What was he writing? A declaration of love. A sonnet? A shopping list?

Finn McHunk

> Yes.

Oh. Well. Fuck me. At least it wasn't a no, I suppose.

> Great. I will drop it off around 6. See you then, Scratch 'N' Sniff.

Christ, I was so lame and so desperate. I'd seen him less in the last two weeks but thought of him more. It was a perplexing paradigm that proved the adage 'absence makes the heart grow fonder.' Apple-brella-gate had pushed me over the edge. Desperation aside, I had a less tragic reason to pop in, even if that was a little more than sketchy.

Since Finn had been home, I had begun planning the first of Wise's retirement events, his official party, and needed—although, not really—Finn's tick of approval.

Initially, it was to be held this weekend, with Jason keen to get the damn thing over and done with. But there was no way I was going without Finn. Much to Jason's ire, we agreed to push it back two weeks, thus allowing me more time to plan something befitting a founding partner, while also giving McHunk time to escape pox quarantine. It was all a matter of perspective. It was also an accidental, genius move. The delay allowed everything to fall into place perfectly.

Asher gave us exclusive access to M.I.X., including full catering and bar service. I booked the disco-loving D.J. that Mr. Wise had name-dropped several times, and when I told the honoree the news, he declared he must have a 70's fancy dress theme. Hopefully, there was enough time for everyone to put their costumes together, but honestly, I didn't give a shit. Finn would be there, I would be there, and the rest was up to everyone else. That's not true. That's how I wanted to feel. In reality, I really did care and was obsessing over every little detail despite the fact I couldn't stand the man it was all in celebration of. It was extremely vexing.

Speaking of obsession, I picked up my phone and re-read Finn's text for the hundredth time.

Finn McHunk

Poetry.

Going to his house was a big deal. *Should I be doing this? Am I prepared? Is my soup Finn-worthy?* I needed to sit, think, and plan my moves carefully.

Approximately three seconds later, I was out the door. I sprinted home, whipped the straightener through my hair, threw the soup I made last night—not for Finn, but he didn't need to know that—and the cookies Mrs. Horowitz had definitely made him into a bag, and I was off again.

I rushed down Sixth and turned onto Bleecker Street with a smile I couldn't wipe off my face. Then, just steps from his house, it hit me. A fist-sized knot of guilt and pre-emptive remorse formed in my stomach.

What the actual fuck was I doing? I promised myself I wouldn't get involved with the hot guy from work. Yet, there I was, planning a retirement party to suit my seduction purposes and preying on my victim as he lay ill and helpless in bed. Me and my chicken soup were going to hell in a handbasket.

Shame should have sent me packing and almost did. But the image of Finn holding me to him by his car and in my kitchen, how his hardness felt pressing against my softness, drove me forward. I never did anything for me. Ben had rightfully been my priority for years.

Hence **Ideology #1 - Ben ALWAYS comes first. ALWAYS.**

But I was still young and deserved some fun. Besides, it was just soup. He was just a man. It was just my shaking hand knocking loudly on his red front door.

The remnants of my WWJD—what would Jane do?—moral code was pushed to the recesses of my mind as footsteps approached. I laughed at the ridiculousness of my nervousness, stood straight, stuck my tits out, and smiled. Slowly, the door opened, and my heart leapt into my mouth, but the beautiful face that appeared before me belonged to a different gorgeous blonde with perfect curls. She was intimidatingly cool, dressed in a vintage surfer-style dress and flip-flops. Her wrists were adorned with turquoise, orange jasper, and braided leather bracelets I would kill to own.

Please let this be his sister. I feared a let-down of epic proportions was seconds away, but then I noticed her striking blue eyes. Finn's eyes. "Hi, you must be Scarlett. I'm Evie, Finn THE COWARD'S," she yelled, looking over her shoulder, "sister."

Thank you, Jesus!

"Yep, that's me. Scarlett, the soup lady, here for Finn, the coward." I giggled nervously and thrust the soup forward into Evie's stomach. "You look so much like him but younger. You're older, though, right?"

"Yeah, three years older, and thanks for that. I'll be sure to let him know." With a wave of her hand, she invited me in. My house seemed to impress Finn on first sighting, and I was no different walking through his. It was huge, stately—regal, even. The choice in furnishings and decoration was all high-end and seemed much more suitable to Jocelyn than to Finn or his sister. "Finn's not feeling the best and is hiding due to his grotesqueness—direct quote. He asked me to thank you for the soup and apologize for not showing his cowardly face."

A loud thump and a series of comical grumbles echoed from the hallway beside us. "I did not say that, and I am not a coward! I am just protecting Scarlett from my hideousness."

"I swear I will kill him by the end of the week. He is such a baby."

"I am not a baby. I am very, very, very sick. Tell her what I found on Google... actually, not all of it, just the brain inflammation and death parts...and stop laughing at me. You'll regret it if I drop dead."

"See what I mean," Evie whispered as she dropped her head into her hands and laughed. "God, it's been a long week. What between him and Iri—"

With an alarming turn of speed for someone so close to death's door, Finn came roaring into the kitchen and smothered his lucky sister and the soup container against his chest, "Hi. Hi, I'm here. Here I am. Hi, Scarlett!"

Evie pounded into his chest until she was released and gave him a look of absolute fire, breathing contempt. "What the hell is wrong with you? You and your poxy hands nearly ripped my head off? Maybe you do have bloody brain fever, you dick. Nice to meet you, Scarlett. I'll leave you to the buffoon." She then punched her brother in the stomach, handed him the soup, and walked out, shaking her head.

"Sisters, eh?"

"Hmm, sisters." I smiled.

"Do you have any? Sisters or brothers? I mean, I don't think we've ever talked about your family," he said. He was standing directly before me and, much like his sister, had his face buried in his hand. Though, I believe he was doing so more as an attempt to hide his spots than out of annoyance, as Evie's had been.

"Nope, an only child. And it's just you and Evie?"

"Yep, just me and horror head."

"Hey, I heard that," Evie yelled, sounding like she was hiding in a similar position to her brother's a few moments ago.

"Then stop listening!"

"You're quite the comedy act, you two." I giggled. "I should book you for the retirement party, which is what I came over to talk to you about. Well, that and to thank you for the umbrella. It's so cute. I love it."

"I knew you would. Evie was shopping online, and I saw the flash of color over her shoulder. I thought of you straight away." He touched his lips and smiled down at mine. "It's my turn to thank you now. I love soup. I think this makes us even, Red."

"Red. You call me that a lot. It's the hair, right?"

"Actually, not for the hair, but because of your name. Scarlett-red, the same color. Though I must say, your hair is lovely. It always looks so soft, but especially when it's straight like today." He reached out, tugged at the one curl that refused to stay straight, and tucked it behind my ear. "Feels soft too." My cheeks blushed the very shades he mentioned as I embarrassingly looked at my feet and lied my ass off.

"Oh, I've hardly touched it today. I must look like a wreck." When I dared look up, I found his spotty, calamine-lotion-covered-but-still-dashing face and dazzling eyes staring right into mine. My bones turned to a liquid runnier than the soup he held, and I needed to lean against the table for support.

"Are you okay, Red? You look a little wobbly."

"Oh, I'm fine, just tired and hungry. I better get going and leave you to it." I began to move away, but his left arm ducked out and grabbed my right.

"Don't go, Scarlett. You, uhh...you need to tell me about the party plans. And maybe I can heat the soup up, and we can split it with some toast. Sound good?"

"Sounds great."

"All done." Finn smiled proudly as he placed an old-fashioned terrine on the table, plus three perfectly toasted and buttered slices of bread. The soup was unrecognizable, resembling a thick chowder more than the chicken-and-veggie soup I had made. Hopefully, it wouldn't affect the taste.

"I love that you have toast with your soup." I swooned as he served me a piping hot bowl. "It's very English. Americans seem to prefer crackers, which are nice too, but it's not the same as having toasty crumbs floating in the bowl."

"Ahhh, you're right. It's toast all the way, especially with tomato soup. Did you make this? It's bloody great."

"Yep, I sure did. It is the least I could do after all the coffee and cake you've had delivered this week. Oh, cake, that reminds me." I dropped my spoon back into my bowl and reached for the M&M cookies. "From your secret admirer, although I don't think it's much of a secret. She told me these were for 'the hottie' when she gave them to me."

"Did she now?" Finn's eyebrow rose and wriggled to the level of epic sexiness as he smirked and nonchalantly stirred his soup. "Now tell me, Scarlett, how did you know I was the hottie she was referring to?"

Fuck.

"Uhh, well. I presumed...since the first batch I dropped was for you...that—" Finn began to laugh. "Oh, fuck off, that's how."

"Ooh, I've hit a nerve, have I? Hmm. Interesting."

14

Finn

"I DIDN'T REALIZE HOW hungry I was until I started eating," I mused as I cleared the table. "Haven't had an appetite since I've been sick."

Scarlett began playing with the cookie container, longing in her eyes. "I wish I had that problem. I rarely stop eating."

As the words left her lips, I realized how often I'd heard her mention eating too much. Sometimes she joked about her weight too. I had no idea what for. Her body was banging. Curvy and tight in all the right places. Fat and plump in the even better ones. "Good. There's nothing worse than hanging out with a chick who pretends not to eat much around guys. We all know they will stuff their faces when they get home."

"Well, if that's your opinion, I better eat a cookie...or two." She slipped her hand under the lip, pulled two out, and took an exaggerated bite of her cookie sandwich. Hot.

"So, it's to be a costume party?" I asked, wondering when I started finding a woman eating so sexy.

"Yep. And it's not my fault. Blame Hermie."

"Oh, I fully intend to. So, what's your costume going to be? Sexy nurse? Sexy librarian? Sexy—"

"I'm sensing a theme here," Scarlett interjected, laughing, and throwing an M&M at my head. "I do have an idea. She's one of my idols, but..." She trailed off, contorting her face till she resembled the eek emoji.

"But what? Tell me." I sat beside her and waited as she blushed a little and began squirming in her seat.

"Don't laugh, but when I was a kid, we'd just gotten our first DVD player, and there was this massive pile of old-school videos on the floor ready to be thrown out. Me being nosy, I went through them all and made an ungodly mess."

"You found your idol in a pile of old movies? Hmm, let me guess who it was. Ummm, Dr Quinn?"

"Nope, she was cool, though. Guess again."

"Okay, so, if your costume is for a 70's party, it must be a 70's show, right?" A cute nod and lip chew was her reply. Fuck she was hot. "70's idols...oh my God, not Farrah?"

"Nope."

"The Flying Nun?"

"What? No!"

"Madonna?"

"Love her but wrong decade. Think more superhero."

Then it hit me, a 70's female superhero.

Fuck no. Fuck yes.

"Holy shit, Red. You don't mean...Wonder Woman?"

"Bingo! She was so strong and independent. Didn't take shit from anyone. Super sexy too. What do you think?"

I know what my dick thinks.

"Uhh, honestly? I think that's a very inappropriate costume for someone like you. I don't think my heart can take it."

"Finn! What the hell? You're crazy. I don't even know if I can pull it off."

"Don't worry. You will. As will I and any other bloke that sees you."

Scarlet's eyes widened as she laughed and slapped my arm. "Oh my God, you're out of control. You really are feeling sick, aren't you?"

"I am. I think I have a fever. I must. It's the only explanation." She leaned closer to me, her nose close to my cheek, and laid her soft palm against my forehead. If the chicken pox didn't kill me, it felt like Scarlett's touch might. Like if I didn't kiss her right then, the world would end.

"You do feel a little warm, but no raging fever. If you don't feel good, you should take yourself off to bed."

Something else is raging. Wanna come with me?

I heard the thought so clearly in my mind that, for a moment, I wasn't sure I hadn't said it aloud. I cleared my throat and brushed some crumbs from the table. "Any ideas what costume I should wear? Should we make it a superhero double act?"

She slapped me again. I fucking loved it. "That would be fun. Imagine the Lycra...and the gossip. We could cause quite the scandal, Finn Austen."

"That we could, Scarlett Grant."

I had a contagious, possibly fatal disease, but Scarlett—insisting she was immune—sat way too close, for way too long, chuckling over something that wasn't funny. The urge to kiss her increased with every freckle I counted on her nose and only paused when Evie appeared. "Finny, I'm just popping down to the shops. Do you need anything? Masculinity? A freaking clue? More ice cream? You've only eaten fifty-eight tubs this week."

Ignoring the barbs, I replied without taking my eyes off the rosy-hued cheeks before me, "Ice cream sounds good. Vanilla, please."

"Boring!" Evie yelled as she headed out the door. "Nice to meet you again, Scarlett."

"You too, Evie." Scarlett smiled, and a million tiny little bubbles of adoration inflated inside me.

"You know, I can always tell when I'm in the presence of someone truly special when my sister doesn't roll her eyes or call them an idiot within the first five seconds of their acquaintance. You got a "goodbye" and a "nice to meet you." I suspect you can walk on water, Red." I gave her a thumbs-up, then noticed chocolate on my nail.

"Hardly. I..." Quieting herself, she pressed her finger against her lips and watched me suck the chocolate off, extricating it from my mouth with a pop that had her twitching and blushing. After blinking at least a hundred times, she cleared her throat and began to speak again. Of course I then noticed my other thumb was dirty, so I cleaned that one too. Scarlett stopped, shook her head, and tapped her hands to her thighs. I enjoyed flustering Scarlett way too much. "Well, I need to leave now."

"Are you sure? Maybe we could—"

"Yes, I think it's best. I need a cold shower— I mean, you need a shower, I think, to ease the itch, and then rest up those muscles to be right for the party. After all, we need a strong and healthy superhero buddy for Wonder Woman."

Enticements to stay were forming in my brain, but then I remembered Iris was in her room, napping. I could be busted at any moment. I wanted to tell Scarlett about her, but not like that. "That's right. I need all the help I can get in the muscle department." I flexed my biceps and delighted in the widening of Scarlett's eyes. "And I will go back to bed. I'm knackered, and I was in the middle of a movie Evie has been bugging me to watch for about ten years."

"What movie?" Scar asked as she rose from her seat and collected her things.

"Uhh, some damn chick flick period piece that's eroding my manhood as I watch it—mainly because I love it," I added in a whisper.

"Oh, I love a good period piece. Which one?"

"*Mansfield Park.*"

We were in the hallway, just by the front door. Halfway through my response, her knees buckled, and she grabbed onto the wall for support. Gasping for air and grasping her chest, she looked at me in a daze. "With Francis O'Connor and Johnny Lee Miller?"

"Yep, that's the one. You know it?"

"Know it! I adore it and could almost speak it word for word." She swooned. Literally swooned. "Fanny Price is another of my idols. Jane Austen is my god. And you like it. You genuinely, honest to goodness like it?"

"Yeah, I do. I didn't think much of it at the start, and I nearly cried when Fanny was dumped at the front door at five am in the cold with no one to greet her. But I have just gotten to the part where the Crawfords have shown up, and I think the shit will hit the fan. Does it hit the fan?"

"My lips are sealed. You will have to wait and see." With the light and magic of an ethereal fairy in her eyes, she touched my chest, gave me a wink, and slipped out the door.

With Evie and Iris snuggling in bed beside me, I finished *Mansfield Park*, then immediately watched *Pride and Prejudice*. Being so heavily influenced by strong women my whole life, I could see why Scarlett admired Jane and her heroines. They were forward-thinking, ahead of their time, intelligent, and funny in a sexy, sharp, I-could-take-you-apart-with-one-word sort of way, just like Scarlett.

I unashamedly loved both and unexpectedly related to the characters, especially one in particular. Guilt ate away at my soul as Darcy denied and struggled to reconcile his feelings. Hopefully, my reasons for doing something similar would be considered less pretentious and pompous than his, but watching sad Lizzy spinning round and round on her swing in the rain was a complete gut punch. I'd been such a jerk to Scarlett that day in the conference room. She was trying to get to know me, asking me about food, music, my family, and Australia. And what did I do in return? I replied with little more than snark and asked nothing of any consequence about herself. Even with my abhorrent behavior, she still forgave me and brought me soup and cookies. Apart from what I'd observed at work, these Jane Austen/Wonder Woman revelations were the first real things I knew were special to her.

Perhaps it's for the best. I should leave it that way. I need to stay focused on work and my promise to Shelby.

Once the girls had settled in their own beds, I returned to my own, turned off my lamp and stared at the ceiling. One of my mum's sayings randomly popped into my head. "You know you're full of shite when you don't believe the crap coming out of your own mouth."

15

Scarlett

"Hello, Miss Grant."

A spot-free, most definitely alive Finn was waiting in the conference room when I arrived on Monday. As part of his recovery, he must have taken an extra pill of gorgeous as his hair was extra curly and floppy and scandalously hung in his extra-blue eyes. The sight of him caused me to pause at the door to take him in. *Click. Mentally saving this image.*

"Why, hello, Mr. Austen." My stomach swooped just saying his name. "You're here early. I usually beat you in."

"I know, but I was so excited to get back to work I couldn't sleep. Which is fine for now, but you'll likely need to prop me up with a stick by two."

"Thanks for the warning." Hoping my thumping heart was only audible to me, I smiled like I was auditioning for a tooth-whitening commercial, placed my bag on the table, and began dumping its contents. My senses were always heightened around Finn, but my body ignited as he sidled up close and set a vat of caffeine before me. "Oh, I forgot, I got you a coffee."

It was huge, and I consumed it immediately. A coffee that size probably cost twenty dollars in this neighborhood. Add that to the morning tea bill from last week, and Finn had been singlehandedly keeping local small businesses afloat.

"Haven't you spent enough money on coffee for me?" I sighed, taking another sip.

"Is it good?"

"It's great."

"Well, it's worth it, then. Isn't it?"

The morning started with us sitting on opposite sides of the table, but the longer we stayed in the room, the closer we got. At ten, we were side by side but still professionally spaced. By eleven, Finn had scooted closer. Very close. Thighs-touching close. Eleven-fifteen saw all pretence of propriety abandoned. I was practically in his lap and keeping up our two-week tradition of doing nothing remotely related to what we were paid for.

After a thrilling debate over what is the correct position for the toilet paper roll to face, things shifted dramatically. "So, Miss Grant," Finn said, his eyebrows dancing with mischief, "I have to ask. Is there someone special in your life? Is there anyone you're romantically interested in?"

This question warranted a thoughtful response, so I replied immediately with none whatsoever. "Maybe. Yes. But doing anything about it is a terrible idea, no matter how much I want him. It would go against many promises I've made to myself."

"What kind of promises?"

"Nope, not going there. It's stupid."

Finn's ridiculously blue eyes bore into the side of my head. "Nothing you do is stupid. Come on, you can't say that and then stop. Spit it out."

I was about to refuse when he began to twirl a curl that laid at my temple. His finger brushed my ear and cheek, and my body instinctively leaned into him. I'm quite sure I looked like a cat rubbing against its owner's legs. "You can trust me, you know, Scarlett."

"Promise?" I purred.

"Promise." The man literally had me wrapped around his little finger.

"Fine! I have this list, you see."

He released the curl and nodded thoughtfully. "A list? Ohh, I love a list. I find this incredibly sexy, Red."

"Well, you shouldn't. This isn't a sexy list."

"Oh, that's a shame. Oh God, it's not some weird manifesto that will be used against you in court one day, is it?"

"No," I laughed, kicking his foot beneath the table. "It's not a manifesto. It's a carefully constructed and well-thought-out list of romantic ideologies I choose to live by."

"Hmm." He stroked his soft and fluffy-looking day-old scruff. "What kind of ideologies?"

"I dunno, just things like, never date a man from work. That kind of thing."

"Oh, so they're rules?"

"No. Not rules. Ideologies. Rules are made to be broken, and these are made to make me better." He cast a cynical look my way.

"Right. I can see you take this very seriously, and I would like to be supportive. Let me see these rules—err, ideologies."

"No. No man will ever see them. Well, Teddy has, but he doesn't count. All you need to know is, by dating...the person I'm interested in, I would be breaking at least half of them."

His lips curved into a smile. "Ahh, I see." Looking proud as punch, the cocky bastard sat straight in his seat and puffed his chest. "Can I give you some advice, Red?"

"No."

"Great. Forcing a set of unrealistic and unachievable rules upon yourself is a recipe for a lonely life. Trust me. I know from first-hand experience." He took my hand and caressed his thumb across my knuckles. "Maybe it's time to draw up a new list?"

"Yeah. I think it would be easier to get a new job."

"Nah, don't do that. I, and whoever this lucky bastard is, would miss you terribly." His voice deepened as he spoke, becoming a low, gruff rumbling that reverberated through me. Slowly, he leaned in. His grip on my hand tightened, and his eyes stayed glued to my lips, which I may have purposefully licked as he pulled me closer. All propriety was lost.

Omg. This was it.

Finn Austen had seen through my brilliant and not-at-all-obvious wordplay. He was going to kiss me. We were so close I could feel his breath on my cheek. I could almost taste him.

"What do we want for lunch, bitches?" Finn and I jumped apart as Teddy burst into the room, throwing a stack of menus at my head. Realizing his shit timing, he cringed but didn't leave. "Bollocks, sorry to interrupt."

Like his arrival, I did not take his apology well. "Fucking choke on it, Teddy." Finn almost fell off his chair, laughing, while Teddy faked offense but continued to insist on taking our order.

"Ladies' choice. What do you feel like, Scar?" Finn asked, still chuckling.

Your lips and desk sex were my immediate thoughts. Thankfully, they stayed in my brain. With two sets of eyes upon me, I had to think of something. A healthy cobb salad or something with quinoa and sprouts should have been my choice, but it wasn't. I needed greasy comfort. "I'll have a triple bacon cheeseburger and large fries...and a chocolate shake."

Finn's eyebrows hit his hairline. "I'll have the same. Thanks, Teddy. But make mine a vanilla shake."

"Sooo, it's vanilla all the way, then?" I quipped.

"Sorry?"

"Vanilla ice cream the other day, vanilla shake today. What's wrong, Finn? Can't handle a little flavor?" Instantly, he pushed his chair out from the desk and ran out the door, chasing after Teddy. "Make that a...a...strawberry shake. Please."

I tried not to laugh as he gave me a proud, wide-eyed look of a man living on the edge. How do you like them apples?

I liked them apples very much. As I did my burger, which I ate sitting in between Teddy and Finn, who bantered back and forth over my ability to make a mess of everything I ate. My sharp and witty comebacks were flushed down the proverbial toilet when—much to their delight—I spilled chocolate shake down the front of my blouse. When the pointing and laughing ceased, Finn came to my aid like a gentleman, lunging at me with a stack of napkins.

Four clumsy wipes around my nipple zone later, he realized the proximity of his hands to my breasts may have been a little inappropriate. "Maybe you should do this." He blushed and handed me the napkins. Teddy could barely contain his laughter. I could hardly breathe.

That was the second time Finn's fingers had been within striking distance of my boobs, and twice nothing had happened. My resolve was weakening. Should he get that close again, and should my best friend not be beside me, I didn't think I would let him pull away so quickly.

I'd spent a week locked away with Finn. Conference room A had become our own private slice for five or six hours a day. It was a wonderful thing, but it was also a non-stop, all-you-can-eat buffet. The boy loved his food, and while he was blessed with the metabolism dreams are made of, I wasn't. I also had a tiny costume to fit into in the not-too-distant future. My impending Lycra crisis and the pent-up sexual frustration coursing through my veins provided the motivation to make some lifestyle changes.

Generally, my afternoon schedule consisted of picking up Ben, stuffing my face with snacks alongside him, preparing and eating dinner, and then tea or wine and toast around eight. If it was a no-Ben week, it was even worse. I worked late most nights and ate takeout hunched over my desk. That shit had to change—along with the jigglyness of my body.

I wanted to start slowly. Any changes I made had to be sustainable. So, I dropped the tea and toast, and eight pm became exercise hour. YouTube provided multitudes of free workout options, and I hit play as soon as Ben was in bed. Growithjo, a Canadian fitspo with fun dance workouts and fantastic music, was an instant favorite. I would either do a curse-filled cardio session with her or go for a jog-walk-collapse if Teddy was available to watch over Ben. Any form of physical activity other than walking or raising my hand to my mouth was entirely foreign and walloped me. Sore, burning thighs left me rolling out of bed and one squat away from peeing standing up.

But I didn't stop, and by the end of the second week, my primary objective had switched from wanting to look hot for Finn to wanting to feel good for me. From losing the cellulite on my arse and thighs to making it around the block without stopping or doing a twenty-five-minute video instead of the quick ten-minute one.

So what if I still had a fat arse? Americans seemed to be obsessed with big booties, and I'm pretty sure Finn checked it out every five seconds. Plus, I was getting fitter and healthier, and even with the ever-present mum shit and constant lustful thoughts of certain burly blonds, my sleep improved too. I woke feeling refreshed and ready for my day instead of like Frankenstein's bride with a hangover. I was proud of myself, and the best part was that Ben even started to do the workouts with me.

"This is much cooler and harder than it looks," he puffed mid-star jump on a grueling Black-Eyed Peas-themed workout. "I can't believe you are doing this every day."

My chest expanded in pride.

Ben was proud of me. I was inspirational, and cool, and felt shit-hot.

It didn't last long.

"It's even hard for me, and I'm not old and dorky like you." My ego couldn't take much of Ben's compliments, so I ran alone the next night.

Music blasted into my ears, the cool air brushed against my face, and my snotty nose ran as fast as my legs. But I kept going. I even added an extra block. Just as I was about to turn and head home, a tall, lean, silhouetted figure jogged toward me. I couldn't make out a face in the dim streetlight, but the blond man-bun halo had my heart rate soaring.

Shit. Shitty shit.

"Red, is that you?"

Why? Why is he here? He can't see me like this, sweating like a pig and an avalanche running from my nose.

"No, it's not me. I mean, I'm not Red."

Only a few paces remained between us. I could hear his laughter as he slowed to a walk and contemplated crossing the street. But knowing me, I'd get hit by a car, and I wasn't lucky enough to be knocked out and would be forced to watch him watch me as I lay in the street, bleeding.

By the time I'd catastrophized myself to hyperventilation, he was next to me, holding my arm and pulling me close. I didn't know where to look. Nowhere was safe. Between his beautiful, flushed face; ripped, toned arms; and massive thick thighs, I was screwed.

"Oh, sorry. You look an awful lot like this cute girl I work with." He then pulled me into the light and almost killed me with hotness. Damn, he was beautiful. His dimples were extra dimply, and his sweat-drenched hair hung low over his eyes in a disturbingly sexy manner. Who the hell looks so good when they're so sweaty? "Well, whaddya know, it is you."

"Surprise!" I laughed while holding my hands over my face.

"Didn't you recognize me?" he asked as he dragged my hands away. "Did you think I was gonna get ya? Rrrr!" He jumped and grabbed me by the waist. Christ, his hands fit well on my body.

"Sorry, sorry. I know how lame that was, but I'm so embarrassed. I've only just started jogging and look disgusting. No one wants to see me like this."

My hair tie spontaneously snapped at that very moment, and my stylishly messy bun fell around my face. Finn's eyes widened. He took a step closer and worried his lips between his teeth. "You greatly underestimate your cuteness, Red." I watched the rise and fall of his Adam's apple. He tucked my curls behind my ears and smiled. "Turn around."

"What?"

"Spin around. Let me help you." A spare hair tie from his wrist was jiggled in my face.

"Oh, that's okay. I'm not far from home. I can manage."

"Nonsense. I insist you can't run with that mop in your face." Not waiting for me to move, he ducked around me and trapped a handful of curls.

It was clear the man was experienced in touching a woman's hair. His fingers brushed my flesh, sending a wave of visible tremors through my body as they twisted through my curls, collecting them in his hands and then binding them on top of my head. The feel of him breathing against my neck as he played with my hair had my lady bits tingling and demanding those fingers give them some attention too.

"There, now I can see you," he whispered into my ear, "and you can see me." He spun me back around and blinded me with a smile that lit up our little section of Sixth Avenue. "Can I run you home? It's been a while since I had a training partner, but I'm sure I can still run and talk."

"I...umm. I dunno, Finn."

My lack of enthusiasm had the poor thing sweating even harder than he already was. His face dropped, and his eyes cast down. I really did want to run home with him, if for no other reason than the shortness of his shorts. But the thought of him listening to me huff and puff and seeing my boobs bounce up under my chin was just too much. Before I could string together a response, his face switched. I could almost picture a lightbulb appearing above his head, and he and his shorts took off ahead of me. "Come on, Red. Don't leave me hanging."

Without seeking permission, my libido and legs followed, but my brain kicked in after a few strides, and I stopped. "Umm, Finn." He slowed and turned but kept walking backward, beckoning me with every step. "Would it be okay if I took a rain check? I'd love to work out with you, but I'm just not ready to be seen by human eyes. Give me a few weeks, and I promise I will be chasing you all over the city."

"Are you sure? I promise I'll be gentle." Cue eyebrow wiggles.

"Finnnnn." I laughed like a dorky teen. God, I was a fucking idiot. Even in the dark, he must have seen me blushing. "While I'm sure I'd be very safe in your big hands, yes, I am sure. Two weeks. Give me two weeks, and I'm yours."

"It's a date, Red."

With my vagina threatening a mutiny, he turned and ran away. The fact that he looked over his shoulder and smiled every few strides settled her rage...as did the bounce of his ass in those shorts.

That night was the first time I struggled to sleep since launching my fitness crusade. When I closed my eyes, I saw a thick, long, veined bicep or rippled quadricep. His expression when I asked for a rain check was there too. Disappointed but hopeful, playful.

Maybe Finn liked a game? Perhaps I made the right choice. After all, as I—more than anyone else—knew, everybody wants what they can't have.

16

Scarlett

GOODBYE, MR. WISE. IT was party night, and I couldn't wait to say those words for the last time—well, almost the last. Technically, the upcoming, unorganized movie night would be the last. I was surprised the old coot's eyes hadn't fallen out of his head. The amount of perving they carried out this week was ridiculous.

Though I often made light of his behavior, I'd come closer to making a formal complaint in the last few days than I had at any other point. No one should have to put up with the objectification I had. Teddy pushed me for months to say something, as had Finn, but I was too stubborn and pig-headed to admit I couldn't handle it. And that I feared the consequences of speaking up. The Me-Too movement may have heralded a new era for women's advocacy, but in my experience, it had yet to be embraced by many men. Unfortunately, some women too.

The final farewell to Pervy McPerv wasn't the only thing I was looking forward to. Finn-fatuation and my lonely, desperate vagina were working in cahoots on what was essentially a hostile takeover of my brain. *Bonk him, marry him, bear one hundred of his blond babies, all of which will have Australian accents like their daddy. Oh, and keep it professional.* These were my thoughts as I slipped my freshly waxed and tanned self into my costume. I was so excited. And so nervous.

Could I get away with a diaper? That was how much I was shitting myself. It was most un-Wonder-Woman-like. There were, however, one or two things I was confident in. One, my costume was HAWT! Even if I said so myself. Yes, my ass was still too big, and my thighs...well, I was never going to be thrilled with them. But my stretch-marked tummy looked surprisingly toned, and for once, when I looked in the mirror, I liked more about my body than I hated. I saw a woman, not just a mum.

As well as ripping almost every hair from my flesh, my beautician did my hair and makeup. Though my locks remained their rare, multifaceted red, not the traditional Wonder Woman black, the styling was on point. Lynda Carter herself would have been impressed. The second thing? Finn was going to flip.

To round out my Amazonian authenticity, I'd been practicing my lasso skills on Ben. The poor kid had barely been able to move without me going for him and had been on the verge of tears several times, especially when I sprang out from behind a door when he wasn't expecting it. Mother of the year.

He looked so relieved when Brett came to get him. I was not. Once again, Bretty was a little too friendly. *Is the guy ever going to get the hint?*

Nerves made me glance at the clock for the one hundredth time. It was approaching six-thirty, and Teddy was due to pick me up any minute. I couldn't wait to see his costume. Finn's too. They'd both kept me in the dark all week. Teddy would tell me nothing, but Finn had at least hinted his was also superhero related. I didn't know if that meant a Superman-Batman deal, or if I would be chasing down Lex Luther or The Penguin.

I was so on edge, so hyped up, that when Teddy did knock, I squealed, jumped to my feet, and ran to the door to greet him, then gracefully fell flat on my face. Hearing the bang and crash as I bit the dust, he burst in and burst out laughing. "Fuck, even lying in a heap, you look incredible, and Christ, look at your tits!" I gave the girls a squeeze and attempted to move. "So, are you already drunk or what?"

"No, no. Just a bit too excited." I bounced back onto my feet, straightened my boobs in my corset, and looked at Teddy, aka John Travolta. "Holy disco balls! You look amazing! Those flares are massive! And your hair, it's so big and floofy."

It looked so soft, almost comfy, and it made an audible *swish* as he shimmied. I moved to touch it but was blocked *Karate Kid* style.

"Don't touch. Aren't the pants great? I found them this morning at a store in Brooklyn. I swear, Scar, it was like the land that time forgot. Sylvia, the lady that worked there, looked like an eighty-year-old Barbie in glitter boots, *and* she was a wardrobe and hair assistant on *Saturday Night Fever*. She fluffed Travolta's tufts!"

"That is cool...but what were you doing in Brooklyn, and why didn't I know you were going? The secrets are mounting, Teddy."

"I did try to call, but by the look of you, you were undergoing deforestation and had your phone on silent. I predict it still is. Anyway, back to me. This morning, I was complaining about my shitty costume, so Asher said he knew a lady. Then he piled me in his car and whisked me to Sylvia's, then his place. Only his mum was there, but she loved me. I loved her. She fed me matzo brei, latkes, and babka. Scarlett, I think I gained ten pounds, and I ain't mad about it."

Pulling me into a velvet-lapel-cushioned hug, he held me tight as we headed outside to the waiting Uber and only released me before he climbed in. There, he paused and ran his hands up and down my bare, cold arms. "Scarlett, I love you. I want you to be happy and I have a feeling tonight's going to be a new beginning. You look fucking amazing, so hot even I would do you. Don't waste it. I've said it before, and I'll say it again. You better lock it down. That boy won't stay single for long."

We arrived at the party minutes later and, to borrow a phrase from Mrs. Horowitz, strutted in, arm in arm, like the complete hotties we were. The bar looked terrific, Asher and the staff had been decorating all afternoon, and it looked just like a—hopefully—cocaine-free version of Studio 54. The guy had gone all out. Think bling, crystal-beaded curtains, gold-sequin drapes, and mirror balls. No doubt the effort had more to do with impressing Teddy than me. It seemed to work too. Teddy quickly dragged him into the darkest corner of the room to show his appreciation. Leaving the boys to get down and busy, I wandered aimlessly, avoiding Herman, checking out the room, and trying not to nervously sweat out of my costume. With every step I took, something new caught my eye. Strobe lights dazzled blindingly across the dance floor as podium dancers did their thing, and private booths to chill and maybe make out had been installed. It was perfect. Or it would be once Finn arrived.

By seven-fifteen he was nowhere to be seen. It had been an hour. I was beyond panicked, and it was obvious. Teddy and Asher tried to distract me as much as they could, but as the minutes passed, not even Teddy attempting the worm during a Donna Summer banger could lighten my mood. He was mid-air on his second go when Jason Wright grabbed the mic from the DJ.

"Welcome, everyone. It's wonderful to see you all—" Blinding light suddenly filled the dark. A caped, muscular silhouette strode in and paused, hands on hips. It wasn't a bat or a penguin. No, it was my hero. My Superman. My Finn. Every set of eyes in the room turned his way, and the confidence he carried in eroded. Hilariously, he hunched over, covered his junk with his hands, slunk backward into the shadows. "Quite the entrance, Austen. Thanks for joining us," Jason quipped dryly before resuming his no doubt boring and lengthy speech.

As a fellow Justice League member, I was honor bound to discreetly save Finn. So, I waved and jumped up and down while yelling, "FINN! OVER HERE!"

Still protecting his manhood, Finn nodded and skirted the edge of the room toward us. "Fuck, he looks so hot, Scar." Whispered Teddy, "he is so ripped, and that ain't padding. Go get him, Wonder Woman." He then gave me an unsubtle shove in the back. I lurched forward, hitting Superman's brick-wall-like body, and was saved from falling by his arms wrapping around my waist.

This feels nice. I like this. The slip of the Lycra beneath my fingers felt almost sensual. He was so soft and warm but also hard and strong. And Teddy was right. There wasn't any padding involved in his suit—not there on his chest where my hands remained, anyway. The costume did feature a comically large codpiece, though. One I could feel poking into my stomach. I couldn't stop my eyes from wandering to it, or my brain from wondering how much he filled it out.

Finn's fingers spanned over the small of my back, and his grip tightened, pulling me so close my head came to rest between my hands on his chest. I closed my eyes, possibly sniffed him, and didn't move. Neither of us spoke. We just stood there, locked in an embrace I never wanted to end. How long we stayed that way was anyone's guess, but at some point, Jason finished speaking. He dropped the microphone onto the table, a dull thud and squeal echoed through the room, and a smattering of applause broke out. It was an unwelcome reminder to the public nature of our embrace. I jumped from Finn's arms, took a step or two back, and watched as he used it as an opportunity to check me out.

"Red, wow. You're... You're..."

I popped my hip. "Wonder Woman."

"Stunning."

"Oh." My blush was a deeper red than my cape. "Thanks, Finn. Or is it Superman? Or Clark?"

"Scarlett, my dear, tonight I don't give a damn. Call me whatever the fuck you like."

My knees buckled beneath me. It was the first time I'd swooned over a Scarlett O'Hara/*Gone with the Wind* gag. It was also the first one to make me snort.

"We should take a seat. Dinner is ready to be served," I said like a robotic waiter. "You're over there." I pointed to Finn's table by the window.

His brow furrowed with concern as he looked at it and back to me. "Scarlett, where are you sitting?"

I pointed to the other side of the room. "At that table, over by the bar, with Teddy, Victoria, and Arthur the IT guy. I did have you with us, but someone I won't name...Jason...made me change it."

The brow furrowing intensified to a scowl. "Uh-uh. No way am I spending the night that far away from you." Seizing my hand, he walked me straight up to Arthur, took out his wallet and handed him a fifty-dollar note. "Mate, I must sit here. Take this and fuck off."

"Yes, sir." Now, I knew how much Arthur made. He told everyone in the office several times when he last had a raise. But he genuinely looked at that fifty like he had never seen one. He choked, jumped from his seat, and left. Finn waved his hand before the empty chair, and I sat with a smile almost as big as the creepy one Teddy was sporting.

"Do people always do what you tell them?" I asked Finn as he adjusted his costume to sit.

"Do you always call Arthur, Arthur the IT guy, like it's his full name?"

"Yes, I do."

"What about Gareth, and Victoria?"

"Gareth the Creep," I started flatly. "I don't have a name for Victoria. I don't know enough about her, and she seems too perfect to make fun of. Teddy calls her Vicky. She hates it. I love it."

My heart spasmed and swelled as he chuckled, "I love it too. And no, people rarely do what I say, hence the fifty. People respect money here, Red. If I tried that at home, I'd probably get my face kicked in."

"That would be a shame. It's so lovely."

FUCK!

I wanted to die immediately. Teddy almost gagged on his mouthful of pina colada, and Finn lit the room with a smile brighter than any damn disco ball.

17

Scarlett

Y OU KNOW THAT FEELING when you eat so much rich and creamy food—apparently everything from the seventies—you think food may fly right out your mouth or your stomach will explode if you move?

Try having that while being tipsy and in a Wonder Woman costume so skimpy it would possibly be illegal in Utah and parts of Texas.

Most of the evening's dishes sounded disgusting when the chef described them to me, but they were delicious, rich—sumptuous, even. Not so good for your breath or waistline, though.

Our appetizers were the height of 70's class and sophistication: deviled eggs, shrimp cocktail, Swedish meatballs, and fondue. There was also Finn and Teddy's favorite—and the butt of many jokes—cheese logs. For entrees, we had a choice of Moussaka, beef bourguignon, or chicken a la king, served with Watergate or three-bean salad. With pumpkin pecan delight, trifle, and some lethal rainbow Jell-O shots rounding out the night, you can see why I, and most everyone else, was a little limp and sloppy.

Listening to the speeches right after eating didn't aid digestion. Long-winded, rambling, and shit were three words you could use to describe them, as were tedious, dull, and mind-numbing. Each of the firm's partners praised the old man, who sat beside them merrily nodding at how brilliant he was and guzzling a never-ending stream of Tom Collins cocktails. When it came to the man of the hour's turn, he was off-his-face drunk, almost unintelligible, yet somehow still dull. Things only got interesting when he started swearing and cursing about his divorces. Muttering something about lawsuits, Jason was quick to snatch the mic from his hand, and that was the end of that.

A series of slow claps echoed around the room. Most everyone sat still, not quite knowing what to do and still immobile from gluttony. Superman was the exception. I'd just finished saying to Teddy that I didn't think I could ever move again when the DJ turned up the volume and invited people to come and dance. The floor filled slowly, and Finn stood, turned to me, and held out his hand. "Scarlett, would you dance with me?"

"God, yes! Umm, I mean, yes, I'd love to, Finn. Can we wait for maybe one song? I'm struggling to move and really regretting that last Jell-O shot."

"Absolutely—"

"If Scarlett won't dance with you, I will." Enter Victoria with the most words I had ever heard her string together. Of course she chose to use them to cut my fucking grass.

Well, not on my watch, lady!

"Actually, I think I will be fine to dance. Let's go, Finn."

I snatched that boy's hand so fast I was a blur. Seeming relieved, Finn tucked my arm into the crook of his elbow and helped me to my feet, then flashed a cheeky grin. "Up, up, and away.... God, that was so corny."

I'd seen Finn dance before—I should say, attempt to dance. A small office party was held a day or two after he'd arrived, and a pitiful dance floor sprung up in the rear courtyard, right beneath my tree. He had no rhythm or coordination but made up for it all in enthusiasm. So yes, he couldn't dance....when alone. But as I quickly discovered, you put a woman in a slinky costume in front of him, and he was transformed. Finn knew how to move alright. He just needed a partner...the right partner.

His body moved with mine. His hands cradled the small of my back. His hips rolled in time to the deep, pounding bass. Our eyes, once locked, remained so for the entirety of the song. When the next began, he smiled, sighed in recognition, and held me closer. His hand dropped lower to lay on the rise of my shiny satin ass, and he leaned in, sending shivers up and down my spine.

I basked in the warmth of his breath against the rose of my cheek as he whispered in my ear, "You, to me, are everything. I love this song. My mum and dad used to dance to it in the kitchen. They were so in love, Red." He hummed to the music and then sang each word in his deep, rich, sexy voice that took my breath away.

I think a glass smashed in the background, or maybe a car drove through the window, taking out several of my innocent co-workers. There was no way to be sure because I refused to look away from the blue eyes that had captured my heart. This dance, him singing, shattered the last of my ideologies. It wasn't just his body—though, that didn't hurt. It was all of him. His heart, his humor, his thoughtfulness, his compassion. The way his eyes seemed to shine whenever he spoke of his family and how slowly, piece by piece, he was sharing his beloved memories of them with me. The way I felt desired and safe when I was with him. If Finn wanted me, he had me.

Voices murmured, people shuffled around us, and I didn't give a fuck. All I cared about was him firmly gripping my ass.

I brushed my cheek against his and whispered, "Finn."

"Scarlett."

"You are very close to me right now."

"I am."

"And your hand is on my bum."

"It is."

"I like it."

"Ahem. Excuse me. Can I cut in? I'd love to dance with THE Superman."

"What? Oh, Victoria." Of course.

For weeks, that asshole had laid dormant, but she chose that moment to erupt and saturate me in her fucking hot lava. And she was hot. She was gorgeous, in fact, and was making goo-goo eyes at my Finn. But then I remembered. He wasn't mine, and I had no reason to say no. I also couldn't scratch out her eyes and drag her outside by the hair like I wanted to.

"Sure, of course." God, how I hated her.

Finn made a gruff, grunty noise as I moved away that almost sounded like, "Fuck no," but he let me go all the same. For a beat or two, I stood immobile on the edge of the dance floor. I watched them. I watched her pull him closer, and I watched her lay her head on his chest, and I watched him sigh.

Suddenly, it was really stinking hot in there. Sweat ran between my boobs and would soon begin to drip on the floor. I had to get out, and did, leaving them together, swaying in time to Billy Ocean's "*Love Really Hurts Without You.*"

Damn straight, Billy.

Behind the dance floor and restaurant, Asher had set up a small, curtained-off area with a few funky ottomans and bean-bags. It smelled of incense and broken hearts and seemed perfect for the moment. I wanted to sit and sulk but wasn't entirely sure that if I sat in either option, I would be able to get back up. So, I just stood there alone, ridiculous tears filling my eyes, my hands wrapped around my waist, imagining they were his, swaying to the music as though he still held me. I was so wholly gone for this guy.

"Your lasso is slipping."

"What?" I spun to face my hero, standing before me with a massive smile on his face. His arms were crossed over his chest, his fists sitting under his biceps, pushing the bulging muscle further. He took one look at me, and that smile faded.

"Scarlett. Are... Are you crying?"

"No. No, I just have, um... I ate too much food, had too many Jell-O shots, and have a tummy ache." *What in the holy shit did I say?*

"Oh." He sucked his lips between his teeth to stop laughing. "Do you need me to take you home?"

"Thanks, but I will be okay. I just needed a break."

"Me too. Victoria was a little too...enthusiastic. A little too close."

"I thought you liked dancing close. You held me pretty close."

He stepped in front of me and ran his fingers down my lasso. I think he liked it. "Well, that's because it was you." Another step closer, a lick of his lips, and a brutally sexy lingering look down at mine. "Let me get you some water."

He turned to walk away, but I couldn't stand the thought of him leaving, even if it was for the seconds it would take to get me a drink. My hand reached to my waist and grabbed my golden lasso. With my tongue poking out to aid my aim, with all my might and a whispered wish, I threw it and snagged him on the first go. His back was toward me, but even over the music, I heard him. Heard and felt the guttural, deep-chested moan. He turned to me, and the wanton sexuality of his expression had me desperate to get my hands on him. With his arms caught behind his back, I dragged him toward me.

"So, what are you going to do with me now? I'm powerless to stop you," he sighed.

Inch by inch, hand over hand, I ignored his continued heckling and my anxiety's valid attempts at sabotage, and wound him in, leaving just enough slack remaining to sling the lasso over my shoulder and lead him outside. Through trepidation more than intent, I remained silent until the whistles of the swirling night air welcomed us to the edge of the balcony. Exhausted and panting in a not remotely sexy way, I turned to face him, gripped his shoulders, and pushed him against the railing. *What the hell do I do now?*

My uncertain eyes flicked to Finn's and betrayed my cluelessness. The cocky bastard held my gaze and smirked, no doubt loving every minute of my awkwardness. He raised a single finger beneath the rope that held his wrists to his sides and brushed it along my bare thigh, leaving goosebumps in his wake and an intensifying ache in my core. "You didn't answer me, Red. You have me at your whim. What are you going to do?"

I poked out my chin, attempting and failing to ooze confidence. "I... Can't you tell? I'm going to kiss you. That's what."

"Oh. Okay, then. Do it." Squeezing his eyes shut, he leaned forward and puckered his lips. Trapped between laughing, grabbing, and swallowing him whole, or running, I did nothing. "I'm waiting."

When I did nothing, he cracked one eye open, again laughed, and shoved the lasso away. That action heralded the end of Funny Finn. There was a new, edgy, sexy boy in town. He clenched my hip, really squeezed me hard, and by God, if I didn't feel it right in the very fiber of my being. "Looks like it's up to me." He tightened his hold on my waist, then slid one hand up my spine to my neck. A tiny gasp escaped me with every inch his fingers traveled until they spanned out, gripping and pulling my hair as he turned us around in one quick move like we were on the dance floor again.

"Whoooo," I squealed, my hair flying into my face as he whipped me through the air, my back making a heavy thud against the balustrade. "I can't believe this is happening," I panted, clawing at his Lycra-covered ass cheeks like a hungry, wild beast. "You're so fucking hot."

"You're so fucking everything." His voice was deep, dark, almost pornographic, then silent. He studied my face, watching me in a way no one had before. I would have thought a gaze so intense would force my eyes away, but they stayed, lost in the blue of his, watching them slowly close as he leaned down and pressed his parted mouth to mine.

This is it. Our first kiss.

Once, twice, three times, he chastely tasted me, each one coming with a tiny sigh and a sweet smile I felt against my lips and locked away in my heart. The tenderness seemed over, though, when he captured my bottom lip between his teeth, gently licking along its edge before tilting my head back and kissing me till I couldn't breathe. He was so demanding, yet so needy. So gentle but rough. I was being worshipped, appreciated, devoured.

My knees buckled beneath me, and he felt it, holding me tighter against his strong body on a grunt, thrusting into me, effortlessly lifting me from my feet. I winced as my bum pressed against the glass, but the stinging chill was almost a relief from the heat raging between us. I moaned as he pulled away and began pressing kisses to the freckles on my cheeks, the very tip of my nose, and the corners of my mouth.

"God, to finally get you beneath me, Red," he growled into my ear. "I've wanted this for so long."

I sighed, licking the salty sweat from his neck, then burying my face into its hollow. "Me too." He pressed a kiss to my hair, inhaled deeply, then raised my face with a finger beneath my chin.

Our gaze remained locked as he cupped my face, whispering, "So beautiful," against my lips as his other hand caressed the curves of my hips. He moved his hand farther south, pulling my leg up to his hip. "I want you, Red. Do you want me?" All breathing ceased as he slipped his hand up my inner thigh, edging closer and closer until he was stroking the damp fabric between my legs. "So wet. Just like I knew you'd be." My head fell against his shoulder, my hands clinging to his biceps as he massaged me lightly, teasing, drawing helpless sobs until...a throat cleared behind us.

"Get a room!"

I peered around Finn's shoulder just enough to see a waiter shaking his head as he cleared the tables, then disappeared inside.

"I'm going to find and kill that guy," Finn huffed in frustration, returning his fingers to the relative safety of my hip and placing another lingering kiss on the top of my head. "I'm sorry I lost control, Red. I completely forgot where we were."

"Don't be sorry, Finn. I liked it. Will you take me home now?"

His eyes rolled back in his head, and he groaned, almost whined as he ducked back down and scraped his teeth along the tender flesh of my neck. "I want to. But I warn you, if I get you in your room"—he kissed me once—"alone"—then again—"and naked"—then once more—"I won't want to leave your bed."

"Who says we'll make it to bed?"

"Ohh, you are a cheeky one, aren't you?" he huffed out a laugh, grabbing a handful of my ass to emphasize his point.

I nodded, kissed him softly and deeply, then took a bite of his perfectly defined shoulder. Rejoicing in the pained cry it elicited, I slid from beneath him, shook my head to clear it from its daze, and elegantly stumbled toward the noise of the party.

"I'll be right back. I'm going to get my things."

18

Finn

*F*UCK. *I'M SO DAMN hard I'm gonna split my suit.*
Unsurprisingly, an erection beneath a codpiece is not at all comfortable. However, I remained eternally grateful I had worn the hard, plastic thingamajig when she slammed our bodies together.

The way she dragged me from the restaurant and out onto the balcony was the sexiest thing I had ever experienced. I could have resisted, but that would have defeated the purpose. I wanted her to take me. And I would happily have followed her off any cliff she led me to.

Running my hands through my hair, I smacked my lips. My mouth was so dry. Sweat ran down my back. Everything about me was tight. The costume wasn't helping, but this feeling was deeper than the Lycra, nylon, and spandex. Scarlett was changing me from the inside out. My muscles, my mind, my heart. All were being dismantled and rebuilt in her image. All I could think of were her soft, parted lips. She'd only been gone for seconds, but I missed their feel and taste. Kissing Scar like that, being kissed by her like that, went against every promise I'd made for weeks, but I couldn't take it anymore. Resistance was useless. Scarlett Grant with swollen lips and freshly hand-tousled hair was the most dangerous creature on earth, and I had to have her.

I folded myself over the edge of the balcony, seeking relief in the cool night air but was foiled again by New York's balmy nights. "In for four, hold for seven, out for eight." Yet again, Evie's stupid breathing techniques were doing nothing of merit.

"Songggg!" Someone was happy with the song choice. I laughed to myself and took another slow, deep breath. And then it hit me... "Bye Bye Baby" by the Bay City Rollers. Shelby loved this song. She was obsessed with Love Actually and played the soundtrack ad nauseum. Three annoyingly catchy and high-pitched lines in, and I was no longer a man on a balcony in New York, waiting for a woman. I was a boy in a hospital room in Byron Bay, saying goodbye.

"Look at her, Finn. Our little Iris is perfect." We shared a sweet kiss—our first as parents—then laughed, and cried, and stared into the beauty of our babe. It was the moment of all moments, the beginning of life. Everything went quiet, and for a split second, all was peaceful.

Until it wasn't.

Until it was loud and frantic and...

"Shelby... Shelby!"

Then it was the end.

Twenty-two minutes and fifty-two seconds. That was how quickly my world turned upside down. Twenty-two minutes and fifty-two seconds of electrical jumpstarts, shots of adrenaline, rib-cracking compressions, whispered promises, and goodbyes. From king of the mountain to...to nothing. From the inception of a family to a single dad. Twenty-two minutes and fifty-two seconds was all it took.

"Taking a break, young man? Me too. It's terribly loud in there, isn't it?" Before greeting Herman Wise, I dried my tears and willed myself to keep it together. "I don't know what I was thinking of asking for a party like this. I'm too old for this shit." I forced a chuckle as he stood beside me and leaned over the railing as I had just been doing. I'd usually been observing the man with such contempt I'd never noticed how big he was. He was almost as tall as me and broad, but old and tired. "Do you know why I'm taking an early retirement?"

"I don't, sir, no." I did. Herman Wise was not retiring. Perhaps it was the strong female influence in my upbringing that impacted my initial skin-crawling judgment of him—one that was justified on seeing his interactions with my female co-workers. The man was one touch away from the predator club, if not already a card-carrying member. His very presence was a cancer to the firm. Scrubbing in on the surgery to remove him and keeping Scarlett and the other women safe via my influential aunt was the greatest achievement and honor in my short career—and yet another secret I was keeping from Scarlett.

An odd, almost relieved look flashed across his face, and he hit me with a sleazy smile. "Enough of that 'sir' garbage. It's Herman. And I am retiring because my fourth wife, whom I met in this office ten years ago, has divorced me. I can no longer afford to pay her alimony and live in the city—not to the standard I desire, anyway." He gulped from his drink, closing his eyes and letting it sink in before continuing. "Austen, I've seen your heart eyes, as my grandkids call it, over that piece of tail Scarlett Grant. It's none of my business, but I want to give you a friendly warning." He poked his bony finger into my chest, splashing me with lemon and gin. "Don't make the same mistakes as me. Don't dip your quill into the office pot."

I nodded in confused understanding and watched as he continued to talk, drink, and drink. "You'd think I would have learned by the time I had divorced the third wife, but I didn't. And now, it's time for me to pack up and move on. And that's exactly what you should do. She's got a bright future, that one does," he said, pointing to the slowly approaching Scarlett, who was watching us speak. "You do too. Don't let long legs and a pretty smile take that future and flush it down the toilet."

Apparently satisfied that he had ruined my mood and night, he staggered away. Passing Scarlett, he tipped his head in greeting and continued walking but looked back and checked out her ass in the process. What an asshole. The damn fool hadn't learned a thing.

"Miss me?" A tiny bag, only able to fit her phone, a bank card, and lip gloss, sat in one hand. The other teased and caressed my chest and stomach. "Take me home, Finn."

Scarlett took my hand and led me toward the side exit. My body followed obediently, but my mind was somewhere else.

"Shelby... Shelby!"

Something shifted inside me. "Wait, Red. I think that maybe...maybe I shouldn't take you home. I think we shouldn't do this. We should stay." A solitary heartbeat was all it took for her beautiful face to twist from playfulness to heartbreak. Her hand, so tiny when held within mine, slipped from my grasp, and she froze.

"What do you mean? Don't you want me?"

I stepped toward her and slid my hand around her waist, fiercely pulling her to me. "Don't want you? Fuck, Scarlett. I want you so bad that thinking, breathing, existing hurts. But my life...it's complicated, and messy, and..." It was a split-second decision. Tell her that the words of my dead ex-girlfriend haunted me? That I was terrified of love, of giving my heart to someone and losing them again? That I was going home to Byron as soon as I could? Or give her a bullshit excuse that would buy me time?

"You did have a lot of those Jell-O shots. They seemed pretty lethal. I don't want to take advantage of you. And, hey, you know what they say about dipping your quill in the office inkpot."

Borrowing the words of a sexist old fool was not a wise decision. It was completely fucking stupid, and rightly, Scarlett did not appreciate the analogy.

"Oh, right. So, I'm the office inkpot, am I? Is that an Australian way of calling me a slut?"

"No, no, I think I said it wrong. I mean—"

"Don't bother, Finn. I know exactly what you meant, and I promise, your precious quill will never, ever be dipping into my pot." She then punched my codpiece. A full fist smash. And it hurt. Her, not me. That thing was hard. A brief wince of pain flickered across her face, and she pressed her lips together to suppress and swallow the curse I knew she was busting to release. Pouting, her bottom lip trembled, and a single tear hung from her long lashes.

I laughed. I couldn't help it. "Fuck, Scarlett, you need to stop. You told me once that you were prone to making snap decisions, and you're doing it now. Please listen. That's not what I meant."

"Why are you bloody laughing? Tell me what you meant and why it's so fucking funny."

I covered my junk. "I will, as long as you don't punch me again."

"No promises," she said with a huff.

"Okay. What I meant to say is, I really, really want to take you home and kiss you a whole lot more." Amongst other things. "And I have the feeling you want that too." She shrugged and crossed her arms over her chest. It made her boobs look huge, and my decision seemed even stupider. "But work is important to both of us, and I don't think now is a good time to become involved. Life's complicated enough as it is. I'm still finding my feet here, and I'm just not in a place where I can give you what you deserve." I cupped her cheek and lifted her eyes to mine. "And the thing is, Red...I think you deserve everything."

Pulling her lips between her teeth, Scarlett exhaled deeply and nodded. "Oh. Okay."

"I need us to be good friends. I really care about you, Scarlett."

"I care about you too. And you should know that I... I think you're right." She began to step back. "This is the smart thing to do. Oh, my phone is ringing. I have to go. Good night, Finn."

Just like that, she turned and ran. I should have chased her. But I didn't. I stayed on the balcony, circling the perimeter like a caged lion, until Teddy, balancing a glass of champagne and a plate of hors d'oeuvres, tapped me on the shoulder. "Finn. What the hell's wrong with Scar? She just left and said she'd cut me if I followed her."

"I think I fucked up, Teddy. I just... I kissed her. Well, she kissed me after tying me up in her lasso, and it was fucking amazing. And, and..." I pulled my hands down my face and resumed pacing.

"And? Most women don't run off after amazing kisses, Finn. Even ones like Scar who have slight tendencies toward extreme theatrics."

"Well, I was going to take her home, and she went in to get her things. But Herman came outside and told me not to dip my quill in her pot. Then I said that to Scar, and she thought I was calling her the office slut. Then she junk-punched me and left."

He took a bite off an essential 70's delicacy, a pig in a blanket, then whistled. "Oh. Wow. Smooth, Finn. Really smooth."

"Yeah. No shit. I swear I didn't mean it like that, and I told her that too. I like her, Teddy. A lot. But I can't get into a relationship right now. I have plans. I was trying to do the right thing for both of us".

"I'm sure you were. But maybe next time, avoid slut-shaming when you try to let someone down. Even if it was taken the wrong way and finished off with sweetness, she deserves better than that. And I know you can do better."

I nodded and began to walk away, but my advisor wasn't finished. He grabbed my arm and pulled me close enough to see the pastry stuck between his teeth. "If you find yourself in the right life position and are lucky enough to get another chance, you better lock her down. She won't stay single for long. The good ones never do."

***

I had never been one to handle conflict well at the best of times, and the predicament I faced in the week since the party, being on shaky ground with three of the most important people in my life simultaneously, was evidence of that. I hadn't spoken to Nate since he called me a monk. Evie and I had barely looked at each other since the letter incident. And now Scarlett and I had skipped the friend zone and gone back to professional acquaintance land.

Talking to her about the best kiss of my life would have been the mature thing to do. But we had been working well together, making some serious headway on the house design, and as much as I missed the fun, I didn't want to rock the boat.

Avoiding confrontation was a habit I fell into when I was a kid. Evie was a firecracker from birth. It was often easier to leave her alone than deal with her wrath. When Mum and Dad died, I delayed my grief by losing myself in Shelby. While Nate understood to some extent, he was less than impressed by our goo-goo eyes and stolen kisses. After almost coming to blows at the beach one day when I may have become a little too handsy in front of him, I again hid from confrontation. Shelby and I went underground and, out of fear, stayed that way until we found out about—and could no longer hide—her pregnancy. Then when we lost her too, I transplanted my feelings into Iris, school, and my job.

The method that had once helped me survive now had me all kinds of messed up. I couldn't sleep, could hardly eat, and felt totally out of control of my emotions, which I hated. I needed to seize it back. I needed to purge, and it needed to start at home. "Eves, can I talk to you for a sec?" She was tucked up in bed, reading and sipping on tea. Iris had one day left before school started, and she was making the most of a late sleep-in.

"You can if you want to. Whether or not I'll listen is another question."

"What are you reading?"

The same eyes I saw in the mirror each morning shifted from the pages before her and focused intently on mine. "'The Truth About Love.' It's beautiful and sweet. Not at all snappy or judgmental of people when they tried to do the right thing." It was hard, but I left the blinding hypocrisy of Evie accusing others of snippy judgment. If I didn't, we'd end up in a bigger quarrel.

That horrible feeling of guilt, of owed apologies you didn't want to hand over, began swirling in my gut. I flopped on the bed and nudged her in the ribs.

"The other night, when I found the letter…I was an asshole. I want to apologize. You were right. You do know Iris as well as me, maybe better. She's spent more time with you since birth and probably wouldn't appreciate her mum's words yet. She'd have it covered in cake, crayons, or both within an hour. So, yeah. I'm sorry."

She dropped her book into her lap. "So, you bloody should be… Me too. I should have told you about it. You deserved to see how happy Shelby was to be having a baby, and you deserve to be happy now, Finn."

"Yeah, probably. Or…" I stopped and decided to keep my thoughts to myself. It was my turn to get a nudge in the ribs.

Evie chased my eyes. "Or what?"

"Maybe it's better that I found it now. Maybe it's a sign for me to remember why I'm here and to remind me to keep Shelby's memory alive for Iris." I hoped to make Evie's life better too. She lived for me and Iris. But I left that inside, knowing she'd find a way to be insulted.

"Maybe. I'm not sure why that means you must be a complete prick, though."

We sat silently, nudging each other repeatedly until Evie grabbed her phone and saw the time. "Jesus, Finn, It's almost eight. What the hell are you still doing here?"

"Oh, well. You know Scarlett from work?"

"The hot chick you wanna bone?"

I rolled my eyes. "No... Yes. Well, she is kind of pissed at me, and being alone in a room with her and her tight skirts is not the best place for me to be at the moment. We were kind of getting close, and then I said something stupid, and now I think she hates me. Working together in such a tight space with no fun and flirtation is...awkward."

"So, you avoid her by apologizing to me? Lovely." Smirking, she sipped again. "You know you can't hide from everyone, don't you?"

"Yeah, I'm a bit slow, but I am starting to realize that."

"Good. About bloody time. Now go. I've got shit to do." She pushed me from the bed and resumed her reading. I began to walk out but stopped at her door and spoke without looking back.

"I don't know what I'd do without you, Evie. I hope you know how much I appreciate what you've done for me...and Iris. You deserve to be happy too."

"Love you too. Now go to work, you big dork."

My issues with Nate were simpler to work through. One phone call, one mention of football, and a question about his latest conquest, and we were back to being BFFs. I could only hope Scarlett would be so easily won over. Even if nothing happened romantically between us, I missed...her. All of her. I missed the banter, and laughter, and friendship we'd built. I wanted things to be the way they were before the kiss, but the way things were before our kiss is what led to the kiss. It was hopeless, and confusing, and basically a classic case of wanting your cake and eating it too.

With all this...this stuff brewing and bubbling around us, somehow, work had progressed on our project. It was beginning to come together, and Jocelyn, who I was FaceTiming with as I walked into Team Finnlett's headquarters, agreed.

"I have decided to extend my stay in France for at least another month." I instantly knew she'd gotten herself a boytoy and dreaded the upcoming discussions this would lead to. Jocelyn was a very open woman. "I've also added some further modifications and a pool house. I'll email it all over later today after my date with Luc. If I can still manage to move, that is." Knew it.

Her instructions continued, and judging by the darting of my intuitive aunt's eyes, the frostiness between Scarlett and me transcended time zones, oceans, and iPad screens. Again, I knew Jocelyn would somehow involve herself in correcting it.

I was right. Though I couldn't prove her involvement, Jason Wright had a spur-of-the-moment idea not ten minutes after her call. The next week, Scarlett and I would join him and Victoria, his PA, to visit the home site. The plan was to stay overnight in Tarrytown and return Friday afternoon.

Well played, old lady...well played.

19

Scarlett

Almost nine years ago.

I CARRIED MY LAPTOP and a giant decaf latte and waddled into my last lecture before the summer break. For me, it would be a break like no other. I was due to give birth in four weeks.

"Slut."

I ignored it, knowing full well who I would find behind me, coughing and sneezing insults into their clenched fists: The Barbies. Three girls, all with platinum-blonde locks, swollen trout pouts, and skin tones akin to an Oompa-Loompa. Not that there was anything wrong with that.

"Slut. Slut. Slut."

It was the same broken record each time since I'd begun to show. I'd tried to ignore it. I'd tried to reason with them. I tried reporting to student welfare. After that, we were all forced to attend group mediations together, but they bullshitted their way through each session, saying everything they knew the counselors wanted to hear. Then, the insults and taunts would start again as soon as we left the room.

Slut, harlot, ho, town bike, and my personal favorite, Cum Pot. That one came about after I ate a kumquat in class. It was disgusting but rather inventive. Any time I was late, had to leave to use the bathroom, missed a class for an appointment, or even if I ate in public, I would be targeted. Accusations of unfair treatment were made because some of my assignment deadlines had been modified. And other students refused to work on joint projects with me because I had been deemed unreliable.

In this class, Fundamental Principles of Environmental Design, the harassment was worse because Teddy had a different lecture time than me. They knew I was alone and easy prey—a lame duck, if you will—and they hunted me as such. Well, on that day, I was done.

"Slut. Oh, excuse me. I must have allergies. Do you have any tissues, Harlett...sorry, Scarlett?"

"No, Stacey. I do not have any tissues, and even if I did, I wouldn't give them to you."

"Wow. Someone's hormonal. I don't know why they let pregnant women loose in lecture halls. Especially this one," she complained.

"She's basically feral. She talks to us like this, and they still help her. It's completely unfair," complained Brooke.

"I can't believe she gets modified schedules just because she can't keep her legs together," added Alisha, my former roommate—the one whose parents had kicked me out.

Tears stung my eyes, but I kept my head down and opened my laptop. The second our professor spoke, they started again.

"Slut. Slut. Slut."

These bitches had pushed me too far. I was retaining fluid. I was having Braxton-Hicks contractions. My ass hurt night and day for some ungodly reason, and I could hardly eat because I had a beach ball squishing my stomach. I snapped, slamming my laptop shut and jumping to my feet as fast as I possibly could jump by that stage. "What the hell is your problem? Yes, I'm pregnant. Yes, I am young. But I deserve to be here as much as you do. I've got the talent. I've got the grades. I got the scholarship. Shut the fuck up and leave me alone."

After a collective gasp and a few claps of what I thought was support, I heard footsteps approach. "Thank you, Miss Grant. I think you should leave." Professor Singh stood behind me, her hands crossed over her chest and her lavender glasses resting on the tip of her nose.

"Me? Why do I have to leave? These three clowns are the ones hurling insults."

"Look, I don't know, and to be honest, I don't care. I heard you swearing, not them, and I have had enough of your"—she looked down at my stomach and then back to my face—"interruptions. You can submit your final assessments for the term like you will all next term's work. Online. Good day, Miss Grant."

"But—"

Her glasses almost slipped off as she dropped her head, narrowed her eyes, and glared. "I said good day, Miss Grant." Snickering echoed around me as I collected my things and left. "Right, now that that uncomfortableness is over, let's get back to work."

Current day

Tears poured down my cheeks. I sat in the bath, drinking rosé straight from the bottle and pulling off the fake lashes I'd put on this morning in a vain effort to cheer myself up.

"Don't dip your quill in the office pot."

It had been a week. A good week, too. Ben had been at home. We cooked together and went skating. He won a sports award at vacation care and helped with the dishes every night. Even at work, Finn and I had made great progress on the house. But I was still raw.

You are such a fucking idiot. Let it go already.

It was an expression I'd heard before. But for some reason, the word *pot* in that context hurtled me back in time. I was that scared, pregnant girl everyone stared at, who one night lost her virginity to an American and became the biggest slut, or Cum Pot, in Cambridge. In a heartbeat, all my deep-seated insecurities over my teenage motherhood, being unworthy, and fear of judgment came together and culminated in a perfect storm of stupid. To top it off, when Finn gave his perfectly valid reasons for sticking to friendship, most of which were my own stupid ideologies and none of which included references to any type of #holife, I still chose to believe the worst.

Then, instead of cooling my heels over the weekend, seeing reason, and talking to Finn like a mature adult on Monday

morning, I doubled down and iced him out. Even alone, half
tanked and stewing in my own filth, I was flushed with embarrassment, the heat of which had me adding cool water to the
already tepid bubbles. I was ashamed not only of my reaction
but because I was continuing to let my past dictate my future.
I'd given those judgmental, nasty twats my power for years. I
let the names, looks, and stereotypes get to me so much that I
hid my son, accused an adorable guy of calling me a slut, and
let my paranoia possibly ruin something that could have been
special. And now, I had to travel upstate with that someone and
be super professional and brilliant while wanting to die on the
inside.

My conundrum led me to HR Jan. Over tea and biscuits, we
had a good, soul-cleansing chat. "There are three things I want
you to remember, Scarlett. One, your fear is understandable and
valid, and you have nothing to be ashamed of in not talking
about Ben. Let's face it, there are men in this firm with kids
that no one has heard of because no one thinks to ask them. It's
just not an issue. Even if they have kids, it wouldn't be seen as a
hindrance to their career. Two, supposedly, we're all adults here.
If it's done discreetly and preferably not with a superior, there
is no rule against inter-office dating. Don't let your fears stop
something you seem to feel is special. Third, over half of America's romantic relationships are formed in the workplace. It's
not the scandal you seem to think it is. You know what, I have
four things," she added, taking a sip of her drink and chewing
thoughtfully on a cookie. "I think I know who prompted these
questions, and the very same person may have already asked me
some similar questions. He's quite lovely—massive too."

Jan was right. Finn was massive. She probably had a point
about the other stuff, but the massive part was spot on. While I
couldn't tell what was lurking beneath the costume, I could feel
every other muscle in that man's body as I begged him to take
me home and fuck me.

Remembering the slight bite and drag of his teeth, I sunk
further into the water and pressed a finger to my lips. Never had
I been kissed like that. It was a panty-soaking, knee-buckling ten
on the Richter scale. Even days later, the mere thought of being

pressed under his body had me clenching my thighs and, if at home, reaching for my bullet.

"You're wet for me, Scarlett. Just like I knew you'd be."

Damn. Such a sweet boy. Such a filthy mouth.

I splashed my face one last time, sipped the final drops of wine, dragged myself from the bath, and lay my still-damp body in my bed. My wet hair flipped forward, brushing the screen of my phone. It lit up, revealing my beautiful Benny's smiling face, ten missed calls, and just as many messages. Ignoring them, I flopped onto my stomach with my head twisted to the side and stared at the mess covering my floor. "So much mess to clean. Such little time."

My phone buzzed again.

Teddy

> You have been avoiding me all week.

That was true. I'd ghosted not only Finn but Teddy too. I couldn't process his level of realism while being so sad and horny.

Teddy

> I gave you time to sulk, but it's done. I know what's going on in that pretty little head of yours, and I'm sick of you not talking about it. He didn't mean it like that, Scar. He was doing the right thing, but maybe in the wrong way.

> I know. That's why I am hiding. I am embarrassed. I was so angry at him. I don't know how to come back from that. I junk-punched him, for fuck's sake.

Teddy
Try sitting on his face.

Sorry, typo. I meant, try sitting next to him and saying just that. I was angry. I thought about it. Now I am not. Sorry for the ball slap.

Then sit on his face.

Goodnight.

Teddy

We all fuck up sometimes, Scar. You gotta stop being so hard on yourself. Talk to him. I swear it will be okay.

Especially if you sit on his face.

My doorbell rang three times. Heavy footsteps climbed the stairs, and Teddy slipped beneath my sheets.

"Teddy, why did you message me if you were at my front door?"

"I wanted to assess your mood before approaching. What are we watching?"

"Apart from my life going down the toilet? Nothing. I just got out of the bath."

"Thought so. You smell good. Wanna make out?" I laughed and pushed his shoulder. "You're right. There is no way I can compete with Finn. I know that already, and you've told me nothing about it. That ends now. Dish."

I took a deep breath, pictured Finn dry humping me against the rail, and quivered.

"WOW. You just orgasmed, didn't you?"

"Little bit, yeah."

"That good, eh?"

"Yup," I said with a pop. "I think that's why it hurts so much to be work-friend-zoned. I'm never going to taste those plump—"

"Ass cheeks?"

"Lips, again."

"Bullshit. I give it a week, and he'll have you bent over the copier, Xeroxing your boobs as he shags you senseless."

I enjoyed that mental image before responding. "Nope. As much as it sucks, Finn was right. We both need to focus on Hudson River House. Maybe things will be different after we're done. But until then, it is strictly business."

20

Scarlett

Y ET AGAIN, I HAD procrastinated to the point of nausea. It was Tarrytown day. I still hadn't spoken to Finn about what happened, but I was determined to do so before we left.

With a lump of remorse the size of Texas in my throat, I approached our building, tossed my head back, and made a wish on the hidden stars. "Please, don't let me fuck this up."

"Scarlett. Are you alright?"

I returned my eyes to ground level and found Finn looking sexy as hell in dark jeans, a navy shirt, and a tailored tweed jacket, scratching his head.

"Finn. Hi. Yeah, I'm fine. Why?"

"You're standing on the street, talking to the sky. I know New York is weird, but..."

"Oh. That. No, that was just... I was just stretching my neck. I've got a real stiff one." I then proceeded to demonstrate stretching in case Finn didn't know what that was. *Idiot.*

"I've heard a good stretch does wonders for morning stiffness." Smirking, he sipped from his coffee like he hadn't made a hard-on joke and nodded toward the building. "Here, let me get the door for you. Are you looking forward to the trip? Do you know where we are staying—"

In classic Lloyd from *Dumb and Dumber* style, I pressed a finger over his lips and shushed him before I had time to think. "I want to apologize for acting like I did at the party." The words burst out in a flurry and didn't stop. "Every day since has been pretty horrendous. I was angry, then embarrassed, and then I got embarrassed for being embarrassed, and it all kind of snowballed. So yeah, I didn't handle it well. I know we have been able to work together, but I miss being buddies, and I hope you can forgive me for being a dick."

"Forgive you? Scarlett. There is nothing to forgive. I stuck my tongue down your throat—oh, pardon me." Two women walked between us and tutted. Finn blushed and held the door open for their disapproving asses. I would have shut it. "As I was saying, I did the tongue stuff and then gave you some lame-ass excuse of why I shouldn't have. I'm the one that needs to apologize. I'm the dick."

We'd just stepped inside, and the word dick loudly echoed through the cavernous lobby, drawing many a smirk and giggle from passersby and more tuts from the door bitches.

"Well, looks like we are both dicks, so I guess that makes us even?"

"I guess it does." He then did that thing he did often, where he stood close to me, breathed, looked, and smelled all gorgeous. I loved-slash-hated when he did that.

"So, we're okay? Mates again? he asked, his eyes wide with hope.

"Mates." I nodded, shaking his offered hand. "Maybe one day we can go out for drinks again and talk some more—if you'd like?"

"I'd like that a lot, Red."

We stood silent, watching our connecting hands shake. Finn was the one to eventually break and pull his hand away. "Are you ready for the big trip? I wish I knew what Jason had planned. He won't tell me a damn thing. I wanted to Google the hotel and check that it was clean looking." As I laughed, I noticed Finn's brown leather overnight bag slung over his shoulder.

"Shit, I left my suitcase at home. Fuck, I knew I'd cock something up."

Finn braced my shoulders and smoothed his hands up and down my arms. "Hey, you didn't cock anything up. It's just a bag. I'm sure we can get it on the way. Don't stress." He then flashed his cheeky smile and leaned into my ear. *Damn, he smells so good. Like chocolate and dreams.* "Besides, it might be a good thing. You could throw some clean sheets in. Just in case. I do wish I knew the hotel's name."

"I'll be sure to do that," I laughed. "You're very good at distracting me from my worries, Finn Austen. I think I can help you with yours, too. Jason gave me a hotel brochure yesterday. It might be on my desk."

I grabbed his giant hand and led him into the elevator without even thinking. My grip was loose initially, but he had taken command and had a firm hold of me by the time we made it to my desk. Regretfully, he had to let go so I could rifle through a mountain of paper strewn haphazardly across my workspace. Surprise, surprise, I couldn't find it. "Hmm, maybe I took it home." I could hear snickering and turned to see Finn smirking behind me. "What's so funny?"

"Nothing, I was just admiring your organization."

I shook my ass, just a touch. "Well, as long as that's all you were admiring, I suppose that's fine."

He sighed, shook his head, and laughed, "Fuck, you can't help it, can you?"

"What?" Batting my eyelashes, I attempted to look all innocent and sweet.

"Being all sexy. Shaking your ass and flirting with me."

"I was doing no such thing. Now, find out where we will be spending the night together and if I need to bring a full case of linen."

He didn't go, thank God. The next ten minutes were brilliant, and I was the happiest I'd been all week. Things just felt right when we were together. Even when Jason and an extra flirty Victoria joined us in the conference room to discuss the plans for the day, Finn's attention remained on me. His eyes ignited the fire I seemed unable to snuff out. It pleased me greatly—Victoria, not so much. Which pleased me even more.

"Thanks for taking me home to get my things, Jason. Sorry again."

"Stop worrying and apologizing, Scarlett. It's fine. What's the address, again?" Jason asked.

While worrying I'd annoyed Jason with my worrying, *and* for apologizing too much about my worrying and apologizing, Finn replied on my behalf. "Oh, it's close. Chuck a uey...I mean, make a U-turn, then take the next two lefts, and it's the third house on the right."

Victoria and Jason looked at each other and smiled at us in the backseat. Seeing their reaction, Finn chuckled nervously and pointed at his temple. "I brought her home when it was raining one night. Have a good memory."

As we pulled up to the curb, my quirky neighbor was out for her mid-afternoon wander and unsurprisingly caught my boss's attention. "Is that woman walking a bunch of cats in a stroller?"

"Yes. Yes, she is," I answered as though it was the most natural thing in the world. "She rescues strays, particularly injured ones, from local shelters and cares for them until they are rehabilitated. I found her quite odd at first, but she is lovely once you get to know her. Isn't she, Finn?"

"Oh, you know the cat lady, Austen? Wow, you have spent some time here, haven't you?" Jason smirked.

Victoria looked as though she was sucking a lemon. It was great.

"Not really. We were introduced the day I dropped Scar off. Mr. Pickles was stuck under the car, and...oh, well, it's a long story." Finn got out first to open the door for me, then stood on the sidewalk and, much to the delight of Mrs. Horowitz, stayed to chat with her while I got my bag.

When I returned outside, she was laughing. Finn, not so much. He looked strained, a bit miffed, you might say. Like Victoria had shared the lemon. "Have a lovely time away. Don't do anything I wouldn't do, Scarlett!" Mrs. H. winked as Finn took my case from me and threw it in the trunk. He then joined me in the back of the car, slumping in his seat much as Ben would do when he's overtired and about to explode into a tantrum.

I went to thank him for taking my case but was distracted by a loud grinding noise. It was Finn, grinding his teeth. Before I could ask what was wrong, he captured my wrist and caught my eyes. "Who's Brett?"

"What? Brett? Why, why? Who told you about Brett?"

"Your neighbor was feeling my biceps, and she said she liked the look of me more than, and I quote, 'that Brett.' So, who is Brett? Is he your boyfriend, Red?" His grip tightened, and so did every muscle in my uterus.

"No, he's not. But he was, I guess, kind of. It was a long time ago, and he is still in my life, but we are not together. It's a bit complicated. I promise I will tell you about it one day, just not yet. But he is definitely not my boyfriend."

Victoria spun to face us, a pure shit-eating grin fixed on her face. "Is he your husband, then?"

"No, I just said he wasn—"

"So, he's your ex-husband?"

The pressure of Finn's hold increased again, and I could feel his eyes boring into the side of my head. Nothing I could do at that moment could stop the verbal diarrhea from flowing. "What? No, Victoria, not my ex-husband, either. I slept with him—well, I didn't even sleep with him. We had sex in the back of a Mini Cooper when I was in university, if you must know. We kept in touch and have been friends since I moved to the States. No relationship. No marriage. Sex once, maybe three times, but it was all on the same night."

The silence was deafening. Finn was no longer holding my hand, and Jason ran a red light. There was no point. No one in that car was escaping the awkwardness. No one. Especially me. So, I did what any mature adult would do. I shoved my Air Pods in, pressed play, and pretended it never happened.

Twenty minutes later, we were still stuck in traffic, I was still beyond mortified, and Finn must have worn his teeth to stubs. Although I couldn't hear the grating any longer over my 90s Brit pop, I could still see his jaw working overtime. He sat silently beside me, watching the traffic, tapping his thumbs, and occasionally looking my way with either a hopeful smile or a worried scowl. I'm sure he wanted to move on from my Mini Cooper sex revelations and talk, but he wasn't quite ready. Neither was I.

So, he forced it.

"What are you listening to?"

"What? I can't hear you." I could. I just didn't want to talk. That didn't stop him. He grabbed my phone and studied the album cover on the home screen.

"Take That, eh? I would have thought you more a Westlife lassie."

"You know Westlife? And Take That?"

"Does this sound like I know Take That? Gary, Jason, Howard, Robbie, Mark."

Wow. He really did. Mark me impressed and a little disturbed.

I must have looked so stunned and puzzled that he explained the reason for his expertise. "My mum and Jocelyn were big fans. I think I have listened to every album they've made."

"Okay, then, what's your favorite song?"

"Hmm, I dunno. Wait, though, I bet I can guess yours. Hmm..." He looked me up and down, twice, sucking his lip into his mouth in a fashion that made me want to climb from my seat, mount, and ride him all the way to Tarrytown.

"All I do each night is pray."

"Wow. You know the words, and yes, 'Pray' is my favorite. Huh. Who's my favorite member, then?"

Again, I was scanned head to toe. "Hmm. Definitely Mark or Robbie, but I sense you greatly appreciated Howard's body."

"Spot on."

Add horny to scared and impressed.

21

Finn

Victoria and Jason rode up front, silently suffering second-hand embarrassment while Scarlett and I butchered our favorite British boy band. Midway through our stellar rendition of "Back for Good", I remembered I had confessed to Scar that I had watched and loved *Mansfield Park*. She was going to think me a complete wanker—or completely brilliant. But at that moment, I didn't care. Her smile and affectionate twinkling as we sang along with Gary and the boys were worth every joke she could make at my expense.

When our driver demanded we stop before he ran us off the road and into a tree, we yielded and reluctantly turned off the tunes. Scarlett read the hotel brochure front to back, and I pretended to nap while watching how cute she looked.

The woman was a non-stop fidget, fluttering between singing to herself, staring out the window, twisting her curls around her fingers, and biting her nails. After a while, her attention shifted again, and she began digging around for something in her bag. "Gotcha," she muttered, then pulled out a well-worn copy of *Emma*. I continued to observe. Smiling to see her eyes widen in surprise or squint with a giggle, even though she had probably read that line one hundred times. She read to herself in a barely audible whisper, and I wondered if she always did that. I hoped so. I could watch and listen to her read for hours.

I was relieved we'd had that chat this morning and cleared the air. Not that things would ever be clear between us. Not with all that chemistry swirling around. Eventually, she caught my gaze and hit my thigh with the book.

"Are you watching me? Why are you watching me, and why are you smiling? Do I have food on my face?"

"Why Jane Austen?"

The novel was placed on her lap as she pursed and twisted her lips. "Well, why not? She's brilliant, funny, romantic, and a feminist ahead of her time. And talk about bravery. She was never afraid to point out the hypocrisy in the world around her or the barriers and injustices women faced. And she did it all with such delicate wit that many readers don't even realize they are being educated with every word they read." She sighed, very near swooned, then suddenly blushed when she caught my gaze. "God, sorry. I do prattle on. I just...ugh, I love her."

"I can see that, and you've completely convinced me. So, tell me, Red, what book would an expert like yourself recommend to a novice?"

"Really, you want to read something of hers?"

"Yep, really. How could I not after that? Why? Is it too un-manly?"

"No, not at all. It's... I think it's lovely." With a clap and a cheer, she leaned down and again fished around in her bag. It took all my strength not to rip her up into my arms. I was so desperate to kiss her. The way she said *lovely*—and *beautiful,* too, come to think of it—all fancy and proper with that fucking accent...drove me insane.

I willed my cock to behave and stared out the window, hoping to spot an accident or maybe some gruesome roadkill. Anything that would clear my brain of impure thoughts of that proper tongue, and all the very un-fancy and improper things I wanted that tongue to do to me.

"Here it is." She gently placed a well-loved, tatty-looking book in my lap and smiled proudly as though displaying a photo of her child, "*Pride and Prejudice*. It's her most famous work for a reason. It can get a little heavy in spots, and some of the terms will be foreign, but..." She shrugged one shoulder and tilted her head, giving me an *ehhh* face. "You're a smart-ish guy. I think you can keep up."

So cheeky. I need to put her over my knee. Okay, stop picturing that. The book was placed on my lap. "Gee, thanks."

"Just look after that copy. It's the only one I have with that cover picture, and it's my favorite."

"Ohh, what will you do if I wreck it? Chuck a wobbly?"

Scarlett's face screwed in a puzzled fashion, and that need to kiss her returned.

"What the hell does 'chuck a wobbly' mean? And that thing you said in the city, 'chuck a uey'. What's that?"

"Oh, I forgot I was talking Aussie. Uhh, a uey is slang for a U-turn. A wobbly is a tantrum. Picture a little kid that didn't get a lolly he or she wanted, face down on the floor, screaming, arms and legs flailing in the air. That's chucking a wobbly."

"Hmm. I like it. I'm stealing that." She giggled adorably and checked with our front seat companions if they had heard the term. Neither had, of course, and it led to a game—what's the Aussie word for? Random words were thrown at me at lightning speed, adding to the ridiculous hilariousness of Aussie slang. Even sulky Victoria got involved.

"Builder?"

"Brickie!"

"Electrician?"

"Sparkie!"

"Toilet paper?"

"Oh, toilet paper is the same, but also dunny paper or bog roll!" That one got a laugh and an, "Ew."

"Doctor?"

"Quack!"

"Wait, a doctor is a quack? Scarlett and Victoria studied me like an oddity. And Jason's eyes narrowed in the mirror as he watched the road ahead.

"Yeah, that's right," I said matter-of-factly.

"So, what sound does a duck make?" asked Victoria.

"Oh, a duck quacks and is still just a duck."

"Well, that's confusing. What about chicken? What do you call a chicken, and what sound does it make?"

"A chicken is still a chicken. Or a chook, and it clucks, which I'm pretty sure would be the same everywhere, surely?"

All three nodded, looking disappointed that ducks are still ducks and chickens still cluck. The game continued for at least another twenty minutes. For me, the novelty wore off after the first five, but Scarlett's laughter and frequent touching of my thigh meant I'd have played for days on end to see her so happy.

Seeming to have giggled herself to exhaustion, Scarlett spent the remaining journey asleep, her head resting on my shoulder. She hadn't started out that way, but much like her constant state of movement while awake, she rolled around like a ship on rough seas during her sleep. The position she stayed in for the longest, and where she moaned, smacked her lips, and nestled in close, was right where she belonged.

On me.

It felt so right. And I knew.

Since the party, I'd been trying to find the right time to tell Scarlett about Iris. I hoped it would prove how much she meant to me. Even if we weren't romantically involved like I knew we both wanted.

As Tarrytown rolled into view, I stole one last glance at her pretty little pout and decided I would tell her tonight.

"Scarlett, sweetheart," I whispered. "We're here."

Like many a man before him, Jason was hesitant to stop along the way, so when we rolled into Tarrytown, it was an all-out sprint to the first public bathrooms we could find, located in a touristy kind of cafe gift shop.

Sticking with tradition, the girls took forever. Jason grabbed a table and ordered some coffee while I perused the shelves. I had no idea Tarrytown was *The* Sleepy Hollow until Scarlett filled me in. As you'd expect, the shelves were filled with ghoulish touristy souvenirs and postcards. One section captured my attention, and it had nothing to do with Ichabod Crane or the headless horseman.

Tucked away in the corner was a display of primarily vintage books that seemed entirely at odds with the rest of the store. The stand was immaculately presented. Several books had small, handwritten cards placed before them with a synopsis and story of where the book had been sourced. I wondered if it was the owner's little bit of sanity, their pride and joy. Perhaps the store started out this way, as a bookstore filled with hidden gems and first editions but ended up becoming just another trinket shop to pay the bills.

Carefully looking through the collection, that old book smell took me back to my childhood. To mum reading me Australian classics like *Blinky Bill, Cuddle Pot and Cuddle Pie,* and *The Magic Pudding*. On the next shelf, I found a vintage copy of *Pride and Prejudice*. Leather bound, it was a rich navy, almost black, with gilded peacock feathers falling like snow over the spine and back.

Scarlett would love this.

"'Tis no' a first edition, but a reproduction. A beautiful one at that." A tiny woman wearing a tartan dress and red apron appeared beside me. She looked as old as the books and kind of smelled the same too. "Ye like Jane Austen, do ye? No' something I see a young lad such a yerself looking at often...unless 'tis for his bonny lass, of course." She giggled and dug her elbow into mine. I had no idea why she was laughing, but there was such warmth and joy on her face I couldn't help but chuckle along.

"Yes, it would be for a lass, but she's not mine."

"Ahh, unrequited love. I've seen that look a thousand times, unfortunately, far too often in a mirror." Without a chance for a reply, she chuckled again, then grabbed my hand and led me into the small dark room. Fluorescent lights blinked to life, revealing a rainbow of books crammed into another series of shelves. "This is my own collection. All these are Austen's works in various editions. Pick what ye like and take it for yer lassie. Maybe 'twill be the thing that wins her heart. Though, I would think a strapping young lad shouldnae have any troubles...unless she's blind, of course. She's no' blind, is she? Lord, I'd feel terrible."

I laughed again, "No, she's not blind, just too smart to mess around with the likes of me." Scolding me before leaving, my new friend left me alone to choose, but I had to make it quick, and I could hear Scarlett laughing from the cafe. A 1970's version of *Sanditon* tugged at my heartstrings, reminding me of our kiss at Mr. Wise's party. I tucked it and the *Pride and Prejudice* book under my arm and headed to the register to pay.

Nodding in approval, my books were wrapped in brown paper tied with string and topped off with a sprig of what Margaret—according to her name badge—told me is dried Scottish Heather. "Och. Aye. 'Tis a fine choice, and she's a lucky lass, even if she doesnae ken it yet."

"Finn! Stop buying headless men, and come drink your coffee!"

Shaking her head, Margaret made a few quips about Scarlett bossing me around and just how typical that is for an Englishwoman. "Ye better take this, then," she whispered, popping a Black headless horseman sculpture on top of my package. "Ye can use it as a cover for the books."

I re-joined my traveling companions, we ate our body weight in cake, then we went to our hotel. Surprise, surprise, it was called The Sleepy Hollow Inn. The plan was to drop off things and then head out to Jocelyn's land, but we'd all eaten so much that the group decided to take a nap first. Jason checked us in while the rest of us collapsed into a row of armchairs.

"Don't fall asleep, noddy." Scarlett teased as I struggled to keep my eyes open.

"Me? You're the noddy. You snored your ass off for half the trip."

Victoria tutted loudly. " What the hell is a noddy? You two are weird."

Like a man about to deliver bad news, Jason returned with bad news.

"Umm, somehow, the hotel had us arriving next week, not today. They only have two rooms. One has two beds, the other just one. So, it's guys and girls to share, I guess?"

"Let me guess, you two"—Victoria pointed between Jason and me—"get the two beds, then you can think about us two spooning all night."

Jason and I looked at each other from the corner of our eyes. The edges of our lips curled. "Let's flip for it," I suggested. "It's fairer that way." I dug into my pocket and pulled out a quarter. "Your call, Red. Heads or tails."

"Heads...tails...heads!"

"Tails it is. Sorry, ladies. You two need to decide who the big spoon will be."

"This is such bullshit." Victoria groaned, snatched the key-card from Jason's hand, and then stomped off toward the room. Scarlett followed forlornly.

"Have fun, ladies." I winked.

22

Scarlett

M Y BEDMATE WAS A mystery, wrapped in a riddle, decorated by barbed wire. On my side of Victoria's wall of pillows, I lay listening to her complain about sharing a room with me while wondering what I did to incite such contempt.

Prior to Finn's arrival, we'd had maybe four conversations in total. All had been formal, business-like, and cold. Post-Finn, she was outright rude. It didn't take a genius to know, her Finn flirtations, and his lackluster response to them, was most likely at the heart of it.

"It's bad enough I had to sit in a car with you for hours. Now I have to sleep next to you!" It was muttered into the wall she faced but loud enough that someone whose hair was trapped under a pillow would hear.

"I'm not thrilled about it either, but we could try and make the best of it. Look..." I pulled my curls free, gagging on the musty scent my movement released from the pillow, and pointed toward the wall-mounted TV. "They have HBO Max. Maybe we can watch an old movie together?"

"I would rather set my hair on fire."

Here's a match. Eat shit, bitch, I thought to myself. What I said was, "Hmm. Okay. Well. Let's just nap, then. The boys will want to go to the lot soon, I expect."

"Yes, and we all know you always go along with what the boys say."

"What's that supposed to mean? In anger, I flopped around, then sat upright, slamming my fists into the pillows and releasing more stench. Finn had been right. I should have brought my own linens. "If you're being like this because of Finn, you're barking up the wrong tree. I know you like him, but nothing is happening between us."

She ignored me. And I couldn't be arsed with a follow up.

Five minutes later, just as drool pooled on my chin, she sighed and turned so far to her side, she was almost face-down. "Please, I see you swanning around him and batting your lashes all day. And not just him, either. You love male attention. Look at the extremes you went to for that creep Herman Wise's party. It's pathetic."

"What the hell are you on about?" I sleepily wiped my mouth and thought back. "Are you talking about his retirement party? I just did what they asked me to do. Creep or not, doesn't the founder of our firm deserve a celebration?"

"Retirement party." She scoffed. "God, you are so naive. He isn't retiring, Scarlett. He was forced out."

"Forced out? But...why?"

"Because, unlike you, I don't enjoy his leering and advances and made a sexual harassment complaint. Jason has allowed him the dignity of early retirement, but it's all a sham. He had no choice. It was this or a lawsuit."

I sat in stunned silence. Yes, I'd seen Herman sleazing onto Victoria too, but..." I honestly had no idea. "I don't know what to say, Victoria. Actually, yes, I do. I promise you, I never invited his attention, and I certainly don't like it. I hate it."

"Yeah?" she snapped, punching into the mattress. "Well, why didn't you say anything, then? Why did you put up with it? All it did was condone and enable his behavior and make it harder for others. People like me. I was his assistant, Scarlett. I couldn't just walk away and hide in the restroom or conference room. I had to be ogled and touched every day. It took me months to build up the nerve to say something, and when I did, it ruined any chance I had with—" She stopped, held her fingers over her mouth, and blinked away her tears.

Vomit rose in my throat. "With Finn?"

"Eww. God. No. Not with Finn. I know I flirted a bit with him, but it was stupid and... Look, it doesn't matter now. It's done. I'm moving on. We have a week or two left, then Herman will be gone, and I never have to see him again."

I nodded and placed my hand on her shoulder. "I am sorry, Victoria. And I think you're very brave. Reporting him was something I thought about, but I was too scared of the repercussions." I swallowed the sickness that lingered and took a deep breath. "I don't know if you know this about me, but I have a son." Her head slowly turned to mine, but she didn't look surprised. "Ben is his name. I had him when I was young, making me a bit of a target at school and at my last job. If I ever spoke up about anything, it only made things worse. I guess I just learned not to make waves. I never considered that I was helping make someone more vulnerable by protecting myself."

"Yeah? Well, you did. But I guess I can't blame you. Jason's mum had him young. People gave her a hard time, too."

"You know Jason's mum?"

Her perfectly made-up cheeks flushed pink, and she turned away. "I've met her a few times."

Leaning over to the table, she picked up the remote and switched on HBO. Marilyn Monroe and Jane Russell popped up on the screen, and we both snuggled back under the sheets, sans wall.

The first words purred from Marilyn's lips, *"It's men like you that have made me the way I am,"* seemed fitting.

"It's a shame we spent all this time hating each other when we could have been helping one another," Victoria eventually sighed.

With a sigh, I turned to face her. "I never hated you, Victoria."

She looked over her shoulder and grimaced. "Oh, that's nice." *Okay, then.*

My roomie fell asleep five minutes later while I sat chewing my nails and eating the mini-bar contents.

The kilojoules consumed came in handy later at Jocelyn's lot. All a bit grumpy after an afternoon nap, we must have circumnavigated that plot a hundred times, and as usual, I was in fine form. I almost careened down a ravine because I was watching the setting sun bounce off Finn's hair. And when he stopped to look over the river and drank from his water bottle, a drip slipped from his lips. My eyes followed it down his chin and neck till it disappeared between his vast moob canal. That was when I walked into a tree.

It wasn't all about Finn, though. Standing in the very space our design could soon inhabit brought the daunting enormity of the project into clearer focus. It was more than a smidge overwhelming, but being surrounded by centuries-old trees, each holding the secrets of generations who walked these paths before us while stoically keeping guard of their own small section of the river, was inspirational.

Despite our deep and meaningful talk, Victoria barely looked at me the whole time. It was a trend that continued at our boozy and flirtation-filled dinner. Keeping with our promise to stay friends, it wasn't Finn and me trading longing glances and suggestive smiles—at least not much.

"Victoria and Jason are going at it hard, Red. I feel like one of those creeps that pays to watch."

"Yes. It's fascinating. I guess I've been so occupied with you...your aunt's project that I've missed a few things." I leaned over the table, and Finn did the same. "Herman Wise isn't retiring. He's been pushed out."

Finn popped an ice cube in his mouth and crushed it as he watched Victoria feed Jason her carbonara. The flex and clench of his jaw had me biting my lip and forgetting what we were talking about. "I know."

"You know what?"

He chuckled and nodded his head sideways. "About Herman. My aunt told me. She was in on the whole thing. After seeing his treatment of you and Victoria, she came into the office one afternoon and let rip. I should have told you this earlier, but I was sworn to secrecy. I don't even think Victoria knows." No time was given for me to process this juicy tidbit before Finn began wringing and rubbing his hands so firmly I could hear the silky *swish-swishing* of his palms. His eyebrows knitted, and he suddenly pushed his chair out, stood, and cleared his throat. "I'm knackered. I might go back to our room and knock out a few ideas before I hit the hay." I understood this meant Finn was tired and was going to do some work and go to bed, but Jason and Victoria didn't. "In American English, please, Austen."

"Oh, sorry. I'm going back to the room to do some work. Scarlett, if you've finished your dinner, would you like to come with me? For the work part, not the bed part." He blushed. "I'm thinking of changing the pitch of the wraparound veranda. I'd love to show you some sketches."

"Sure, Finn. If that's okay with you two—"

"Night, guys." Victoria turned her back to us and continued to offer her fork to Jason, who didn't seem to mind one bit as he waved.

My chair dragged across the slate floor as Finn gripped my wrist and pulled me to my feet. "Ohh!" a little squeal escaped. Remaining unaffected by the relative ease in which he controlled my body, how big his hand was, and how it easily swamped mine was as hard as swallowing the lump of desire wedged in my throat. But I had to. *Because we are friends and friends don't notice how big other friends' body parts are. Or fantasize about the stinging red welts those body parts might leave on my ass.*

Once he'd stabilized me from my totally unrelated giddiness, he ducked down and collected the bag he knocked off the chair, shoved it in my hand, and whispered into my ear. "I've just got a call to make. Then I'll come to your room. See you in ten, Red."

My recent jogging paid off as I sprinted to my room. With hardly a puff or hair out of place, I called Ben, blew him a hundred goodnight kisses, chastised Brett for feeding him waffles and ice cream for dinner, even though I had done the same thing three nights ago, then had the world's quickest shower and shave down. Yes, it was unnecessary. This was a work meeting, after all. But I'd always found I thought clearer with a neatly groomed hoo-ha. I'd just finished cleaning the shower when there was a knock at my door.

A burst of color, in the form of flowers and a flush-faced hottie, greeted me.

"Pansies," Finn puffed. "I stole them from the garden. The concierge was watching me through the window and looked pissed, so I may have crushed them a bit as I ran." He looked edgily over his shoulder, and I sucked my bottom lip into my mouth to stop the laughter. "I think I lost her, though."

"The blonde concierge with the ponytail? The one that can barely see over the desk. You ran from her?"

"Hey, I live with several little blonde people, all of whom kick my ass frequently."

"Then I guess you better come in before she hunts you down." I stood to the side, leaning against the door frame as Finn strode in. It looked like he'd showered too. His hair was damp and in a bun, but tiny curls clung to the nape of his neck. His arm brushed mine as he passed, and my thighs clenched on impulse. Hoping not looking would make the want go away, I forced my eyes closed and held them so tightly I could hear my lashes collide. But it only heightened my senses. I could taste the memory of his lips on my tongue, and damn, that boy smelled good. With one discreet sniff, I was at the beach, by his side, face down with my bikini undone while he wrote his name on my back with sunscreen.

"You like the scent? It's a lovely, sweet smell. Very delicate." I looked at him blankly. "The flowers. You sniffed them as I walked past."

"Oh. Yes. The flowers. Right." Smiling like the idiot I was, I watched as he took a glass from beside the mini-bar, filled it with water, and neatly arranged the pansies he then placed beside the bed.

"There. They look pretty. Just like you."

"Number three. Number three. Number three," I repeated as he stood facing the bed, his eyes on the ugly carpet. "Scarlett. I lied. I didn't come here to talk about the veranda."

"This might be hard to believe, but I know. I saw through your brilliant ruse. You came to tell me about Herman, right?" I took two beers from the mini-bar, handed one to Finn, and then flopped onto the bed. "I'm ready. Give me everything." I opened my beer and took a large gulp.

Finn gasped with his mouth open, swallowed, then said the last thing I ever expected. "Scarlett, I have a daughter."

Swallow the liquid in your mouth before you reply. I gulped again.

"You have a what now?"

"Iris. I have an Iris." He shook his head and made a cute nervous grunt that warmed and tickled my belly. "A daughter. I mean. Her name is Iris and she's amazing." He reached into his pocket and pulled out his wallet. "Isn't she beautiful?" he asked, sliding out and then handing me a photo. "She's sweet and kind, and up till recently, has been the single best thing that's ever happened to me. I've hated every minute of hiding this part of me from you, and I wanted to tell you for a long time, but I didn't know how. That may sound cowardly or deceitful, which I guess it is, but I can explain and hope that one day you can forgive me."

Two things were happening in my body simultaneously. My heart was aching. I could see the pain in Finn's eyes. It hurt to see it. It hurt to know and feel it. The other was tingling. Not like a stroke or anything, but with need. I was desperate to hold him, to kiss him and tell him, '*I see you. I know. I understand. I forgive you.*' I felt utterly incapable of saying anything remotely close to that, though, so I did the next best thing.

"I understand more than you know, Finn." With my tingling fingers, I took my phone from the nightstand, opened my gallery, and passed it to Finn.

Nodding toward the screen he couldn't take his eyes from, his cheeks grew a deep, ruddy pink, and his eyes shone with tears, "Scar? This is why you leave at four. This is your little boy." It was a question and an answer.

"Yes, it is. That's my son, Benjamin. He's seven, too. Only Jason, HR Jan, and Teddy know about him. I made it that way because...well, I think you can understand why."

A single tear sat on his cheek as he turned to me and smiled. "Yeah, I think I can, Red." My stomach swooped. It's amazing how such a simple act could mean so much. It could heal so many years of loneliness. "He's a handsome boy. He looks just like you. The same freckles in the same spots. I hope he doesn't throw a cock punch like his mum, though."

"Hey. My mum was Spanish. I carry the Latin temper within me. But yes, he is much better tempered than me. There is no way I would have put up with all the lasso practice I submitted him to before that damn party."

Finn laughed, and we then fell into contemplative silence as we studied our babies' faces. I couldn't stop smiling. Iris was the cutest red-haired, blue-eyed little girl I'd ever seen. She had the same dimples as her dad and the same cheeky smile. I lost myself in thought, not only about Iris and Ben, but about what this all meant. The level of trust between us meant something that couldn't be ignored.

A gentle touch on my hand broke my contemplation. Finn was kneeling before me. I hadn't even noticed him moving.

"Promise me, Finn. Promise you don't mind that I have a son and I didn't tell you."

Finn shook his head and thumbed my cheek with so much tenderness I could cry. "God no. I think it's brilliant. Besides, I can hardly be upset with you for something I did myself." His body inched closer. "I understand why you didn't tell me, Scarlett. You needed to know you could trust me. I get it. We were just kids when we were blessed with *our* own. Life can be cruel and hard, and we've done what we need to survive."

The door of our room swung open. "Goodnight, Jason." Drunk as a skunk, Victoria staggered into the room but stopped when she saw Finn on his knees, at the foot of our bed. It was understandable. "Oh, so '*nothing is happening*' between you two, huh, Scarlett? God, you're so full of shit."

23

Scarlett

"J ESUS, HELP ME!" I woke with a fright, my room echoing the hollow moans, sobs, and begs for mercy of a distressed woman.

Victoria? My eyes shot open, searching the room for the raven-haired beauty, but she was nowhere in sight. Neither were her bags. *Weird.*

"Victoria? You here?" Nothing. Not a peep. Stumbling from bed, I padded in the dark to the bathroom, then blinded myself with the buzzing harshness of the fluorescent light. The month's supply of cosmetics she's set up like a store display was gone too. My immediate thought was that I'd slept in and been forgotten, just left lying on the bed like some smelly old teddy bear. But no. I returned to the bed and checked the time, 1:07. *You've only been asleep for two hours, dork.*

I slid back beneath the sheets and replayed the events of the evening. Victoria definitely returned to our room twice. The first time was when she cockblocked me—well, lip-blocked at least. When Finn begrudgingly left, she took a shower, and I did what any reasonable woman would do. I lay on my half of the bed and worried and cried like a pathetic loser. *Is it time to give up? We were alone, baring our souls and hidden secrets in a romantic—if you squinted—hotel room for god's sake. If nothing happened now, maybe it never will.* Looking me over with a fresh face of make-up and expression of absolute disgust, Victoria whipped through the room, told me she was going back to the bar, and left.

Things went downhill from there. I took my own shower then, lathered myself in body lotion, and slipped into the inappropriate sleeping attire Teddy insisted I pack. *"Just in case Finn wants to slip his bill into your platypussy."*

Bored. Lonely. All dressed up with no one to bone. There was nothing left to do but consume the remaining contents of the mini-bar and cry myself to the point of dehydration until Victoria returned just before eleven. She refused to play Uno with me, or watch a movie, so I just fell asleep in a pile of candy wrappers and tissues.

Man, I must have been dead to the world not to hear her packing her things. And why did she pack her things? Accompanied by banging, my headboard shook, and the moans increased in volume and frequency. *Screw this. I need a drink.*

With a frightful head of wild curls and my skimpy nightie, I opened the door and poked my head out to check if the coast was clear. The corridor to my left was empty, but much to my horror, the first thing I saw when I turned right was a forlorn Finn sitting cross-legged on the floor with his overnight bag at his side.

"What? Finn, what are you doing out here?"

He looked up at me through his own wild hairdo, his eyes brimming with that undefinable Finn-ness and a look that almost drove me face-first into the floor. Bam. Dead. Just like that. Goodbye, Scarlett. Death by hotness.

"Honestly, I'm trying to work up the courage to knock on your doorrrr..." His voice trailed off. He'd noticed my attire. And he dug it.

Feeling quite thrilled with myself, I watched his eyes widen and felt the burn as they journeyed upward over my long bare legs, my smooth satin stomach, my lace-lined breasts—where there was definite lingering—and eventually up to my face. I casually tucked my hair behind my ear and then hung onto the wall...just a little bit, though, and just to help me stay upright. And maybe to cover my bum. "Why aren't you asleep?"

"I...uhh... I was, but...umm... Do you always wear things like this to bed?"

"Finn, concentrate. Why are you on the floor and not in bed?"

Those eyes slowly blinked in time with his words. "Oh, right, yes, I was, but about twenty minutes ago, a little Victoria-shaped birdy tapped me on my shoulder and kicked me out. She and Jason have been going at it ever since."

"What? Really? Oh my God. I knew they were flirting all night, but—Wait. Isn't he married?"

"Yep. She is too."

"What? Victoria's married?"

"She sure is. She told me all about her heinous hubby one night at the pub."

"What? You went out for drinks with her?"

"Scarlett, stop what-ing and start breathing, or you'll hyper-ventilate." He was right. My heart was racing, and I didn't think I'd taken a breath since I walked out and saw his gorgeous body slumped on the floor. "I didn't go out *with* her. I just happened to be out, and she was there with a group of friends."

"Oh. And did you have a good time with her and her friends?"

"I guess we chatted for a bit, danced for a bit—"

"Wha—I mean...you danced with her?" The utter devasta-tion this was causing in my body was not right. I knew Victoria wasn't interested in Finn. She had told me hours earlier. But the thought of them dancing made my skin crawl. Clearly, the horror within me was showing on the surface.

"Nothing happened, Red. We all danced as a group for one song, and then I left." Rising to his feet, Finn shuffled closer. "I'm not interested in Victoria." His eyes drifted again.

"I know you're not. And she's not into you either."

With raised brows and a sweet blush, he leaned on the wall beside me. "Nope."

A series of expletives celebrating the length and girth of Ja-son's dick hit us with gusto, reminding us both that we were in the hall, and I was half-naked. Finn dragged his hand down his face. And I became even more turned on.

Fuck he's sexy when he's frustrated.

"Water. I needed water. That's why I came out here," I stated robotically.

"Right, water. I see. Water's good...important...for life in general."

"Yes, it's vital." There was a long pause filled with X-rated moaning. Again, not from me. "This is pretty uncomfortable, Finn."

"For us, maybe. But Victoria and Jason's massive cock seem to be enjoying it."

I wanted to laugh. Chuckles tickled my throat with a desire to burst free, but the continued moaning and talk of taking it all and riding it harder were awkward and weird, and I had too many memories of someone else's massive dick rubbing against me to find anything funny.

Finn, who continued to have trouble keeping his eyes off the pretty white lace, came up with a plan. "Right, well, let's make a deal. I'll get some drinks. You and that nightie get back to your room...oh, and if it's okay, maybe it could be my room too?"

Oh, my goddamn God, yes.

My lips screwed to the side to emphasize my pondering. "So, in theory, that would make it...*our* room. Yours, mine...and the nightie?"

"Yep. It would be...*our* room. Just the three of us."

"In one bed."

We both gulped and seemed to lose the ability to speak. As such, I grabbed his bag and dragged it into *our* room, and he bolted down the hall in search of water like a fireman.

It seemed like a good idea at the time. Share a room and a bed in a romantic hotel with your dream guy while wearing sexy lingerie. But when the guy insists on sleeping on the floor, and the only sex sounds are made by your married boss and his equally married assistant next door, that idea quickly loses its shine. It was surprising that with the recent *we-both-have-kids-we've-been-hiding* revelations, we didn't talk about them. But we didn't. Maybe it felt too heavy or icky with the sexual soundtrack. I wasn't sure. We discussed the house plans, played another round of *What's the Aussie word for*, and rock, paper, scissors, then braided each other's hair.

After all that, our athletic neighbors were going at round three. I don't know if Jason had swallowed a whole box of Viagra, or if he—and she, for that matter—were just lucky, but it was pretty incredible. The longer—no pun intended—and louder they got, the more awkward and silent we got. Conversation stopped altogether, and we lay there, staring at the ceiling, saying nothing, but hearing and feeling everything.

For my part, I wanted to be the better person and say those feelings centered on our emotional connection, but no, I was horny as fuck and desperate to jump him. The memory of his lips, his body pressing against mine, that ocean scent of salt and sand that lingered wherever he went...

God, I want him so bad. Does he feel the same? Does he think of me? Of that kiss? Of my body like I do his? Is he miserable and suffering just as much as I am? There is some definite heavy breathing going on.

Ultimately, we could ignore it no more and both pretended to be asleep. I knew we were both pretending because he looked at me each time I would sneak a peek at him.

After what felt like an eternity, the grunting, groaning, screams of, "Fuck yes, Jason, give it to me!" and other sounds of euphoria ceased, and we were left with only the quiet hum of the AC. Legitimate sleep seemed only a heavy breath or two away, and despite pretending for a while, I still wanted to hear him say goodnight.

Who knows, this may be my one and only chance to hear it.

"Finn, are you awa—"

"Yep. Sure am. Not sure if I'll ever sleep again, to be honest." Both laughing, I rolled over and hung my head off the bed. He looked so cute snuggled up on the floor. Cute, but uncomfortable.

I tutted and patted the mattress. "This is silly. We are both adults. Come and hop in bed with me."

"No. Sorry. I can't do that. I think it would be safer to sandwich between Vicki and JJ."

"You can't possibly mean that," I laughed.

"Oh yes, I can. I'm unsure if you remember what happened to my body the last time it was close to yours, but I have struggled to stop remembering it."

"I remember just fine." *And frequently.* "But that was before we officially became buddies. And buddies' bodies behave." This was an attempt to convince myself as much as Finn.

"You should put that on a t-shirt, Red. I still wouldn't believe it, though."

More laughter filled the room. *Fuck. He makes me happy.*

"Please, Finn. I can't rest knowing you're down there. Look, I'll put all the pillows between us like Victoria did. That way, we won't have to touch at all."

"You didn't touch at all. Not even just a bit?"

"Nope."

"That's disappointing."

"Finn. Come to bed."

"Nope."

"Finny, please. I'm cold and alone. I need you," I begged in my softest, sexiest voice.

"Fucking hell, I'm weak as shit." He huffed and climbed to his feet. "That's not fair. Build the damn wall, woman, and build it high."

24

Finn

"BEFORE I GET INTO bed, I'm just going to shower quickly." *A cold one in the hopes it will handle my erection issue,* I thought to myself. I grabbed my bag, half the contents of which fell out as I held it in front of my boner, and then slipped into the bathroom.

Who am I kidding? Just knowing she was in bed...in the next room...with her ass in that nightie with its shortness and lace and frills...while I was there naked, wanting. It was getting painful. I was certain I was nearing the point of a medical emergency, and I was *not* getting wheeled out of the shower naked after suffering a penile implosion. Handling it myself—if you get what I mean—was the only option. Resting my forehead against the wall, I bit my lip to keep from grunting her name, pictured laying her over my knee and smacking that ass, then sliding her onto her knees and watching as those plump lips replaced my fist. I exploded into my hand with embarrassing efficiency. It almost took longer to wash the evidence away with the shithouse water pressure than it did to create it. When physically, not morally, clean, I stepped from the shower to dry and dress.

Damn. My sweats must have fallen out of the bag, Shit. No briefs either.

It was a predicament. I was still dripping, hearing each and every *plop* against the tile as I tried to decide what to do. It wasn't like I was worried about Scarlett seeing me half naked, I took care of myself and had no issues there. Rather, I was worried how I would react to *her* reaction. As quietly as I could, I slunk back into the room and slipped my boxer briefs and sweats on beneath my towel—something I was very used to doing after years of surfing and changing in public. I was about to pull on my tee when I heard a breathy "whoa" behind me. Glancing up, I spotted Scarlett, one eye open, watching me in the mirror.

"I see you watching me, Miss Grant."

Both eyes blinked shut...almost. There was some definite squinting going on. "I'm not watching you. I'm sound asleep."

Running a hand through my wet hair, I made sure I flicked some drops of water in her direction and chuckled, "With one eye open?"

"Yes. I do that sometimes. It's a terrible affliction, and I'll thank you for sparing me your judgey judgment."

"Sure. That sounds believable." Not one to disappoint, I turned to face her, giving her the full view as I slipped the white cotton over my head. Even then, I still earned an extended boo and wet-sounding raspberry from the peanut gallery. "Red, come on."

"What? Just one friend letting the other friend know she's disappointed he covered his body."

"Hmmm. You're right. You are being very friendly. Why don't we swap spots? I'll lay in bed and, real good friend-like, watch you change out of your silly little nightie into something less frilly."

"Well, that's just ridiculous. No one wants to see me half-naked, and besides, I can't change beneath a towel. Only guys can do that."

I was flabbergasted—about the nakedness, not the under-towel action.

"What? I... No one wants to... Wha? Red, I dunno what trick mirrors you're looking into, but I would kill to see you nak—uhh...I mean, I know heaps of guys that would kill to see you naked."

"I said, half-naked. Not naked."

"Half-naked, then." Daring to edge closer, I slid my foot over the surprisingly clean maroon shag carpet. My knees hit the edge of the bed, and I almost accidentally fell on top of her. *What a shame that would be.* "Look, I don't want to sound like a total creep or anything, but Red... You do know how hot you are, don't you?"

"Pfftt." She waved me off, wriggling in a fashion that had me needing another relieving cleanse and began playing with her hair. I couldn't tell if she was appreciative of my compliment or if I was making her uncomfortable, so I changed the subject. Sort of. "Also, what you said about changing beneath a towel is nonsense. Shelby used to do it all the time." *Shit*. My stomach flipped. I stepped back and pretended to look for some socks while Scarlett, who seemed to sense and share my unease, delved further underneath her sheets till her lovely face was only visible from nose up. Hidden, she watched me dig through my bag while I watched her in the mirror. Eventually, our eyes found each other in the reflection.

"Who's Shelby? One of Evie's friends back home?"

I dropped my gaze and unrolled a pair of socks. "Yes, well, she was Evie's friend, twin sister of my best friend, Nate. My girlfriend and Iris's mum." Then I re-rolled them and looked back up.

"Oh. That's nice. Shelby is a lovely name. I've never met a Shelby. Does she still live in Australia?"

"Umm." Deciding my next move, I grabbed the spare blankets at the foot of the bed and began to fold. *Just tell her.* "No, Red. Shelby passed away when Iris was born."

A rush of air and feminine warmth swept over me as Scarlett leapt from the bed, ripped the linen from my hands and climbed me like a monkey on a tree. "Christ on a bike. I'm so sorry. I shouldn't have been so nosey."

My grief should have been enough to distract me from the effect being hugged by her had on me, but bloody hell, that nightie was so, so short and felt so soft, and she...she smelled so good. That gentle, sweet vanilla with a touch of spice or fire that burned right into my soul. Her body fit perfectly around mine. Her head nuzzled so neatly into the crook of my neck, and how my hand sat right on the small of her back was perfect. It was all perfect. She was perfect. The timing was not. I gently slipped from her embrace. "It's fine, Red. I promise. It's probably good to talk about it. I don't do it a lot."

She sat on the bed, tapped the spot beside her, and smiled. "I'm here. You're here. We have a wall. Let's talk."

I had no intention of ever doing what I did, of revealing part of my soul. But the minute my thigh aligned with hers on the edge of the bed, my past leaked from me like water through a sieve. "Like I said, Shelby was my girlfriend. We got together after Mum and Dad died. She was such a cool chick. We grew up together, surfing and mucking around. Anyway, she fell pregnant and had a great pregnancy. Everything seemed fine. Her labor was long, and she lost a lot of blood, but Iris was the cutest baby. I know everyone thinks that about their kids, but she was perfect. Shelby was holding her and talking and laughing. Then suddenly, all these alarms started going off. The nurses all swooped in and took Iris away, and then, she was gone."

"Finn."

A violent gasp caused her whole body to shake against me as she lay her head on my shoulder. "It was a heart condition. We didn't even know, and the pregnancy and birth...it was just too much."

"How old was she?" Scarlett asked, her voice raw, cracking, sexy in a way I shouldn't have noticed in such a moment.

"Seventeen. The same as me."

"Bloody hell, Finn. It's such a tragedy. I'm so, so sorry."

"Please, Scar. Don't be sorry. I don't want sympathy. I just want you to know that I do think about you. I want you. I crave you, and I've only kissed you once. I had never felt anything close to that before. I catch myself thinking about you and feeling like a horrible person. I keep comparing what I think could be possible with you to what I had with Shelby. Every time we're together, at work, in your kitchen, at the party when I kissed you, the guilt is there in the back of my mind. I can't seem to make peace with it, and it's part of why I can't give you what you deserve. I just feel so guilty. Especially because her death was my fault. She died because of me."

Scarlett grabbed my hand and held it to her soft cheek. "Finn. Look at me." My eyes closed, but then opened and looked into hers as she traced her thumb over my skin. There was no pity in them. No disgust or judgment either. Just unconditional acceptance and empathy. "Shelby died because she had a heart condition. You just told me that yourself. How is that your fault?"

"Because if I'd listened to Nate and kept my fucking hands to myself, she wouldn't have gotten pregnant. Her heart problem might have been discovered another way. She could have gone on meds. She could be alive this day if it weren't for me fucking her because I was selfish and sad about my mum and dad!"

She held me tighter. "No, Finn... Have...have you ever said that to anyone before? Have you even acknowledged that to yourself before?"

Have I? "I dunno, maybe. I don't think so."

Pressing her lips to my temple, she sighed heavily, her warm breath tickling against my ear oddly soothing. "It's just simply not true. What happened to Shelby was a tragedy. Yes, she was pregnant with your child, but you didn't force yourself on her and didn't do anything with malice or selfishness. Shelby may have had a heart attack surfing or jogging. Anything could have set it off. You have to believe me. Shelby's death was not your fault."

A guttural groan, an expulsion of grief and trauma that had been trapped inside for seven years, surged my body forward. Violently shaking, my head clunked against her shoulder. "I'm so sorry, Scarlett. This is why I don't talk about it. It's too much."

"It's not too much. I am your friend. I care about you as much as you do me, and I understand. My life has been no picnic. I'd only known Teddy for weeks when I fell pregnant. Within hours of finding out, I went from his new friend, the promising scholarship student, to a homeless, knocked-up loser crying on his shoulder and moving into his house. Youth, babies, and grief...that's hard stuff to deal with. And you have done it so well. Look at you, Finn. You've graduated, raised a beautiful girl, moved to New York—"

"Met you."

My eyes closed again. Her beautiful smile caressed the back of my hand. "Met me." She giggled and raised my face to hers.

"Never apologize for being emotional or genuine. It's one of the things I like most about you."

Even in a moment so raw, the temptation of playfulness was too strong. "What are some of the other things? My body, obviously."

"Obviously." Pressing her lips into a thin line stifled her smile, but it still shone clear as day in her eyes...once she stopped rolling them. "Your taste in music is pretty good. I heard you singing Taylor the other day."

"Hey...look, I only know the lyrics to almost all her songs because Evie and Iris play her constantly. It has nothing to do with me seeing the *Reputation* tour twice, *Folklore* changing my life, her hotness, or her being the most talented songwriter of our generation."

"Obviously."

I sighed heavily and scrubbed my hands over my face. "Red."

"Yes, Finn."

"Promise me I haven't put you off with all this. I know it's heavy. But I need us to be mates."

"Promise." She winked and elbowed my ribs. "We're still buddies. Now, stop all this blubbering, and let's get drunk."

I feared my nervous breakdown would send Scarlett running to the hills, but it seemed to bring her even closer. Physically and emotionally.

After talking till three and sharing the two bottles of wine I "borrowed" from the bar as Scarlett distracted the bartender with her lingerie and a knock-knock joke, we fell into bed in a fit of giggles.

"Tops and tails!" she declared, spinning around so her surprisingly nice-smelling feet laid on my face. "Finny. I think I'm a teeny, tiny tit bipsy."

"I think you mean a bit tipsy, Red. And I think I am too. I can't remember why we're here or where here is. I'm glad we're wherever we are, though."

A giggle I would remember forever hiccupped from deep inside her as she spun again, shimmied closer, and laid her head on my thigh. My fucking thigh! *Do not get a boner!*

Exhaling loudly, she blew a curl from her face, then glanced up at me. "What do you love most about America? Apart from meeting me, which is number one obviously."

"Oh, obviously. Hmmm, let me think." Hoping she may slide off me, I tried to move farther up the bed, but she came right along with me. *She's bloody closer to the trouble zone than she was before, dick.* I stared at the ceiling and focused on her question. "Favorite thing... I think the people and their approach to success. People pump each other up more. Like at home, we have a tendency toward being knockers."

Two ripe, delicious breasts were cupped in her hands and bounced. "I would have thought you liked knockers."

I forced a smile and focused on her eyes. "Big fan of that type. But I mean more of the tall-poppy-syndrome knockers. Everyone loves an underdog, but they'll also tear him or her down the second they make it. I haven't noticed that as much here."

"It's a bit like that in England too. That's a good one." She nodded, then rolled to her side. That little nightie didn't shift with her body, and her boobs were on full display. I tried to look away immediately, but I was a man, and she was a woman...with the most beautiful breasts and what looked like the loveliest pink nipples I've ever seen. A nun and the Pope would have had trouble diverting their gaze. Eventually, I did. *Look at the ceiling. Think of nanna.*

Seeming not to notice her flashing, she asked, "Okay, what do you dislike the most, then?"

"Bitch," I said flatly, too distracted by a bothersome mold-like stain I spotted in the far-right corner of the ceiling.

Scarlett bolted upright, "Pardon me?" Her movement drew my eye for only a second before I looked away again. "Who are you calling a bitch, and why do you keep staring at the ceiling?"

"No! Not you. I'd never... I mean... I'm looking up here because of...that." I pointed at what I thought was her chest.

"Oh, oops." I heard the slip and shuffle of satin over skin as she thankfully adjusted her nightie. "Okay, you can look at me again. The knockers are gone."

I released the breath I didn't realize I was holding and smiled to see her cute face again. "Bitches, in general. I hate that so many guys my age, and some chicks too, call women bitches. Like, I get it in a joking manner between friends, like how Teddy does it. But just calling random women hoes and bitches? Yeah, nah. It's disrespectful."

A wicked smile played on her face." And that is why you..." *Oh God, she's on her hands and knees. Shit, she's crawling closer.* "Must refer to me as ma'am, or your majesty, from here on in."

"I like Red better." I swallowed. "But if you stay in that position, I'll call you whatever you want."

Once shoulder to shoulder, Scarlett leaned in and pressed her lips to my cheek. "You're so sweet." Her hands shifted to my shoulders before she leaned over my body, crushing her boobs into my chest, stealing my air, and mirroring the soft kisses on my right side. "And such a gentleman."

Again, she repeated that tortuous, maddening pattern. Sure, they were only drunken, sloppy, messy kisses on cheeks that edged closer and closer to our lips meeting, and I told myself it was all innocent fun. But the lingering looks between each one soon lingered a little bit longer. Breathing heavied. My *accidental* grazes of her bare skin became deliberate caresses, and fuck if it didn't feel amazing and right.

This time, there was no one to interrupt. It was just us, and I knew if I was serious about being friends, I had to be the one to say stop. But before I could, Scarlett ghosted her lips all the way to the side of my face and breathily whispered in my ear, "Do you want to go to sleep now?" Deep and raspy, her voice was shaky, full of hope and uncertainty. It was also sexy and damn near impossible to resist.

Agony. Not taking her face in my hands and kissing her the way I wanted, the way she deserved, was agony. But I had to stay strong—for her. *You can't be what she needs.* I nosed her hair, breathing in her scent, and fuck me, she smelled amazing. "No.

No, I don't. Not at all. But I think, after the chat we had, we probably should."

She sighed heavily, her breath tickling every part of me as she pressed one last kiss high on my cheekbone, then sucked the lobe of my ear into her mouth, releasing in with a pop. "I thought you might say that."

Everything suddenly felt different. The evening revelations had shifted things up to a level I so desperately wanted and feared. That was why, one by one, a wall of pillows was erected. We topped and tailed again, then both pretended to sleep.

The pillows were nowhere to be seen when I woke at six a.m. with a throbbing headache and Scarlett's ass firmly wedged against my painfully hard cock. It had been there for the few hours of "rest" we managed. Conscious of my condition, I slid my hips back an inch or two, but she made a delicious moan and chased them, nestling back against me, then sighing happily. I tightened the grip I already had around her waist, splaying my fingers over her softness and massaging lightly. "Good morning, Red," I whispered, smiling, pressing my nose into her curls, and inhaling her pure goodness. She muttered something, and I think she smiled as I could see her glowing cheeks rounding. Then, she molded her round ass cheeks further into me. "Lord, give me strength."

After a solid hour of lying with a stiffy and watching Scarlett sleep, spread-eagled across her bed, breathing with her curls covering her face and her lovely round bum sticking and poking from the blankets, I snuck out and took another shower. My second boner issue in hours was handled with equal yet unsatisfying efficiency, and I was out and dressed before she woke.

Only time would tell where things went between us. I knew what I wanted. I was pretty sure I knew what she did, too, and I felt that a small portion of the weight I always carried had lifted. But whether or not I could listen to Scarlett's all-too-familiar words—the same ones I'd heard from Nate, Jocie, and Evie so many times before—and finally let go and forgive my self-declared sins was an entirely different matter.

Sitting on the edge of the bed, I buried my head in my hands. "What the fuck am I going to do?"

"Morning, Noddy. What are you going to do about what?" Her raspy, sleepy voice had my dick ready to party again.

"Breakfast. I'm starving." *Do I say anything about last night? Wait and see what she does.*

"Mmm. Me too. Some poor innocent pig has my name written all over its ass." She sat up against the headboard, yawned, and stretched. I watched in awe as curls fell over her shoulders and perfectly highlighted her boobs and her pebbled, satin-covered nipples. "Speaking of food, I wanted to ask you something. There is a new Italian restaurant near my house. I was wondering if you wanted to join Teddy and me for dinner before Herman's movie night next week."

"Sure. That sounds good. I like melons."

"That's great, Finn. But I just asked you to come for dinner. Not what you wanted for breakfast."

Fuck, you're staring at her boobs. Blink and look away. Say something.

"Sorry. I was just…"

"Thinking of melons." She smiled, ducking her head to chase my eyes.

A knock on the door and a remarkably chipper Jason shouting at the top of his lungs saved me.

"We are starving. Meet you two in the restaurant. Buffet breakfast is on the business!"

We looked at each other glumly. "Time to head back, I guess." Scarlett sighed and rubbed her palm down my thigh as she slipped from the bed. My favorite nightie in the world earned further admiration by taking its sweet-ass time to fall, and I got the briefest glimpse of her lovely cheeks before she covered them with her hands. "You go ahead and get your hands on those melons, Finn. Me and mine will meet you there."

She sashayed away, and I watched every step she took like the besotted fool I was, torn between doing what was right and what I wanted.

25

Finn

"YOU'RE SO DAMN OBVIOUS, Finn. Jocie picked it up the minute she saw you two together. I had my suspicions. But since your work trip, you haven't shut up about her and have fluttered around like a lovesick puppy." *Stare straight ahead. Tap to the music, and she might stop talking.*

"The fact that you're a nervous wreck before dinner and a movie are just confirmation. You're gonna hurl in front of her and make a fool out of yourself. I'm gutted I won't see it."

Okay, you can't leave that alone.

"You're projecting now, sis. I'm not the one who blew chunks over everyone at every school Christmas concert and dance recital ever. That was all you." This was true. Evie had been a nervous chucker for years. I cry. Evie pukes. I was never sure which I'd prefer.

"Whatever. All I know is *you*"—she emphasized *you* with a poke in my arm—"are a goner. And if Scarlett ever drops her standards and gives you a chance, boy, are you gonna be whipped!"

"Put a sock in it, Evie. I'm trying to concentrate on the road." Horror head's merciless—perhaps, on-point—teasing had begun as soon as I arrived home from Tarrytown, and a week later, it had yet to cease. Until today, I'd been able to take it in good humor or ignore it because I was high on life, and I probably *had* fluttered. The house concept was progressing, and Scarlett and I continued solidifying our relationship—I mean, friendship. She'd also ordered sushi for lunch three times. I very much enjoyed all the yum-yum sauce and finger-licking.

Resisting those sweet and salty lips for eight to nine hours in the office was hard, especially with the memory of their pillowy softness still so fresh, but it was achievable. I found respite at home in my nightly routines. Even though I thought of her constantly, of waking with her ass pressed against me and the smell of her hair as she lay in my arms, I could distract myself with family life. Tonight's dinner and movie farewell for an undeserving asshole removed that small window of breathing time. It was going to be Tarrytown all over again. I had ogled her satin boobs, spilled my guts, cried, and jacked off twice in the shower. That couldn't happen tonight.

Thank God Teddy is tagging along.

Still, Evie was way off base with the nervousness thing. Yes, I may have showered and dressed an hour earlier than required, then paced the house while dusting several hundred times. But that didn't mean I was nervous. I was apprehensive at best. And I wasn't going to chuck. I also wasn't going to lean over, open the car door, and push her out like I wanted. Iris would be disappointed.

Dinner together after dance class was part of our Thursday-night routine, and Iris loved routine as much as I did. We always went for pizza at Rubirosa. It was the restaurant owned by the family of Iris's friend, Cole, and they had the best slice in the neighborhood. Tonight's altered schedule added to my apprehension—*not* nervousness. The pizza was being picked up on the way home, not eaten in, and this was the first dance class I'd missed since Iris started. It was also her first day of the new school year, and she walked directly from school with the cool mums of her new friends, Olivia, and Grace, and didn't want her dorky old dad hanging around. Those were her exact brutal, cut-me-to-the-bone words this morning. Words that became another weapon in my sister's already hefty arsenal. "Iris was right to call you dorky. Who gets nervous about dinner and a movie? She's never called me dorky. She thinks I'm cool."

"That's not what I've heard. She told me you were a dork and smelled like a stinky stink butt. She just didn't want to tell you because you'd cry like a baby."

"She did not say that." Evie snorted.

"I swear she did. And she called you a sooky sooky la la, too."
That one had us both laughing. Evie especially.

"God, I haven't heard that expression for years. Shelby and
Nate used to call you that when you'd hurt yourself surfing and
cry."

"I did not cry." I probably did cry. "What assholes. Bloody
Nate could talk—he was always sooking to me about you, but
did I tease him? Nope."

"Nate was sooking about me? Why would he be sooking
about me?" Evie squawked about three octaves higher than
usual.

I shook my head and rolled my eyes. *And this woman is calling
me pathetic.* "Uhh...because he liked you and was madly in love
with you?"

A sharp blow was delivered to the side of my sizable head.
"What? Nate liked me? Loved me? Since when?"

"Since we were like...born. You're honestly telling me you
didn't know?"

"No, I didn't know! How did you know? Why would you
know and never tell me?"

"I knew because I was his best friend, my girlfriend was his
twin, and he talked about you constantly. But we made a deal
when we were fifteen. Neither of us would go near the other's
sister. We all know I broke that deal, and Nate didn't. That
was part of the reason he was so upset when Shelby and I got
together."

My sister was at a loss for words. It was a rare occurrence,
one I had experienced only a handful of times throughout my
life, and I can honestly say I found it entirely refreshing. She
remained quiet as she slipped from the car and into the rain
to sign out Iris while I waited in the parking lot. Serene silence
would not be long-lasting. A still-flushed Evie and an overtired,
overhyped Iris returned. Her blow-by-blow account of the cute
dog they saw walking to class and Cole's epic backflip and sick
dance moves took care of that. No one else could get a word in.
Almost.

"He emails me a few times a week, you know. Texts me sometimes too. He always says it's to check in on Iris, his number-one girl. Do you think he...? No, no, that's silly."

"Evie, I've told you before. I don't know what you are talking about when you start mid-sentence. Who emails you?"

After a long pause, she replied, "Nate."

"What? Nate? Nate emails you a few times a week? I'm lucky to get a message once a month, and you've been getting weekly emails and texts? For how long?"

"Since we left Byron. And he has messaged you. You just bloody ghost everyone all the time."

I ignored her factual ghosting remarks and focused on gross Nate stuff.

"Jesus, Evie. He's still into you. Fuck. That's rich. That bastard gave me so much shit for chasing Shelby, and he's been doing the same thing behind my back this whole time."

"Daddy, you said sweaws!"

"Shit, sorry, bubs."

Iris was in hysterics. Evie and I were not. "You said anothew, Daddy!"

After flashing Iris an apologetic grin in the mirror, I focused on my sister. "Evie. I am putting my foot down on this. I insist you end this...this...online relationship with my childhood friend. A friend who happens to be your niece's uncle. It's fu—freaking weird." Catching my swear earned me a clap of approval from the swear police in the back, but my words did not sit well with the other passenger.

"My God, Finn. You're such a hypocrite. Number one, Nate is not chasing me. He is checking on his niece, which he wouldn't have to do so often if you pulled your head out of your own ass and called him. Number two, even if he was, I am not related to him, and neither are you. Iris is the only one who is, and there is no difference between Nate and me being together and Shelby and you. And on that subject, I'm pretty sure Nate got over that years ago. It's ancient history, and you bloody well know it."

"Now that Aunty Evie is sweawing, can I sweaw too?"

"No!" Evie and I chorused in agreement.

The heated discussion continued until I pulled up at Rubirosa. Before Evie jumped out, she leaned into my shoulder, pinched my neck, and whispered through gritted teeth, "I'm not talking about this with you anymore, Finnley. Who I choose to talk to is none of your damn business. You need to focus on controlling your boner around Scarlett and not my life." In a chilling change of tone, she then turned and flashed a smile to Iris. "Back in a second, bubs."

Evie was right. I did have a boner issue.

Sitting across the table from a woman as beautiful as Scarlett, feeling the way I did but holding myself back, was exhausting, oddly exhilarating, and not enough to stop the party in my pants. I hadn't had this many spontaneous hard-ons since I was fourteen. I was starting to feel like Nate.

The lousy mood I carried with me into the restaurant dissolved when my lips caressed her cheek, and she removed her black trench coat. Hidden beneath it was a pale-pink dress that could be best described as a slip, black pantyhose, the ones with the line up the back that led all the way to trouble, and stilettos that could be classed as a weapon. I was tempted to drop to the ground and ask her to stand on my neck, but I resisted. Her trademark red-stained lips finished off the killer look that had me discreetly adjusting myself within seconds.

To make matters worse...

"Teddy isn't with you?" I asked, pretending to look behind her but really looking at her round ass.

"Nope. He ditched us for Asher. He's going to meet us there once they've finished dinner."

"Oh. So, we're alone?"

"Yup. Just you, me, and the other people eating—which there are very few of." We looked around the near-empty restaurant. "God, I know this place is new, but there are three other people here." As she spoke, a couple at one table paid their bill and left. "Make that one other people...person."

"At least we won't have to wait long for the food." Nudging her in the elbow, I smiled and tried to ignore how it shook her boobs. "I could eat a horse." I couldn't. Again, as Evie Nostradamus Austen predicted, I felt like I was gonna chuck. But I didn't want Scarlett to feel bad about the forthcoming food poisoning.

"You might be in luck." She smiled, scanning the room again. "Maybe they serve horse meat, and that's why there's no one here."

Twenty-five minutes later, we'd ordered our mains, were enjoying our appetizers, and I had decided there was no way I could keep this up. I wanted her and was falling for her. I knew it. She knew it. And so did almost everyone around us.

Which was no one. We were the only customers.

"I'm so relieved the food has been good...so far. What's in these crumbed egg-looking things again?"

"Rice, tomato, some egg to bind the breadcrumbs, and the most important ingredient of all...fresh mozzarella," explained Spiro, our waiter and part owner. Spiro was Greek. His wife, Natalie, the chef, was Italian, and as their only customers, they brought us a selection of entrees and their family history.

"So, there's a lot of cheese?" Scarlett asked, her face full of concern as she sucked a long string between her lips.

Spiro nodded, then left to get his drinks and call his yia-yia.

"You don't like cheese, Red? I'm sure I've seen it on your burgers, and pizzas, and sandwiches, and—"

"Yes. I eat a lot of cheese. I get it. I love cheese. It's just..." Pausing, she held her hand over her mouth and looked between me and the cheese. "It's just something Teddy said to me once. Never mind." She dropped the fried rice ball and started nibbling on olive-oil-soaked Focaccia.

The cheese thing really piqued my interest. As did the sheen of olive oil highlighting her plump bottom lip, but it was clear she wanted to move on. So, I did.

"I had an interesting conversation with my sister tonight." I winked, watching her chew and swallow. "Are you ready for me to dish, Bish?"

Scarlett pursed her lips and chuckled, "Ah, obviously, but first, you need to know you're spending too much time with Teddy. You're beginning to sound like him."

"I know. It's freaking me out, but he just gets under your skin!"

"Tell me about it. I spoke to him once—once—in class and haven't spent a day without him since. Anyway, tell me what Evie said. Gawd, was it about me? About the brightness of my clothes? I've been getting a lot of negative feedback about that lately."

"Relax, Red. Nothing was said about your clothing, which I love, by the way. But she did mention us."

"Us," Scarlett said with a smile. "That sounds...interesting."

"Hmm, it was. Apparently, Jocelyn picked up on our chemistry, as she called it, the first time she saw us together. Evie said she had her suspicions too. What do you think about that?"

Tapping her chin with her index finger, Scarlett looked to the ceiling as though the answer was there and then replied, "I would say they were observant."

"Evie also said if we ever got together, you'd have me whipped."

"Ah, I see. Make that extremely observant. I knew I liked the look of your sister. Not only does she look younger than you, but she's also wiser too. You should take any advice she offers from now on." With a wriggle of her brows, Scarlett leaned over the table and gripped my hand. "Now, tell me what else she said about us."

"I'd hate to disappoint you, but that was about it. We kind of moved onto a different topic then, and the less said about that, the better. Unless you want me to blow chunks all over the table."

"I don't want you to vomit, but I want to know what she said more. Tell me, and I will shield behind my napkin in case you do puke." She held her cloth napkin over her face. "Go for it."

Through my laughter, I relayed the whole story about Nate, about how he had fawned over Evie for years when we were kids. That he never did anything about it, even after I broke my promise not to get involved with his sister. And how they had been secretly communicating since we moved.

"Just because they're talking doesn't mean anything is going on. Maybe he does just miss Iris. And maybe he's embarrassed to ring you all the time cause he's a dumb guy. No offense."

"None taken. We are pretty dumb. I dunno, though. I have a weird feeling about the whole thing. Nate has never been mates with a chick—not without trying to get in her pants."

Spiro re-emerged with a beer for me and another margarita for Scar. The consumption of which soon had me forgetting all about Nate and Evie. Envy filled me as Scarlett took her straw between her lips, chewed it a little, sucked in the most beautiful manner I had ever seen, and then licked away the tiny drop that sat on her lip. She began to talk, and I did my best to pay attention while picturing my cock replacing the straw.

"Seems you and I are quite the point of discussion. I was going to tell you some gossip involving us too."

"Blimey, I'm starting to understand how Taylor Swift must feel. People are as obsessed with our love lives as they are hers."

"I know! And it's as close to famous as I want to be. So, I was in the bathroom, innocently washing my hands, when none other than Victoria walked up behind me and just eyeballed me in the mirror."

"What? What did she say?"

"Nothing. She just looked at me like this." Scarlett held my gaze, knotted her brows, scowled, and pushed out her lips like a fish. It was so cute.

"Really? Shit, well, what did you say?"

"Okay, this is a long story. Try and stay awake. Right, so I stared back for a bit. I didn't know what to say, then I noticed her hair looked nice, so I asked her where she got her hair done. She rolled her eyes and said, *'You couldn't afford it.'* Then she said, *'Have you and Finn got together yet? Because I overheard Gareth and Arthur talking about people bonking in the conference room. If you and Finn are together, maybe I could tell people it was you and not me and Jason.'"* Scarlett made a shocked *O* with her lovely mouth, then wrapped it around and sucked on her straw again. I lost all feeling below my eyes, and then she continued,

"I said, *'No, sorry, we haven't yet,'* and then she said, *'Oh. Well, Jason and I are splitting from our spouses. Once it's all done, we're going public. We just wanted more time.'* I felt sorry for her. I think she loves him."

I nodded, trying to process what she was saying while being stuck on one word. "Yet?"

Scarlett dropped her straw and looked at me blankly. "Yet what?"

"You said Victoria asked if we had gotten together yet, then you said not yet. Not yet implies that you think we will."

Potato alley turned a gorgeous, flushed pink. "Okay, so I just told you all that, and that's all you took from it. Yet?"

"Yet..." I teased. "Sorry, I mean, yes. That's all I heard."

Sighing, Scarlett tilted her head to the side and sighed. "You have nothing to say about Victoria?"

"Oh, I have plenty to say. I think she's scared. She's in love with her boss. She's had a terrible time with Herman and is clutching at straws. I'm just more interested in *the yet.*"

The cutest, worried little frown appeared on her face, and all I wanted to do was pick her up and hold her. Of course, I didn't. "Finn. We talked about this in Tarrytown. I think you know how I feel about things. But I hope you know I respect where you're coming from, and I'm not going to push you on anything. I just want you to be happy."

My eyes twitched as my mind flicked to Shelby, but the lure of the woman before me was too strong. "And what about you, Red? What would make you happy?"

She bit her bottom lip, then beamed a smile across the table, "I am happy. I have an amazing son, my dream job, an interfering best friend, and maybe a new second-best friend too."

Shit. She means me. DO NOT CRY. Taking a moment, I sipped from my water, cooled the hell down, and continued. "There's nothing else you want, though? Nothing just for you?" I brushed my foot against hers.

A look of mischief settled on her beautiful face. "There are a few things I could think of. But I'm being respectful, remember." A dull thud sound came from beneath the table, then a shoeless foot rubbed against the inside of my ankle.

"Respect is very important. But so is adaptability," I whispered. Scarlett slid a little in her seat, and that foot slipped up and under the leg of my pants. "Flexibility too." My glass was emptied as Scarlett continued to rub.

"Oh, I agree. I'm very adaptable and flexible."

"I always liked that about you, Red. It's very sexy."

"Why, thank you. You told me my laugh was sexy once. Now my acrobatic style. Is that all you think is sexy about me?"

My dick hardened instantly.

"No, definitely not. That, my girl, is just one of many things on my very big, long, long, long...list. Maybe if I give up and let you be my girlfriend, you could show me *your* secret list, and I could show you mine."

"Ahh, you remember my list? You're very clever and cocky. But who says that I want you to be my boyfriend?" She swirled the pink straw that sat in her margarita. "I really do fancy getting my hands around that list. Probably not now, though. It seems quite large. I don't think we'd make it to the movies."

I, too, began to doubt if we would, in fact, make it to the movie.

By the time we finished our mains, the vixen had her foot between my thighs, and it stayed there, gently caressing and inching up right through dessert. I'm not sure if you've ever eaten tiramisu with a sexy woman's foot rubbing against your cock, but it's an experience I'd recommend and one I hope to have repeated many times in my life.

Preferably with this woman. There are an awful lot of desserts, after all.

With every ounce of strength, self-restraint, and adjusting a young couple so obviously in lust could possibly possess, we left the restaurant and walked to my Jeep. Like a nervous fifteen-year-old, my little finger tickled against her finger before my hand tentatively claimed hers. I'm not sure why I was so nervous. Her black pantyhose-clad feet had been molesting my cock half the night. But holding hands out in the open for the whole world to see felt like a big deal. It also made me extremely happy.

I smiled down at her, admiring how the streetlight's glow bounced off her flushed cheeks. "Thanks for dinner, Red."

"No, thank you. I had a great feeling—I mean time." She stopped, balanced on her toes, and pressed a kiss right on the edge of my mouth. "Allons au cinéma et touchons dans le noir."

Distracted by her closeness, it took my brain a while to translate. I'd unlocked the car, held Scar's hand as she climbed in, and was walking to my side when it finally hit me. *Allons au cinéma et touchons dans le noir.* Let's go to the movies and touch in the dark.

26

Scarlett

FINN SCOFFED ANGRILY AND pointed at the screen. "I find it both fascinating and insulting that the partners are okay with a French movie when they can barely understand me...and I speak English."

"Aww, poor Finny. Remember, you don't come with subtitles on your chest like the movie does." I patted my fingers against that very chest, which turned into giving his pecs a good poke, testing out their firmness. When I realized what I was doing, I flicked my eyes to Finn's. He was watching my finger intently, just as he was when I played with my hair at dinner and when I twirled my fork around my Bolognese and sucked the non-existent sauce from my thumb. "Sorry about the poking." I wasn't a tiny bit sorry.

I returned my hands to the safety of my popcorn bucket, but Finn's eyes stayed fixed on me. Rationally ignoring it was sustainable for only so long. *Maybe this isn't just intense sexiness.* I knew who I was. What I was. What I often looked like. A mess. "What? Why are you looking at me? Do I have something on my face? God, is it pasta sauce from dinner? Have you let me walk around like this all night?"

"No, not at all, sorry. I was just...you look great. Really pretty. Promise." Like me, he didn't look sorry, but his compliments and smirk appeased my fear.

By this point, we were an hour into the movie. I couldn't remember any characters' names or a damn thing that had happened. Hopefully there would be no test at work tomorrow. Should there be one, I would be fucked. But honestly, how was I supposed to focus on some French guy with a big nose climbing a mountain, when Finn was next to me and I could study how his quads flexed in his pants? I kept telling myself I would be fine, and an exam was very much in doubt. Hopefully.

Things in the office had been super tense over the last week. Jason finally reached his limit with Mr. Wise boob-eyeing Victoria and had security escort him from the building. He wasn't even permitted to come tonight. Since everything had already been ready and paid for, Jason and Bernstein decided to go ahead with the evening, turning it instead into a team-building exercise. A reset, of sorts. A pop quiz seemed ill-suited.

Finn's elbow bumped my arm, my thighs clenched together, and my thoughts returned to where they should be. My attraction to him had hit the next level since I had slid my foot between his legs. It was only two hours ago, but it felt like an eternity.

Damn, I want him to kiss me.

My eyes drifted back to his face, and his gaze locked on my mouth. "This staring is becoming a habit, Mr. Austen. At work, in the car, and now in the cinema. You're supposed to be watching the movie, not me."

"Hmm. That's very hypocritical of you, Grant. You were looking at me too. And honestly, you're much prettier and more entertaining than Big Nose."

He pointed to the screen as I chewed on my lip and giggled. "Well, stop. It's quite distracting."

"Fine. You do the same, then."

"Fine."

I managed to look at the screen for maybe twenty seconds when Finn shifted in his seat and again stole my attention. His hot breath tickled my face, and a featherlight kiss was planted on the swell of my cheek. Goosebumps covered my flesh, so he made them worse by brushing them with his thumb and kissing me again. This time, adding a hint of tongue. "You're beautiful, Red." Nuzzling into the crook of my neck, he took the lobe of my ear in his teeth and bit it gently.

"Should you be doing that?" I sighed, leaning into him and praying he didn't stop. "We shouldn't do this. Everyone can see us."

"We shouldn't. We definitely shouldn't. But we also absolutely should." He backed up his words by sweeping the hair from my neck, peppering my collarbone with a series of kisses, and licking his way back to my ear.

"Scarlett."

"Yes, Finn."

"Meet me behind the cinema."

He was up and out of his seat before I could react. Chasing after him while tearing off my clothes like I wanted wasn't an option. I had to wait.

Be discreet. Inconspicuous.

I planted my ass in the seat, sunk my nails into the disturbingly stained velvet arms, and tried to resist watching him bound up the stairs. My heart pounded so hard, I was sure everyone would hear it and instantly know what was happening. This was going to change everything. For me. For Finn. Maybe for our careers.

Relax, Scarlett. Relax. It's just a man. Just a kiss.

A flash of light in my periphery turned my head *just* as he glanced over his shoulder, gave me a cheeky wink, and then disappeared through the doors.

"Holy shit. Am I doing this?" I muttered.

A hand came to rest on my shoulder, and a soft, deep voice whispered in my ear, "Why are you still sitting?"

Patchouli cologne hit me, and I turned to find Theodore's mouth oddly close to my ear. "What?" My head spun left and right. "When did you even get here?"

"I can sense sex, Scar. I got here just in time to see him eating your neck. Now, go get him."

"Oooohhhh, I don't know if I should, Teddy. My ideologies strictly—"

"Fuck your rules," Teddy said, digging his fingers into my skin. "You've spent your life trying to make everyone around you happy. It's time for you to be happy too."

The French guy fell off his bike, and laughter rolled through the theater. Teddy gave me a quick pat on the arm and kissed the top of my head. "Go."

"Christ on a bike! I'm gonna do it." I made my break. "Sorry, bathroom." I winced as I squeezed past a series of squashed legs. "Sorry, I shouldn't have had the large drink."

Absconding from a work function to make out with a colleague who had friend-zoned me only to have me ignore that and feel up his dick with my foot as he ate was a new low. One that had me so excited and terrified I could hardly breathe.

I left the safety of the cinema and my scared, but horny, English ass hit the mean streets—well, one alley—of New York.

"Finn? Finn?" He was nowhere in sight. But the minute my foot turned the corner at the rear of the building, a familiar scent and strong hands possessed me. All air was forced from my lungs as a muscular arm hooked around my waist and pushed me against the wall. He held me there with one hand and ran the other along my side till he cupped my cheek. "I want you, Scarlett." His gaze dropped to my lips.

"I do too. Want you, I mean, not me. But I have to say this first."

His brows pinched. "Okay, but make it quick, 'cause I need to kiss you."

"Yes, right. Well, the thing is, I know you're not ready for this. You told me you're not ready for this. But I need this, and I think you need it too. Maybe this can be a one-time release valve, letting off steam, and then we can go back to being friends."

Finn's eyes wandered to my boobs as I spoke and stayed there as he replied, "Is that what you want, Red?" It was *not* what I wanted. "To go back to being friends? 'Cause I have got to tell you. I want to do bad things to you, Scarlett. Very, very bad things that could change the way you see me, and I don't think there's any coming back from that. Just tell me what you want."

I want you to fuck me senseless. I want to be yours. I want to have a million of your blond babies...

I ran my fingers through his hair and tugged his face until his eyes met mine. "I want whatever you can give me."

A visible shudder rolled through his body, and he sprung to action, removing my trenchcoat, running his hands beneath the fabric, and pushing it down my arms until it fell to my feet. Disappointment over the filthy street germs covering my coat disappeared as he groped his way to my ass and lifted me from my feet. My core pulsed with need as he sunk his fingers into the fat of my ass and squeezed. I wrapped my arms around his neck, my legs around his waist, and linked my ankles at his back. Never had I been happier for the size of my butt.

"You have no idea how often I dreamed of this sweet thing," he growled, molding it in his hands. "It's perfect."

"Kissing me right now would be even more perfect."

Every inch of my skin ignited in anticipation as he licked his lips, bent down, and sealed his mouth over mine. He pressed his hips forward simultaneously, and the double assault had me seeing stars. My whole body shook and tensed.

"Relax for me, Red," he whispered against my lips, and my body obediently followed his command, melting into his touch as he ran his fingers along my spine. The curtain of hair blocking his path was twisted into his fist until he was free to taste the nape of my neck. "I'm going to savor you." His words came hot and breathy in my ear. I expected his next move to be gentle and soft, but his firm and rough handling flicked that thought to the trash, just what I needed to do with my ruined knickers.

Finn gave me everything I never knew I liked—hair pulling, head tilting, teeth grazing, neck biting. An embarrassingly high-pitched, girly squeak burst from inside me, but it was silenced by his mouth closing over mine, the clashing of our teeth and his desperate, angry, and possessive tongue. Every thought, care, and worry I'd ever carried was torched from my mind. Heat surged through me, soaking my panties. I was wet. So wet he would feel it through my dress should he touch me, and God, how I wanted him to touch me right where my desire pooled.

My core clenched as the strokes and flicks of his tongue became more aggressive. More demanding. I responded in kind, sucking on his tongue, maybe biting it a bit too, then joining in, stroke for stroke, till we found a rhythm that had us both moaning for more.

Time no longer existed. All that mattered was being eaten like a cheap tart at a bake sale by this beautiful man.

And coming. Coming mattered.

I wanted to come.

Goddamn it, Finn Austen, make me come!

Eventually, the ridiculous need humans have for oxygen forced us apart. Panting into each other's open mouths, we continued to touch, and his hips maintained their bucking.

"Doing this, touching you like this, shoving my face in your tits...I've thought of nothing else since you walked into the restaurant. And this dress, Scarlett. Fuck. You're so hot." He then buried his face exactly where he wanted.

"You like it?" I asked with a squeak as he bit my satin-covered nipple.

"The boobs or the dress?" he mumbled, tit in mouth. "'Cause the answer to both is yes. Yes, I do. I really do."

"I meant the dress. And good. I do too. But I'll like it even more when you rip it off me."

All sucking ceased. Finn looked up. His face was as serious as it could be with flushed cheeks, swollen lips, and boob-tousled hair. "Red," he said, swallowing heavily. "I need... I need to take you home. Can I please, please take you home? I need to be inside you. I can't wait any longer to watch you come."

My body screamed, *Yes, fuck yes!* I was one nipple bite away from orgasm and wanted it bad. I could taste the release on the tip of the tongue he'd just violated. Just as I went to launch myself at his face again, my brain kicked, reminding me of my life outside this alley, away from the god of pure sex.

"Bloody hell." I pushed my hands between us, pushed off his chest, and slid down his body. "We can't. Ben is with Mrs. Horowitz, and I have to pick him up once we're done here. Shit. Shit! I'm so sorry." I began to pace. "Maybe, maybe we can just fool around a bit here in hooch alley, and a bit in the car, and then pick up where we left off next week?"

"Next week? Scarlett, this cannot wait another week." Finn pointed to the boner that was pointing toward me. "I don't want to beg. But I'm begging."

I had to agree. I could hardly wait five seconds, let alone five days, but... **Ideology #4 - ABSOLUTELY no 'friends' are to sleep over**. It was clear. I did *not and should not* bring men home. Even ones as hot as Finn. Yes, I was smashing #3 as much as I was smashing my pussy onto his leg, but two ideological infractions in one night was a bridge too far.

"Okay. Let's think about this. We are intelligent, creative, horny people. Surely we can come up with a solution."

Finn gripped my arm and pulled me back against him. "How about we—"

"Scaaaarrrrrleeeettttttttt! Are you back there with Croc Dundee, or are you being murdered by a stranger? Moan once for Dundee, twice for murderer."

I pressed my hand over Finn's mouth and, for some reason, my own too. "Shh, if we're quiet, he'll leave. He has a ten-second attention span."

Finn sucked my fingers into his mouth and laughed. Teddy's voice gained volume. "I'm not hearing any moaning!"

I'm going to fucking kill him. "It's okay, Finn. I'll deal with this. Theodore, I AM FINE. PLEASE FUCK OFF!"

"Yes! I bloody knew it! Have fun, kids. Do everything I wouldn't do."

Finn claimed my mouth again, kissing me so profoundly I forgot my name for twenty-five seconds. "I know we have to leave, but can I at least drive you home? Be a good girl and say yes, Scarlett."

Now, I'm a feminist, and I should find the concept of being called a good girl condescending and sexist. But from this man's lips, it left me wetter than a slip n' slide and bordering on begging to take him in my mouth. But before I could drop to my knees before him, my jacket buzzed on the ground.

"That might be Mrs. H, Finn," I said, mentally undoing his fly. "Sorry, I have to suck it—check it. The phone. I have to touch and check my phone."

Finn followed my gaze down to his crotch, shoved his tongue in front of his top teeth, and exhaled heavily. "Of course you do, Red. It's fine. I'm fine." Finn looked far from fine. He bent over on his haunches and started sucking in some deep breaths. "I just have to calm myself down."

I peeled my eyes from Finn and rifled through my once-favorite, now germ-encrusted coat.

Teddy

> I will collect Ben from Cat Lady, and he can stay at my place. Take that man home. Take off his clothes. Ride him.

> Be a complete slut. Be safe. Love you.

> You better tell me everything or I'll cut you.

"Finn. That was Teddy. He's picking up Ben. If the offer still stands, I'd like you to take me home and make me come."

27

Scarlett

GOD HIMSELF WANTED ME to fuck Finn Austen.

He wanted us to get into my house and tear off each other's clothes and bang, good and proper, to hell with the consequences. I knew this because there was an empty car space directly in front of my door. I had lived there for almost two years, and that had never happened...not once. But there it sat, as empty as my vagina had been for an unmentionable number of years.

Our drive had only been three miles, but a three-car pileup and massive overreaction to it by New York's finest ensured it felt like three hundred and seventy-five thousand. Finn's free hand roamed up and down my thigh the entire torturous, completely silent time we were trapped in his khaki Jeep. The feel of his fingers dragging and slightly sinking into my flesh drove me insane. I couldn't wait for bigger, harder, shaftier things to sink into me. My eyes kept wandering to the bulge in his pants. The one he kept adjusting with a grunt and pretending like he hadn't. I contemplated riding his lap the whole way home or using the cover of darkness to go down on him as he drove, but he was a terrible driver as it was. My tits in his face or mouth on his cock would ensure our evening was spent in a hospital bed, not mine. Still, I wanted to so badly that I had to sit on my hands to stop myself from mounting him.

In the alley, we'd been like nymphos on speed, unable to stop touching and dry humping. In front of my house, we were shit-scared virgins doing nothing and dying of our own ineptitude.

Teddy's face popped up in his window several times. He was curtain-twitching so hard I wondered if he was attempting morse code. When he abandoned the blinds, and his front light began to flash on and off, I knew it was time to make a move. Otherwise, he would be here, dragging us both inside, and then I'd struggle to get him to leave.

"Finn, would you like to come in?"

His reply was immediate and came in the form of a strangled kind of grunt from deep in the back of his throat, followed by an attempt to get out of the car without removing his seatbelt.

I would like to say each second of this momentous entry to my home was burned into my mind, and I could see it as clearly as a golden tattoo that stained my flesh.

But that would be a filthy lie.

I had little memory of how I got inside. I knew it happened. I knew I was so nervous I could barely walk or breathe. I could still feel the tremble and tingle in my hands and the caress on his lips on my neck. I vaguely recalled the thud of the closing door and the clunk of my phone on the side table, but the first clear memory I had was the rattle and clunk of brass keys hitting the floor after Finn swept me into his arms. It splintered through the air like a starter's rifle, signaling the shedding of attire. I had little to remove as I'd refused to wear the germ jacket, so it was mostly me who tore at him.

My hands, desperate to see and feel what laid beneath his shirt, dispensed of that first. "Holy shit, Finn. You're ripped!" After that classy declaration, I stood back and admired the view. "Can I touch it?"

Finn's eyes widened and shot down lower than his 8-pack. "I mean your stomach." He exhaled, huffed out a laugh and nodded as his trembling hand took mine and placed it between his pecs, right above his heart. I left it there for a heartbeat, feeling his chest fill and expand while mine did the same. Then, with a wee squeal and a little too much enthusiasm, I let my fingers roam his smooth skin, trace the rise and fall of perfection, circle his nipples and belly button. I ducked and felt Finn's body turn to stone as I kissed the goddamn ridiculous cut of his V. I looked up and whispered, "Perfect. Now, I want to touch your other hard thing too." From my angle, it was hard to tell if the flush of color to Finn's cheeks was modesty or lust, but I didn't have long to ponder. I was too distracted by the contracting muscle beneath my lips, then his greedy hands lifting me up, skimming the sides of my body, gathering the hem of my dress, and lifting it over my head.

"Oh, you will. Never mind. But first, I have a feeling I'm about to see real perfection." Once removed, it was tossed in the air beside me, and despite its flimsy nature, I swear I heard a thud as it fell against the floor. Or perhaps that was my heart? I stood before Finn in my heels, bra, panties, and stockings, fighting the urge to cover my body as he ran his thumb over his bottom lip. The pulse in his neck was visible from three paces away as he studied me. "I've wanted you from the moment I first saw you. I can't believe this is real. That you're real."

"I'm real. Are you?"

"I am," he said, his voice deeper than I'd ever heard as he stepped closer.

"I'm nervous, Finn. I know I came at you like a feral animal in the alley, but it's been a long time for me. I know I come off as loud and outgoing, but—"

Finn shook his head, closed the space between us, and held my palm over his chest. "I don't know if I'd call you loud or outgoing. I think you're quite shy, maybe a bit nervous, like me. Anxiety can trick people into thinking we're the life of the party. But our flailing arms aren't crazy dance moves or lively storytelling. We're just drowning on the inside and desperately grasping for anything to keep us afloat."

Okay. Wow. So, if still waters run deep, does that mean shallow ones run rapidly? My poorly timed metaphorical questioning came as my heart hit near tachycardia, and my hoo-ha throbbed so fast I couldn't breathe. The sweet, and deep, and fucking sexy man's perfectly accurate study should have forced me into contemplation. But we were half naked. He looked like he looked, and his potent purity served only to increase my need to bone him. *I AM THE SHALLOW ONE.*

I placed my free hand over his, pulled it from his chest and placed it on my boob. "Finn," I said as I squeezed. "I'm going to

be honest. I need you to stop making sense and just fuck me."
I clutched his face in my hand and pulled his lips to mine. My
nerves and tummy self-consciousness slid from my body like
sweat down my temple. I released his cheeks and went straight
for his belt, undoing the buckle in record time and pulling it,
loop by loop, till it swung in my hands. I threw it to the ground
and celebrated by starting on his zipper.

That was a long process. Finn was playing with my boobs,
groaning, and sucking so hard I momentarily lost all motor
skills. I only seemed able to palm him through his jeans. "You
need some help with that, Red?" he panted between licks.

I wriggled my fingers in his face. "Yes. I think that would be
useful. I can't work my thingies."

Finn smiled against my lips, assaulted my tongue again, and
undid his zipper. In one flick of the wrist, his jeans were at his
ankles, and my eyes were hanging from my head.

"Holy shit, Finn!" I pointed at the thing pointing at me
through thin, black cotton.

"Yeah, sorry about that." He pulled me against him and began grinding in a bone-melting manner that implied no remorse
at all. "This has been brewing for a long time."

"That's a good brew. Can I touch it?"

"You do make it hard—pardon the pun—to be sexy, Red.
You asked me to fuck you, remember? And I would very much
like to." Finn slid his hand between my legs and ran his finger
over my soaked panties. "I need to be inside you, Scarlett. I can't
wait to watch your pretty face come."

An unrecognizable whimper shuddered from me as I worked
my fingers inside Finn's boxer briefs, and a second later, they
joined his jeans at his feet. His cock sprang free. My eyelids and
vagina fluttered uncontrollably. He stepped free of his briefs,
shaking them from his ankles, and then pushed me against the
wall, pinning me between his arms and spreading my legs open
with his knee.

"Do we want this slow or fast?"

"Fast, fast. Now. God, please, I'm going to explode."

Looking thoroughly pleased with himself, Finn dipped his
knees a little, slid his hand between the wall and my ass, then

pushed my pelvis forward. The thick head of his cock slipped between my thighs, and we both moaned. Finn may have cried a little. I rode my pussy over his cock, and he began to thrust. "You feel so amazing, and I'm not even inside. You blow my freaking mind, Scarlett."

"Keep rubbing me like that, and your mind won't be the only thing I'll blow."

Finn's body—well, not all of it—appeared to go limp for a moment or two, and then he smiled and huffed a laugh, but he was back with gusto and pumping away seconds later. "I want to take you to bed and do this right, but I also wanna be in you yesterday."

"I vote for yesterday, too. Teddy has an emergency stash of condoms in the bathroom, I think. I've never had to....doesn't matter. Wait right there, Big Boy. I'll be back."

Realizing I had addressed Finn's cock as Big Boy, I slipped from his grip and scooted to the bathroom, my hands covering my ass the whole way. I closed the door and collapsed back against it. Filled with joy, I laughed as my mirror reflected the atrocious state I was in. Lipstick was smeared from one cheek to the other, and my eyes resembled those of a giant panda, but I knew Finn wouldn't care. Still, I washed my face, ran my wet hands through my curls in a vain attempt to control the uncontrollable, and stole a few long deep breaths while searching for the condoms. *I could kiss you, Teddy,* I thought as I found them and made my hasty exit.

My naked man was not where I left him. He and his massive frame were sprawled on my couch, his curls a gorgeous mess, his cheeks and lips red and raw.

"I thought I told you not to move."

"Big Boy wanted to spread out."

I shook my head and the condom box as I approached. "Are you still up for this?"

"Does it look like I am?" With a raised brow, he fisted himself with one hand and gripped my hand with the other, pulling me between his parted legs. He leaned forward, held my calves in his palms, then indecently followed the seam with his thumbs all the way to the garter. "These stockings are sexy as fuck, Red.

The sight of you in satin and lace is enough to make me come right now." Snapping the strap sharply against my skin, he then slid his tongue along its edge and bit into the swell of my ass. "Did you wear these for me?" he said between mouthfuls of cheek. "Were you teasing my cock with your foot at dinner while your pretty little pussy was keeping these a secret?" He shifted suddenly, my body jolting as the sound of tearing fabric buckled my knees. I'd normally despair over the most expensive lingerie I owned being torn in such a brutal fashion, but I was surprisingly okay with it. Handling the rush of hormones with my usual poise and grace, I dropped the condoms and almost fell head-first into his chest. As always, Finns hands were there, gripping my hips and steading me before hooking his fingers inside my panties and discarding the tattered remains. "They were almost too pretty to ruin. Almost."

My world blurred when he traced the line of my slit with his nose, breathing me in, then planting a kiss against the lace. "Are you trying to fuck or kill me, Austen?"

"Most definitely the first. Now, step out of them, Red. Then sit on my lap like a good girl." Two seconds later, my thighs were straddling his, his hands were gripping my waist, and he was rolling me over his hardness, "It's good we had that chat cause friends don't normally sit like this, do they?"

"Not in my experience, no. But we are very good friends."

"That's true."

My thumb came to rest at the edge of his insanely hot, partly open mouth. I ran it along his bottom lip, dragging it down slightly. Finn's tongue darted out, licked the tip, and my whole body quivered. "I'm a bit nervous again, Finn."

"If it makes you feel any better, I'm nervous too. But I also know we will look after each other like no one else ever has. I'm so into you, Red."

"I know. Me too. And you're right. We will look after each other." I nodded in agreement with myself and shook away the fear. "Okay, I'm good. Sex me now, please."

A smile I knew I would treasure the rest of my days lit Finn's face. "Consider it done. Now lift your hips, baby."

While considering what little I wouldn't do if he kept ordering me about and calling me baby, I raised myself from his lap. The smoothness of his words didn't carry over to condom application. It was adorably obvious Finn hadn't used one in a while, and it took several curse-filled tries to get it rolling. I enjoyed the process while hovering over him, running an unhelpful commentary, and kissing his chest.

"Gotcha, ya bastard!" He celebrated by gripping my waist and sucking my right boob till I was begging for him to be inside me.

"Take me hard, Finn. Hard and fast and rough." I dropped my hips and slid down, groaning as his thick, already glistening tip slipped inside. Finn's head fell back and hit the couch as I continued to take him in.

"Such a perfect little pussy, baby. So wet, warm, and tight for me. Just like I knew it would be."

Inch by glorious inch, he filled me like no one ever had, and the animalistic sounds coming from my body were unlike any I'd heard myself make. I rolled front and back, leaned side to side, and bounced up and down, every new angle delivering a new sensation.

"Your boobs look amazing. I could watch them bounce forever."

"And you feel so good...amazing. But Finn, I need you to break me. I need you to hurt me." It was a desperate sob, a pathetic plea that had him bracing me in his palms and flipping me onto my back and repositioning us lengthwise on the sofa. Somehow still inside, he pulled out before driving into me.

"Now I can rail you as you deserve. Christ. You're tight as sin and need to be fucked like the devil." Again and again, he repeated his pattern, drawing all the way out and slamming back in. Each thrust increased in ferocity until he was fucking into me so hard I feared I would shatter into a thousand pieces and thank him for doing it.

My soul left my body when he draped my legs across his shoulders, lifted higher onto his knees, and absolutely annihilated me. My head rolled back and slammed into the arm with each pounding thrust. I cried for more so loud and long my voice was hoarse.

Sweat dripped from Finn's forehead onto my breast. His effort, the all-out punishing force, was unsustainable. His arms gave way, his chest dropped, and I discovered that the weight of Finn Austen's body against mine was everything I'd been missing. That and his lips. Lips that kissed and breathed life into me with every thrust in a way no other had and, I knew, ever would.

We lay skin to skin. Connected. Moving as one.

"I can feel you clenching around me, Red. I have to slow down. I can't take much more."

"Don't stop, please, don't stop!"

The desperate crack in my voice seemed to spur him on. I could feel he was losing control, his thrusts wild and messy, but the boy was nothing but determined. He gritted his teeth and continued to smash against me with an almost violent force.

Life changed as I clawed into his back, and an orgasm stronger than I'd ever believed possible swept through my body.

"I feel you coming. You're squeezing me so tight! I'm, I'm. . ." Finn's hips bucked and then stilled, and I felt the release and relief in his body as he spilled inside me. A sweaty, sated mess, his face laid between my breasts, and he continued to roll his hips as our bodies met at their peak. I buried my face in his curls, kissing the top of his head, then fell back against the cushions.

"I'll never forget this, Finn."

"I'll never give you the chance."

28

Finn

I'D BEEN AWAKE IN Scarlett's bed, mentally tossing between jubilation and fear while watching her sleep and breathe like a creep, for hours. I'd had one of, if not the best night of my life, but I couldn't let myself enjoy it.

When I slipped her the big one, a bit of my heart accidentally snuck in too. One teeny-tiny morsel of me floating around in a whole other person shouldn't have been an issue. But the problem was I'd *slipped* inside her, fully protected and with consent of course, I think four times, and on each glorious occasion, a bigger piece of me remained. That's quite a lot of my heart in a woman I already knew would never be mine—not like I wanted, anyway. I was going back to Sydney. New York was not permanent for me.

How can I give myself to her when I know I'm leaving?

A brilliant idea came to me at five a.m. I should stop being a pathetic bitch and have fun. Scarlett said it herself in the alley. Maybe this could be a one-time thing, and we could go back to being friends. Not one piece of my being wanted that, but maybe it was for the best. I decided to wake her and talk it through before I left, but then she rolled over, pressed her ass against Finn Jr., wriggled it around a bit, and I forgot. Instead of a serious, heartfelt discussion over where we stood, I distracted myself by raising the sheet and admiring her nakedness. Shimmying underneath, I positioned myself between her legs, with a hand on her boob and my mouth on her pussy.

Her whole body shivered when I kissed the very top of her slit. She sighed, her hips lifted from the mattress, and her fingers wove through my hair. "Finn," a sexy, sleepy voice purred. "Finn, what are you... Oh, you don't... Oh, that's nice. Oh, oh, oh...but, Finn, wait. Wait." I glanced up and found Scarlett, staring at me flushed face and wide-eyed and not in a good way. She looked horrified and left me face-planting the mattress when she pulled her legs to her chest and scooted from my grip.

"Scar. I'm sorry. I shouldn't have presumed. Please, I'm so sorry." I propped myself up on my elbows and wiped my mouth with my shoulder. Never in my life had I wanted a fiery pit to hell to open at my feet as I did at that moment. And by the look on Scarlett's face, she would be pushing me out of the way to drop through first.

"No. You don't need to apologize. It felt lovely. It's just that you don't have to do that. I mean, no one else has ever..." She began to chew her nails like it was her last meal. "I'm just gonna say it. Finn. I'm like...a virgin."

It was not the time to laugh. She looked so sincerely worried. So, of course, I laughed so hard it hurt—as did the warranted whack to the back of my head. "Um, okay. Look, I hate to break it to you, Red, but just tonight, we've had sex in this bed, on your couch, in the kitchen, and in the bathroom. *And* you have a child. I'm pretty sure your virginity expired some time ago."

"Yes, I know that, smartass. I mean with tongue...down there." She pointed down to her pelvic region in case I didn't know what she meant. Cuteness personified. Then, for some reason, maybe to break the news gently, she whispered, "I'm an oral virgin."

Slow blinking with my jaw at my feet felt like a natural and justified reaction. As was taking a moment or two to process and choose my next words wisely. My laughing hadn't gone down too well, and with the shock wearing off, I realized this was a fucking tragedy...for her. For me, it was a pussy goldmine. "Scarlett, what I am about to say is deadly serious." I took a deep breath, scooted to her side, and held her hand. "I think this may be my mission, my reason for being. Eating you out for the first time is my purpose in life. Please let me do this for you. Let me be your first." *And last.*

She worried her bottom lip between her teeth and picked at her nails again, "But what if you don't like it?"

"Impossible. I can guarantee I will love it. And you will too. It's the best fucking thing in the world, and honestly, I've thought about tasting you from the very first second I saw you strutting through the office in that little pink skirt. "

"What if I taste bad or look weird up close?"

"Again, I guarantee that won't be the case. Look, I am never going to do anything you don't want to do. If you say no, it's a no. You know that, right? You trust me?"

"Of course I trust you."

"Good. Then, you have to believe me about this. Tasting a woman, making her scream your name as they come on your tongue, is the ultimate. Most guys love it, and I think you'll love it too. Look. Look at my dick. It's rock solid, just talking about it."

Scarlett admired and patted the boner but still shook her head and buried it in her hands. "I just don't get it. Understanding quantum theory would be easier than following this, and I flunked humanities three years in a row, Finn."

"You learn quantum theory in physics, Red."

"Point made."

I pried her hands from her face and kissed the insides of her palms. "I don't know what dud's you've been with that haven't wanted to do this for you, the joke is on them."

"That's the thing, I guess. I've been on maybe three or four dates since I had Ben. All when I was in England and most ended within seconds of me disclosing I had a son. I was tired of feeling rejected, so I decided to give dating a break. The longer that break became, the harder it was to put myself out there. I was anxious about never meeting anyone, but the thought of meeting *the one* and it not working out was ten times worse. I was so scared that I stopped trying."

Everything Scarlett said was a hundred percent relatable. But it was still shocking when I slowly did the math. "Okay, so wait... I get it. Totally get it. But are you telling me you've been with no one, not one person since Brett?" She nodded, and I slapped my palm to my forehead. "What the fuck? Wha...how... How is that even possible? Look at you. You're gorgeous and strong and sexy. How could you not have been beating guys away with a stick?"

"There were interested parties from time to time, but nothing that took my fancy. You look upset, Finn. Is this going to be a problem?"

"No, no. God no. I just... I'm surprised and...to be honest, stoked."

"Stoked?"

"Yeah. Happy."

"Because...why? Is this some Neanderthal-caveman thing or—?"

"Because I haven't been with anyone since Shelby."

"Get out!" she yelled in my face and pushed me in the chest so hard I almost fell off the bed. "Jesus Christ! And you're asking *me* how I haven't been with anyone? Have you looked in a mirror?"

Like two naked idiots, we sat staring at each other, like, well, naked idiots trying to understand what seemed unbelievable. There was only one thing to do. Make her laugh and resume begging.

"Scarlett Elizabeth Grant, would you do me the honor of letting me feast on your furless fur burger? I promise you'll love it, and if you don't, you can beat me with a stick."

A spark ignited in Scarlett's eyes as she shook with laughter. "I can really beat you?"

"It worries me that you seem excited by that, but yes. You can definitely beat me, and I feel safe in saying that because I know we are both going to enjoy it. The tongue, not the violence."

Squinting with one eye, inhaling through clenched teeth like a cute little Popeye, she nodded.

"Is that a yes? You'll let me...you know. Go deep muff diving. Pig out on your pie? Skim the quim?"

"You're a damn fool. If I say yes, will you shut up?"

"Well, yeah, 'cause my mouth will be basking in your beaver."

"Oh, my God. You're crazy. Alright, let's do it. Well, you do it. I will receive it."

I gave her a wink, sucked her boobs a bit, and then ran my hands down her body to her ankles. "Lay back, baby girl. I've got you."

The joy of a thousand Christmases had me releasing an ungodly growl as I kissed down her fucking gorgeous stomach, spread her open, and kissed her wet lips. "Scar, baby, your pussy is perfect. I knew it would be. I knew you'd taste sweeter than honey too." Scarlett wriggled beneath me but remained silent.

Starting slowly, I licked in teasing circles, getting closer and closer, but never quite hitting her clit directly. I watched her hands clinging onto the sheets, gripping tighter and tighter. When I hit a spot she really liked, I could feel her hips lift off the bed, and she made the cutest, frustrated noises when I shifted away. *Damn, I love her.*

Never in my life had I wanted so badly to do my best. To prove myself worthy.

"How are we doing, Red? Is it too much?"

"No!" she puffed. "No, it's just right, please. I like it. Don't stop."

I returned my mouth to her clit and gave her several long, slow licks and a bit of suction, and her whole body stiffened and lifted from the bed like she was possessed. She liked the suction.

"Finn, there. Right there. Do that more. Please."

Fisting my hair, her fingers twisted and tugged, her nails digging into my scalp when I did the licky-suck combo again.

"Don't move. Don't move. Yes," she sighed. "Fuck me with your dirty mouth."

I didn't move. I almost came. But I did not move. If anything, I doubled down, focusing on that one spot, teasing, smoothing, tormenting. She cried out, and I wasn't sure if it was in pleasure or pain, but I wasn't stopping to ask. I trusted she'd let me know.

The fact that what I did to her with my tongue, with my lips, even the tip of my chin, had never been done to her before was the ultimate turn-on. I was as hard as a rock when we started, but I became desperate to bury myself inside her. This wasn't about me, though. This was an experience for both of us to remember. Scarlett deserved the best, and I was the one giving it to her. True, I was no expert in the matter, but instinctively, I found the hidden, sublime parts of her that she maybe didn't even know existed. Secret spots and ways to tickle and tease them. I sighed and told her how good she tasted, how often I'd dreamed of doing this to her body, and brought her orgasm after orgasm until she was unable to take any more and begged me to stop. "Finn, I can't feel my...anything."

I sat back on my knees, panting, feeling her body tremble as I traveled kisses up her body until we were face to face. A single tear fell to her cheek as she pulled me onto her lips, where I knew she could taste herself on my tongue. "Thank you. I had no idea it could feel like that."

Waiting what felt like a year to see and taste her like this was worth it. It was everything I imagined and more, and she was thanking me. I pulled myself up beside her, wrapped her in my arms, and held her tight. She fell asleep as I whispered sweet promises I prayed I could keep into her ear.

29

Scarlett

I WOKE THE NEXT morning feeling like I'd slept on a cloud, held high above the earth by the massive, lickable arms of Finn Austen. He eventually unwrapped himself from my body and left just before six. Sleep overcame me instantly, and I woke again at seven when Teddy brought Ben home. I must have been quite the sight when we met at the foot of the stairs. My darling son eyed me inquisitively but said nothing and went straight to his room. He'd been without his iPad for twenty-four hours and missed it more than me.

As for Teddy, he took one look at me and burst out laughing. "Did you just come up for air? Shit!" His hands braced my shoulders, and he bobbed side to side, looking behind me. "Is he still in your room? Is he naked? Is he rigged up in the basement or, as it's now known, the sex dungeon, naked?" He was dismissed with a coy smile and a confession.

"He's not here. I didn't trap him in the basement...*this* time, and we didn't make it to my room."

With a look of pride, Teddy kissed me then squinted, "You banged on the couch, didn't you? In the kitchen too."

"What! How do you know that?"

"How many times do I have to tell you I can sense sex, Scar?" He rolled his eyes and pulled me close. "So, was it good? It must have been if you didn't even make it to bed."

"It was amazing, Teddy. So freaking amazing. We did it, like, five times, and he, you know, licked...stuff. And we did go to bed, but I took him to the guest room instead. There was no way I was letting him in my room."

"You're a smart, filthy, lucky woman, Scar. Whips and chains are one thing, but that room of yours would scare the bravest heroes off. As for lickity-split, thank God you've finally had your muffin munched."

The sudden blaring of Teddy's phone ended all sex talk, and he rushed off to meet Asher at M.I.X. before work.

After finally receiving a delicious Benny cuddle, our morning routine was completed without a single logical thought crossing my mind. I had no idea what I dressed myself in—or Ben, for that matter—until I floated past a store window after dropping him off. Luckily, I wore a cute-as-hell outfit that Finn would hopefully ogle me in, and yes, I said I was floating. Well, it felt like floating. Technically, I skipped my way down 6th Avenue like an unhinged child on the world's biggest sugar rush. Singing Taylor Swift at the top of my lungs, I was entirely oblivious to the outside world, with little to no regard for how many people were avoiding the crazy, singing, skipping woman.

Regrettably, my sweet, semi-psychotic bubble lasted a bitterly short time. Popping occurred within one or two steps inside the office. Suspicious eyes followed me everywhere. Presuming I had food or coffee splattered somewhere, I looked down. Nope, the clothes seemed fine. There was no apparent nip slip or side boob, either. My dress was *not* tucked into my knickers, and no toilet paper was stuck on my shoe. It was highly likely that food was stuck to my face. I couldn't see that, but also, everyone was used to that. My mess had never drawn this much attention. I began to sweat in and on every orifice of my body, creating a whole new set of stains. My trembling hands could barely hold onto my coffee, and if it dropped to the ground, so would I.

What if...? Was it possible? Could my colleagues tell I'd spent the night ravishing the body of their hunky co-worker? Was the foul stench of hoochie emanating from my very being?

No, it had nothing to do with me or my debauchery. Just hours after I had finished fiercely shagging her nephew, Jocelyn Crane was back in town. She was at my desk, and she was looking straight at me with a disconcerting smile. I wasn't sure what was worse: publicly reeking of sex or that grin.

I gave her my best *nothing-to-see-here* greeting. "Ms. Crane, you're back. It's a pleasure to see you."

"The pleasure is all mine, I assure you." Her squinting eyes assessed me as I dropped my things on my messy desktop and then leaned against it for support.

"Are you here to see Finn?"

"Finn and you, yes. I just flew back in this morning and wanted to talk before I went home and slept for a week."

"Ahh, so, you had a good time, then?"

A look of bliss and wistfulness crossed Jocelyn's blushed face, and she rubbed her neck slowly and stared into space. "You could say that. Never underestimate the simultaneously rejuvenating yet exhausting power of a French vineyard and a hot, young man."

Speaking of hot, young men. Looking gorgeous and not at all like he had an hour of sleep and bonked my brains out all night, Finn appeared. Tiptoeing behind his aunt, he gave me a wink, held his index finger to his lips and mouthed, *Shhhh.* Then, he slammed both his massive hands on his unsuspecting victim's shoulders. "Old lady!" Poor Jocelyn shrieked, clutched at her chest, and then slapped her nephew sideways. "Finnley James Austen, you will kill me one day. Is that what you want?"

"Not at all," he laughed, wrapping her into his massive arms and squeezing. "I promise, I love you dearly. I just love scaring you almost as much."

Still recovering, Jocelyn wiped her brow, then took a relaxing, deep breath. "A nice, "Hi, Aunty," and a kiss on the cheek is all I ask of you. Why must your love be so rough and bruising?"

Bruising? Rough? Rough Finn was almost my favorite Finn last night. Rough Finn pinned me down, slapped my ass, and ruined me. I was a big fan of Rough Finn.

"Miss Grant, are you joining us?"

"Hmm, what?" Jocelyn and Finn paused. They were halfway to the conference room, looking back at me, probably wondering why I was frozen on the spot and drooling.

"Yes, yes, of course." Rushing to grab my bag, I took two steps, fumbled, and fell flat on my face. I watched in horror as my coffee hit the ground, the lid popped off, and my liquid life juice spilled onto the floor. It was horrific. Then I noticed another color liquid dripping onto the ground. Blood. My blood. I was bleeding.

An echo of, "Scarlett!" filled the room, and multiple sets of feet ran toward me. Finn was the first at my side, and with little effort, he picked me up and almost threw me over his shoulder. No amount of blood or the sudden sharp pain stabbing me in the temple could un-sexify that.

Things then got a little blurry from there. I'm not sure if I had a concussion or if Finn was singing songs from Disney's *Tangled* as he carried me off into the sunset, but either way, I was good with it. Once inside the castle-themed conference room, he placed me on a throne. My hand slipped from around his neck, ran down his chiseled jaw, and cupped his chin. I could taste the blood trickling from my lip, and it felt as though I might have some oozing from my forehead too, but I couldn't be sure. Finn was too close and looking too deep into my eyes to be bothered by a drop or liter of blood. Two Jocelyns were bustling around behind him, shooing everyone else out of the room and closing the door.

"You need to stop that bleeding, Finn. Have you got a first aid kit here?"

"I don't think so, but there's one in the kitchen. Jocie, could you run and grab it for me?"

Finn's worried face was right in mine as Jocelyn nodded and disappeared. He was so sweet, kissing me on the nose and asking if I liked doughnuts in Spanish. It was hard to concentrate on translating because he was also taking off his shirt and holding it to my temple. I began to feel woozy and dizzy, and my eyes were getting heavier with each blink. I knew I was in trouble, and if I didn't die from the blood loss, I might from the image of him shirtless and kneeling before me.

"Yes, Finny! I mill warry us!"

"I'm not asking you to marry me, Red. I'm asking if you're okay. You hit your head. It's a nasty cut. I think I need to take you to the ER."

"Hero my." I swooned, making perfect sense and patting his face.

"Okay, I definitely need to take you to the E—" I swallowed his words with a sloppy wet kiss, and I returned my arms to his neck.

"Me take, Finnley."

Finn laughed and kissed me back but tried to unglue me at the same time. My mouth was fondling his neck when Jocelyn returned with the first aid kit, an ice pack, and a smug grin. "Sorry to interrupt."

"You're not interrupting, Jocie. Scarlett is just being a little extra friendly. I think I need to take her to the emergency room. That gash on her head looks nasty, really deep."

I snorted. Loud. "Nasty? Ha ha, I thought you liked my deep gash, Finny." My medic turned and flashed a gorgeous smile and turned a brighter shade of red than the bodily fluids on his shirt while Jocelyn kicked him in the bum.

"So, how long have you two been sleeping together?"

"We're not sleeping together," Finn lied, his voice two octaves higher than normal.

"Yes, we are, Finny. We sleeps together five times last night, and my bum is sore."

"She's definitely concussed," he muttered.

"Well, I like her concussed," said Jocelyn. "I also like how she makes you smile, even through *five* layers of shame. I haven't seen you smile like that in a long time." She then took out her phone and began pacing back and forth. "David, yes, can you bring the car around? We need to take Miss Grant to the ER."

Hanging up, she returned to Finn's side as he again picked me up like I was nothing, carried me from the room, and nobly whisked me through the office. Of course, we made it to the front door the very moment Teddy walked through it. "What the hell is going on here? Shirtless and carrying my girl across the threshold? Did I miss something?" He then saw the blood. "I did miss something. Shit, what happened?"

The story was relayed as I was carried then hauled to and inside the waiting car. The last thing I remembered was Teddy waving goodbye, Finn's eyes watching me protectively as he laid me down across the backseat, and the dull thud of the black town car door closing behind me.

"Christ. Why is it so bright in here? Where is here?"

Blinking my eyes open, pink and white peonies were the first things to greet me. Tied with a pink bow and sitting in a makeshift coffee-cup vase, they leaned sharply toward the light I was shielding my eyes from, desperate to enjoy their last days before shriveling and dying. After realizing where I was and who I was with, I wouldn't have minded shriveling and dying myself.

Shirtless and hot, Finn stood to my right. Fully dressed and lukewarm-at-best, Brett stood to my left. My future, hopefully, and my definite past stood directly opposite each other, eyes darting back and forth between us.

"You're awake," they said in unison, exchanging a stern stare.

Following an excessively loud throat clearing, Brett sat on the bed and possessively claimed my hand. "I was worried about you, Lette."

I pulled free of his grasp and shifted away. It was exorbitantly rude, but my tolerance for his shenanigans was at an all-time low. "Why are you here, Brett? How did you even know what happened?"

Smugly smirking, he replied, looking at Finn, not me. "*I'm* recorded as your next of kin, so the hospital called me when you were admitted. How are you feeling?"

"Oh, right. Umm, I'm okay. I think. Bit of a nasty headache, though."

Finn joined Brett in sitting beside me on the bed. This time, I didn't move. I may have leaned in a little and nestled into his warmth. "The doctor said you would. You gave yourself a nasty egg, a pearler of a bruise, five stitches, and a concussion. All before ten a.m. It's impressive, Red."

"Red?" Brett scoffed.

"Oh, it's just a nickname. Finn calls me Red—you know, as in Scarlett red?"

"Cute," he said flatly. Judging by the way he screwed his face up and by what he said next, Brett didn't think it was cute. He thought it was complete shit. "Well, thanks for bringing *Scarlett* in, but this is a family matter. I've got it from here. You can go back to work now."

"Actually, I feel okay," I said, grabbing Finn's hand and stroking my thumb back and forth. "I think I'm fine going back to work, too. You can go, Brett. Finn can take me back to the office in his town car."

"You...have a town car?" Brett folded his arms across his chest and nodded to Finn. "Is it as big as mine, Lette?"

For fuck's sake.

If Finn had an apple, he would be polishing it proudly on his chest. I could just picture it. "Well, it's a family thing really, but yes, I do have a car here, and I can take you back to work, Scarlett," he said, looking away from Brett and smiling at me with such warmth I began to tan. "But I'd much rather take you home and tuck you into bed."

Brett skulked around the edge of the bed, firing off a round of questions. His tone and disposition became more aggressive with each step until he was face to face with Finn and pointing his finger at his chest. "Tuck her into bed? So, you know her address? You've been there before, have you? Have you met my son?" Accusatory eyes darted in my direction. "Who the hell is this guy, Scarlett?"

"*This* guy is a colleague and close personal friend of Scarlett's who would really appreciate it if you removed your bony finger from his chest...Bretty." Finn's forearm muscles flexed like crazy as he poked Brett back. It was immature and stupid, but he looked so hot and angry. Switching from sweet and caring to macho and territorial really suited him. Brett didn't back down, though, and they stood chest to chest, just glaring. As much as I enjoyed the testosterone flying around and the image of Finn's veiny arms and puffed-out chest, their competition of sorts—although kind of flattering—was stupid, and it was up to me to end it.

"Finn is my friend, Brett. He brought me to the hospital, and no, he hasn't met Ben...yet."

"Yet? So, you plan on him meeting *our* son, then? I don't like it, Lette."

You don't like it? My temper flared. I moved to sit, but my stomach violently protested the sudden movement. I really didn't feel great. I cradled my head in my hands and then sucked in a few deep breaths. Noticing my discomfort, Finn fluffed my pillows behind me and helped me sit. Brett didn't notice. He was replying to a text he had just received. Apparently, it was more important than the dick-measuring contest. The one he would lose. "I really don't care if you like it or not. You don't have a say in my life, Brett, and I don't have a say in yours. Now, if you'll *both* excuse me, I'd like to get changed and go home."

"You're not going anywhere, Miss Grant." A nurse arrived, looked at me threateningly, and pointed at the bed. "We need at least four hours of observation after a concussion, and judging by the increased bruising, you may be here longer...bed!"

"But I have to collect my son in a few hours!"

Shoving his phone back in his pocket, Brett pounced. "I can do it. Let me get him. I am his dad, after all. I can take him back to my place or bring him back here, and we can all go home...together...as a family."

Cue savage glare to Finn.

Showing her expert bullshit detection, the nurse rolled her eyes and changed her look to one of sympathy. "I don't care who takes her home. She's just not going yet. She doesn't need to be stuck in between you two peacocks either." Continuing to stare threateningly at the boys, she took my vitals, popped my chart away, and made her exit, checking out Finn and giving me an approving nod in his direction on her way.

"Well, you heard the nurse, *Flim*. Scarlett needs to rest. Best you toddle off back to work and draw your little pictures. Or maybe there's a crocodile or alligator you can wrangle from a toilet somewhere." His phone buzzed again. "Hey, speaking of crocodiles, Lette...remember when you and Ben first arrived, and we took him to the zoo as a *family*? We should do that again sometime."

He was back on his phone as he spoke. *What a dick.* I wanted to vomit in my mouth. "Sure, Brett. Sounds great." I left Brett on his phone and turned to Finn. "Did you find out why Jocelyn came back early?"

His dimples popped, and that sexy, cheeky grin spread. "*Romantic misfortunes*, I believe she called it. I don't know all the facts, but I do know it caused quite the Austen-esque scandal in her petit village français."

"Ooh, continuer de parler."

I leaned in. My head spun, but Finn was leaning in too, so I ignored it. We sat huddled over the edge of the bed, nose to nose. "Rumor has it, a much younger but equally wealthy man was persuaded to believe himself in love and called on her late one evening to propose marriage. His family and, from what I've understood, Jocie herself, objected to the union, and she fled that very night, leaving the poor little rich boy broken-hearted, alone in a sea of Famille Perrin, Fromage and Foie gras."

"Who's Jocie, and what's Famille Perrin?" Brett barked. I'd almost forgotten he was here.

"Famille Perrin is a French wine-making family, and Jocie is Jocelyn, Finn's aunt. Finn and I are designing her house."

"Together," Finn added, slapping my thigh. "We are working very closely on it, aren't we, Red?"

"Oui. Oui, ensemble, Finn." I then burped. It was a gross, sick burp. I was not well.

"For fuck's sake." Brett had had enough. "I'm going to head out. Lette, do you want me to pick up Ben or what?"

"Oui—I mean, yes. Yes, please, Brett. That would really help— Oh God!" I slapped my hand to my mouth, but I was too late. A tsunami of puke blew all over Finn. It went on and on. I looked like that kid in *The Exorcist*. If I weren't so ill, I would have died of embarrassment. Covered in my barf, he still stood to aid me, grabbing my hair, and holding it back as the spew-nami rolled on.

Brett, on the other hand, screwed up his face and wet himself laughing. "Looks like I'll be getting Ben, then. Call me later, Lette, and let me know what you want to do with him. I'm good either way." Halfway out the door, he stopped. "Enjoy the clean-up, *Flim*."

30

Finn

BRETT WAS A DICK.
I took an instant dislike to the bloke the minute I saw his weasley face, and he backed up my inkling by laughing and walking out on Red when she was so sick. Giant dick. Though, I doubted he was endowed with one. My beliefs over his phallic-ness were not disclosed to Scarlett, of course. Like it or not, Little-Cock Brettles was the father of her child, and I wasn't going to openly disrespect him, no matter how minute I believed his dick was.

My contempt for the man was almost a blessing. It provided me with a distraction.

I hated hospitals. People died in hospitals. People I loved. Once Brett left, I occupied myself by dishing more family gossip, this time regarding Evie and the part-time job she'd found at Iris's dance school. After that, I turned to refolding the blankets on the foot of Scarlett's bed, color-coordinating the pens and charts, and fixing them again each time a doctor or nurse messed them up. My unsubtle fastidiousness was noticed.

"Finn, you've folded that blanket five times. I think it's as neat as it's going to get. Are you worried about Evie and her job?"

I shook my head, dropped the blanket, then immediately neatened it again. "No, not all. I think it's great. I'm stoked for her. And please, you shouldn't be worrying about me when you're so sick."

"I'm not sick. I'm clumsy. So, tell me what's wrong, and then I don't have to worry."

The folding resumed and may have increased in vigor. "Hospitals. I don't like them. Actively avoid them, actually." Scarlett tilted her head to the side in sympathy. That simple motion had her eyes rolling into her head, and her face turned as green as a go light. I jumped to her side, passing her a sick bag, then sitting carefully so as not to move her. "Are you okay, Red?"

"Yup. I'm good." She wasn't good. But she still gave me a cute thumbs-up. She caught her breath, her complexion returned to its sweet pink tone, and the questions resumed. "Your hospital thing. Does that have anything to do with your mum, dad, and Shelby?" I didn't respond. Instead, I began to sweep the damp, sticky curls away from her forehead. "You do know that if it is that, it's totally understandable. That kind of trauma can stay with you for a long time."

A pathetic nod is all I could manage. I was struggling to maintain my cool. Somehow, as unwell as she was with a freshly stitched head wound and an asshole ex, Scarlett was in better spirits than me. If she could put on a brave face, so could I.

"No, it's not that. Not all of it, anyway. It's the...smell mainly. It's too, um, bleachy."

Scarlett raised a brow. "I don't believe that for a second. You'd wear bleach as an aftershave if you could, but I'm not going to push you. Just know if you ever want to talk about it, I'm here."

"Noted, Red." I leaned down and kissed the top of her head.

Continued vomiting meant the doctors ordered an MRI, which saw the end of Scarlett's calm disposition. An MRI meant a contrast dye. This meant a needle, and apparently, Scarlett was terrified of needles. She lay trembling in the cold, stark-white room, and I sat beside her, holding her soft, warm hand with a machine that looked like a giant metal doughnut whirring steadily behind us.

"Promise you won't leave me, Finn? I know it's ridiculous to be scared, but..."

"I promise. I'll never leave you, Scar." That brought a cute little smile. "Besides, it's not ridiculous. Heaps of people fear needles. It gives me an excuse to hold your hand too."

I stayed with her as long as I could, bravely defying a nurse who looked like she was twelve when she tried shooing me out of the way to explain the procedure.

"Strictly speaking, it's not a needle you're getting, Scarlett, but an IV. It's basically a needle that stays in your arm, and once it's in, you'll feel nothing but a light scratch." If that was supposed to make Scarlett feel better, I'd failed. The staying in a bit seemed to ramp up the freak-out. Her grip tightened until it got to the point I was being put at risk of amputation. My fingers were purple by the time the damn thing was in, but her calmness and my circulation returned quickly once it was all done.

Disregarding my promise to stay, the nurse then successfully ordered me from the room. I valiantly fought her on it, but I couldn't fight radiation.

They say idle hands are the devil's playground, but with nothing but time on my hands, it was my brain that was getting up to mischief. *What if there's something wrong? What if it wasn't just a concussion? What if...?* And it wasn't just Scarlett on my mind. Each time I heard a call over the PA or a shuffling scrunchy walk of a doctor in scrubs, I was flooded with teenage memories of hospitals, and buzzing alarms, and crying, and death.

Fuck it, Austen. I can't believe you've put yourself in this situation again. I had done what I said I would never do. I'd let down my guard. Let someone in. Was falling in love.

I shouldn't be here. Brett was right. She should be with her family. I should slow things down. Maybe step back altogether. I'm only going to hurt her.

I was ashamed to say I was seconds from walking when Scarlett returned to her bed. "Hey, I'm back. And guess what? I finally discovered a doughnut I didn't like."

Thank fuck I didn't leave. I snorted out a laugh, and my hand returned to hers. "Hey, yourself." *I promise I won't let go again.*

Logically, I knew that was a promise I couldn't keep, but God's will, evil scheming, or convenient coincidence meant I would be able to hold it for the rest of the day, maybe the weekend too.

Scarlett's MRI came back all clear, and she was to be discharged that evening on one condition—she was not to be left alone.

It thrilled me to no end that she refused to stay at Brett's, so that left only me and one other person. Teddy. He popped into the hospital around three but was mysteriously unavailable to play nurse. Who could say if my dragging him from the room, placing him in a playful but threatening headlock, and promising he would come to suffer further physical harm if he so much as offered to watch over her had anything to do with it? All I had to do then was sort out where to take Scarlett. My house or hers? We were in the midst of deciding this when Daddy Pig's grunts alerted me to a message.

Evie

> Jocie and I are kidnapping Iris and having a girls-only mini-break in Tarrytown. See you Sunday night, Nurse Finn.

Normally, I would be super pissed. But the prospect of a whole weekend with Scarlett was too good an opportunity to miss.

> Thanks, Eves. I'm going to be staying at Scarlett's.

By six-thirty, we were in Scarlett's house, approaching her bedroom, and still hand in hand. My hospital-induced anxiety was well-hidden, if not altogether gone, and I was selfishly thrilled, maybe even giddy. Not because Scar was injured and needed me, of course. I would never want her to feel pain, but the thought of being in her house, in her room, alone... I would be lying if I said I wasn't happy.

"Here we are again," I said, pausing outside her closed bedroom door.

Scarlett smiled sheepishly, kept walking, and then came to a stop about five paces away at the end of the hall. "Thanks for staying with me, Finn. I'm not sure why Teddy couldn't, but it's kind of nice to have some more time together...even if I do look like Frankenstein's monster."

"You do not. You're cute as a button." To be honest, many people may not have agreed. But to someone as besotted as me, Scarlett was still the most beautiful woman in the world. Swollen lip, bruised, stitched forehead, and all.

The nail-biting began as she looked at the door behind her. "God, this is so embarrassing, Finn. That door you're at, the one we spent the night in...it's not my room. This is, and well...if the state of my face doesn't scare you off, *it* might."

The four-panel timber door swung open, and I stepped inside. "Wow, this is..."

"A pigsty?"

"Yes. That's the word I'm looking for." Not once in my life had I had anxiety-induced hives, but fighting the need to bleach that room was so strong I swear I could feel each individual spot breaking out.

"Thanks for being honest. It makes me almost believe what you said about my face."

"Scarlett Grant." I grabbed her hand, raised it to my lips, and kissed the soft flesh on the inside of her wrist, something I discovered she enjoyed last night. I also kept an eye on the floor because I swore I saw something move. "I am being honest about your face. So what if you have stitches and a bit of bruising? Nothing can conceal your beauty. It's irrepressible. Also, do you have a hamster?"

"I'm not sure why you're asking that. But no, I don't have a hamster." Scarlett began to kick a path to her bed and led me in. "Since you don't think I look like a freak, and my room didn't make you run, I need to remind you of something."

"A tetanus booster?" I asked in all seriousness.

"No, not a bloody tetanus booster. This is not needle-related. It's lip-related."

"Oh. I like your lips."

"Good. I like yours too. That's why I wanted to remind you that we haven't kissed almost all day."

"Trust me. I am well aware of that. I want to remedy it immediately. I really, really want to, but what about your lip?"

"Fuck my lip. After I shower and sterilize my teeth ten times, you should take off your shirt and kiss me."

Like every man should, I did what I was told.

"I hope it's okay to ask... I'm just curious. We've talked a lot about my family, but not yours. I know they passed away when you were a little kid, but would you tell me what you remember about them?"

Scarlett lay on my bare chest. An ice pack covered one temple, my fingers stroking the hair on the other. She'd managed to grab a few hours of sleep, but the painkillers administered in the hospital were wearing off, and the plain old aspirin and ibuprofen combo was doing little to ease the throbbing pain. I'd been telling her about Mum and Dad and their dancing in the kitchen while they cooked and shaming us by kissing in front of our friends. It was serving a dual purpose for me, learning more about this most magnificent creature and divulging pieces of myself. For her, it was maybe the same but also a distraction. The mood had been light. But the dark and heavy storm clouds rolled in at the mere mention of her past.

"How you and I deal with grief is like two people looking at a hologram. It's the same picture, but viewed from such different angles, the image reflected is completely different. You've said talking about your parents helps keep them alive. Maybe that's because even though they died too young, they had lived an amazing life. They'd known true love and watched their kids grow up. My mum and dad were just beginning. They never got a chance to have more kids or to see me grow. Remembering the good times is hard because I feel so guilty about everything they missed. That I missed."

"Like dancing in the kitchen and embarrassing your kids with public affection?"

"Yeah. Stuff like that," she whispered, snuggling against me. As I kissed the top of her head, my mind conjured an image. Scarlett in my arms, me wiping pasta sauce from her rosy cheek as we swayed to the music. It was so real I could hear it... *You to me are everything.* "My mum, Sofia, was Spanish. She had red curly hair like me, and I can remember her calling me *Gordita.* Chubby girl. And I was too. I had the fattest cheeks. I remember Dad, Christopher Benjamin Grant, had brown hair like Ben, and he was really tall. He used to carry me on his shoulders everywhere and pass lollies up to me. I guess that's why I was gordita. Oh, and Mum had the most amazing laugh."

"Like you," I said with another kiss.

"I hope so. That would be nice."

"Do you remember anything else? Like cousins, aunts, and uncles?"

"Nope. It was just me, Mum, and Dad. I can vaguely remember the house we lived in. The kitchen cabinets were stained glass, like my front window is now. And Mum used to sing all the time, but that's about it." She stilled, then turned her face to look up at me. "Finn...are you crying?"

"What? No. I just have a bit of a cold." I was totally crying. I moved her head with mine, then wrapped her even tighter in my arms so she couldn't look back up. "I'm so sorry for pushing you about it, Scar. I can't even imagine how hard it must have been."

"There's no need to be sorry, Finn. And you didn't push. You just want to know me better. It's nice. Other than Teddy, you're the only one who's ever asked me, which is probably a good thing, really. I hate people feeling sorry for me or giving me that *Aww, the poor little orphan* face."

"Ahh, I know that face." I shifted till she could see my face, dropped my bottom lip, and tilted my head to the side.

"That's it," she said, wiping my tears without a word. "And I get why people do it. It's bloody tough on a kid. Life was hard. But I did have fun times too. Like lots of kids that grow up in England, I had trips to Brighton and Scarborough, days at the zoo, and naughty adventures with my friends at school. It's just that those trips were with foster parents or volunteer programs, not my mum and dad. And I changed schools a lot, so the friends were few and far between."

"Lucky you found Teddy, eh? And now me too. We can make up all the lov—umm, lots of affection and friendship." *Shit, that was close.* I cleared my throat and continued. "I want you to know you can talk to me about this stuff, Scar. You never have to hide anything from me."

"Same, Austen." Scarlett pressed her lips to my chest and nuzzled back under my arm. "Since my vault is cracked, do you have anything else you want to ask me?"

"Brett." I said it so fast I almost coughed. "What's the deal there? You've said before it was a one-time thing, but was he ever in the picture? Did you love him?"

"Uh, nope. Brett was... Brett was a mistake made by a horny, lonely English girl being naughty on her first week at uni. He was already back here in the States by the time I knew I was pregnant with Ben. Even if he was still around, I don't think we would have been together. We're completely different people and not in the sexy, opposites-attract kind of way. Just the opposite-and-nothing-to-say way."

My breath caught in my throat, terrified of what I was going to hear next. "So...just to confirm, you *didn't* come to America to be with Brett?"

"God, no! Not at all. Brett and Ben being closer and having a real relationship was part of the decision, no doubt. I want Ben to have the family that I never had. That's so, so important to me. But there was no notion of romance involved. Not for me, anyway."

"Red, you know Brett sees it differently, don't you? He was marking his territory at the hospital. You should have seen him when you were asleep. He practically hovered over you with his arms spread out to stop me from getting close. I'm surprised he didn't take a piss on your leg. He kissed you too."

Scarlett's hands slapped into the mattress on either side of her thighs, and her whole body tensed. "He what?"

"He kissed you. Smack bang on your chops the minute he came in and saw me sitting by you, holding your hand. He didn't talk to me at all. Didn't even ask who I was or what happened to you. He just...hovered."

"Ughh. He's such a creep. I understand he wants us to be close and do things together for Ben, but he knows I'm not interested. Hopefully, he'll take the hint now that he knows we're together...uhhh. Um, I mean, not together, but you know."

A blush rose from the swell of her breast to her ears. I elbowed her arm playfully. "Together. Are we together, then? You and me? We're *us*?"

She chewed her lip and grimaced so cutely my heart hurt. "Would you like that? To be...*us*?"

You're going back to Sydney. You can't be the family she wants. I hoped Scarlett didn't notice the brief hesitation. "Very much so, Scarlett. I wanted to be *us* the first moment I saw you."

"Me too."

At the most inopportune time, as I leaned in to kiss my girl, I was hit with a sudden realization, a bolt from above. "Holy shit!" I jerked upright and sent Scarlett rolling from her position on my chest. Dazed and confused, she landed awkwardly, face down, on my lap.

"What? What holy shit?" came a crotch-muffled reply.

"Brett and Scarlett! RHETT AND SCARLETT!" Scarlett rolled her eyes and then buried them into her hand.

"Oh God, you just realized?"

"How did I not see it before?" Laughing so hard I almost fell from the bed, I carefully pulled the mortified Scarlett off my crotch and into my arms.

"It's not funny, Finn," she whined, "Teddy had a bloody field day when he first found out and teased me relentlessly the whole of my pregnancy. I'm incredibly traumatized." Entrapped in my embrace, her body shook as mine did until she laughed along with me.

"You are fucking Rhett and Scarlett! Shit, I wasn't really threatened by the dork before, but I bloody am now. You two seem to be fated."

"Oh, please. You want to hear something even worse. Rhett's...fuck, I mean Brett's parents...their names are...Bill and Hillary."

That was it. I fell from the bed but moved quickly to not take the very much unimpressed Miss O'Hara with me.

31

Scarlett

S MASHING MY FACE ON a thinly veiled concrete floor and the subsequent hospital/homestay really brought Finn and me together.

Amid my mountain of mess, Finn ignored the need to clean, folded his body around me like a blanket, and held me all night. Not even the sticky, late-summer sweat sheathing our bodies induced a shifting of his weight. He talked, kissed, and nursed me back to health. He was perfect. It was perfect.

Until the next morning. Morning light streaming through the crack in my blinds woke me at seven.

Finn's scent, somehow still clean, fresh, and aquatic, filled my room. Like a bloodhound, I sniffed time and time again. I breathed him in.

How does he always smell so good?

A biteable arm was slung around my waist. His head buried into my curls, and his impressive hardness pressed into my ass.

I could get used to this.

It was the first time I'd ever had a man spend the whole night. Sure, Finn was here the day before, but he'd had to leave before dawn, so it didn't count.

I celebrated the momentous occasion by squealing internally, lifting the sheet, and ogling his body, especially the hard-on. *Bloody hell, he's beautiful.* I felt like Emma Stone looking at Ryan Gosling in *Crazy Stupid Love*. He really did look photo-shopped. When he began to stir, probably because I was poking at his cock and laughing at how it twitched, I ran to the bathroom to look in the mirror. There were no Hollywood special effects there.

You bitch!

You know things are bad when you're swearing at a reflective surface. In the cold light of day, it was worse than I'd hoped. The swelling had reduced, but the bruising extended from my eye to my temple. My lip looked like one of those split screens, before and after commercials for lip fillers. It was not good.

Oh my God, he's gonna run.

Emergency makeup application started immediately. I was almost done with the concealer when a deep and scratchy morning voice called out, "Scarlett, come back here right now. I'm going to make you breakfast in bed. And an essential component of breakfast in bed is being in bed. Hop to it, Red."

A flurry of butterflies took flight in my belly. *Finn Austen is in my room and wants to make me breakfast. And I look like this. Christ on a bike. What should I do?*

"Morning. Breakfast sounds great, but I can make it. I hope you got some sleep. I didn't move too much, did I? How do you like your eggs?" This was mumbled in the small space between my ensuite and bed, all while pretending to dry my face with a huge towel.

"Don't hide from me, Scarlett. Don't you know how beautiful you are? Bruise or no bruise, you're the hottest chick I know. Let me see you."

Hummanaa, hummana, hummana.

"I don't think that's a good idea. I have excellent natural lighting here this time of day, and I don't want you to leave. I like having you here."

"I like being here, too. But if you want me to stay, I need to see your face."

"Promise you won't run screaming?"

"I definitely won't scream." I could hear the smile in his voice, and it made me all gooey like honey. I was a second away from revealing myself when I realized he'd omitted something important. Still holding the towel up with one hand, I stopped, threw the other hand onto my hip, and pointlessly gave him a stink eye. The message was received. "Oh. I won't run either. Promise."

"Alright then. But don't say I didn't warn you." I closed my eyes and dropped the towel.

"You were right." He closed his eyes and shook his head.

Oh, fuck. I knew it was too good to be true. Stupid Scarlett, stupid. "Your tits look incredible in the morning light."

"Fiiiinn," I gushed while accidentally rolling back my shoulders to stick out my boobs. "Be straight with me. Tell me what you're thinking."

Like Poseidon rising from the sea, every muscle in Finn's naked body flexed as he rose to sit on his knees. "What I'm thinking is that I want to kiss every inch of your skin and use to that delicious ass of yours as a pillow for the rest of my days."

FUCK ME. FUCK ME NOW.

Playing it cool, I responded, "Oh. Well, that's lovely. But what about my face?"

"I don't think it would be as comfy as your ass, but I'm willing to give it a shot." He lunged for my arm and guided me to him. "Your face is bruised, and your lip is swollen, and you're gorgeous. There is not one damn thing I would change about you or your fucking insane body, except make your face stop hurting. You are everything I want, Scarlett. Everything I've ever wanted. Now, I'm going to lay down and make you forget all about your face while you sit on mine."

Saturday passed in the blink of a swollen eye. A steady stream of takeout was consumed while I read Austen to Finn, and Finn read Bronte to me. We watched movies, and slept, and talked about absolute crap, and when my head finally stopped thumping, the humping began. Seven years of celibacy was smashed like Finn smashed me. Honestly, I had no idea I would, could, or should like sex that much. Or laugh so much while having it.

What I adored most—well, *almost* the most because I was really enjoying the oral stuff —was that Finn Austen was just as wonderful out of the bedroom as he was talented in it. A kindness, intelligence, and loving spirit oozed from his every pore and had me falling faster than my knickers. It was terrifying, exhilarating. Then there was how he spoke of his baby girl. The love he felt for her, what he'd done and sacrificed for her was... I didn't even know the words.

By Sunday afternoon, Iris's impending return, his need to clean the filth we lay in, and the fear of developing bed sores became too much for Finn. He climbed from the bed, dragged me with him, and began scurrying around the room like a sexy, naked Cinderella. Ignoring my objections, the bedding was stripped, clean sheets applied, clothing that had been strewn on the floor was collected, and it reached the point where I had to remove my laundry hamper from his hands forcibly. "Finn, stop. I can do it."

"But...but...Red, just let me help you tidy up before I go home. I can't leave an injured woman alone to do it all herself."

"Excuse me? After the sexual heptathlon you've put my body through, I would think you'd know I'm quite capable of more than a little physical activity."

"Yes, but I want to help you. I like doing things for you."

"I know you do, and it's very sweet, but you need to go home, shower, and greet that beautiful girl of yours. I promise I will be fine. I will miss you, though."

Finn swept me into a deep, passionate kiss. "Miss me? I should hope you will do more than miss me, Miss Grant." I was then tossed back onto the freshly made bed. "I would very much like to believe you will pine for me, so much so you are forced to take to your bed and touch yourself while you think of me."

"Oh, really? And will you do the same for me, Mr. Austen?"

"Most definitely," he growled. Crawling over my body, he buried his face into my neck and began tracing his nose up to and along my chin.

"*Finn,*" I sang, "*Iris.*"

"Shit, shit." The weight of his body collapsed atop me. *Damn, I'm going to miss that.* "You're right. I should go. I want to be home when she gets there." Halfway off the bed, Finn stopped and glanced over his shoulder. "Hey, maybe we could finally get together for that run this week? If you're feeling up for a thrashing, that is?"

"You know, I do love a good thrashing. It's a date."

A final gentle kiss was placed on my lips. It quickly deepened before we reluctantly slid apart and began to dress. With a heavy heart, I walked him to the door, not wanting the weekend to end but knowing it had to. Finn, while holding tight and kissing me goodbye, seemed equally downcast over our separation. "Christ, this was fun. You should knock yourself out more often."

"Hmmm, perhaps not, but yes, it was fun. Thank you for all the sex. I'll never forget it, Finn. Or walk straight."

"Me either, Red. It's been...well, it's been incredible." Showing how much Austen I made him sit through, he then took a step back and bowed. His blond curls fell over his eyes, he kissed my hand, and I might have fallen a teeny-tiny bit in love. I mean, really, how could I not fall for this complicated man with layers I'd only seen the very outer edges of? Who was masculine, strong, and physically intimidating, yet vulnerable and prone to tear up at the sight of his little girl in pigtails or a cute kitten video on TikTok. Who was sexy and funny, a complete dork who clearly possessed a jealous, slightly possessive nature but wore his heart on his sleeve and would give a stranger the shirt off his back.

Not that I'd thought about it much.

"Till tomorrow, Miss Grant."

"Yes, till tomorrow, Mr. Austen."

32

Finn

"DADDY! WAKE UP! I'M home!"

"Who's home? Who is that? Whose bony little body is bouncing on my belly like I'm a trampoline?"

"It's me, silly Daddy! Iwis!" I loved how she said her name. Not pronouncing her Rs bothered her greatly, but I secretly, selfishly, hoped she never grew out of it. With a quick flick of my wrists, I grabbed her ankles and flipped her upside down. Bubble-gum-scented curls tickled my nose, and I took a mental picture of an extraordinary everyday moment. "You're not my Iris. You're too grown up to be my Iris. I demand to know what you've done with her!"

"It *is* me, Daddy. I think maybe I gwew over the weekend. I did eat lots of waffles. Do waffles make you gwow?"

Spinning her the right way up, I dropped her back onto my stomach. She blew, then brushed her hair from her face and gave me a cheesy grin—the same one her mum would give me as she lay on her board, watching me and not the waves. My heart gripped, but I swallowed it down for Iris. "Well, whaddaya know, it is you! And yes, I think, for sure, waffles make you grow, especially if they are covered in strawberries and cream. Were *your* waffles covered in strawberries and cream, Iris?"

"Yup, and I loved it!"

"As much as you love me?"

Her precious little face filled with naughtiness, her eye twinkled, she screwed her lips to the side and tapped her dimpled little chin as she looked toward the ceiling, "Hmm...almost."

She then ran for it, knowing her reply would result in a fierce tickling.

Chasing her down the hall and listening to her laugh bounce off the walls, I was so genuinely bloody happy. God, I didn't even know the word. I was home with the girl who owned my heart after spending the weekend with the woman who was rapidly claiming half. As they tend to do, hard times may come. Down the track, Scarlett and I still had the whole kid-introducing thing to go through and the possible fallout at work, too. But for once, these moments of pure joy and brilliance outweighed the burden and ever-present flicker of guilt. I was okay with not knowing what was coming, with not being in control or punishing myself. I was okay with a little happiness.

Growling like a hungry ogre, I pursued Iris into the living room, where she sought refuge behind an exhausted-looking Evie's back. My aunt sat opposite her in her favorite chair, her favorite Aussie beer in one hand, the other listlessly waving.

"Welcome home, ladies. Did you walk home from Tarrytown? You two look knackered."

Jocelyn looked at me, feigned a smile, and then pointed to the collection of shopping bags sitting beside her. "May as well have. We stopped off and did a little shopping."

"A little?" I scoffed, peering inside to see if there was anything for me. "Looks like a whole lot." Iris, who was still hiding behind my sister and seemed to believe herself invisible, giggled and then clapped her hand over her mouth. I watched her from the corner of my eye as I circled the room. "Gee whiz, I sure do wish my Iris was here. I'd love to see all the things she got while shopping. Oh well, never mind."

"If I come out to show you, pwomise you won't tickle me?"

"Cross my heart." I was lying to my child and felt no remorse. No one ever tells you how much you will lie to your kids. They should teach that in birthing classes.

"Ta-da!" She leapt out from behind Evie, jumped from the couch, and hopped on one excited foot to her loot bags. Seizing the opportunity, I grabbed and tickled her till she could hardly breathe. "You promised, Daddy!"

"My fingers were crossed. Always check the fingers, Iris." I continued to tickle, only stopping when her wriggly little legs began to twist together in the universally known body language for *I'm gonna pee my pants!* With the energy only a child can possess, she bounced up onto her knees and crawled to the bags. A series of sweaters and dresses and shoes were held up for my inspection, then came a few toys—My Little Ponies, of course—and then a gift for me.

"We found these for you, Daddy. They awe just like the ones you have in your woom." Iris handed me a familiar-looking bundle wrapped in brown paper, tied with string, and a sprig of heather tucked beneath it.

"Can I open it?" I asked, genuinely curious as to what she picked for me.

"Yes, please. I hope you like it."

"Of course, I will, bubs, because you gave it to me." One tug on its frayed end had the string falling away, and with delicate precision, I opened the package. Just as I suspected, Jane Austen's *Northanger Abbey, Persuasion,* and *Emma,* and they all looked even older than those I had for Scarlett. My heart swelled. My affection for her was permeating every aspect of my life, and I was more than okay with it. "Thank you, Iris. They're perfect. Just like you."

"And they are vewy old, just like you, Daddy."

She bolted from the room before I could catch her and apply further tickle punishment. Jocelyn laughed, then cast her wicked, I'm-going-to-tease-you smile and eyes over me. "We thought you may like to add these to your collection, though I don't think it's you that you're collecting for."

"No, you're right. They're not for me. They're for...a friend."

"Perchance, would this be the same friend"—the *friend* was highlighted with air quotes—"I ferried to the hospital on Friday?"

An irrepressible smile bloomed as I shrugged. "Perhaps."

"Excellent. She's special, unique, and so very beautiful. I like her, Finn. I like her very much."

"Me too, Jocie. Me too."

Getting an overtired child to sleep is never easy. Getting an overtired Finn to sleep is even harder. And it seemed I wasn't alone in my restlessness. Just after midnight, my phone began beeping repeatedly, and I almost fell from bed in my rush to retrieve it. I knew it was her.

scar

Are you awake?

Can't sleep. Is it okay if I say I miss and want you?

No. I'm asleep right now. Hand on cock, dreaming of this sexy woman I spent the weekend with.

Also…I miss you too.

scar

Is Iris asleep? Wanna sneak over? Just for a bit?

I want to. I really do. But I don't think I should. We have work and school. Must be an adult.

Scar

But we can be quick :)

A pic of her boob accompanied this message. My favorite one too, the right one.

> Oh, I can be quick. Be there soon. Don't start without me.

My perhaps stubborn insistence on driving in New York had been a constant point of ridicule by all my acquaintances, but for some reason, this was the one time I didn't get behind the wheel. I ran. I ran so fast I could hardly breathe and fell several times, but I made it to Scarlett's street in impressive time, and I spotted her two houses away. Wearing a robe and hopefully nothing else, she paced the sidewalk, biting the nails of one hand, and running the other through her twisted curls.

"Red," I called her name, and she looked up, her smile lighting the dark New York night. She dropped her hands to her sides and ran into my arms, jumping when she reached me and wrapping her legs around my waist. My shirt lifted as she ground against me, and I could immediately feel the slick, wet heat of her pussy.

"Finn. What, now you decide not to drive? What took you so long?"

"I ask myself that every damn day, Red." I stumbled toward her house, crashing loudly into two trash cans waiting for collection on the curb then stepping on one of her neighbor's cats. Scarlett's reprimand quickly silenced its ear-piercing cry. "Oh, fuck off, Jerry."

Taking two steps at a time, I raced up her stoop, burst through her unlocked door and kicked it shut behind me. "I want to kiss every inch of you, Red, and I want to take all night to do it."

"Finn, a quickie, remember?"

"Shit, right, right. Let's just fuck, then." I threw her down and would like to say she bounced onto the plush bed, but no. We'd only made it halfway up her staircase, and it was more of a crash and thud than a bounce. She laughed beneath me as

I slipped her robe off her shoulders and discovered that frilly nightie she wore in Tarrytown. The one that barely covered her ass and perfectly highlighted the cherry plumpness of her nipples. I mouthed them through the silk, and as she moaned, I slipped my hand between her legs and trailed my fingers through her wetness. "I'm so happy to see this silly little thing again. God, how I have dreamed of fucking you in this."

"Me too. I need it now!"

The timber creaked and groaned beneath us as I lowered my body over hers and captured her mouth. Her lips parted instantly, and she welcomed my tongue with a flick of her own before groaning and biting my lip. A sharp sting and metallic taste had me rearing back and sucking my bloodied bottom lip between my teeth. "Oh, poor baby," she crooned, "let me kiss it better."

"Lucky for you, I like a bit of pain, Red." I brought my hand down on her thigh with a stinging slap. "Giving *and* receiving." I kissed her deeply, punishing her mouth with aggressive, possessive strokes before pulling away. "I'm going to fuck you now," I said, fumbling in my pocket for the condom and placing it on the step beside us. "And you're going to lay back and take it like a good girl. Okay, Scarlett?"

"Yes, Daddy."

Before I could respond as I wanted or died due to lack of blood to the brain, she grabbed the hem of my shirt. Sighing as she lifted it over my head, she then dragged her nails down my chest and traced the lines of my abs. "I know I say this a lot, but I will never get over how hot you are, Finn." Her fingers continued their noble trek south, following the light dusting of hair that disappeared beneath my jeans. Relief washed over me as she palmed my cock, and the holy sound of my zipper sliding down reached my ears. Her soft hands wrapped around my length, and with her eyes on mine, Scarlett grabbed the foil packet, opened it between her teeth, and then carefully rolled it down me. "I must say, you really do have the most beautiful long, thick cock."

"Why, thank you. May I use it to plunder you?"

"Yes. Yes, you may."

I gave her a nod and my cheekiest smile, then gripped her ankles, slid her ass lower and spread her open. After one last kiss, I took a deep breath and lined up at her entrance. The sound the raw slap our bodies made as I drove into her warmth pierced my soul.

"You're so damn wet. So wet and sweet and tight. If I weren't buried inside you right now, I'd lick you clean." She was shaking, her pussy clenching around me. "Would you like that, Scarlett? Would you like me to eat you out?"

"Yes. I would. But I need you to fuck me hard first."

Another brutal thrust slid her body farther up the stairs. I chased her, gripping the balustrade beside me for extra purchase. The thud of my knuckles against the solid wood made Scarlett flinch, so I caught her eyes, gave her a kiss for reassurance, then slipped my other hand to the small of her back.

Wedged between my body and my palm, she was fully mine at that moment, and I moved and molded her to suit. Lifting her hips in sync with my thrusts. Licking and sucking her nipples. Kissing the swell of her stomach. Her skin smelled amazing, like a springtime garden blooming just for me, and she was my rose. My sweet pea. My cherry blossom.

Something shifted inside me as I breathed her in. Something unlocked. She sensed it too, and we calmed, our kissing slowing but intensifying. All thoughts of that quickie vanished as we became lost in each other's eyes. It was like the initial fury had passed, and we found a deeper, more intimate connection. I still fucked her hard like she'd asked, but slower, my rhythm falling in line with the ticking of the clock in the hall.

This is making love. I'm in love.

I sealed my mouth over hers and captured her cries. I swallowed them down along with the three words I wasn't yet ready to say. I felt them flow through me, each one reverberating through every cell in my body. Our lips stayed connected, and as I began to throb inside her, the urgency returned. I released the balustrade, dug my fingers into the fat of her hips and gave her everything I had, driving her hard into the stairs as I began to lose control.

"Yes, Yes. Finn. I... I... " She came first, her legs trembling, her eyes closing as she called my name and coated my cock in her sweet release.

God she's beautiful.

"I love...I love watching your sweet face come, baby." Seconds later, I was coming inside her with such force I feared my heart would never recover.

Still deep inside her and never wanting to leave, I laid my head between her breasts and listened to the pounding of her heart beneath me. We were still. Our rapidly rising and falling chests were the only movement between us. When capable of any logical thought—apart from how soon I could do it all again—I looked up at her face. She was aglow, her lips red and swollen, her cheeks flushed, trailed with tears.

"Red, why are you crying? Was I too rough? My God, did I hurt you? Is it your back from the stairs?"

"No, no, you didn't hurt me. It's just. Finn, I had no idea it could be like this, that I could feel so good and bad and naughty and right all within the same heartbeat. You make me feel everything. I...just—"

"I know." I swallowed her words with a kiss. I didn't need to hear what I was feeling, breathing, or living.

After carrying Scarlett to bed, I pressed a kiss to her forehead, carefully avoiding the still tender bruise. "I don't want to leave, and I don't want to ask this and sound like a prick, but I have to. What should we do—"

"What are we going to do about work? Hmm, I was about to ask you too."

"I can't believe you, Scarlett. What a prick of a thing to ask."

"FINNNN!" Her palm slapped against my collarbone, and I was promptly pushed from the bed. "Stop. Tell me. Are we out and proud, or chilling on the down low?"

"Well, first, I have to say how cute your accent is when you say down low, and second, would I be an ass if I said option two?"

"Not at all. I think it's a wise move, especially with us working one on one."

Still on the floor, I nodded in agreement. "So, it keeps our hands to ourselves at the office, and, as fun as they are, maybe this should be the last midnight visit for a while. After all, we are mature professionals with kids and shit. You must control yourself and keep those sticky, wandering paws off me, Red. In the office and at home."

Ignoring these rules completely, we had sex twice at work the next day, and not twenty-four hours after our little chat, at the stroke of twelve, my phone buzzed against my shoulder as I lay thinking of her.

Scar

> I can't sleep. Are you awake?

>> I think I'm going to be awake for the rest of my life after last night. What are you wearing? Doing? Touching?

Scar

> Wearing nothing. Doing nothing. Wrapping my hands around the pineapple I got from the market today. I'm just about to split it open. Want some?

>> Knew you couldn't resist me. Be there in five.

She opened the door wearing a black robe over her naked shoulders, the still unsliced pineapple covering her questionable modesty.

"Hello, darling. Hungry? I am." Her voice was low, husky, and different. It was also hot. Very hot.

Slightly taken aback but fully into it, I was slow to move. Scarlett wasn't. Catching me by surprise, she dropped the pineapple and grabbed me by the scruff of my shirt. The thing must have split open as it was all I could smell as she dragged me inside and pressed me against the wall. "Jeez. Have you been lifting weights or something?" I teased.

"No. I just know what I want. And right now, that is to slip my face between your massive thighs."

"Oh, my God. Red, what the fuck are you doing?"

Scarlett said nothing, just winked and raised my finger to her lips, "Shhhh." I'd never seen a pair of sweats pulled down so seductively. I didn't know it was possible, but it was apparently, and by the time they were around my ankles, my cock was ready to go, in her hands, and being licked by her soft tongue.

Biting my bottom lip between my teeth, I swept her hair away from her face so that I could enjoy the view. And what a view it was. Her plump, red lips pressed kisses down my length and back again, then when she reached the tip, already wet with pre-cum, she wiped it clean with her little finger and then sucked it right off. "Mm, tasty."

"You like?"

"Yes, baby. I love it. Like I knew I would."

"Fuck, Red. Are you trying to kill me?" With an evil smile, she shrugged, wrapped her lips around my tip, and then gently sucked. "Holy mother of fuck." My palms were plastered against the wall, my flesh burning, my nails catching as they struggled to find purchase on the rough, exposed brick. I looked down just as she pulled away and almost came on the spot. The sound of her wet slips sliding off my flesh was unlike anything I'd ever heard. She licked her lips and then repeated the process again. And again. Taking me all the way in, then pulling back just as my knees began to buckle. She was teasing me. It was torture. The kind I wanted to live through every day for the rest of my life. But I also needed it to end. I released my futile grip of the bricks, threw my hands into her hair, and scratched my nails against her scalp. "Do it. Please, Red. Take me in. Let me fuck that smile right off that pretty little mouth." She moaned and did as she was told. She took me in deep...then deeper...then deeper again.

It. Was. Incredible. The pressure, her touch, the smoothness of her tongue, everything. She once shared her disbelief that sex could ever feel so good. That what it was between us could be real, and I'd known exactly what she meant. But watching her bobbing up and down and listening to her grunting, gagging, and licking took my understanding to a whole new level.

I never wanted this to end, but I was so damn close already. Desperate to hold on, I threw my head back, thumping it against the wall and staring up at the stark-white ceiling. I focused on the patterns carved into the ceiling. I listened to the persistent whining of a car alarm on the street and the buzz of my Apple watch congratulating me on making my step count. Anything I could just to hold on.

I allowed my mind to wander, but that was equally dangerous. Each time I let it roam, an image of the very thing I was trying to be distracted from would flash before my eyes. Then I had a thought. *Holy shit!* "Look at me, Red." I twisted my hands through her hair and tilted her head back slightly till I could see her eyes. "Have you done this before?"

"Never," she purred, still sliding up and down me, never stopping, never losing speed.

Half of me felt bad. She was so innocent. So pure. The other half fucking loved it and thrust even harder. "Do you like choking on my cock, Scarlett? You like being a bad girl?"

Nodding and giggling, she then lightly bit down, and that was it. I was done. "Shit, I'm gonna come, Red."

She laughed and pulled off with a pop. "I may not have done this before, but I think that's kinda the point." With a hum of pleasure that sunk into my bones, she took me back in and three long, slow, tickling-the-back-of-her-throat bobs later, my body seized. That rush, that feeling like no other overcame me. I spilled inside her mouth, my hips continuing to thrust until she'd swallowed every drop I gave her.

Utterly boneless, I slid down the wall, my shirt catching on the rugged finish and tearing in the process. Scarlett, her face flushed and glowing, joined me, falling to her side between me and her tropical treat. I reached for the nearest chunk that had made no contact with the floor, took it between my trembling fingers, then used it to trace her lips. "Lie down, Red. I think it's my turn to dish out dessert."

33

Finn

I RIS WOKE UP IN a mood the next morning. One that had me dreading the teenage years to come even more than I already was. Her initial buzz to start grade one had well and truly worn off after the first week, and it took Evie, me, and the promise of a Jocelyn-funded gourmet breakfast to subdue the teary-eyed demon that had possessed her. It was almost enough to ruin my lingering high from Scarlett's surprise blowie. But not quite.

Once exorcised by waffle syrup, we again piled onto the sidewalk and headed to school. For most of the way, I walked with my hands on Iris's shoulders, steering her through the masses as she played Candy Crush on my phone. I'd just apologized to yet another victim of her feet when she looked up at me, then held the phone into my face. "What's that? Daddy, what is this in your phone? It kind of looks like a boobie."

"Shit!" All too late, I made a dive for the phone, clutching and snatching it from her tiny hands. But the damage was done. Tutting smugly, Evie dropped her sunglasses to her nose to cast the evil eye at me while Jocelyn's legs buckled beneath her. I remained silent, looking at the store windows we passed like nothing happened.

"Is it a boobie, Daddy?"

"Ahhh, yes, yeah. I think, yeah. That looks like a boobie. Someone sent it to me last night by mistake. Wrong number, I think."

"Why would someone send a picture of a boobie on their phone?" *Pray she still wonders this in ten years.*

"Yes, why, Finn? Why would someone send a picture of a boobie?" *Thank you, Jocelyn.*

"Well, uh, well...not having boobies myself, I'm not one to answer that question. Evie, why would you send someone a picture of your boobie?" If looks could kill, I'd be sixty-five feet under.

"What? Me? God, I don't know. It's not my bloody boob. Jeez, I, uhh... I imagine it was supposed to be sent to a doctor...to check if it's healed after surgery. Yeah, surgery."

Evie's gasping for air and Iris's determined questioning of what type of doctor would receive such a picture were suddenly drowned out by the thumping of my heart. Fresh as the breeze that tussled her curls, I spotted Scarlett on her walk to work.

"Oh, there's Scarlett. Gotta go, bye now, love ya!" I gave Iris a quick kiss on the head and was off before anyone could argue. "Red! Wait up," I called, weaving through people to catch her.

"Finn? What are you doing here?"

"I might ask you the same. You're not following me, are you, Red?"

"Pfft. You wish. Besides, you walked up behind me. I think an essential part of following someone is being behind them.

"Good point." I nodded and tapped my temple. "That's why you're the brains behind Team Finnlett." I smiled into a kiss and took her hand. "Now stop proving me wrong and being all cute, or you'll make me late for work."

Scarlett swung my hand through the air like she had no cares in the world as she almost skipped down the sidewalk. She was so damn cute. Unfortunately, her carefree demeanor didn't last long. "Iris saw my boob?"

"Yep, Evie and Jocie did too. It is a very nice boob, Red. You've got nothing to worry about."

"That may well be the case, but how would you like me to show everyone a dick pic?"

"Scarlett. I've never sent you a dick pic. Dick pics are gross."

"They are, but that's not the point. The thing is, it's different for men. You can flash your..." We drew closer to our building, her anti-cock-shot rant continued, and I stole tiny glances at her lips every two or three steps and tried to pay attention. It was really hard—for once, not my cock. It wasn't far from it, though. But it was the prospect of letting her hand go and not touching her the way I wanted when I wanted. The temptation to take what I could while I could proved too strong. As we passed beneath the neon sign from the 24-hour drugstore next door, a deep, hungry growl rumbled from my chest, and I hooked my arm around her waist and dragged her into the alley.

Wedging her between my body and the brick wall, an arm on either side of her face, I bent down and roughly captured her lips. "Sorry to interrupt." I wasn't the slightest bit sorry. "I just needed this before we go in," I said when I came up for air.

"Gahh, you're so polite. I love that about you. But there's no need to apologize. Feel free to interrupt me with your hot tongue at any time." Scarlett then wrapped her arms around my neck and pulled me back onto her lips.

Our all-too-hot, all-too-short make-out was interrupted by a family of rats deciding my Converse was an ideal breakfast. "The vermin may be a sign that I must let you go," Scarlett said, not fazed in the slightest as she kicked them away, "but we could bail on work. Perhaps, I could pick up some wine and some handcuffs, then drag you back to my place and do some nasty, possibly illegal things to your body. Ooh, that makes me think of all the hiding spots I could drag you into in the office."

"I have a list, you know," I said, shaking the last stubborn rodent from my foot. "It's been a little game of mine for a while, imagining all the dark and private places I would ravage you."

"You do enjoy a good exploration of my dark and private places."

"I do. I really, really do. Kiss me again, Red."

"Okay!"

After that one last kiss, I was painfully hard, thinking things I shouldn't and still crushing Scarlett against the wall. Glancing to our building, back to Scarlett, and then grimacing, I whined like a brat. "I don't wanna go to work. Tell me to go to work, Red."

She ducked under my arm and, facing me, walked back out onto the busy sidewalk. "Go to work, Finn."

We walked those final few paces toward our door, not looking at each other, not holding hands, not touching at all. Those paces sucked. Jason Wright approaching, looking mighty pissed for a man with a steaming coffee and jelly doughnut, didn't make them any better. With a knotted brow, he glanced at his watch, then back to us.

"You two decided to join us, did you?" he grumped. "Nice. Maybe you could see your way into going inside and doing some work too?" Barging through the door I held open, he brushed past us, staring disapprovingly over his shoulder as he stuffed his face and then disappeared.

I waved Scarlett through the door and gave her a quick pat on the bum for good measure. "He's right. We better head upstairs. I need to find that list."

Scarlett should have known I would *never* joke about a list.

Twenty minutes later, proud as punch and grinning like a fool, I wandered into Team Finnlett's HQ and dropped it like it was hot—a list of sins and debauchery, not my ass.

"Wow. This is thorough, more fun, and way less Judgy Judgerton than my ideologies. Neater too. I should have known even your fantasy make-out sessions were meticulously planned and located in exceptionally clean but snug spaces."

Leaning in close, I ran my thumb down her neck. "You know I love a good, snug space, Red."

All work was suspended at that point, and we set to the task of trying out as many spots as we could as quickly and inconspicuously as we could. The one Teddy finally busted in on us—thank the Lord it was him—was beneath the staircase that led to the outdoor garden. In theory, it was a perfect spot, but Scarlett's bright-pink skirt and yellow shirt meant someone on Mars could have spotted her between the open metal grating.

"If you two wanna keep this on the down low, you'll have to stop dressing like the pride flag, Scarlett. You gotta camouflage that shit up!"

"He's right, isn't he?" she asked as she buttoned her shirt.

"Little bit, yeah."

We did much better the next day. Looking dark and sexy and kind of like she was off to a hot-girl funeral, Scarlett dragged me into the server closet, and no one noticed. When I swept her into the emergency stairwell, let her grope me like a ninth grader, and got us locked out, only Teddy, who I called to let us back in, knew. It especially worked the next day when I pressed her up against me in the copy room and photocopied the world's best boobs.

This pattern continued for possibly the best month of my life. I didn't once think of my three-year plan or going home, and even considered what the USA forever future may look like. The guilt and grief I carried constantly were lifted from my shoulders with every kiss, and the weeks flew by in a blur of inside jokes, shared lunches, and sneaky sleepovers, where, to put it plainly, we shagged so hard that I could barely walk most days. Scarlett felt much the same, but obviously, my pain was worse as a male. Treatment for repetitive strain injuries of the pelvis may have been Googled.

As thrilling, and fun, and sexy as it all was, our dirty little secret was perhaps a secret no more.

34

Scarlett

S WEATER WEATHER HAD ARRIVED, and Jason and his blue cashmere were onto us.

Honestly, it wasn't hard to see why. Finn and I were as discreet as Wednesday Addams at a Spice Girls concert. Like a hawk hunting its prey, he'd stalked us for a good portion of his morning, floating in the wasteland between his office and our HQ, just waiting for us to slip up so he could capture us in his hawky talons and feast on our carcass. On each fly-through, he would stop, pop his head in the door, maybe raise his brows, look at Finn, look at me, nod, and motion between us like he could entice us into a confession. A thorough rub of his chin would follow his failure, and then he'd just grunt and walk away. Even when in his office, his predatory stare rarely left us, especially when Victoria joined in.

These looky-loos started the day before after he'd come alarmingly close to catching Finn and me going at it like rabbits on the fire escape. We managed to pull apart before he saw anything...or so we thought. Then, this morning, Team Finnlett was kicked out of our beloved conference room A. Apparently, it was needed for an upcoming pitch worth more money, but the timing was highly suspicious, and my fear was unwarranted and kind of stupid. I knew he and Victoria were in a relationship, and he knew I knew. Jan had given us the thumbs-up on interoffice dating. The woman had practically smooshed our faces together and forced us to kiss. But despite all this, my anxiety, my need to please and do the right thing, raged.

Between eyeballing Jason and Victoria and trying to do any-thing remotely useful, I also kept my eyes on Finn—a tough job, but somebody had to do it. He was so sweet. He'd been showing one of the new interns, Ronald, how to use our design system with such patience and kindness I wanted to push Ronnie out of the way and hump his leg. Even while helping the kid, I could see Finn was just as stressed about Jason busting us as I was. He'd given me the she's-all-good-mate thumbs-up twice but countered that by tapping his fingers against his thigh and extra heavy-duty desk arranging. *Classic stressed Finn.* We needed a distraction, though probably not the one that kept popping into my mind. No, wandering over to my man's desk, straddling his luscious thighs, and enjoying the ride would not be helpful to our predicament.

As time ticked away, my anxiety and lust hit their peaks. Honestly, I felt as though I'd been struck down with some stress- and lust-induced stupidity. Just that morning, I spilled my coffee twice. I called Arthur, the IT guy, Gordon three times, and much to the delight of Gareth the Creep, I had strutted into the men's restroom instead of the ladies'. As I shielded my eyes and ran, Gareth's enthusiastic invitation to stay and give him a hand was not accepted.

Around eleven, while hunched over my desk, pretending to work but really practicing my Scarlett Austen signature, some-thing struck me in the back of the head.

"Fuck it, Teddy!" It lodged in my nest of curls, and my im-mediate suspicion was that my bestie was throwing spitballs at me again. But when I reached into my messy bun, it was not a disgustingly moist wad of paper but a paper plane with the words 'OPEN ME' written on its wings.

Finn's handwriting!

Inside the meticulously folded paper was a handwritten note and a sweet caricature of me. *Of course, he can draw too.*

Meet me under the cherry tree at one. Bring your sexy ass, a coat in case it's cold, and your appetite.

At the stroke of twelve, Cinderella-style panicking over Ja-son's lingering presence struck. It had also been a whole thirty minutes since I had looked at Finn, so I needed a hit *and* some reassurance. With all my usual elegance and grace, I spun my chair to go and check and came face to face with his crotch.

"We're still on for lunch, right?" he deadpanned, smiling down at me, pursing his lips, and not moving an inch.

I replied, as emotionlessly as possible, "Yes...yes, we are," while blinking uncontrollably, looking at my non-existent watch, my feet, anywhere other than straight ahead. "Do you need me to help you with something?"

"What? Right now?" he whispered, covering his man bits with his hands and bending down to face level. "Scarlett, not here."

Half-wishing I could, I looked up to his eyes, full of endearing cheekiness and mischief, and slapped him on the leg. "For lunch. Do you need me to help you with anything for lunch?"

"Oh, lunch. No, everything is taken care of. As the note said, all you need to bring is your ass, coat, and appetite." With a precious wink, he wandered back to his desk, spinning in his chair with a mile-wide grin. It was then I realized that, at some point during our highly inappropriate interaction, Jason had escaped his enclave and was nowhere to be seen.

"Damn it!" I slapped my hands on my desk and turned to Finn, who shrugged, shook his head, and walked back toward me.

"I think he knows, Finn."

My nervousness all but disappeared when Finn attempted to slide an errant curl back inside my messy do. Melting into a puddle of lust, I sat still as he made a few unsuccessful attempts before giving up and, instead, tucked it behind my ear with a tickle. His face was right in front of mine, so close I could hear each shaken inhale and exhale and wouldn't need to shift an inch if I kissed him as I wanted. His warm breath caressed my cheek, his lips dangerously ghosting mine, which seemed to be all he could look at. "I think he does too, but I don't think I care. I don't want to hide how I feel anymore." Finn placed a sloppy wet kiss I could hear on my nose, then nodded toward the garden. "See you at lunch, Red."

Twelve-fifteen...twelve-seventeen...twelve-eighteen and twelve seconds.

Never in the history of clocks had staring at one made time go faster. In fact, they said it usually had the opposite effect—a watched pot never boils and all that. Today was *no e*xception.

By the time one p.m. rolled around, I'd handed my anxiety over Jason or anyone knowing about us over to the gods—or attempted to, at least. The problem was that a small but loud voice of doubt had settled on my shoulder. And despite all the evidence pointing to the contrary, the fear of doing the wrong thing, of judgment, lingered. I'm not sure why I couldn't shift it. Thankfully, my desire to secure Finn's happiness, and the gratifying prospect of healing his mighty splintered heart, was more vocal than my own fears.

Carrying a large wicker picnic basket in one hand, a tartan blanket under his arm, and a grin I would remember forever on his face, my date had already ventured outside. He returned a few moments later, collecting another box from the kitchen before disappearing again.

With my curiosity piqued, I raced through the office, almost knocking poor Ronnie off his feet as I careened through the kitchen, burst through the door onto the landing, and looked down over the garden.

Fall was rapidly approaching, so my tree stood barren and bare in the center of the yard, but it had never looked so pretty. Adorned with fairy lights, a picnic blanket laid at the roots. Upon that sat a terrified looking but undeniably beautiful Finn. Next to him was the empty basket, two grape juice boxes, and what looked like an entire patisserie. "Hope you're hungry, Red. Come sit," he called.

Finn watched my wobbly descent with his lips between his teeth and his body shaking as he held in his laughter. "Don't fall, Scarlett," I mumbled, "Please don't fall in front of the pretty man." My choice of footwear, though stylish, wasn't the only fashion issue I faced. The length of my skirt was a major regret as

I approached and knelt by Finn's side. Luckily, the abnormally loud thud of my heart had me quickly forgetting my flashing concerns.

My ass hit the blanket, and Finn's hand cradled my chin, caressing my cheek with his thumb as he chastely pressed a kiss to the edge of my lips. "You're so beautiful, Scarlett."

Though only twenty-four, I'd already resigned myself to never finding love. It was inconceivable that I could be loved when I could barely tolerate myself. That someone could take the things I vehemently tried to disguise—the hated, broken, ugly fragments of a child that had been so alone and lost—and see something they found beautiful. Someone they didn't want to run from. That they wanted to stay with. Build a family with. To me, that was true love, and at that moment, I was close to finding it.

My gracious host gave a detailed description and sample bite of each pastry before lying on his back and sighing. "I know we're only out the back of work, but this is nice. I like this. This is good." He punctuated each statement with a nod of his head and began tapping the ground beside him.

"Are you nervous, Finn? "

"In general, or right this second?"

"Right this second."

"Oh. A little, I guess. Can you tell?"

"A little." I nodded to his still-tapping fingers. "You tap your fingers like that when you are. Are you nervous that people can see us?"

Taking a bite of his smoked salmon croissant, Finn chewed thoughtfully while watching me from the corner of his eye. Not nerve-racking at all.

"No. I'm not worried about that. I was just thinking about how you're the most incredible woman I've ever met. You're so damn sexy, and you don't even know it, which somehow makes you even sexier. And I don't know if you've noticed, but the more time I spend with you, the more I want you. I think about you all the time, and well..." He edged closer. "I would very much like to tell you—" *Oh my God, Oh my God. He's going to say he loves me!* "My best friend Nate is coming for Christmas, and I wanted to know if you would like to meet him?"

Okay, not quite the same, but still good.

Christmas? A shimmering, tinsley bubble of joy appeared in my belly and inflated rapidly as my mind skated away with itself. Finn was thinking of us being together at Christmas. CHRISTMAS. That was over two months away.

Do not do a happy dance.

I was included in his future. This was big. Not only because he wanted me to meet his bestie and would still be mine in two months' time, but because I FREAKING LOVED CHRIST-MAS! Growing up, I hated it. I was always lonely and sad. But since Teddy, Ben, and I formed our own little family, I'd worked hard to make it special, to build new and happy memories. Now I had more to look forward to. Shopping for gifts, baking, decorating, wrapping myself in a red bow, and lying naked in Finn's bed.

My answer came in the form of my arms around his neck, pulling him down, and sealing my lips over his. As I moaned yes into his mouth, my worries melted away. The man had the lips of a god. Every kiss was like the first. My body came to life. Reborn again and again. No man had ever made me feel like he did, had kissed me the way he did, felt the way he did. His lips were soft as a cloud, and the smell of his skin set a fire within my soul. His tongue was smooth and wet and caressed the edges of my bottom lip like it was the sweetest candy on earth. I parted my lips, welcoming that irresistible tongue inside, and gently massaged it with my own firm, possessive strokes.

"God, I wish I could get you naked right now," he breathed into my neck, pressing his firm body harder and harder into me. We chuckled as my head clunked against the hard ground, but neither removed our lips from the other.

"Tell me, nephew. Is Scarlett part of the menu, or do you always eat her face like that?"

"Poop! Jocelyn!"

Being familiar with the wit of his aunt, Finn took her jab in stride. I did not. I snorted, blushed, and then slipped behind his back. "Don't let me stop you, Scarlett. I only wanted to talk to you about the design, but I can come back later. It's much more fun to kiss each other than to talk to an old lady like me. Enjoy your time together."

"Oh, we will, Jocie. We will." Finn smirked.

Laughing and puffing her way up the stairs, I took a mental note not to add too many to her house and resumed kissing her nephew. When she finally made it to the top deck, she took a few deep and heavy breaths, then leaned over the railing and yelled down to us, "Don't do anything I wouldn't do, Finny!"

After eating more and making out for a good twenty minutes—most of which was watched through the window by popcorn-eating Gareth the Creep—we packed up and headed inside.

"Austen. Grant. My office. Now."

"Shit! Jason!" My stomach dropped, but Finn grabbed my hand and spun me to face him before I could freak out.

"No matter what happens, Scarlett. I'm not letting you go. I want everyone to know. I lo—"

"Austen, Grant, I said now!"

"For fuck's sake! Shut up! Shut up!" The words flew out before I could slap my own hand over my mouth to stop them. Finn and others around us erupted into laughter, including Teddy, who maturely added pointing. Jason didn't seem to find it so funny.

35

Scarlett

"S HE WANTS MY DESIGN. I got the house?" Pinching his nose between his thumb and forefinger and huffing so loudly his hair shook, Jason nodded and then repeated himself slowly.

"Yes, Grant. For the third time, yes. Jocelyn had a change of heart and decided to go with your original concept."

Logically, I understood this. Yet somehow, it was still beyond my comprehension. "So, let me get this straight. I haven't blown my career by dry-humping Finn in the garden?" Jason's slow nodding continued, as did my verbal diarrhea. "You don't give a crap about Finn and me? You just wanted to tell us about the house?"

"Yes. Scarlett."

"But, Jason, what was with all the staring and hovering?"

"Victoria and I had a bet over how long it would be before you two banged—"

"And also, Finn and I have worked really hard on this for weeks. Jocelyn said she was happy. What exactly changed her heart?"

"Okay, we're moving on already?" Jason seemed a touch exasperated, threw his hands in the air, and stalked back to his desk. "Well, it seems that after spending some time at her land, she reviewed all three designs, and yours just felt right. Is there more to it than that? Perhaps. Frankly, as long as we have her business, I don't care. Finn, you can still act as a consultant and help out when needed, but otherwise, she's all yours, Grant.

Congratulations." On an elongated sigh, he began shuffling papers and gave us the why-are-you-still-here look.

"But—"

Finn slapped his hand over my mouth and whispered, "You need to stop talking now," as he slowly backed us toward the exit. The second the door closed behind us, I broke free of his grip and spun to face him.

"I'm sorry. Maybe I can talk to Jocelyn and—"

"No. No, you will do no such thing, and you will not be sorry, Red. This is exactly how it should be. You're brilliant and deserving. No one else could do anything close to what you can, and everyone knows it."

"I dunno, babe. It doesn't feel right. I loved working with you."

"Babe?" He smiled, pulled me closer, and tugged on a curl. "Did you just call me babe?"

Embarrassed as all fuck, I snorted and punched him in the arm. It was a mistake, not only because of the immaturity, but because the man's arms were so freaking bulky it hurt like hell. "Shut up and stop changing the subject."

"Ahh, okay, bully. I'm not sure I want to since you're bashing me, but Jason said I'm to act as a consultant." He looked around and dragged me into an empty meeting room—the only one without walls of glass—and locked the door behind us. "You do know what this means, don't you? You're kind of my boss. I like it, Red. I like it a lot." He thrust his hips into me, and yes, I could feel that he really did like it.

"Finn, you can't be walking around here with that."

"So, help me get rid of it, then, boss." He threw me onto the table. My legs were roughly kneed apart, and my underwear ripped. Ripped! It was so fucking hot.

"Fuck, Finn. We are going to get caught. We can't keep doing this."

"Nah, it'll be alright. I'll be real quick." Houdini the Second produced a condom from nowhere and unzipped his fly, but with the wrapper in his mouth about to be torn, there was a knock on the door. We both froze—kind of. Finn kept thrusting into me but at a reduced rate.

"Is everything alright in there?" Fucking Gareth the Creep. *Had to be him.*

Finn was having trouble maintaining his composure and had a rubber in his mouth, so I spoke for us. "Yes, it's fine, Gareth, thank you. I'm just..."—cue fake tears—"on an...uhh...emotional phone call. I'll try to keep it down."

"Are you sure you don't need a hand?" he sleazed.

"Pfft, he wishes," scoffed Finn, spitting the still sealed condom from his mouth. Fighting the urge to laugh was as hard as the erection trying to pummel my core, but I had to try.

"Shh, he'll hear you, Finn." I took my turn to cover his mouth, then replied, "Yes, all good. Thank you, Gareth."

The impeccably timed fool may have managed three steps down the hall before Finn's lips were on me again. I was pressed back against the table. The front of my dress was pulled down, and the same hunger he exhibited when ravaging my neck was devoted to my breasts. But just as my body began to melt, the footsteps returned, and I swear I heard a dull thud as he leaned against the door.

"Finn, as your boss—"

"Gahh, God help me, that's hot. Say it again."

"No. Well, okay. Finn, as your boss, your superior, I demand that you stop."

He pulled his head from my boobs and looked at me hazily. "Stop?! What? Why?"

"Gareth," I whispered, pointing to the door. "He's right there. Can't you hear him?"

"Nope, potato valley is really soundproof." I gave him a slap and shushed him again. Further shuffling and a rattle of the door handle had him zipping up in seconds. "Yeah, we gotta go. Mark this as *to be continued at home*, boss. Hey, you don't think he's got a camera in here, do you? I would have thrown in some fancier moves had I known."

In NYC, a week is a long time where a whole lot can happen. Especially when you're a single parent whose child is spending an extra-long week with their other parent. Because of my hospital visit, Ben had been gone for four days already and still had a few to go. Keeping busy at work had always gotten me through the Ben-free days, but the evenings were always long and lonely. Life was changing, though. The nights remained long...but not so lonely. Instead, they were filled with blond hair, blue eyes, crumpled sheets, and laughter.

Oh, and sex. Really, really, really incredible sex.

I was a greedy, greedy Finn-whore, desperate for more, shaking for his touch, constantly seeking out my next pounding. But it wasn't just the shagging. An element of loved-up domestic bliss crept into my world.

Each evening, once Iris was settled for the night, Finn would race to my place for a late dinner. Just as his parents had done, we'd cook side by side, he'd take my hand and dance me around the kitchen, and kiss me across the table when we finally sat to eat. While he did the dishes, I made our lunches. Then, we'd bundle ourselves on the couch or in bed, watch Netflix, drink wine, and fold laundry. We went for runs in the dark and made love as the sun rose. Even at work, the freedom of not hiding our affection, of bookending our days with a kiss, holding hands over lunch, and receiving high-fives from HR Jan when she caught us kissing in the hall became the norm. Never had I known such contentment. Such balance.

Unfortunately, it wasn't the same for Teddy, and after a long, sweaty Wednesday-night run, Finn and I returned home to find him face-down on my sofa, surrounded by empty lollipop wrappers.

"Teddy? What's going on? You're eating sweets after seven p.m. You only drink carbs after sundown."

He raised his head, glanced at Finn and me, sighed, and then flopped onto his back. "Please tell me you didn't do the nasty on the sidewalk."

"No, we didn't do the nasty. Not all of it, anyway." I walked to his side and went in for a high-five but was left hanging. "What's going on, Teddy? And please, don't say nothing because I know you're full of poo."

His reply was like a slap in the face with a wet fish. "Just drop it, Scar. I don't want to talk about it. It's too personal."

As I gasped and clutched at my heart, Finn padded up behind me and pressed a kiss to the top of my head. "Uhh, why don't I go take a shower? Catch ya later, Teddy."

Normally, Finn mentioning taking a shower would have me in a hot flutter of dirty thoughts, but neither Teddy nor I paid him any attention. "Too personal? Too personal? Theodore William Henry Digby, you were at—"

"The third."

"Oh, for fuck's sake. Theodore William Henry Digby the third!" I corrected. "You were present for the birth of my son. You saw my lady bits stretch and tear and get sewn back together. I think we crossed the line of personal boundaries a long time ago."

"Well, this is not about me. It's about Asher, and I don't know if he wants me to tell anyone. But I have to tell you because it's stupid, and I need him to understand that it is."

"So, tell me, then!"

"Fuuckk!" he groaned while whacking his arms and legs against the sofa before flailing dramatically into the beaten cushions. We really were two peas in a pod. "Fine, then. Remember how I hid the fact that Asher and I were dating when we first got together?"

"Yes. I was super annoyed and am still low-key bitter, by the way. I know I hide it really well."

"Hmm, yeah, you keep telling yourself that. Anyway, I didn't tell you because Asher wasn't really out."

"Oh. Shit."

Teddy sighed, sat up, and snuggled into my boobs. "Yeah. Oh, shit. Only his parents and a few staff at the bar know he's bi. We rarely go out, and if we do, he won't hold my hand or show any affection."

"What? But I've seen you kiss at the bar."

"Only with those specific staff and none of his regular patrons around. All the time we spend together is at my place or his, but only if his dad isn't around. And I don't even know what the deal is with that because he won't tell me."

I chewed on my nails as I thought. "Mm... Have you thought about talking to his mum? You got along well when you went to get the costumes."

"We did get along," Teddy said, flashing the briefest of smiles before frowning and planting his face in his hands. "She loved me, and fed me, and I did think about talking to her, but I don't know if we're solid enough for that. The other day, I asked him if he would come on a double date with you and Finn. He said yes, but only if we ate in damn Jersey where no one knows us. When I pushed back, he got all weird and huffy. I called bullshit, we had a massive fight, and now I'm pretty sure he hates me. I can't see how talking to his mum would make things better." He then raised his head and broke me with a puppy-eyed glance through his sad, floppier-than-usual hair. "Scar, I don't know how to make him feel safe with me."

I grabbed his face and shoved it back in against my boobs. "Teddy, darling. Asher doesn't hate you. He's nuts about you, babe. I know he is. Obviously, something deeper is going on with his dad, but you have to know it's not you that makes him feel unsafe. It's the world. Remember, you came out at, like, twelve. You were so brave and comfortable in yourself, but not everyone is like you. Maybe he just needs more time."

"And I want to give him that time. I want to show him the world can be safe and that he is okay with being his authentic self. But he keeps holding back, and it's hard not to feel like he's ashamed of me. I don't know. Maybe I'm selfish, but I want to go out and show the world he's mine, and I want him to do the same."

"God, you are such a beautiful man." I beamed sloppily, applying a heavy dose of smoochy head kisses that had my mind traveling back in time, trawling across years of heartbreak and happiness that Teddy and I have helped, nursed, and loved each other through. "I love you so much, and I believe with all my heart that if you give Asher the time, he will love you too."

"You think so, Scar? You really think that we boogers from across the pond can finally find happiness here?"

"I do, Theodore. In fact, I know so. We are deserving of it, and we will have it."

For maybe the first time in my life, I actually believed that.

Thursday saw Theodore taking a personal day and Finn and I working late. It was the norm for me on a Ben-free week, but one that was made even more enjoyable with my man humming away behind me. The office was empty, and it was just Finn, me, and the romantic glow of Sixth Avenue streetlights.

"No hanky panky tonight, Big Boy," I bossed. "We *must* finalize this exterior, or Jason will bloody shank us."

"Uhh, I'm pretty sure I can keep my hands to myself for a few hours. You just worry about yourself, Little Miss Grabby."

"Alright, then, let's put some money on it....say, twenty quid?"

"I honestly don't know how much that is, but since you will be paying, I guess it doesn't matter. You got yourself a deal, Red."

Cocky bastard. I'll show him.

It should have been easy. As Finn said, it was just a couple of hours.

It was not easy. The man had turned me into a nympho. I tried to distract myself, to focus on other things. The mountain of work that covered my desk, for one. But it was Finn. Finn and his perfectly highlighted silhouette. Finn and those arms and how the muscle tensed and flexed just gripping his pen. Finn and his V-tapered back and powerful thighs that could hardly squeeze under his desk.

How can I leave him alone when he looks like that? I can't. It would be a crime against sex itself! Shards of the pencil I chewed fell like gray confetti, littering my dress and desk and smudging into a further mess when I tried to clean it away. My eyes stayed fixed on Finn until the pencil finally snapped in half. It was discarded—as were my knickers—and I stalked my prey.

"I thought we were working," he said, sensing my approach.

"Can't concentrate. You're too pretty and distracting." Before I could whisper, "Fuck me," into his ear as I'd planned, he spun in his chair, grabbed me by the waist, and pinned me against his desk.

"Thank God. I haven't stopped thinking of having your tits in my mouth all day." They'd been in his mouth only two hours before, but he was literally tearing me out of my dress, exposing, and gorging on said tits, so I didn't bother to correct him. My skirt was hitched around my waist, and his eyes nearly popped from his head when he saw my naked flesh. "Red! You're not wearing any underwear."

"I know. I've been sitting there bare, just waiting for you." It was a lie, but it was sexy, so...worth it.

Every hair on my body rose as he scraped his teeth along my neck and released a deep, dark chuckle. "Ohh, you are trouble, aren't you? And I bet you're so wet, too. I want to dive right in and drown inside you."

"I want that too, but I want your cock inside me even more." I pushed him away, draped myself over the desk, and ground my ass against his cock. "Take me now."

Mumbling something about going to hell and loving it, Finn began rifling through his drawer. "We weren't going to do this, remember? We made a bet. You owe me... Oh, fuck. I don't have any condoms left."

"Noooo...." I slammed my fist into the timber, then remembered my half-decade-length spinster lifestyle. "Well, I'm on the pill..."

"And we both haven't been with anyone for a long time, right?" He nodded with extreme enthusiasm. "I went and got tested, too. I'm good to go."

"Me too! Let's fuck!"

"Yeah?"

"Yeah. Let's do this, Big Boy!"

I leaned forward, resting my cheek against the desk and rubbing my ass against Finn's hard length.

"Holy mother of..." slipped from his lips as his cock nestled between my folds. He took a deep breath, teased my entrance once, twice, then pushed inside. Hard, slow thrusts had me clenching my fists, my nails digging into the flesh of my palms. The sound of his hard body slapping against mine, the silky smoothness of his bare, throbbing cock pushing inside me, was so intense I couldn't speak. I could only take.

"God, to finally feel you like this," he groaned, taking a grip of my hips, holding, and drilling me harder and harder until halting altogether. "Sorry, just give me a second. I have to stop. I can't move, and please God don't squeeze me like that." Of course I ignored him and put my Kegel training to work. "Fuck, when you flutter around me, I want to live and die inside you!" His poetic compliments continued as he pressed a series of kisses up my spine, pulled out slowly, then drove back in. "Ahhh, God, I want to taste you again so bad, my Scarlett. I wish I could eat you out and fuck you at the same time. I've waited my whole life to do you... Scarlett, your cunt is so fucking tight."

My very own Neruda.

Unusual creaks and cracks soon accompanied his filthy ramblings and my whimpered begs for more, but it was hard to focus on anything other than the warm rush of orgasm beginning to build. Suddenly, the earth moved beneath me. Literally.

CRASH! The desk collapsed beneath us. I hit the floor first and was then flattened by the full weight of Finn crashing down on top of me.

Laughing so hard I could hardly see, six feet of bulk shifted off my back and was replaced by huffs of laughter and tender kisses. "Sorry, sorry, sorry. Shit, Red, are you alright?" I flipped to face him, dug the pencil out of my armpit, and gave Finn two thumbs-up.

"Yep! All good. Carry on."

"Carry on?" Finn snorted. "You're so fucking amazing, Red. I love you so much."

All merriment ceased, and I swear a full philharmonic orchestra began to play. Fat little cherubs scattered rose petals above us, and I lay motionless, silent, dazed beneath the man who loved me. Understandably, my lack of response caused concern. Those blue eyes filled with tears, and the smile I adored began to fade. "Scarlett, it's okay if you don't...if you're not—

I wove my hands through his hair and pulled his lips to mine. "No. No, God, I love you too, Finn. With all my heart."

"You do?"

"Yes! Of course I do. More than I ever thought possible. You're incredible, Finn. You're sweet, and thoughtful, and protective, and so freaking fun. How could I not love you?"

"Red." He smiled through his continuing tears, brushing my own away with his thumb, kissing me till I was breathless, and looking at me the way no one ever had. "How did we get so lucky?"

"I don't know, but I need you to stop fucking crying and celebrate by fucking me."

He exhaled a laugh and swiftly kneed my legs apart. "That's the filthy girl I love so much."

Entering me with unmatched tenderness, Finn slowly began to push deeper and deeper, moaning with each one until fully sheathed. He slipped his hand between our grinding bodies and played with my clit till I was screaming his name. It was the fuck of ages. He seemed twice as hard and twice as big. Taking everything he gave, my body stretched and clenched around him. Grunting, with his eyes locked on my bouncing boobs, he leaned back, ran his hands down my thighs as far as he could, and then raised and rested both legs on his shoulders. "You're so fucking hot, Red." The new angle stirred an instant orgasm and a promise to do anything he ever wanted. My nails dug into his back, and I pulled him closer but couldn't get him close enough. The harder I pulled, the more I gripped and scratched, and the more he moaned. He was losing all control, his thrusting increasing and then slowing as he tried to hang on. He moved me again, grabbing my ankles and holding my legs in the air. I was open, spread out in a sinful V, and being pounded hard and deep.

"Finn!" Riding that fine line between pleasure and pain, I closed my eyes and clenched my fists.

"Open those eyes," he demanded. "Look at me, Red. I need you to watch me ruin you for anyone else."

A sea of blue greeted me, and I didn't think I'd ever forget the unbridled love, bliss, and ecstasy I found in its depths. Or the groan and hot rush of him coming inside me, claiming me, and promising me a forever I never believed I deserved.

What started out as picking splinters from each other's asses, turned into making out like a pair of horny teenagers, desperate to steal one last kiss before curfew. We even had the grumpy parent-type person to ignore. After the fourth ring, Finn resigned, released my boobs, and rolled off me. "Bloody Evie. I better get it, Red. She'll bloody kill me otherwise."

The second he picked up, I heard her bellow, "What the hell, Finn! Lucky I'm in a good mood. Now, get off Scarlett and get your arse over to M.I.X. I have a surprise for you."

36

Scarlett

S EX HAIR CAN RARELY be hidden or denied when you have a head full of curls. Not that I would have bothered. I rocked that hairdo as I proudly walked into M.I.X. with Finn's arm around my shoulder. Evie took one look at us, rolled her smiling eyes, but said nothing. She was too busy pointing toward Teddy *and* Asher, who were smugly holding hands across the table she was standing by.

"Teddy? What's going on? How did you and Evie meet?"

"Well, to make a long story short, I was here at the bar with Asher. I'll fill you in later"—he winked—"and Evie overheard us talking about you crazy kids and all the humping. We got to chatting, I fell in love, and here we are. She's quite the firecracker, Finn, but I must tell you. Our fabulous bond is *not* your surprise. Is it Evie?"

"Nope, not even close." Evie began to bounce on her toes, and Finn lost patience.

"Not to sound ungrateful or anything, but you look happy, Eves, and I gotta say it's freaking me out. I need you back to your grumpy self, stat. Where's the surprise?"

"Right behind you." An incredibly hot, tall, surfer-looking dude with sandy hair and a dangerous swagger threw himself into the back of Finn. After a short bro-hug, Finn grabbed his hands and twisted his body to face him.

"Nate?"

"G'day, bro.

"Nate!" he repeated, blinking rapidly. "What the hell! You're not supposed to be here till December!"

"I know, but things changed at home, so I decided to come earlier and sample my first Thanksgiving. Evie helped keep it a surprise, and here I am." Midway through speaking, Nate's eyes shifted to me. "And who's this draped around you, Finny? Looks like I'm not the only one keeping a few secrets." He winked at Evie, who replied with a twinkling eye and slap to the back of his head, immediately piquing my interest.

Normally, I would consult with Teddy and investigate, but I was too distracted by Finn almost pushing off me like I was a brick wall. "Nate, this is, um, Scarlett Grant. A work colleague."

Colleague? Colleague? Why the bloody hell am I back to a bloody colleague?

Teddy, Evie, and Asher studied Finn with raised brows while I focused on remaining upright. "Nice to meet you, Scarlett," Nate said, shaking my hand wildly. "Keeping the big fella in line at the office, are ya?"

Still reeling from Finn's shithouse introduction, all I could manage was a stupid laugh and nod as Teddy guided me to and plopped me into a chair. Things didn't improve. Adding to my disillusionment, Finn ditched me, walked to the other end of the table, and pulled out the chair next to Evie. Luckily, Nate practically pushed him out of the way to claim the prized position, but Finn wasn't happy. He grunted then begrudgingly shuffled to sit in the only free chair between Teddy and me. "Are you okay?" I whispered, leaning into his arm. "You seem a bit out of sorts."

"Yeah, of course. I'm good. I'm great. I'm fine." His Ross-from-*Friends* pitch and super shifty, darting eyes seemed at odds with that.

"Are you sure? 'Cause you don't look it. Shit, are you sweating?"

"Yeah, nah. Like I said, I'm fine. Just a bit shocked to see Nate, I guess. It feels weird, him being here, us being here. But I'm definitely fine, though. I'm good. Great."

"Hmm, so you said." I smelled bullshit, and Teddy, who was leaning into me listening, hmm-ed like he did too. His eyes flicked between Finn, Nate, and me with a deserved suspicion before defaulting to his natural state of indiscreet interference.

"It's nice to meet you at last, Nate," he said, wrapping his arm around the back of my chair and shaking me by the shoulders. "Scarlett and I have heard a lot about you. We both work with Finn, though their work is much more...intimate. Wouldn't you say, Austen-tatious?"

Finn blushed slightly, shrugged, then rested his elbows on the table and began talking about the Long Island swells to his bro. Undeterred, Teddy tried again. "So, Evie, you were telling me you've met Scar at your place?"

Picking up what Teddy was putting down, Evie added, "Yes. Yes, I have. Scarlett brought soup for Finn when he was sick. There was a ridiculous amount of flirting, maybe even snogging. It could have been sniffing. It was hard to tell because I was hiding in the hall."

"Snogging, eh," said Nate, suddenly interested in something other than waves. "You go around snogging all your co-workers, do you, Finny?"

"Gosh, I hope not. Although our HR lady is very handsy with you, Finn. Do you need to tell me something?" Along with the rest of our friends, I laughed at my hilarious joke, then reached to take Finn's hand. Seeming to sense the incoming affection, he pulled it from my grasp and placed it under the table. It was the second blow to my pride in as many minutes, and the tears began to well. The whole thing was mortifying, and not only to me. It was all too much for poor Asher, who jumped to his feet and almost ran to the bar to escape the awkwardness. "Why don't I bring us some drinks?"

After an hour of being ignored, blessed alcohol blurred the menus, dulled my senses, and brought me back to some semblance of happiness. Even Finn, the relationship denier, seemed to relax with a disgusting number of tequila shots in his system. His hand had finally found its way to my knee and his thumb brushed back and forth over my skin. Each stroke brought me a sense of calm *and* another excuse for his behavior.

Perhaps he's just nervous? He hasn't seen Nate in such a long time. He was just shocked. Nate is Shelby's brother. Introducing a new woman is bound to be awkward...even though it's been years and he did ask me to meet him.

Once I'd fully gaslighted myself, I forced my way into the conversation. After all, everyone was getting along. Finn was touching me again, even if it was only under the table where no one else could see. Nate seemed like a cool guy. I just needed to chill and loosen up. And what better way was there to do that than swapping traumatic stories about your past?

"So, Nate, tell us all something embarrassing about Finn," I said with a cheeky wink. "What was he like when he was little? As obnoxiously perfect as he is now?"

"Unfortunately, yes. He was exactly the same. Ridiculously good-looking, tall, ripped, and the life of the party. He was also the first at the bar, the worst dancer on the floor, and the dork who started cleaning while the party was still raging. Oh, and he called the teacher mum one day in class and was so embarrassed he fell off his chair."

"Aww, poor Finny." I grabbed and played with his cheeks. "Why were you so embarrassed? Lots of little kids call the teacher mummy."

"Not when they're fifteen, they don't," added Evie, who was laughing so hard she had to cross her legs so as not to wet herself. Her beloved brother looked like he was going to throttle her and Nate or melt into a pit of shame at his feet. Being the loving girlfriend I was, I wriggled closer and moved to press a kiss to his flushed cheek. But just as my lips brushed his skin, his eyes widened, and he sharply turned away. My kiss landed on the back of his head, and to add further insult to injury, he leaned forward so my face planted on his shoulder with an audible thud.

Okay. That was not okay. That was humiliating and cold.

Thankfully, our friends had been too busy acting the fool to notice, but still, I felt like absolute shit. I had just enjoyed dirty, incredible, desk-breaking, fucking floor sex with this man. Not only that, but he told me he loved me. Then, hours later, he wouldn't blink, touch, or look at me for more than a few measly seconds.

A spectator again, I sat and watched the conversations flow. I could feel the slow descent into the self-blame game but was powerless to stop it. I loved him. I wanted him to be happy. *He just needs time. Am I being too sensitive? Taking things personally? Remember what he went through with Shelby.*

A large celebratory cheer rose from the table, pulling me from my mental wanderings. I presumed it was for yet another round of drinks being delivered, but it wasn't. It was for me. While I was spiraling, Teddy was boasting. Sharing the news that Jocelyn had chosen my design for her home.

"Sorry to be the party pooper, but who is this Jocelyn?" Asher asked.

My bestie, the world's most indiscreet individual, explained. "Right, so Captain Koala and Scarlett were designing a house for a mega-rich client, Jocelyn Crane. It's no secret now, but at first, Finny didn't tell anyone that Jocelyn was his aunt. He'd sworn her to secrecy and everything, but the minute she arrived in the office, he hugged her, kissed her cheeks, and blurted out, 'Hi, Auntie!'"

Finn's cheeks bloomed with an adorable blush, undoubtedly intensified by the whiskey he'd moved onto. "Ha ha, yeah, yeah. All laugh at the idiot. All worked out in the end, though, eh, Red?"

"Wait, wait, wait," interrupted Nate, "Scarlett's the hot girl you rescued from harassment and forfeited Jocie's house to? Ah, see, now I get it, Finn. Wise move, brother. "

Spinning in my chair, I shot Finn a look that could melt metal and started poking him in the arm. "You rescued me, huh? What exactly did you rescue me from, and what the hell is this about Jocelyn's house?"

Teddy jumped to his feet and started doing something resembling the Macarena. "Hey, guys, who's up for some shots?"

"Not now, Teddy," I snapped, with my eyes still scorching and finger still jabbing. "Answer me, Finn. What did you do?"

"I swear it's not that bad, Scarlett. Nate is being a dick, as per usual, and blowing this way out of proportion."

"Oh, really. And exactly what proportion should it be?"

"Well, um...I never said I rescued you. I just told him about Herman and how Jocie and I intervened when you wouldn't make a complaint, which you knew. And as for the house, all I did was tell Jocie to...well, I didn't tell her. I advised...recommended that she let you pitch to her...and then maybe choose your design. But that's all."

"That's all!" The sound of metal scraping over polished concrete drew every set of eyes in the bar. I jumped to my feet, my chair fell, and I nearly went with it. "I got the job because you told her to give it to me?"

"No, no, not at all. That's not what happened."

"How is it not? You just said you recommended she choose my design. Was this a pity thing? You thought you had to rescue the damsel in distress and give her work? Or...or was it just a way to get into my pants and slip me something else?"

Finn became defensive, rising to stand beside me. "Hey, that's not fair. I did it because your designs were better. You deserved to get the job, Scar. It was pure admiration for your work."

"Oh, I'm sure it was admiration for something, but I don't think it was my work."

Grimacing, Finn scratched his head and said the thing a man should never say to an angry woman. "Calm down. You're over-reacting, Red."

"Oh, God," muttered Evie.

"Calm down? CALM DOWN? Huh? Funny how being dismissed as a colleague, treated like an idiot, and told you're overreacting by a man—the very man who, only hours ago, told you he loved you for the first time—can work a girl up."

In my periphery, I saw Asher slap his hand over Teddy's mouth to mute the he-*said-he-loved-you* squeal of glee we both knew was coming.

The tears I continued to hold in burned my eyes, but I was determined that not one would fall. No, I was going to leave and hide in the restroom and cry like a mature adult. After getting my foot caught on the leg of the chair and almost falling flat on my face *again*, I made a most gracious exit and hightailed it to the restroom.

Unsurprisingly, but not wisely, Finn followed, protesting his innocence and begging me to stop. But his attempted appeals to my sense of reason were futile. Any ability I once had to appreciate logic left the building when the word *rescue* left his bestie's mouth. I refused to even look at him, and once locked into an awful, single-stall, unisex toilet I bloody hated, I collapsed against the cold tile wall. There, safe and alone, I placed my hand over my mouth to stifle my sobs and waged war on the conflict in my mind.

Seconds later, the ginormous shadows Finn's clown feet cast appeared beneath the door.

"Scarlett, please..."

"No. Go away. I will not put up with this. I worked in an office full of men that treated me as a dumb teenage mum and coffee girl, little more than a toy or object. I refuse to do it again, Finn. I am strong, intelligent, and talented. I don't need my boyfriend—who, for some fucked-up reason, refuses to acknowledge me as his girlfriend to his best friend—to set me up with work. I've gotten where I am by myself and will bloody well get further by myself."

"I agree with you, Red. You are all those things and more. You're strong, talented, and bloody brilliant. I didn't tell Jocelyn to hire you because you were a young mum I wanted to get with. Fuck, I didn't even know about Ben then. I swear, all I did was give her my honest opinion. Your portfolio was better. I knew it, and Jocie knew it. And look! Look how it worked out in the end. It's been amazing. We got to work together, fall in love together..."

"Oh, so now that I'm locked behind a door, crying like a freak, you can admit that you love me. I should have just thrown myself on the floor the minute you saw Nate, and we could have avoided this whole freaking nightmare!"

"Scarlett. Please don't cry. I can't handle you crying."

"Why can't I cry? I've seen you cry plenty."

"Yes, but I'm a baby. You're not."

"Well, I guess you better leave then 'cause I have a shitload of tears, and I can't see them stopping any time soon."

"No!" he growled. "I'm not going anywhere. You have to listen to me."

I have to listen. That was it. I burst through the door and knocked Finn clean off his feet, sliding across the floor, and into the wall. The ever-present angel on my shoulder told me to reach down and help. But I flicked that sucker to the curb and went with the devil. "I'm not helping you up, and I do *not* have to listen. Not to anyone or anything *but my own conscience.*"

Haughtily thrusting my head back, I left him on the floor and huffed away, dismissing the pleas of my friends as I passed our table and marched out the door.

Unsure if my whole-body shiver was the result of anger, humiliation, the cool autumn air against my coatless skin, or a combination of all three, I stomped my way down Sixth Avenue, refusing to acknowledge the voice of the man who claimed to love me. "Scar, please. Just stop." I didn't. I angry-walked in silence, and after multiple failed attempts to have me stop, Finn took the hint and did the wisest thing he'd done since Nate opened his trap. He shut his.

Home was in sight, and the surety I'd felt dissipated. My old friend panic set in. A lifetime of massive quick judgments and massive overreactions played in my mind. I thought of how quick I'd been to jump to conclusions when I first learned of his aunt. Of how I'd judged Victoria and let myself and her down by staying silent. Of the firm's partners and my colleagues and the unvalidated certainty I held regarding their judgments over Ben.

Am I doing it again? Am I misreading this? Is this an overreaction? The thing was, I had no way to tell. Years of people-pleasing, of thinking myself less than, had eroded my gut instinct, leaving me in no place to judge a thing happening within my own damn brain. With each step toward my door, my thoughts flipped, from reinforcement to regret, doubt to determination.

Two steps remained. Finn was right on my heels and would never let me get inside without him, but Mrs. Horowitz and her new cat, Macon, appeared just at the right time. "Oh, Finn, my key is stuck in the door. Could you help me please? I need to get in and give Macon his furball medicine."

Despite Finn's need to stalk, he was too soft-hearted and kind to ignore an elderly woman asking for help. His delay, though only momentary, gave me just enough time to hit the door, slide in, and turn my key. I heard rather than saw him coming, and my door was almost knocked off its hinges when he pushed his way in and captured my face in his hands.

"I swear to you, Scarlett, on everything I love and hold dear. It was only a recommendation. I purely wanted you to have an opportunity, and that was it. I never told her to pick your work. Once you get to know Jocelyn better, you'll understand no one tells her what to do. She is strong, proud, and capable, just like you, which is exactly what I love about you. Your fierce, stubborn independence is the sexiest thing about you."

"And what about Nate? What about refusing to hold my hand or acknowledge to him what you said I meant to you? I felt like shit, Finn. Like a piece of crap stuck to the bottom of your giant shoes."

He smashed his fist against the wall and growled at the floor. "God, fuck. I know. I just... It felt weird and confusing, and I didn't know he would be there, and I didn't know how to react. And once I called you a colleague, I didn't know how to take it back and kept digging myself deeper. I'm an idiot, Scar. I didn't mean to make you question yourself. Or us."

"But you did, and I feel like a bloody fool."

"You are not a fool. I'm a fool. A very sorry one. You have to forgive me. I've waited my whole life for you, Scarlett. Please, you have to forgive me."

"Stop telling me what I have to do. You may not believe it, but I am capable of making my own decisions. I need to know that you see me as an equal, as someone you're proud of, and as someone you trust. I want a partner, Finn, and not just in the bedroom. I want you to see and value me just as I am in every aspect of my life. Just like I do you. I refuse to be treated like a plaything or silly little girl that can't fend for herself."

Two strong hands braced my shoulders, and he ducked and weaved until I met his eyes. "Scarlett, I've never thought any of that for a minute. I do see you. Everything about you is what I've fallen so hard for. I know I messed up with Jocelyn and Nate. I get it was shit. But none of it was intentional. I won't do it again. I'm so, so sorry."

"You better mean that, 'cause remember, the proof is in the pudding. All the sweet promises in the world mean nothing if you don't live up to any of them. Words matter, but actions do too."

"I know. I promise."

"Good, 'cause God help me, Finn. If you bloody well pull anything like that Nate crap or talk about my work with Jocelyn without consulting me first, I'll..."

"You'll what?"

"Well, I was going to say I would cut your dick off with a knife and feed it to the cats next door for dinner, but it may be a little extreme. Still...do you hear what I'm saying?"

He winced, and a sly smile passed his lips. "I swear, I get it. I will work hard every day to show you how much I love and value you. I never want to hurt you again, Scarlett."

"I kind of hate you right now, Finn Austen."

"I kind of hate me too. I really, really like you, though. Love you, in fact."

He edged closer and closer. "I need you to forgive me. Do you forgive me?"

"Possibly. But first, you have to tell me if you had anything to do with her changing her mind and giving the project solely to me."

Three fingers were raised to his temple in salute. "Scout's honour. I knew nothing about it. It was as much a surprise to me as it was to you."

Biting back a smile, I forced my pout to remain, so he took my hand, placed it over his heart, and held it tight. "How about this? Cross my heart and hope to die, stick a needle in my eye. I had nothing to do with her choosing your design. To be honest, I think she only ever included me to try and get us together. Once that happened, I was discarded."

"Promise?"

"Promise."

A smug grin had his dimples popping, but it didn't make my heart flutter like normal. Okay, it did a bit, but it kind of pissed me off too. *He thinks he can flash that smile and be all cute and you'll forgive him.* He ducked lower and softly, tentatively, possibly wisely after my castration threat moved toward me. I could taste him, smell him, almost feel the press of his lips.

I wanted it. My body ached for it. But a voice from within, something loud and clear, told me no, and this time, it was me who turned their head.

"Forgiveness takes time, Finn. I'm angry and hurt, and I need to be alone."

"Scarlett, please. Let me make this right."

"No. I'm sorry, Finn. Not tonight. I need to sort things out in my mind. I promise I'll give you a call tomorrow. But please. If you love me like you say you do, you can show me by listening, taking a step back, and saying goodnight."

My hurt was mirrored back to me in the watery blue pools that studied me as he nodded and did just that. "Goodnight, Scarlett."

I closed the door, collapsed against it, and cried. Judging by the thud I heard on the other side, I was pretty sure he did the same.

37

Finn

THUMP!

THE DULL THUD of my giant, stupid head smacking and sliding down the door ended my night. I remained on Scarlett's stoop, awake and hoping she'd come down, until two a.m. After that, I either fell asleep or succumbed to hypothermia and dreamed of Scarlett's warm breath tickling my cheek as she pressed her lips to my temple. *"I love you, Finn. Come to bed."*

I woke at four with a blanket covering my freezing body and a thermos of hot cocoa resting at my feet. *Maybe that kiss wasn't a dream?* At six, I gave up and left, the question of who had taken pity on me unanswered. If it wasn't Scar, perhaps Teddy had discovered me on his way home, or Mrs. Horowitz spotted me on one of her regular curtain twitches.

Converse in hand and a possibly permanent crick in my neck, I snuck into the house, quiet as a church mouse but with none of its agility.

"You slut!" Nate was alone in the kitchen, smugly smirking with my copy of *Pride and Prejudice* in one hand and scratching his head with the other. He seemed confused as he turned the page and returned to reading. Being the bigger man, I ignored the slut-shaming and went for his intelligence instead.

"It's called a book, Nate. It has lots of words and tells a story. Some even have pictures."

"Yes, I am familiar with the concept. What I don't get is how a girl that clearly has you so twisted that you've begun collecting and reading Austen is the same girl you treated like shit in my company last night."

I threw my keys on the table and sauntered to the fridge. "I didn't treat her like shit!" I argued, grabbing the milk. "Well, I did a bit, I guess... But Scarlett will forgive me. I think."

"You think? Nate's eyebrows met his hairline. "You doing the walk of shame at dawn implies you already made up."

"We did a bit. But not fully."

"So, where are you creeping in from?"

Not wanting to answer, I delayed as long as I could, checking that Evie was nowhere in sight and taking a hearty mouthful straight from the carton.

"She wouldn't let me in, so I slept on her doorstep."

Nate clenched his eyes shut and scratched at his neck. "Jesus, Finn."

"What? I thought she'd come back down. Waiting for forgiveness on her doorstep seemed romantic, but then I fell asleep and woke up with a cat licking my face. She did bring me hot cocoa and a blanket, so she can't be too pissed. And I'm sure she'll wake up and see I didn't mean to hurt her. I was just trying to be respectful."

"Respectful? Respectful to who? Pretending you're not in a relationship with someone you apparently love doesn't seem very respectful."

"Isn't it obvious? To you and to Shelby. I didn't want to make you feel awkward by flaunting Scarlett in your face."

"For fuck's sake, Finn. Shelby's been gone over seven years, and while I miss her every day and always will, do you really think I—or she, for that matter—would want you to grieve forever? You deserve to be happy, to have a life of your own outside of the amazing one you've built for Iris. We all do."

"But—"

"But nothing. You made Shelby happy her whole life. Those last few months were precious to us all, but you have to move on. Be young, have fun, have sex. Fall in love!"

I had no comeback. Another milk swig drew the ire of Evie, who walked in mid-gulp. Naturally, she punched me in the gut and took the carton from my hand. Nate laughed. I wanted to, but the predatory way he watched Evie strut in her sleep shorts and tank top made my skin crawl.

"I heard the words fun, sex, and love," she quipped, looking directly at Nate. "Do I want to know what you're talking about?"

"We were talking about Finn and Scarlett and no one else," Nate snapped with a shake of his head. Further skin-shriveling uncomfortableness was caused by Evie mouthing, *"What?"* and shrugging. My hackles were up. Steam fogged the glass splashback as the kettle boiled. Nate took it from the stovetop and began shuffling around behind me. I watched as he made Evie a cup of tea without asking and precisely as she liked it, two sugars and flooded with milk. The milk she handed him with a lingering, twisting, almost flirtatious ticking of fingers. He then passed her the bread without looking. It was oddly intimate. They didn't say a word but knew the very thing the other wanted.

Puzzle pieces began sliding together. The weekly emails Nate had been sending my sister. His premature trip to the States and Evie knowing about it before I, his best mate, did. Pushing me out of the way to sit next to her at dinner, ordering her food and her favorite drinks. And her joyful insistence and enthusiasm to play tour guide so I wouldn't miss any work. Evie was rarely enthusiastic. Joy was almost unheard of.

Then, she dropped her spoon. In unison, they bent, clunking heads and giggling nose to nose, hovering over it before Nate picked it up without shifting his eyes from her smile. *What the actual fuck?*

"Oh, my God. You fucked my sister!!"

Evie squealed, leapt to the bench, and started buttering toast as though nothing had happened. Nate gulped, huffed out a sigh, and cautiously approached with his hands outstretched, calmly waving me down like I was a man whose vest was strapped with bombs. "Finn. Mate—"

"Don't fucking *mate* me. Are you or are you not sleeping with my sister?"

The butter knife hit the counter, and Evie spun to me, her eyes ablaze. "Yes, he is, and there is not a damn thing you can do about it. Like Nate said, you deserve to be happy. We all do."

"Eww, this is...is...disgusting. You are practically related. She's my sister, for fuck's sake."

Equally fired up by my outburst, Nate squared up and stood right in my face, "Yeah, and Shelby was *my* sister."

"Pfft," I scoffed. "That is completely different."

Not backing down, Nate jerked closer. "Oh really, and how is that different?"

"We were stupid kids who didn't know any better, that's how," I spat. "You two are fucking adults—well, you're supposed to be." Evie jumped between us, and her hands fell onto Nate's chest. Her tiny back may have faced me, but the heaving of her body betrayed her tears.

"That's enough. Please, Nate. Let me handle this."

"Handle what, Evie?" I snapped, "There is nothing to handle. You two cannot be a thing, and I forbid it, and Nathaniel is going home...today. I want you gone by the time I get back from work...mate."

Hell hath no fury like my sister scorned. She spun on her heels to face me. I didn't know if I'd ever seen her so angry, and that was a massive statement. "You forbid it?" she snarled, her whole body tight with rage. "Bloody hell, Finn. Who the hell do you think you are?" Even at the height of my rage, I was too scared to answer. I also didn't have the chance, which was probably for the best. "You have absolutely no right to say that to me. I have dedicated my fucking life to you and Iris. I have been happy to do it, too, but I deserve to have something for myself. That something is Nate, so you bloody well better get used to it." She then grabbed Nate by the scruff of his shirt, planted a massive wet kiss on his lips, and dragged him from the room, screaming at me as she did. "The people in your life are not your pens, Finn. You cannot organize, order, and control us to behave in a manner that suits you. This is my life and my house as much as it is yours. Nate stays. If you don't like it, piss off!"

I didn't like it. I didn't like it one bit, so I did just as she said. I pissed off.

In my car, I turned off my phone and put the windows down, music blaring. It was freezing, but I didn't care. I played death metal and screamed. I played Taylor Swift and cried, and when

I stopped to get a burger, the lady at the drive-thru took pity on my woeful state and gave me extra fries and a box of cookies. "You look like you need it, love."

The last twenty-four hours played on a loop through my mind. The dinner, flinching at Scar's touch, the fight, the stoop, Evie, and Nate. I kept driving, hardly noticing a stop sign or landmark till I ended up by the beach on Long Island; the sand and sea drew me to it, just like it had always done at home in Byron.

I watched the families at play, singles walking their dogs, and couples walking hand in hand. It was cold and wet, but no one seemed to mind. They needed the water, sought its peacefulness. Maybe it helped them think too.

The people in your life are not your pens, Finn. You cannot organize, order, and control us to behave in a manner that suits you. You deserve to be happy. We all do. I heard Evie's words again and again. They did deserve it. Perhaps I did too. Recognition of their truth came slowly and painfully. I watched the waves roll endlessly across the ocean. Trampled on each grain of sand. Smelled the yellow flowers thriving despite the cold, salty air and sharp rock bedding, and admired their beauty and determination. I wanted to smell, and see, and touch Scarlett.

But is that the real problem? Did it all start there? After all, I'd done what I knew I shouldn't. I let myself fall in love and become distracted. Lost sight of my purpose. My plan.

How could I *not love* Scarlett, though? The mere thought of her ruby lips, her eyes, and her skin could leave me hard as stone. I wanted her constantly, but it wasn't just her physicality. Her heart was as pure as any I'd ever known, and she was so funny and witty, fierce, and determined. Strong and loyal.

After hours of sulking, I'd had enough of being alone. I'd been alone for too long, for too many years. Knowing a tsunami of shit was likely headed my way, I turned my phone back on. Missed calls, texts, WhatsApp, and IG messages filled the screen. Scar, Nate, Evie, and even Teddy had tried to reach me, and I honestly didn't know where to start.

So, I didn't. I ignored them all, turned my phone back off, and pulled out from the parking lot. There had to be a way to make things better, to make it right again.

I just had to figure out what it was.

38

Scarlett

"KNOCK, KNOCK." I POPPED my head into Jan's office, finding her flushed, and fanning herself with a wad of papers. Looking decidedly cagey, she promptly switched her screen from *Firemen of New York,* to our office email and winced.

"Sorry, I didn't realize the door was open."

"No need to apologize. I was looking at the same site yesterday." I was not. "I'm a big fan of Mr. December."

"I'm a Mr. April woman myself. He can torch my tamales any day." The fanning increased, and she refreshed herself with a sip of water. "What can I help you with?"

"I just wondered if you've heard from Finn today. His sister, Evie, can't reach him, and neither can I."

"Oh. Yes, Finn called and left a message early this morning. I can't disclose why he's not in, but he seemed fine. Just had an appointment." Her glasses slid to the tip of her nose, and she made no move to correct them. "Is everything okay? Are you okay?"

Well, if going to bed sobbing after a fight with your boyfriend, then waking at three a.m. to find said boyfriend asleep on your porch is fine, then yes.

"Of course. Um, I think so. It's been a stressful few days with all the changes here and at home, but yes. Yes, we're good." *I think.*

Offering me a seat, Jan stood and closed the door. "Finn mentioned earlier in the week that you two had revealed your little secrets to each other. Have you introduced the kids yet?"

"Finn told you about the kids?"

"He sure did. I've been watching you two watching each other for weeks. I always thought to myself, *Does she know? Does he know? I think they both know.* I caught him singing in the kitchen the other day and harassed him until he spilled. I think it's fabulous. People were even gambling on when you'd finally get together. Teddy won. Didn't he tell you?"

"No, he didn't," I sighed. "It would seem I'm quite out of the loop with the men in my life."

"Two hundred and fifty dollars he pocketed. He seemed to have an unfair advantage over everyone else since you have such a close friendship, but I digress." Moving to sit beside me, Jan patted my leg and gave me a sympathetic smile. "I'm sure everything is fine with Finn. He seems a lot like my husband. Hard-working, determined. Always looking to make sure things are just so, and so fixed on his ideals. Just look at his three-year plan to set up a firm in his hometown. It's a lot of pressure for a young man. Self-inflicted, but still pressure all the same." *Three-year plan? His own firm? His hometown?* Not sure, willing, or able to say what I wanted, I nodded, forced a smile, and began picking at my nails. "Sometimes I forget you're only twenty-four and twenty-five. You both had to grow up so fast, and you're so mature in so many ways. But I sense you're both still babies when it comes to matters of the heart. Take it from this wise, old woman. You can't control your heart or a stubborn man any more than you can control the weather. If Finn is off in a huff, let him sulk and lick his wounds. He'll come paddling back once he sorts things in his mind and has all his ducks lined up in a row."

With my head spinning, and after assuring her I didn't think Finn would be interested in being a cover boy, I left Jan's office determined to stop chasing Finn, just as she said. But also, even more determined to learn why our company HR lady knew his future goals when I, his girlfriend, didn't.

Ten minutes later, I had called him six times and left messages varying from,

> Hey, me again. Just checking in. You don't need to talk. Just let us know you're okay.

to...

> Finn Austen. I am going to throttle you if you don't call your sister or me back.

Teddy sat beside me and began playing with my pouting bottom lip. "Any news on the Finn-inator?"

"No, Teddy. There's bloody not, and I'm getting really worried. Evie said he hasn't '*chucked a sickie*'"—Teddy's eyes crossed in confusion—"taken a day off," I explained, "since high school. That's not exactly true because he had a day in bed with me not long ago, but still. Why won't he just send a message to say he's okay?"

"That, I can't help with, my pet. But I can help with this. Grab your bag and hang onto your curls. I'm taking us out for lunch."

"Would you be paying for this lunch with the two-fifty you earned gambling on your best friend like a racehorse?"

"Uhhh."

"Yeah, uh. I hope you haven't spent it all already. I'm comfort eating."

Once seated in the most expensive restaurant I could be bothered walking to, I called Finn again, then threw my phone across the table when he didn't answer. "Tell me again, why do people get into relationships? Having no one to worry about seems awfully attractive right now."

"As attractive as Finn shirtless?" Teddy asked as he retrieved my phone from his caprese salad.

"Obviously not," I snapped.

"Didn't think so. Trust me, Scar. The land of singles is highly overrated, *but* it is once again the land I call home."

My own worries disappeared as I almost choked on my Pimm's. "What? Teddy! Did you and Asher...?"

"Split like a gymnast? Separate like your tits in that push up bra? Yeah. Yeah, we did."

Throwing myself across the table, I wrapped my arms around Teddy's neck and squeezed the living shit out of him.

"I'm so sorry, my love. You looked so happy the other day. What happened?"

Teddy's reply was just a grunt and wriggle, but I realized it was because he couldn't breathe. I relaxed my grip, and after two or three steadying breaths, he replied, "Don't worry about it. You have enough on your plate with Bindi Irwin missing. Let's just talk about you and Finn and how proud I am of you for standing up for yourself and not shagging him senseless."

"Thank you. I was kind of proud of me too, but now it's backfired. Finn's run away, I feel like rubbish, but I will not marinate in my misery anymore. I want to talk about yours." I squeezed him tighter and brought out the big guns. "Bloody tell me what happened, or I will call your mother and tell her how much rent I pay."

"Fine. Fuck, there's no need to bring the Queen of Mean into it. I will tell you if you get off me and stop squishing my salad."

"Oh. Sorry." I slid off the table, wiped the dressing off my pink-and-white-polka-dot dress, removed the olive from my neck, and returned to my seat. "Go ahead."

"So, last night, after you stormed out, Evie, Nate, Asher, and I were sitting around, bitching about—I mean, *talking* about—you guys and the whole dual hot-orphan thing. Then Evie shared some memories of her mum and dad. Nate told us about his folks, and I complained about the duke and duchess. All eyes turned to Asher and his contribution was, '*They're great.*' That was it."

"Hmm. Okay, so how did you go from that to breaking up?"

"I'll get there, but it's a long story, so bear with me." After taking a few mouthfuls of lettuce, he continued, "I could see by Ash's body language that he didn't wanna go there, so I let it slide. But when we left, I asked if he wanted to go to his place or mine. Of course I didn't want to go to Brooklyn—it was more of a test. Asher said, *'No, we can't go home. Dad's home.'* Then he just froze."

"Okay. Getting weirder."

"I know, right? So, I asked, *'Why can't we go there if your dad is there?'* And he said, *'I'm so sick of this pressure, Teddy. Why can't you get the hint? I don't want you to meet my dad, okay? It's just not going to happen.'* He then told the cab driver to pull over, which was stupid because he hadn't taken off yet. Asher got out, turned around and said, *'I think we're done. I can't do this.'* And that was it. He walked away, blocked my number a few minutes later, and bada-bing bada-boom, I'm single." Our cutlery bounced as Teddy slapped his hands on the table, then skulled his Pimm's in one go.

"Wow," I sobbed, wiping my eyes with the back of my hand, "that was a long story. A bloody sad one too. I really wish I didn't order a salad. I need some grease after that."

"Good old grease, eh. I won't be needing any for a while."

"Teddy," I cry-laughed.

"What? It's true. I'm done, Scar. I am officially done with men. I think I'm going to get a British Blue and buddy up with Cat Lady. Maybe we can start a trend and become known as the cat block. Ooh, even better, pussy parade."

Remaining seated, I grabbed the bottom of my seat, held it to my ass, and shuffled like a turtle to Teddy's side. "I know you're making fun of it, but you care about Asher. I know you do. It's okay to be vulnerable and hurt. Not everything has to be a joke."

"Why not? What else should it be? I'm not sitting around crying into my caprese, Scar. I can't believe I'm about to do this, but...as your bloody Jane once said, *'The more I know of the world, the more I am convinced I shall never meet a man whom I can really love.'*"

"*Quoting Austen!* Are you trying to kill me?" I dropped my head against Teddy's shoulder and howled like a banshee. "You got a few bits wrong, but that was close and bloody heart-breaking. And you will, Teddy. You will meet a man. A wonderful, hot man with a massive schlong who you can love and fuck for the rest of your days, and the best thing is, you may have already met him."

"Uh-uh, no way."

"Yes way. Asher most likely is that man. You are so good together—perfect, even. He will be back. I just know it. I can feel it in my bones."

Teddy dropped his fork and spun it around on the table, gloomily following the trail of dressing it left behind. "Ah, but the question is, do I want him to be back?"

"And the answer is...?"

After a long pause, a rush of tears, and a monster boob cuddle, Teddy sobbed, "Yes."

Teddy and I picked up Ben from school, made dinner, and laughed ourselves silly over SpongeBob. But when he left to go to the gym and Ben disappeared into the world of Minecraft, I was alone with my thoughts. And when you're me, that's a scary place to be.

I didn't know where my boyfriend was. He'd ignored me all day. He seemed to have plans to return to Australia before I was scheduled to pay off my last pair of shoes. It was only yesterday, when I declared my worthiness for love, that I dared to wonder, to dream that I, Scarlett Grant, was in line to find my own happily ever after. *What a joke.*

KNOCK. KNOCK.

39

Scarlett

"C HRIST ON A BIKE, Finn! Where the fucking hell have you been? I could fucking kill you!" *And damn it, why do you look so good, all dark and moody!*

I couldn't name the expression darkening his face, but whatever it was, it was hot as fuck and really annoying. I was about to ask why he was on my doorstep and if seeing me caused him such distress when he cut me off. "Red, I know I shouldn't have avoided you all day, and I was a butthead last night, but...well...I was thinking..."

"Butthead? What are we, six? Spit it out, Finn. You're making me fucking nervous as well as pissed."

He grimaced again and then smiled through his clenched teeth. "Sorry, I just wondered if...would it be okay if we come over for a playdate?" He stepped to the side and turned toward the pavement. Toward Iris. His daughter. There she was, standing on the bottom step with a bunch of flowers clutched in her little hands. Finn turned to face me again, placed his finger beneath my chin, and closed the gaping hole. "Surprise!"

How dare he? The bloody nerve of the guy. Turning up to my house after dodging me all day looking so bloody gorgeous, his curls a mess, his dimples dimplier than ever, and bringing with him the cutest little girl on the planet. What an asshole.

"I'm going to fucking kill you, Finn Austen," I spat between gritted teeth before switching deftly into my super peachy keen mum voice, "Iris! Hello, sweetheart. I've heard so much about you. Come in!"

Dressed in striped, knee-high, rainbow leggings, a bright-green sweater, a pink beanie, and rainboots, Iris Austen, who had clearly chosen her own ensemble—one I'd be proud to wear—bounded up my stairs and pushed herself between her asshole father's legs and into my house. I was seconds away from closing the door in Finn's face but thought better of it when I finally looked him in the eyes—his red and puffy eyes. The man had been crying. It was plain as the nose on my face, and it hurt like hell. So, I averted my gaze and retained my threatening tone. "We need to talk, Austen."

Iris skipped down the hallway, stopping at the crossroads between stairs, hallway, and kitchen. She was adorable, a mini version of her dad but, in my current mood, much more tolerable. "Daddy said you had a son named Ben. Is Ben home, Ben's mum?"

"You can call me Scarlett if you like, Iris. And yes, Ben is home. He's upstairs. I'm sure you'll find his room. It's the one with the floor covered in toys and odd socks." An evil glimmer of joy washed over me as I pictured the horror and pathological need to clean that my son's room would give to Neat Freak Finn. "Why don't you sneak up and surprise him."

It took all my strength to wait and stay calm, but the minute her rainboots disappeared from sight, the nice-mum smile faded, and I grabbed Finn by the scruff of his delicious-smelling shirt. "What the hell are you playing at? You disappear, ignore everyone's calls, then show up here with Iris, which I'm fudging delighted about if you can't tell, but you probably can't because you've lost your goddamn mind!" Super calm.

Finn smirked. He smirked. "Fudging? You dropped the F-bomb fifty-seven times in front of Iris, and now you're giving me fudging?"

"Well, I think she's heard enough of my potty mouth for one day, don't you?"

"Possibly. I do find it incredibly sexy tho—"

"Don't you fuc—freaking dare flirt with me. We're fighting."

"We are? I think maybe you are. I came to say sorry, not fight."

Cocky, arrogant asshole. Dammit, he's sexy.

"What exactly are you apologizing for, Finn? The whole Jocie-house debacle? Sleeping on my stairs like a bum? Skipping work? Ignoring me? Or bringing Iris over here to soften me up when we hadn't discussed telling the kids yet? Which, again, I am freaking ecstatic about."

Finn nodded to each point made and tried to kiss me, but he was too slow. I spun my head, and his lips landed between my cheek and ear and made a horrible squelching noise I would usually laugh at.

"All of the above." He grabbed me by the shoulder, and this time, a big wet kiss landed. "I freaked out over an argument with Evie, and I just needed to cool off. But I do have to clarify one thing. Yes, Iris is here, but I have no intention of telling the kids about us. I need to protect her, and Ben, for as long as I can. If they got close to us and something happened, I would never forgive myself. I just thought they could run off and play, and then we could run off and play, and it would be like a super-fun playdate."

I could not have rolled my eyes any harder. "Christ, Finn. *You* have no intention of telling them? *You* need to protect them. Do I get a say at any point? You arrange work opportunities without consulting me. You skip work, go completely off the radar, and turn up here with Iris without checking with me. Do you see a pattern here? 'Cause I do. Oh, and don't you worry, I know all about Evie. I called her looking for you, and if you think the reception you're getting here is rough, wait till you get home." My rant continued, and Finn just stood there, his expression halfway between amusement and regret, with his arms crossed over his chest. "Even with Evie, you're trying to decide her relationship status, but you"—I poked his chest—"can't always be in control...even if you're convinced what you're doing is right. People aren't—"

"I know, I know. People aren't pens."

"What?" I wanted to tell him to shut up. I hadn't even mentioned his plan yet, but the pen thing threw me. So did the continuous wandering of his eyes toward my unfolded laundry. "I don't know what you're talking about, and are you even listening? You're looking at my laundry basket."

"I am listening. It's just..." His eyes again darted between me and the basket of clean laundry waiting for my attention on the kitchen table. Unable to deal with it, the doofus began folding it as he spoke. "It's something Evie said about my pen organizing. She thinks I try to sort and control people like I do my pens..." His voice trailed off as a particularly cumbersome fitted sheet stole his attention.

"Well, she does have a point." I grabbed the sheet and, much to Finn's horror, threw it back haphazardly into the basket. "Look, you couldn't even let my laundry sit unsorted for five seconds while we spoke. Remember folding all the blankets at the hospital? And don't think I missed how you color-coordinated my underwear drawer. Nice touch with the scented liners, by the way." Finn slipped me a wink. "I know you want everything to be perfect and in order, but life is not perfect. It's complicated and messy, and you alone cannot organize and determine the fate of people you care for or maybe even love."

"Maybe? Red, you're not talking about us, are you?" I shrugged, maybe pouted a little too. "There is no maybe here. We're new, I know, but I knew I would love you the first time I saw you, and even more so the first time I heard you say, 'Christ on a bike.'"

"Don't be cute," I snapped.

"You do make apologizing challenging, Miss Grant. No sexiness, no cuteness. What's a bloke to do?"

I caught a smile with my teeth and forced it into a frown. "Well, among other things, you can start by sitting down and telling me what happened today. And I want the truth. No fudging lying or telling me it's no big deal. I can see you've been upset, and I want to know what is knocking around in that thick fudging noggin of yours."

Tea was offered, made, and consumed in relative silence. Finn's bravado disappeared, and the only chatter or laughter in the house was floating down from upstairs.

"Cat got your tongue?" I said, bobbing in his field of sight till I caught his eye. "Come on, Finn. Are we just going to sit in silence?"

"No, I'm sorry, I just...watching you make the tea made me think how much I enjoy everyday things with you." He sighed and ran his palm down his face. "I've just fucked up so much, and I feel so selfish. I tried to do the right thing for you, to look out for you with Herman because you seemed so scared to stand up for yourself, but I overstepped the mark. Now, I've done exactly the same thing with Evie and Nate. I can't seem to help myself, though. What if she falls for him and goes back home? What will that do to Iris? It will completely throw off her routine. I mean, Evie's the only mum she knows. And what happens if she *does* go home, and Nate breaks her heart? How can I do anything about it if she's on the other side of the world?"

Seeing and hearing his distress pushed my own down the list. I leaned over and began rhythmically rubbing circles on his back, "You have to back it up, Finn. For starters, worrying how Evie's relationship might change things for you isn't self-ish. Anyone with half a brain and an ounce of love for their family would have the same thoughts, but you can be happy and apprehensive at the same time. Look at me, I was equally excited and terrified of being alone with Ben when Teddy and I got separate places, and he was two doors away. But I'll tell you this, if Evie were to leave—which she is bound to do at some point—yes, it would be a massive change. Iris will probably be sad, and you will be sad too. But you will all be okay. You have to trust the universe will only give you what you can handle."

Finn sat back in his chair and scoffed, "Pfft. The universe? I dunno, Red. I think both you and I drew short straws as far as the universe goes."

"We absolutely did," I agreed, "but I think you and I were also kind of lucky. I think we were allocated two straws. Maybe the first one was a bit of a sick joke, one of those crappy paper ones, but look what the shiny, silvery second one has brought us. We have beautiful kids, homes, *and* friends. We have our dream jobs in the most exciting city in the world." *A city you want to leave in under three years.* I pressed a kiss to his lips, swallowed my fear, and swept his curls from his eyes. "And we have each other. And even though I am still mad at you, to me, that seems like some pretty bloody long straws with a lot of sucks left in them."

"That sounds far too sensible and positive for my level of tiredness." His face dropped loudly onto the table, "So, all-knowing one, what's the other thing?"

"Huh?"

"You said, *'For starters'*"—insert terrible, snobby English accent muffled by timbre—"which implies that there's more. What's the other pearl of wisdom?"

"Oh, yes, number two." *Ask about the plan. Ask about the plan.* "Do you even know how serious things are between Evie and Nate?" *Idiot.* "From what I heard, up until you stomped out, they'd had one kiss. This relationship may turn out to be a harmless couple of nights of rumpy-pumpy, and that's it."

Finn lifted his head from the table and feigned dry-retching. "God, I think I'm gonna puke. Please don't ever say rumpy-pumpy when referencing my sister. Actually, never say it again about anybody. It reminds me of my nanna."

I slapped him with a towel. "My point is, you've already got her barefoot and pregnant and shipped back to Byron before you even know what's going on. Slow down. Talk to them and see where things go. Evie is a big and terrifying girl, and I'm confident she can handle herself."

"No, no, you're right. It's just...the thing is... it hit me today how fast things are changing. I like and am used to routine, Red. And please don't get me wrong. I'm not saying I'm unhappy with everything, especially you, but I'm scrambling to keep up with the pace. I drove to Long Island this morning just to sit and think, but my brain just kept going round and round in circles." He suddenly stood, carried the empty mugs to the counter, and began to fill the sink. "Since Shelby died, things have been tough for us, Scar. Really tough. And I know I am not alone in that. I know single-parent life has been bloody hard for you, too." He added some soap with a farty sound and began to wash. "For years, my world was tiny—just work, home, and Iris. That was it. Now, I'm here in New York. Iris is growing like a weed, Evie is sleeping with my best friend, and I'm here, washing the dishes of this amazing, stunning woman my brain doesn't possess the power to dream up. Sometimes...it's all a bit much."

Joining him at the sink, I stood behind him with my arms around his waist and my head tucked between his shoulder blades. "I get all that. I know how hard change is, and these kids are growing up so fast. But change can be a good thing, too. If Evie and Nate are serious, they could be great together. And look at us. If I never hog-tied you with my golden lasso and then dry-humped you over a balcony, things may not have changed between us, and you'd still be at work, thinking about me as you flog off in the toilets."

"Ahh, if anyone was rubbing it out in the toilets at work, it was you. And they would be great together," he said thoughtfully, "but Nate has a habit of being great together with a lot of different girls at the same time. He's never been in a monogamous relationship that lasted more than three days, and Evie is innocent." He paused, huffed, and grunted in disapproval as he scrubbed a particularly unbudging piece of cheese from a plate. Once satisfied with its removal, he continued. "She hasn't been in a relationship for years. Iris and I have been her life. All she wants is marriage and a family, and I don't think Nate would ever want that. I don't want her to be hurt, and I could never forgive myself if Nate, my buddy, was the one to hurt her."

"Look. Yes, she is your sister, and you want to look out for her, but she's also a grown woman, and she has to be able to make her own decisions...and mistakes."

"Shit. I just want to protect her."

I slipped around his thick body. Inserting myself between the sink and his belly, I grabbed his face and pulled his lips to mine. "I know you do, and the love you have for your family and your need to look out for them is one of the things I love most about you. I can't promise things will work out for them, because no one can promise such things. But there is one thing I can almost guarantee... Wherever you or Evie end up, if you'll have me, I want to be there. That and the quality and quantity of your future rumpy-pumpy."

Finn dipped his finger into the bubbles, bopped soap on my nose, and then brushed it off with a kiss.

"Since we're talking openly," I said, pulling away for a breath, "Jan mentioned something to me today."

"Let's not talk about Jan. Let's talk about us." Finn captured my face in his hands. "I do love you, Scarlett. I'm sorry."

"Eww!"

"Puke! Told you your dad had the hots for my mum," snipped Ben, sounding an awful lot like Teddy. I could feel the tension zapping between Finn and me, but for some reason, we remained pressed together, frozen solid, lip locked.

"Well, duh, Bunny," Iris said, rolling her eyes and elbowing nonplussed-looking Ben in the side. "We knew that weeks ago."

"Christ on a bike!" A delayed reaction kicked in, and I pushed Finn in the chest and sent him flying backward. "We knew? I mean, you knew?"

"I knew, our teachers at school knew, Dad knew…" Benjamin added.

"Wait, wait, wait," I said, not remotely freaking out or breaking into an instant sweat. "What do you mean *your* teachers knew?"

Ben sighed, looked at Iris like, *Can you believe this idiot?* then pointed to Finn. "Well, you were hugging and kissing my mum on the street, and our whole class walked past you to go to the museum, and you didn't even sawed us."

HOLY SHIT!

"Ben! You and Iris go to school together?" I spun to face Finn. "Finn, they go to school together."

"I know. I heard. They went to a museum, too, apparently. Are we really shit parents or what?"

My nodding, glassy-eyed stare at Finn was broken by Iris waddling up beside me and tugging on my shirt, "I saw Daddy kiss a pictuwe of you on his phone. That's when I knew. I saw boobies on his phone, too. Wewe they youws?"

"Christ." Finn released the edge of the counter he was clinging to and did his best to keep his voice calm and steady. "Hi, Ben, or should I say *Bunny?* I'm Finn." he said, walking to my side and rustling Ben's hair.

"Nice to meet you, Finn. You're really tall."

"I am. And you're very affectionate from what I hear." He then straightened and leaned into my ear, "Now that I know Bunny isn't a girl, I think I need to have a word with you about your son's intentions. All this handholding and cheek kissing I've been hearing about is a matter of concern."

"So, awe you my dad's giwlfwiend, then, Bunny's mum?"

"Ummm." I looked at Finn and shrugged. "Ummm."

In a move that both threw me for a loop and made me fall even harder, Finn got down on his knees, placed one hand on Iris's shoulder, and did the same to Ben. "Would you mind if she was, Iris? You too, Ben. Would you mind if your mum and I were dating? 'Cause I know you're the man of the house, Ben, and we need to have your blessing."

Ben held out his pudgy little hand and shook Finn's. "I think it's great! Mum smiles all the time now. I like it." My heart exploded with joy, Finn's eyes with tears, and all focus turned to Iris. At seven years old, her ability to hide her emotions was far superior to her father's, who looked like he was waiting for the apocalypse. I had no idea what she was going to say. And clearly, neither did he.

At first, she said nothing, just twisted her lips from side to side. But then she moved closer to me, stood on my toes, and pulled me by the hand down to her level so both Finn and I were on our knees. She then planted a big, sloppy kiss on my cheek and smiled. "Can I stay for a sweep ovew?"

Once we'd had our fill of grossing the kids out with kisses, we had as honest and frank a chat as you can with two sev-en-year-olds, one of whom sat upside down on their head for the majority of the time. It was likely easier to catch farts in a jar, so we gave up and went out for gelato instead.

The kids chose the flavors and then played in the park. Finn watched, laughed, and sexily licked his cone. I dropped mine down my shirt, and everyone rolled their eyes at me. And when Finn crossed the street and brought me another double scoop with sprinkles and nuts, he also got a wad of napkins to tuck into my shirt like a bib. I knew I needed it, so I didn't make a fuss.

There was no denying that our talk continued to play on his mind, but it was playing on mine too. I was happy we'd talked and made up. But I had a sick feeling in my belly that wouldn't shift. The longer I stewed on it, the more intense the feeling became. We sat there, side by side, watching the kids do what kids do while we did what we did. Kissed and talked and laughed. But that feeling, that dead weight, lingered.

I was angry. And not at Finn. Well, I was still angry at Finn, but not *just* at Finn. For some time, all the arrows in my life had been pointing in one direction, but I was only then realizing where. I did things to make people happy. To make people like me. Maybe to help them to love me. Pleasing people relieved my anxiety. But by doing what other people wanted, what secured their happiness, I was often neglecting my own. I put up with things I shouldn't put up with because I didn't want to rock the boat. I stayed quiet when I should have spoken up—stayed small when I should have become big. And the more I did it, the more anxious I became and the more I needed to please. I'd set myself up to fail in a vicious circle of self-neglect.

Those arrows all pointed at me. My anger was squarely focused on me. But I didn't have a clue how to change directions.

"Penny for your thoughts." Finn's face popped in front of mine, and he planted a long, deep kiss on my lips. "Are you okay, Red? We're okay?"

Swallowing my own needs again, I plastered the brightest smile on my face and lied. "Yeah. Yeah, of course we are, Silly Billy. Everything is fine." I returned the kiss and continued to do so until Ben and Iris appeared by our side, my son looking unimpressed.

"Eww. Are you ever gonna stop kissing?"

"Hmmm, let me think." Finn kissed me again, a nosy, sloppy, gross-even-for-me one. Ben pretended to gag, and Iris swooned. "Nope. Never stopping."

"Awe you two going to get mawwied and have babies?"

"Ohh, good question, Iris. Answer your daughter, Finn." I rested my elbows on my knees, propped my chin on my hands, and waited.

"Uhh, I...well... How about, for now, we do this instead? Let's go to the Christmas tree lighting at Rockefeller Center together. Remember the big one I showed you on the telly, Iris? That would be fun, wouldn't it?"

"Hmm, that would be fun...but that's ages away. I want something now, Dad!"

"I hate to burst your bubble, kiddo, but babies take much longer. I'm sure you can wait for a couple of weeks." Iris flopped to the ground with disappointment.

"I have an idea. Thanksgiving isn't too far away. Ben and I didn't celebrate either last year, and you two were still chasing kangaroos in Australia. Why don't we make this American holiday season our first official one and spend it together?"

That did the trick. Iris's lethargy disappeared, and she was up on her feet, flossing with joy, and back on the playground, and I got my people-pleasing dopamine fix.

"Nice save, Red." Finn smiled with relief.

"Thanks. I could see you were shitting bricks. Now I have a question."

"Am I gonna shit myself again? God, it's not about babies, is it?"

"Relax, your little swimmers are safe for now." *ASK HIM ABOUT THE PLAN.* "It's about...turkeys and if you know how to cook one."

40

Finn

"**W**HERE HAVE YOU BEEN, Finn? Iris is almost frozen solid." *What is with women asking me where I've been?*

"Yes, thank you, Evie, but I do know how to take care of my child."

"Oh my God. I never said you didn't. I was just—"

Nate walked up behind Evie and dragged her away. "Let him be, Lil Gidge. He's a big boy. He knows what he's doing."

Lil Gidge? The affection sent a shiver to my core.

The nauseating lovebirds headed toward the kitchen, but I reached for Evie's arm and squeezed her hand. "Guys, wait, I need to talk to you." I turned to Iris, picked her up, and gave her a quick kiss and cuddle. "Thanks for a fun night, bubs, but it's time to get ready for bed."

"Aww, okay. Love you, Daddy. I weally like Scawett. She's weally pwetty." I was kissed again and watched my baby waddle off to her room.

Evie eyed me with suspicion. "Iris met Scarlett? You were so dead against it. What brought that on?"

"You and your big mouth did, sis, and for once, that trap of yours was right. I owe you an apology. You too, Nate."

"Well, well, I'm all ears." Evie sat on the couch and crossed her arms, legs, and face.

"You're not going to make this easy on me, are you?"

Evie shook her hair, her blonde curls tickling Nate's face. He really seemed to enjoy it, almost basking in each golden swish.

I didn't. "Nope. I don't get an apology from you often. I'm gonna make this count."

"Jesus Christ," I mumbled under my breath as I sat before my sister and my best friend. "As much as it makes me want to vomit and gouge my eyes out, I accept that you two are a couple and that there is a chance you may actually be good together."

With a beaming smile, Evie nodded. "Thank you, Finn. That means a lot. Not that we need your approval, but still, it's nice to have it." She then smooshed closer to Nate, who took her hand.

I looked away and continued. "Yeah, well, as I said, you are probably perfect for each other. You're both complete pains in my arse and have a particular knack for knowing what's best for me. You both may also be excellent people, fun, and have the same taste in equally horrible music. Now that I think about it, I'm surprised you weren't together when we were kids, despite our deal."

Nate leaned in and whispered something in Evie's ear that had her all blushes and giggles, then turned to me. "Well, it wasn't from a lack of trying on my count. That was partly why I was so pissed off about you and Shel. I was so jealous I couldn't see straight. All I wanted was to get a hold of that sweet little as—"

"LA LA LA LA!" I threw my hands over my ears as the chunks rose in my throat. "Alright, alright, I get the picture. I've apologized and don't need to hear all the details."

Evie jumped from the couch and covered me in gross sister kisses, then sat on Nate's lap—which was even more repulsive—and did the same to him. "And what about you and Scarlett?" she asked, wiping her spittle from Nate's face. "I take it since you took Iris over, you told her about your relationship?"

"Sure did. And yet again, I did it wrong. I kind of forced it on her, in truth, but she handled it with grace, as she always does. I don't know what I did to deserve her, but I bloody hope I get to keep her."

After throwing a cushion at my head, Nate snuggled into Evie. "Aww, look at us Byron kids, all happy and shit in NYC!"

The two love birds began to swap spit again, and I was gone. At the foot of the stairs, I remembered Thanksgiving and had to turn back. With my eyes closed, I stuck my head into the living room and hit my head on the wall but kept my eyes shut tight. "By the way, we are all invited to Thanksgiving at Scarlett's. Do you know how to cook a giant bloody turkey, Evie?"

Halloween came and went in a costumed, sugar-filled blur. Before Scarlett and I knew it, we were at the end of our third month together and co-sniffing the pumpkin spice, toasty cinnamon, and pungent clove that flavored the air and lingered deliciously on her neck. It was our first Thanksgiving, and it was a bloody madhouse of chopping, blitzing, and roasting meat and fingers.

I felt like a real Yankee and like I had a real home. A home that was bursting at the seams. Jocie, Iris, Evie, and Nate were there, along with Teddy and Ben. Even Mrs. Horowitz had been invited after Scarlett discovered she would be alone for the holidays.

In the lead-up to the big day, all the prep, planning, shopping, and buying turkey-shaped decorations and table adornments had been done together. We ate candy corn, which I seriously loved, and did possibly the most American thing I had yet experienced—taking a trip to a pumpkin patch. After soothing Iris, who had confused a pumpkin patch with a Cabbage patch and spent the first ten minutes searching for dimpled, plastic babies, we rode tractors. Tractors. Who knew a tractor could heal a wounded 7-year-old soul? Next, it was apple bobbing, then carving ridiculous faces into even more ridiculously priced pumpkins.

Other pre—Turkey Day activities were not as wholesome or done in the presence of children. There had been lots and lots and lots of jogging, sneaky sex, and secret sleepovers. Scarlett was insatiable, as was I. Never before had I experienced the kind of want, all-consuming, soul-deep need that I felt for this woman. Never before had I been so scared of having something taken away.

At times, I was so overpowered by such absolute bliss and moments of tenderness, love, and lust that I feared it was all an elaborate and cruel dream. And that when I woke, I would again be alone and lonely. But it wasn't a dream. Her every touch, kiss, and laugh confirmed that. What we had was real and powerful, and with every day spent with Scar and Ben, I fell deeper and deeper in love.

Today, I watched her in adoration, running around searching for ingredients, swearing under her breath, and adding finishing touches while nervously chewing her lip.

The table was set, decorated with fall leaves, pumpkins of every color, shape, and size, and two—let's call them interesting—centerpieces made by the kids in school. The parade was done. She was a sweaty, hot, but always sexy mess. Even covered in cinnamon, marshmallows, and turkey grease, she was a complete turn-on, and I couldn't wait to get her alone. I just had to be patient.

Clearly frazzled but proud, Scarlett wrangled her guests into the dining room and was the last to collapse into her seat. "Okay, everyone, we have cornbread stuffing, mashed potatoes, sweet potatoes, and marshmallows. Don't look at me like that, Finn. Apparently, it's traditional. We have gravy, cranberry sauce, for some reason, and the biggest bloody turkey I have ever seen. Now, let's eat, and for Christ's sake, if you don't like it, keep it to yourself, or you may end up deader than the bird."

I proudly elbowed a potato-covered Teddy in the ribs. "That's my chick."

"Hmm, yes, I know. Congratulations. Be a good lad and pass me the stuffing."

After a prayer for those loved and lost, we dug in. I made a point to snag all the white meat I could for Iris and me but discovered Scarlett liked the white too. Of course, I gave most of mine to her, and I'm not going to lie. It hurt. Marshmallow yams tasted weird, and chewing on a drumstick was gross. But the foot I felt slowly sliding its way up my inner thigh before coming to rest snugly between my legs felt great. Suddenly, the slimy, brown meat didn't bother me so much.

Scarlett was sitting opposite me on the long dining table she'd bought just for this occasion. Next to her sat Mrs. H, who seemed to be flirting with me as much as my girl was. I prayed to God it was Scar's foot and not hers, especially when it began to circle up and down my zipper. This foot knew its way around my bulge. It was clearly Scar. The way she kept sinking lower in her seat with each stroke was another tell. I was half tempted to undo my zipper and let her foot have its way with me, but I was already struggling to remain composed as it was—a fact Scarlett was well aware of.

"What do you think of the yams, Finn? Going down okay?" she asked, fiercely batting her eyelashes.

"Yes. They are going down very smoothly, thank you."

"Not too hard for you? Not hard...lumpy, I mean."

"No, not too hard or lumpy. Just riiiiight...perfect, in fact." I was beginning to sweat. "Can't wait to taste your other sweet goodies."

Evie dropped her fork. "For freaking sake. Can we please drop the innuendo for five minutes? This is a holy day, for Christ's sake!"

"I don't think it is, actually," butted in Teddy, shaking his head and picking a piece of meat from his teeth. "Holy, I mean. Isn't it about pilgrims or something?"

"What the hell is a Pilgrim?" and "What's a pilgwim?" Iris and I asked in curious unison.

Teddy looked away thoughtfully. "I don't exactly know... I think they were the first English people to arrive in America."

"Oh, shit." I rubbed my forehead and pointed to the imperialist Brits sitting at the table. "So, we're celebrating British colonialism? Are you two happy?"

It was Scarlett's turn to drop her fork in protest. "Hey, I'm only half English. My mum was Spanish, remember? Not that they were shy of a bit of land grab, but this is more Teddy Rich-boy the Twelfth's scene."

Mrs. H disapproved of our dinnertime topic. "Scarlett, I think it's best we don't look too deeply into it until after we eat. Let's just enjoy the beautiful food you and Teddy prepared." Seeing as she was the only one here to have experienced a proper

Thanksgiving, we all took note and shut the hell up. Well, I didn't. I was solid as a rock under that table and was two seconds from swiping it clean and taking Scarlett in front of everyone. Not a usual Thanksgiving custom, I would imagine. I had to get out of there, and as such, I finished my meal at lightning speed.

"Uhh, excuse me, I just need to use the bathroom." With my napkin discreetly covering my shame, I fled the scene and made the uncomfortable jog to the toilet. As I pondered whether to handle the situation or wait it out, Scarlett burst in behind me.

"What? I locked the door! How did you get in?"

"It's a child lock. I can open it from the outside. Now, shut up and stuff me like you did that turkey." She was right. I had stuffed the turkey, and it was my only genuine contribution to the meal apart from stirring and tasting. It was so gross I refused to do anything else.

I was then accosted. Scarlett came at me like a wild beast, ripping at my jeans, corraling me against the tub, and then pushing me right into it. My spine cracked against the enamel base, but I made no complaint. She had whipped her boobs out, and I would go through any pain she could put me through when she had her boobs out. She lay her body on top of me. I suckled and bit her, licked her from nipple to chin, then back down again. I cried when she slipped away from me but got over it post-haste when her warm, wet, heavenly pussy slid down my cock.

This was a super-speed fuck, and I loved it. Scarlett bounced on me like a kid on a trampoline. I was merely along for the ride, and again, I didn't mind one bit. She felt so good, better than ever, and I was just about to mention that when she stopped.

"Fuck, Finn. I don't think I can keep going and stay quiet! Everyone is right outside, but you feel so good I wanna ride you till I collapse."

"Oh. Well, that does sound good." I continued to push into her, and I pretended to think. "Should we stop? 'Cause I really don't want to."

After a quick think and nail chew, Scarlett declared, "Ahh, fuck it," and we were back at it. She rode me even harder, leaning over me with her hands on my chest and her head either rolling back or forward as she glued her lips to mine.

"This is so hot, so good. So—"

"Finn, mate. Are you still in there? Hurry up, bro, I'm busting." It was Nate.

Scarlett bit her hand to stifle her glee and laughter and continued to bounce. "Piss off, Nathaniel. Go upstairs," I cursed.

"Nah, I can't make it. Just come out." She stopped pretty damn quickly, though, when the door began to rattle, and the lock began to slide. Nate had figured out the door had a child lock.

"Stop flogging off, Finn. You've got ten seconds before I come in." He then started to count. "Ten, nine, eight..."

"What do I doooooo," whispered Scarlett, her face glowing from her oh-so-close orgasm.

"Seven, six..."

I was not helpful. I was hard as a rock, my brain could barely function, *and* I was too busy laughing.

"Five, four, three..."

Scarlett slapped me, jumped off my cock, and out of the bathtub. I followed her out, painfully shoving my boner back into my pants, and endeavoring to make myself half-decent, then ushered Scarlett back into the tub. "Shh, be quiet, and he won't even know you're here."

"Two..."

I ripped the shower curtain around her, turned, and opened the door.

"One. Halle-fucking-lujah!" chided Nate as he pushed past me, shoved me out into the hall, and shut the door.

"Fucckk!" I had no idea what to do apart from laugh. I could hardly wait around for him to come back out, so after pacing back and forth, I headed to the kitchen, washed up, and returned to the dining room.

Way too many minutes later, Nate returned looking lighter and refreshed. "Oh, God, no," I mumbled. Nate looked at me and laughed, and I was up and in the bathroom in a flash, ripping the shower curtain back and revealing Scarlett. Pale. Shell shocked. Traumatized.

"He took a dump, Finn. I heard it. Farts and all. It smelled so bad I gagged, and he heard me, then tried to have a conversation." Laughter rattled through me. I knew I was in trouble once she recovered, but it was just too funny. "I think he's ill. Is he ill? I mean, like with a bowel disease or something?"

"No, he's just a guy, and we are disgusting. I'm so, so sorry."

She nodded slowly. "It's okay, Finn. I'll be okay. Just take me home so I can rest."

"You are home, Red. This is your house."

"Oh, God. I need to move."

When I returned the still-shaking Scarlett to the table, Nate greeted us proudly. Evie looked us up and down in pure disgust, and later, as I stood at the buffet where the seventy-six flavors of pie were laid out, she told me in no uncertain terms what she thought...after she hit me in the head.

"What the hell is wrong with you? I cannot believe you had a quickie in the bathroom while we celebrated Thanksgiving."

"Hey, I was thanking Red for the food."

"Oh, so you'll be sneaking the cat lady into the toilet next? She made the apple pie, after all."

"Mrs. Horowitz, you mean? No way. I can't tame that vixen. She and her titanium hip are too much woman for me." My giggling sister cut such a tiny piece of pumpkin pie I didn't quite know why she bothered. "Whaddya reckon, Evie?" I asked with a nudge. "Scarlett and Ben seem to fit in nicely, don't they? Jocie seems quite taken with the little man." We turned to find Jocelyn smirking as Scarlett wiped the kids' faces free of toffee, cream, and bananas she'd almost force-fed them.

"She does like him. How could she not? He's a sweet little thing, almost as sweet as Iris. I think they'll fit into the family perfectly—if that's what you want, of course."

"Of course that's what I want... I think it's what I want."

"You think?" she asked, adding another tiny slice, this time of the pecan.

"Well, I still have a few concerns, mainly about me, not Scar or Ben. I know she is perfect for me. I just hope I'm what she needs and wants." Perhaps sensing someone overlooked her dessert, Scarlett looked up and eyed Evie's plates. "Shit. Quick, for fuck's sake, Evie, take some of Scar's banoffee pie, would ya. Look at her watching you." I cut a hearty piece and slapped it on her plate, then grabbed a slice and ate it from my hand.

"But I don't like it, Finn. I tasted it a bit before, and it's weird and gritty. Lumpy too."

"I know. It tastes like shit, but the poor thing's recovering from the incident I will now refer to as The Shitting, and she needs a bit of a boost. Crap! Shh, she's coming. Just take some damn pie!"

Evie laughed again, patted me on the shoulder, and headed toward the kitchen, most likely to throw out the banoffee pie. "Good Lord. You're whipped better than her lumpy cream. Called it!"

Hastening Evie's retreat with a push in the back, I took another mouthful of yuck and almost choked on some well-disguised but misplaced banana peel.

"I'm so happy to see you like my pie."

"Scarlett, I think you're well aware of my regard for you and your sweet pie."

"Finn." She blushed and kissed me on the cheek.

"What?"

"You know exactly what. Stop being so cheeky and come and watch football with us. Ben wants to tell you all the rules, and I want to watch Tom Brady."

"Pfff, Tom Brady? Do you like him? What a joke. I'm the same height as him, and I play proper football like rugby and AFL. Not this rubbish where they are covered in pads and helmets and prance around in shiny leggings."

"Aww, Finny. Do I detect a hint of jealousy?"

"Pfft, not at all. I just think it's weird you'd fancy someone like that."

"I don't fancy him. I just think he's extremely attractive."

"Pfft."

"Would you stop pfft-ing? You're covering me in spit. Now sit down and watch the bloody game."

I did as I was told and saw Evie and Nate mockingly whip me in the background. I could understand Evie, but Nate? Like he wasn't going to be just as whipped by my sister.

Nestled between the kids and Scarlett, whose feet leisurely rested on my lap the entire time and who had absolutely no idea what was happening, I watched and cheered along for the first half. Despite my lack of knowledge and newfound hatred of Brady, it was entertaining. I hoped this would be the first of many holidays spent in this manner, leaving me with a warm, fuzzy, bubbly feeling that filled me as much as the food I'd consumed.

When Bruno Mars hit the stage for the halftime show, all the boys cleaned up and did the dishes. It was a good thing I was on trash duty and not Scar. Almost every piece of her pie was a quarter eaten and laying amongst the turkey carcasses. She was so proud of that damn thing. I felt terrible for her.

As I hovered over its remains, Teddy stood behind me and sighed. "She makes it at Christmas too. She's just so damn proud of it that I've never had the heart to tell her it tastes like banana-flavored poo. Oh, and her trifle... Christ, Finn, it's even worse." The remainder of the pie was plopped into the trash bag Teddy carried while I took the other. It felt like we were two crooks, disposing of the evidence before the cops arrived and hauled them away.

We remained undetected all the way to the curb and had just trashed the evidence when a familiar voice called out from across the street.

"Theo, hey, man, how's it going?" Brett crossed the street and shook Teddy's hand in an overly aggressive manner.

"Hi, Brett," Teddy replied with a forced smile. "I didn't know you were invited. Good to see you."

"You too, buddy. You too." The handshake was lasting way too long, and Brett's eyes were fixed on me the entire time. "Flimm, right?" the wanker asked, nodding in my direction.

"Finn. Finn Austen," I said, snatching his hand from Teddy's and squeezing the absolute crap out of it. "Scarlett's boyfriend."

"Boyfriend, huh? News to me."

"Well, all the important people in her life know. In fact, they're all inside while you are out here."

"Dad!" The door swung open, and little excited footsteps hurried down the stairs. "I didn't know you were coming, Dad.

Can you stay and watch football with us? I have been teaching Finn the rules, and he's taught me about Aussie football. They don't wear any padding and are real men, you know."

"Really? Well, I played football all through high school. Maybe I can teach Finn a thing or two."

I had several witty comebacks lined up and ready to go. *You can only teach me one or two things about a game I know nothing about? Fuck you!* But Scarlett appeared at her door and called us back inside. Cross-armed and leaning against the doorframe, a less-than-impressed Scarlett smiled half-heartedly as Ben led his dad inside. Brett stopped at the door, whispered, and kissed Scarlett on the cheek before disappearing into the warmth. Teddy and I followed, both mumbling about assholes under our breath. Scarlett grabbed me as I passed, her face a blend of annoyance and concern.

"I'm sorry he just turned up. I didn't invite him, but he's Ben's dad. I can't send him away."

"And I would never ask you to," I said with a smile so fake I felt ill. "You're a family, Scar. I get it." Perhaps sensing my insecurity, Scarlett gripped me tighter, pulling me flush against her body, and kissed me deeply. "Brett is not my family. He is Ben's. *You* are my family."

"Muuuuum, come and watch with Dad and me."

"Shit, I—"

It took all of my strength not to pin her against the door. To not mark her with my teeth. To not carry her inside over my shoulder and tell everyone that she belonged to me. To say what I said next... "It's alright, Red. Honestly. Go sit with him and get your funk on with Bruno. I'll finish cleaning up." Scarlett kissed me again, let go of my hand, and left me to sit with her son and his father. Someone and something I knew—no matter what I did, how hard I tried, or how much I cared—I would never be.

41

Scarlett

FOR WEEKS, EVERY TIME I looked at Finn, Jan's gentle voice hummed *three-year plan* and *his own firm back home* in my mind. The litany of questions I was desperate to bombard Finn with were always there, sitting on the tip of my tongue, but I never dared let them slip out. I was too scared of rocking the boat, so life continued, and it was wonderful. It really was. Especially Thanksgiving. Apart from being locked in the toilet with some questionable bowel issues, our day was a blast.

So, by 12:01 on Thanksgiving night, I decided I'd spent enough time worrying and was fully prepared to let it all go and move on to bigger and better things. Namely Christmas. The presents, the food—especially my world-renowned banoffee cream pie—the hustle and bustle, and the decorations.

As a kid, waking on Christmas morning sans gifts was not unheard of, so I unashamedly went overboard to make the holidays special for Ben. This year's frivolities were extra frivolity-ish because I, Scarlett Grant, was in love.

It was also the one time of year I was organized. Though only the end of November, my shopping was done. Gifts for Finn, Evie, Jocelyn, and, of course, Iris and Ben were hidden amongst the empty suitcases and boxed-up memories in the attic, wrapped and ready for the big day. My excitement had spread to Ben, who had insisted on selecting Iris's gift, a gorgeous My Little Pony charm bracelet. There was only one gift I hadn't yet wrapped, and that was only because it might die if I did. Flotus, one of Mrs. Horowitz's cats, named in honor of Michele Obama, had just had kittens, and one of the cute furballs was to be our first family pet.

Another first I hoped would become an annual tradition for Finn, the kids, and I was attending the lighting at Rockefeller Center. Playing tourist in our hometown, Finn had planned the day down to the finest detail. We were chucking a sickie from school and work and hitting the Empire State Building, Times Square, the Central Park Zoo, the Statue of Liberty...THE WHOLE LOT. If we survived all that, Rockefeller would be next for skating, and then, courtesy of Jocelyn, our no doubt bruised asses would be filling VIP seats at the tree lighting.

In all honesty, I didn't know if I had ever been more excited to walk so much in my life...until I was trapped in a metal sweatbox halfway to the top of New York.

"Are you alright, Red? You're sweating bullets, and you're holding my hand so tight my fingers are blue. I haven't seen you like this since you had that bloody needle."

I loosened my grip. "It wasn't a needle. It was an IV, and yes, I'm fine. Just excited is all."

Finn didn't look convinced but said nothing—until we came to a halt, and the doors slid open. To everyone else, it was an elevator door opening to the observation deck of the Empire State Building. To me, it was a portal opening to the fiery pits of hell.

The elevator emptied. No one remained inside...no one but me. After blindly reaching for my non-existent hand, Finn realized I wasn't beside him, turned back, and laughed at my attempts to hide in a place with literally nowhere to hide. "Are you coming out or trying to recreate a Lionel Ritchie video?"

"Hmmm, you know what? I left something in the car." I hadn't. It had taken weeks of lobbying, but Finn had finally begun to leave his precious Jeep at home. Today we'd taken the subway like normal people. "And...and...I need the bathroom. I'll go back down and find one. You guys go ahead, and I'll come back and meet up with you."

The elevator operator, Jerry, smiled and pointed out the doors. "There are bathrooms on this level, ma'am. Just to your left." What an asshole.

"Oh. Um. I..." I began to panic.

"Sorry, ma'am, I need to return to ground level. Are you exiting?" I couldn't move. "Ma'am? Ma'am?"

I spun on my heels and snapped, "Give me a break, Jerry. I'm freaking out here!"

"Red, what—"

"I'm sorry. I'm sorry, Finn, kids...Jerry. But I can't do it. I thought I could, but I can't. I'm bloody terrified of heights. You've seen me move, Finn. I'll trip and smash through the glass and fall to my death, I know it. Please don't make me do it." My heart was pounding through my chest, vomit rising in my throat, and I was crying. Not cute, feminine tears either. This was Kardashian-level ugly crying.

Finn held up his hands, waved and moved slowly toward me as though approaching a raging, red-headed Tasmanian Devil.

"Take it easy, Red. It's okay. I'm here. I won't let anything happen to you. It's perfectly safe. No one dies here. It's a fun tourist spot, right, Jerry?"

"Well, no one's died recently, but many have died in the past by—"

"You're not helping me, Jerry." Finn grimaced. There were now more eyes on me than on the view, and the kids were becoming upset. Finn remained calm as he continued to move toward me until he was close enough to peel my hand from the handrail. Holding it tightly in his, he looked me straight in the eyes and gave me a wink. "I won't let anything happen to you. You trust me, right?"

"Yes. Yes, I trust you."

"Right, then. You need to trust me that it's safe to let go of the rail. Just hold on to me and walk out of the lift, step by step. I promise you will be okay. You don't even have to go outside. You can just sit and wait here, and I can take the kids out for a peek."

"I can really stay inside?"

"Absolutely, you can really stay inside. But not of the lift. The lift you have to get out of." Ben and Iris joined Finn's rescue mission, making me feel even more pathetic.

"C'mon, Mum. It will be okay. I will wait inside with you if you like."

"Me too, Scaw." They looked so sad. I didn't want them to miss out because of me. But I also didn't want to die. It was a tough decision made no easier by the ever-present mum guilt kicking in.

Jerry tried again. "I promise it's safe, ma'am. Millions of people visit us every year. Listen to your family." *My family.*

"Okay. I'll do it," I said the words, but my body didn't respond. Didn't move an inch.

The corners of Finn's lips twitched, but he held the laughter bubbling away inside. "You need to lift your feet, Red. One at a time."

"I'm trying. They won't work."

"Okay, then. We'll do it this way." Two seconds and two giant strides later, Finn's arms wrapped around my body. Without so much as a puff, I was lifted off my feet, flung over his shoulder, carried out of the elevator, and set down on the polished tile floor. The kids rushed to my side, cuddled my legs, and sang my praises while Finn continued to hold me tight and kiss the top of my head until I calmed. "See, Red. You're out. You're alive."

"I'm a complete fool."

"You're not a fool. You're courageous. I can't believe you were planning to do this when you have acrophobia."

"Oh, I'm not afraid of spiders. Just needles and heights."

"No, that's arachnophobia. Acrophobia is the fear of heights."

"Oh, well, yes. As you know, I have acrao....aroflo...fear of heights. Sorry, I'm still scared. My brain isn't working."

"You're so freaking cute." Finn squished me between his bulky, deliciously smelling moobs as he shook with laughter. "I love you, you big baby."

"Hey!"

"You know, I've heard they have a cure for acrophobia. A bloody great needle right in your ass." The kids giggled along with the comedian. I didn't. "Too soon?"

"Oh, shut up. You go now. Enjoy the view while I stay here on the solid ground, shitting myself and dying of embarrassment."

"Are you sure you don't want to come, mum?" Ben asked sweetly while walking away.

"Yes, darling. I am sure. You go with Finn and Iris and have fun. I will be right here, not panicking at all, when you get back."

"Promise?"

"Promise."

God knew how Finn managed to keep two seven-year-olds entertained by looking off the edge of a building for that long, but twenty minutes later, three excited, rosy-cheeked, windswept faces returned to the exact same spot they left me.

With the man I loved holding my hand and keeping me safe, I bravely left my seat and, without incident, ventured into the souvenir shop. "Did I tell ya you look very sexy today, Red?" he whispered, his warm breath sending the best kind of shivers down my spine.

"Do you mean that, or are you taking pity on me because I made a fool of myself?"

"I mean it. I was watching you from the edge of doom." He smirked. "I couldn't take my eyes off you. Sitting all cute and trembling, biting your nails and sucking on your bottom lip. You know how I like it when you suck on your lip, Scarlett."

While our out-of-control, unsupervised kids excitedly ran around, looking at and picking up every piece of crap they could find, Finn continued his attempts at sky-high seduction. "It's great to have the kids with us. But I'd love nothing more than to find a nice quiet hiding spot, taste every inch of your skin, and bury myself inside you."

"Daddy, can I get a monkey building?"

"It's not a monkey, Iris. It's King Kong. He's a gorilla," said Ben dryly.

"Well, can I have a King Kong building, then, Daddy?"

"Sure, get whatever you like, kids." Without looking, Finn handed over his wallet. "Would you like that, Scarlett? Would you like me to bury myself inside you?"

"I would."

"You would?" His finger ran from my ear down my neck, then along the exposed lines of my collarbone. "I thought you were a good girl, Scarlett? But you'd let me do that to you in public? Plow you senseless?"

"Yes." His voice dripped with sex. I was weak. Putty in his hands.

With his nose, Finn tilted my neck to the side, allowing his lips to roam as they pleased. "Would you now? What else would you let me do to you?"

"Everything," I sighed.

The make-out continued. It was completely inappropriate and insanely hot. Too hot. "Red, I don't know if I'm completely turned on or thoroughly shocked and disappointed."

"Daaadddyyyy, looook!"

Finn removed his face from my neck, and we both turned to find Iris smiling, ear to ear, with her arms full of swag. Actually, it wasn't swag because it wasn't free. She'd bought half the shop, and Ben had done much the same. "Christ, bubs. You said you wanted a monkey building! How is this a freaking monkey building?"

Her lip dropped, and tears welled. "I asked, and you said yes. Scaw did too. Didn't she, Bunny?"

"You did, mum. You said we could have everything."

"When did I say that?" I squawked.

"When Finn was licking your neck."

"Oh," Finn and I replied in unison, but only I began to laugh...and laugh and laugh. I think all the nervous energy trapped inside me chose to escape through my wide-open mouth. Finn seemed to be the only adult in the situation and took control.

"Well, then. I guess that's a lesson for me and Scarlett to keep a better watch on you two monkeys. Now, let's get a bag for all this...stuff and get the hell out of here."

We didn't learn a damn thing. The kids did, though. When we went to get ice cream, Finn spent more time watching my ass as I bent over the counter to choose a flavor, and both kids ordered triple scoops. At the zoo, they slipped away as we shared an innocent kiss by the hot dog stand, and it took us ten panic-filled minutes to find them, and then they chose the most expensive tree decorations from a very chuffed street vendor. That wasn't because we were canoodling. That was just fatigue, and in all honesty, I wasn't too upset. Unlike the array of King-Kong-covered Empire State Building toys, these were super-cute baubles and would look amazing on our tree. Ben picked a Santa Mickey Mouse, and Iris chose an angel that she insisted was a fairy, no matter how many times my dear son tried to correct her.

Halfway to Rockefeller, with Iris on Finn's shoulders and Ben on his back, we decided we were all too tired for skating, so we made our way slowly to our VIP seats and collapsed. As the crowd began to fill in around us, Finn and I were kept busy umpiring the great *who-had-the-better-bauble* battle and compared notes on our many successes and failures of the day.

"This has been great, hasn't it?" I beamed, my heart full of everything good.

"It has, Red. It's been brilliant."

"Are you as exhausted as I am?"

"Well, I'm knackered and think I have spinal damage. So, if you're knackered and can't feel your toes, then yes."

I laid my head on his shoulder and yawned. "Two kids is a lot harder than one. I kind of thought they would require less attention as they had a buddy. I was wrong."

The contagion spread to Finn, who smiled and yawned as he answered, "We were both wrong. It was worth it, though. Look how happy she is."

Iris was before us, twirling on her tippy toes, spinning her decoration, and singing a little song she made up as she went along, totally oblivious to the crowd of thousands surrounding her and being at the foot of the biggest Christmas tree she'd ever seen. "Spinning, spinning...yawn...spinning like a...yawn...fai-wy on a stwing!"

"Sometimes, I never thought I'd get to share days like this with someone. I hope you know how much this means to me, Scarlett."

I did because I felt the exact same way. Not wanting to ruin the moment with the tears I could feel brewing, I simply nodded and pressed my lips to Finn's. It was a picture-perfect moment, made all the more so by the first snowflakes of the season, the Austens's first in America, falling upon us.

"Daddy! It's snowing!" Iris continued spinning as Finn brushed the flakes from my nose.

"Snow or no snow, if you don't stop spinning, you'll get dizzy and chuck," laughed Finn.

Ten seconds later, all dizzy and about to chuck—just as her father predicted—Iris gripped what she thought were my legs but belonged to a lady standing beside us.

"Oops, sowwy!" she squeaked and quickly jumped to my side. Her eyes widened as she caught a glimpse of Iris hiding behind me and smiled warmly.

"That's alright, darling. My, aren't you a cutie? And look, you have beautiful red hair, just like your mommy."

For a brief moment, it seemed New York fell silent. No one knew what to say or how to move. Except Iris, who didn't blink and replied with the type of innocent, blunt, kick-you-in-the-teeth frankness that only a kid can manage. "Scawett is not my mummy. My mum's in Heaven. Scawett is my dad's giwlfwiend. We just have the same haiw."

Horrified, the poor woman slapped her hand over her mouth and looked as though she might cry. "Oh my gosh, I'm so sorry."

Giving as much affection as socially appropriate with a complete stranger, I gave her a smile and patted her on the shoulder, "No, it's fine. Please don't feel bad. I'm the biggest idiot in the city and say stupider things than that daily. Not that what you said was stupid. No. It's an easy mistake to make."

Finn said nothing but avoided our gaze by fidgeting in his pockets and looking down to his shuffling feet.

"Well, okay, then. Have a lovely night. Merry Christmas." The rosy-cheeked woman and her family moved away as quickly as they could, and Finn and I made no mention of it again all evening.

42

Scarlett

"HELLO THERE, SLEEPY HEAD," whispered Finn as we shuffled down the hall toward Iris's room, "You've been asleep since we left the tree lighting. Ben's been dropped off at his dad's, and we're at home. It's time for bed, bubs."

Her little hand laid on his chest, and she smiled when she noticed me walking a step beside them. "Hi, Daddy. Can Scawett please tuck me in?"

"Uhh, if that's okay with Scarlett, sure."

I caught up, leaned over Finn's arm, and kissed her on the forehead. "I would be honored, upside-down Iris."

"I'm not upside-down, Scaw. You awe."

"Follow me, Red," chuckled Finn. We walked the few remaining steps to Iris's room, and Finn delicately transferred his baby girl into my arms. "Goodnight, bubs. Love you."

"Love you too, Daddy."

Just before he slipped away, Finn leaned into my ear. His breath was warm, carried the scents of Christmas spices, and had every hair on my body standing to attention. "I can't wait to have you naked in my bed." I'm not going to lie, the thought of tossing Iris into her bed from there and running down the hall while shedding my clothes did pop up. But it was instantly dismissed. Almost instantly.

No tossing was involved as I tucked Iris into her white, mini four-poster bed. Pink sheets I wanted to steal for myself were pulled back. Her forty-five layers of clothing were removed and a Peppa Pig nightgown slipped over her cute little head.

"Would you sing me a song, Scawett?" she asked as she finally lay down.

"Sure, I will. But I must warn you. I'm not a good singer like your daddy. What do you want me to sing?"

"Have you heawd of Taylow Swift? She's my favowite."

"What? Iris, did we just become besties?" I laughed at my own *Stepbrothers* joke, then realized—hoped—Iris had no idea what I was laughing at. "Yes, well, Taylor is my favorite too!" Iris giggled the cutest-ever giggle, jumped to her feet, and threw her arms around my neck. "I love you, Scawett, and I'm glad my daddy does too."

Believing myself likely to drown in my own tears, I wiped my eyes, cheeks, and neck dry and got on with it. "What Taylor song is your favorite, sweetheart?"

"Nevew gwow up."

"Oh, good choice, one of my favorites too. I sing it to Benny sometimes."

"I know, we sing it togethew at school."

More tears. The kid was trying to kill me. "Okay, lie down. Let's get you tucked in. Okay. Close your eyes. Are you ready?"

Iris swiped the back of her palm over her forehead, brushed away the baby ringlets, then nodded, closed her eyes, and held my hand, just like the little girl in the song. Then, just like Taylor—but not at all like Taylor—I sang about dreams and love and quiet worlds. Of fluttering eyelids and never, ever growing up. Finn's sniffles behind me were a pleasant accompaniment, but after a heavy sigh, he shuffled away. Knowing the guilt he carried over Shelby, the sight of me where she should have been couldn't have been easy. My body wanted to go to him, but Iris's grip on my hand tightened. She needed me too. So, I stayed and kept singing.

Another two Taylor classics were butchered. Iris tried with all her might to stay awake, but slowly, her breathing heavied, and her chubby little hand released its grip and fell from mine.

"Goodnight, my sweet girl."

Tiptoeing from her room, I followed the sounds of clumsily played piano downstairs. Each note drew me closer until I found him freshly showered, bare-chested in his PJ pants sitting behind an ebony Steinway. The windows beside him were all open, and the chilling night air blew the curtains toward him, almost caressing his skin. Perhaps that same breeze carried my scent through the air as he smiled lazily on a deep inhale and opened his eyes.

"Red. Are you ready to go to bed? Hey, that rhymes. I'm a poet, and I didn't know it."

"Oh my God. You just looked so sexy and then ruined it by saying that."

"What? I thought poetry was the language of looovveeee." He melted into me as I snuggled beside him and laid my head on his shoulder. "Control yourself, woman. The door is open, and Evie and Nate are in the room above us. That means no Scarlett moany snuggles. Not in here, anyway." I chuckled and nuzzled closer, allowing his lips to attach to my neck.

He continued to play, and much to my relief, his piano was as good as my singing.

"It's so nice to finally find something you're rubbish at."

"Ouch. That's a bit rough. And here I was, considering taking you to bed and pleasuring you."

"Oh, did I say rough? I mean, remarkably well. Liberace would be intimidated with your skill."

"That's right. Mum was the real pianist. I just played alongside her sometimes. This is her piano, actually. It cost a fortune to ship and only arrived last week. But it's nice to have another piece of her here. Especially since Iris never got the chance to know her."

"You're so sweet, you know?"

"Eh. I'm okay. But you, the way you sang to Iris..." he whispered between slow, wet kisses, "that was very sweet, Red. Very sweet."

"She told me she loved me, Finn. You don't mind, do you?"

He stopped playing, sighed heavily, and rested his head on mine. "Why would I mind my little girl falling for the woman I've fallen for?" His words were convincing, but his face was not. There was a glimmer, a twitch of pain.

"I dunno. I just...I know how much you worry about Shelby."

Finn shifted, held my face in his hands, and caressed the lines of my cheeks. "Shh, it's okay. None of that tonight. Let's go to bed." Sorrow swam in his eyes, but perhaps foolishly, naively, I let it go.

Hand in hand, he led me to bed. A tiny knot formed in my stomach with every synchronized step. Finn's room. The great unknown. I had no idea what to expect, except I knew it would be spotless. He opened the door, moved to the side, and waved me in.

A dark-navy feature wall stood behind the dark-chocolate timber, white-linen-covered bed. Black-and-white photography filled the walls, and luxurious floor-to-ceiling drapes floated by the windows. They were closed, but I shifted the heavy fabric and peeked out to the night sky. His scent enveloped my senses. My underwear dampened with each timid step inside. It was so clean, so sexy, so masculine...so perfect, so Finn.

I paced the room. Taking it in, my fingers ran the expanse of his bookshelves across the immaculately organized desk where his precious pen containers sat, along with a photo of Iris, a few books, a sketchpad, and two parcels. One was wrapped in brown paper, tied with string, fastened with a near-perfect bow, and finished with a sprig of an unusual dried purple flower. The other appeared to have been wrapped in the same fashion but was open, and three vintage books sat within its still-pristine paper. I stepped closer and gasped on reading the titles along their frayed, worn spines: *Emma, Northanger Abbey, Persuasion*.

"Finn?"

He rushed to grab them, but it was too late. "Shit! They were supposed to be your Christmas gifts. I was so excited and nervous to finally get you alone in my room that I forgot all about them."

The remaining books on his desk were other favorites of mine, not only by Jane Austen but Emily Dickinson and Charlotte and Emily Bronte, all of which were earmarked.

"You're reading them too? Even Wuthering Heights?"

"Well, I've only flicked through some, but I'm most of the way through *Pride and Prejudice*. Lizzie reminds me so much of you, Red. The same beauty, fierce independence, rotten temper, and sharp tongue."

"Hmmm, those traits do seem vaguely familiar. I don't know if you mean it as one, but I'll consider it a great compliment."

"Of course I do. There's nothing sexier than a strong woman." His eyes scanned up and down my body before settling on my lips. I traced my fingers down his biceps and forearm and then tapped on the still-wrapped parcel.

"Soooo, can I open this?"

"Nope, you have to wait for Christmas."

I stepped back, stamping my foot like an impatient toddler. "Damn it. I can't believe you bought me vintage bloody books and will make me wait for them. And I really, really can't believe you're taking the time to read them. God, you're such a surprise packet. Next, you're going to tell me you painted those." Still sulking, I pointed to two black-and-white abstract pieces on the wall behind his bed.

"I did."

"Bahhh! Christ on a bike. I am feeling really, really inferior right now." Finn blushed, and my stomach flipped. "You're beautiful, you know. Did I ever tell you that?" I stepped closer again and brushed his hair behind his ear. "But not just on the outside. Look at what you create. You're so talented. You play and sing and paint. Why, I believe Mr. Darcy himself would find you adequately accomplished."

"Don't forget that I fuck like a god. Darcy, the horn bag, would rate that highly."

"Finn, I'm serious. Everything about you, everything you do, is beautiful. You even make me feel beautiful."

"Make you?" he scoffed as though that was the most ridiculous thing he'd ever heard. "Scar, you're the most perfect creature. Nothing can *make* you beautiful. You just are."

"I haven't felt that way for a long time—if ever. I've always felt kind of unworthy, or...I dunno." I swatted the air dismissively, but Finn wouldn't leave it alone.

"Unworthy? That's mental and couldn't be further from the truth. What else? Come on, spit it out."

"I dunno, you know, like perhaps unwanted. Undesirable, unattractive, unappealing, undeserving, unseen."

Finn aggressively captured my face in his hands and kissed me so hard I almost lost my footing. "You are incredible and absolutely none of those things. Tell me you know that." I shrugged, and he shook his head in disbelief. "Here, let me show you." Dropping his firm grip on my face, he grabbed a sketchbook from his desk and flipped it until he came to a charcoal drawing." I drew this the first day I saw you. I got home from work, ran in here, and locked myself away so I couldn't forget anything about your face or body. I needn't have worried. I could never forget you, Scarlett. You're unforgettable."

He studied me, sketched, and perfected me. How is this real? How is this my life?

"See, I was one kind of 'un'," I whispered, tearing up as I took the image in, "maybe just not the one I thought."

I took the sketch from Finn, looking it over one more time before placing it back in his hands and resting my own on his chest. "Will you draw me now, Finn?" Discarding my clothes, I moved to the bed and lay naked on my side. "Draw me, then make love to me."

"Jesus, Red. You really will be the death of me." He stalked to the bed, but I placed my hand on his forehead to keep him at bay.

"Draw first. Sexy times later."

Studying me silently while licking his lips, he spun his empty chair and sat. Without blinking or taking his eyes from my body, he reached behind himself, slid open a drawer, and took out a fresh box of charcoal.

In silence, he began, his eyes shifting between my body and the paper. His jaw clenching and relaxing, his perfect features contorting as he chewed his gum. He stopped, stood, and studied me again, moving around the room to find the light. The expression on his face was slightly concerning, displeased almost. But then he walked to the other side of the bed and flung open the drapes, allowing a dim, almost eerie blue light to fill the room. I watched his silhouette before me, watching, considering me again, then resuming his seat.

"You should see yourself in the moonlight. You're glowing like a fairy."

"Do you have a lot of naked fairies in Australia?"

A deep chuckle shook through his body. "Yes, if you believe in them, we do have fairies. Gumnut babies. They have yellow willow blossoms or gum leaves covering their bottoms. So not entirely as naked or sexy as you."

Silence fell over us again, and time disappeared. I have no concept of how long I posed for him, how long I watched his tongue poke out the side of his lips, his brow wriggle and furrow in concentration, or how long it took me to fall asleep. But I certainly was aware of how I woke up.

Blond curls tickled the tender flesh between my thighs. His eyes looked up at me, and his tongue searched and discovered. Like a sculptor, he shaped me and molded me, repositioning my body till he found his desired light and angle, then hovered between my legs, one knee draped over his shoulder. My back arched from the bed as my hands grasped his head and pushed him deeper. His moans filled me, as did his fingers. He was so gentle and tender, yet hungry and demanding. I'd never known such pleasure. Before Finn, it was inconceivable.

When he found the perfect spot, I pushed into his face, begged, and pleaded, "Don't move! Faster, faster. Never, *ever* move." My heart fluttered, faltered, and my legs trembled. Finn was my everything. My end. My forever. Nothing on earth could feel like this.

This must be what it feels like in...

"Heaven, you taste like heaven." He stole my thought, and I allowed him to with no argument. He could take what he wanted from me. I yielded. Surrendered my all.

When I called his name and came in his mouth, he drank me in, demanding more, swearing he could never have enough. He kissed me down and climbed over my body, hovering above me with an elbow on each side of my head, and I tasted myself on his lips as he kissed me till I couldn't breathe. I was immobile, incapable of movement, or thought, or speech...well, almost. "Make love to me, Finn."

I accidentally stayed the rest of the week. I didn't mean to. It was just that one kiss, one touch, one night led to another and another. Saturday appeared out of nowhere, and adulting—as it always bloody does—came calling. I was due to pick up Ben and go home at three, and Finn had some things to do around the house. As did I, but he was much keener on actually doing his stuff than I was.

Apparently, Saturday was waffle day in his house, and as Finn, Iris, and I sat and ate our Nutella, strawberry, and cream-covered breakfasts, I had a brilliant idea—well, I thought it was brilliant. Finn, maybe not so much. "Guys, since you have some things to do, how would you feel if I took Iris out for a girl's day—well, morning, actually? I am supposed to be getting my hair cut at ten. Maybe Iris could come with me, and we can get our hair and nails done, do a bit of shopping, do a bit of lunching. What do you think?" Iris was up out of her chair, doing a happy dance, but Finn's eyebrows twitched suspiciously. "What's that look? Good idea? Bad idea?"

"No, no, it's a good idea. Great idea. I just... I don't know."

"Daaadddyyyy. Pllleeeaasseeeee."

"Iris, don't moan," he grumped.

She slumped in her chair and flopped lifelessly side to side while not moaning. "I am not mmooaanniinnggg."

"Bubs, Scarlett has been with us since Wednesday. Maybe she needs a little time to herself?"

"No, really, I mean it. That's why I offered. I would love to take Iris. Ben has no interest in doing this stuff with me. It would be fun. But you are the boss, Finn, and it's completely up to you."

We then stared him down, and when Iris fell to the ground and took up a kneeled praying position, Finn rolled his eyes and conceded. "Fine. You win. But Iris, no toys, no shoes, no crap. I think you've been spoiled enough lately. Got it?

"Got it, Daddy." She smiled like butter wouldn't melt.

She hadn't gotten it at all. I knew it. Finn knew it. So he turned to me, eyeing me with a steely determination softened by the hint of a side smirk. "That means you too, missy. No letting this little devil fool you into buying everything she wants."

"Got it, Daddy," I purred.

A fire I was all too familiar with lit in Finn's eyes, and his bottom lip disappeared beneath his teeth. His thoughts and intentions were clear, but cute little fingers grabbed mine and pulled me away. We winners then happily danced around the grimacing, horny loser.

43

Finn

I WAS ON THE edge—literally and figuratively. Perched on the edge of Iris's bed, I picked up the stray parts of Mr. Potato Head that littered the floor while listening to the lengthy recount of her big girl's day.

"Scaw and I both had ouw haiw washed next to each othew, and they wubbed my head, Daddy. It felt all wawm, and tickly, and nice. When Scaw's haiw was done, we went to the nail lady and picked the same nail colouw, and we didn't even mean it. And then..." It went on and on, and it was gorgeous. She was so excited and happy, beaming. But then her face changed, and her voice filled with hope, fear, and sorrow mixed into an innocent, heart-breaking tone I'd never heard before.

"Daddy."

"Yes, bubs."

"Is it okay if I want Scaw to be my mummy?"

The potato hit the deck. "What?" It may have been dark, and she may have been seven, but I'm sure she rolled her eyes.

"Is. It. Okay. If. I. Want. Scaw. To—"

"I... I heard you, bubs. I'm just surprised. You have a mummy already, Iris. Shelby is your mum."

"Yes, but she lives in Heaven, Daddy, and I don't even know hew. I know Scaw, and I weally like hew, and I think she likes me too." She looked at me through her curls. "Do you think she likes me, Daddy?"

I swallowed the lump in my throat and resumed the potato reconstruction as though my heart had not just been mashed into a bloody pulp. "Yes, I do. I think she likes you a lot."

"Wight, and you love hew. And when people love each othew, they get mawwied. So, if you mawwy Scaw, she would be my mummy, wight?"

"Well, kind of. She would be your step-mum."

"But I could call hew Mum? Oh! And Bunny would be my bwothew."

"Technically, I guess. But I think—"

"Okay, then. So, you mawwy Scaw, and then I can have a weal Mummy and bwothew." She then yawned, sat up, kissed my cheek, and snuggled back under her quilt. "Goodnight, Daddy."

This kid's brutal.

Picturing an imaginary pink and glittery dagger lodged firmly into my bloody, mashed pulp of a heart, I slunk from the room and left my innocent savage to sleep.

All too soon, I was back by Iris's side, kneeling on the floor as she violently tossed and turned in her polka-dot bed sheets, caught in the space between sleep and wake where confusion reigns supreme. A haunting cry had woken me, but who she called for right before her eyes shot open woke a fear in me I thought I had laid to rest.

"SCAWETT. I WANT SCAWETT." It tore through me like a bullet, dislodged something inside me, leaving me open and raw.

"Bubs, bubs. Daddy's here. It's okay. Don't cry, sweetheart. Everything's okay. It's just a dream."

"I WANT SCAWETT."

"Scarlett is at home with Ben, bubs. Shhhh. Daddy's here. Daddy will always be here."

In the dim glow of her nightlight, I witnessed her eyes change. Recognition of time and space returned, and she jumped into my arms, her tiny body gripping onto me so tightly I almost lost my footing. She continued to cry, mumbling the ludicrous atrocities she'd witnessed in her sleep as she yawned and rubbed her face into my shoulder. After several minutes, the kid wasn't budging, and I had lost all feeling in my crookedly twisted legs. I stood, cursing as an upside-down potato mouth lodged between my toes, and then carried her from the room. I was pretty sure she was asleep before her red curls hit the crisp white cotton of my pillow—a pillow blessed only hours ago by a much deeper Scarlett red.

Light footsteps on the squeaking timber floor roused me from my impending and much-craved slumber. I held my breath, rolled away from Iris, and found Evie's face popping around the doorframe.

"Is she okay?" she whispered so quietly I could barely hear.

"Yeah. She was asleep before I even laid her down."

Her features remained fixed. Even in the quiet dark of midnight, she knew something was wrong. "And you? Are you okay?"

"Yeah... I think. I mean..." I looked down at Iris, so cute, so sweet, so peaceful in her sleep, when the burn of Scarlett's name tearing from her lungs was still ravaging me. "Evie, do you think I've rushed into things? Introduced Scar and Iris too soon? Iris has become so attached to her already. Is it too..." Iris shifted in her sleep, kicking me in the stomach with the back of her heel, then rolling to face me and doing the same with her toes. She then smiled and stilled.

Evie giggled softly, and the rest of her body followed her face into my room, awkwardly pulling down the baggy T-shirt that almost reached her bare knees. Nate's baggy T-shirt. She tiptoed and sat on the edge of my bed. "You've done nothing wrong, Finny," she whispered. "Scarlett is the first woman you've opened yourself up to and the first you have brought home. I believe she will be the only one too. Iris loves her because she's fantastic and because she sees how much you do. We all see it, Finn. Everyone. Please don't try to control what's unfolding. Just let it be." Leaning down, she kissed my forehead, the back of Iris's, then tiptoed away.

"Evie," I whisper-yelled till her head floated back in. "I'm sorry I've been weird about Nate. You guys are terrific together and deserve to be happy too." One chubby tear dropped onto her cheek. She let it sit there, whispered thank you, and then disappeared.

$\cdot\heartsuit\cdot\heartsuit\cdot\heartsuit\cdot\heartsuit\cdot\heartsuit\cdot$

I woke with a toe in my nose, a foot resting against my neck like a blade, and a headache that could take down a football team. Careful not to disturb Iris, I removed the toe and crawled from the bed. An all-too-familiar feeling shrouded me as I walked to the kitchen, and it wasn't hunger—although I was bloody starving. No, this was guilt, an over-familiar and ever-present companion of mine for far too many years. The late night, or was it an early morning, conversation with Evie had done little to ease the doubt I was feeling over Iris's affectionate overtures toward Scarlett. In fact, my restlessness had confirmed it.

Scarlett was right to be pissed at me when I had made that clandestine visit with Iris. It was a mistake. I had used my daughter to manipulate her into forgiving me and, in the process, left her open and vulnerable to another crippling loss. It was selfish and short-sighted, and I was ashamed of it. Protecting Iris and fiercely guarding her heart was the most important thing in the world to me, but with one weak and stupid decision, I had undone all those years of work. For a heartbeat, I paused, realizing I'd been safeguarding my own heart all those years as much as Iris's. Regardless, I needed to fix the mess I'd made. I needed to secure Iris's future, and I had a crazy but brilliant idea of how to do it.

A work in progress as I walked to the closest key cutter, my plan was set into motion at the counter while a smart-ass kid with a face full of piercings gave me attitude. In all fairness, it had taken me a while to choose a key, but if they want people to be quick, they shouldn't have so many styles.

This was a big deal. I needed this key to make the right statement. *Should I go with clean and modern? Antique, novelty, or colored?*

Metal face didn't appreciate my indecision." Dude, could you pick a key already? I'm busting for a leak."

"Lovely," I muttered. "Ahh, give me that one, the old brass-looking one."

"Classy," he mumbled back.

While the metal-face smartass cut my key, I began to sweat. One second, I was pumped. The next, terrified. I knew my idea would be confusing for her. I myself had been confused an hour earlier. But everything was suddenly clearer than it had ever been.

With the key in my hot little hand and a head full of steam, I headed to my girl.

My enthusiastic and persistent knocking went unanswered. I pressed my head against the cool door, listened for signs of life, and could faintly make out Taylor Swift wafting down the hall. Smiling to think of Scar inside, dancing while making breakfast, I tested the doorknob and found it unlocked. "Scar? It's me. I'm coming in." As I hung my coat on the hook and quickly tidied the others that were hanging haphazardly, Scarlett's voice clashed with the music before it was turned off. Hoping to catch her unawares, I tiptoed toward her, the knot that had been holding my stomach ransom easing with each step. But then I heard another voice—a man's voice. Brett's voice.

Maybe I should have left, knocked, or again loudly announced my arrival. But I didn't. I softened my steps, edged closer, and snuck my head around the kitchen corner.

"C'mon, Lette. You don't have to love me. But you do have to do what's best for Ben. We can be a family. I know that's why you came to the States. For us." Then the asshole grabbed her, groped her, kissed her.

Jealousy and anger blurred my vision. Thanksgiving flashed before my eyes—Scar, Ben, and Brett on the couch, sitting together. A family. Just like she wanted. But I could hear her voice, and this was not what she wanted.

"Get off me now, you creep." Before I knew what I was doing, I was standing beside Scarlett, my chest heaving. My white knuckles twisted around Brett's sweater, releasing the sickening stench of whiskey and tobacco as he lay on the ground before me. "She's not going to make a family with you, dickhead. She's making one with me. I should kick your ass, you stupid son of a bitch."

"Finn. Stop. It's okay. I can handle this. Brett is a little over-hydrated and enthused after a big night out, but he was just leaving. Weren't you, Brett?"

"It didn't look like he was leaving, Red. It looked like he was making himself at home."

"What's the matter, Flim?" Brett sneered. "Can't handle a little competition? We could always share, I guess."

With all my strength, I lifted that asshole from the ground and was just about to strike when Scarlett jumped onto my back and wrapped her arms around my own. "No. No fighting. I am not some prize pig to be fought over. There is no violence in this house. Brett, you can't be here. You have to leave. And Finn, I think you should go too."

"Me?" I said, twisting my head side to side to try and catch a glimpse of Scarlett, who was still riding my back. "Why do I need to leave? I'm defending you. I came here to ask you to marry me and find this asshole pawing all over you, and you're asking me to leave?"

"Marry you?" Scarlett slid from my back and landed with a thud. "You were going to ask me to marry you?"

"Oh, God. This is precious. Haven't you two been together for, like, five minutes?" Brett scoffed.

"Shut up, Brett!" Scarlett and I yelled in unison. With a grunt, she kicked Brett's unsurprisingly small feet out of the way and positioned her body between us. Her face was flushed red and full of confusion I couldn't understand. "Finn, you can't be serious."

"I was. I am, I mean. Just hear me out, okay." I captured her face in my hands and caressed her soft cheek. "I decided that, yeah, we should get married. Iris needs a mum, right? And that lady at the tree lighting thought you were her mum. Then, after you left last night, Iris had a nightmare and was calling for you. When I woke her up, she wanted to know if she could call you mum. And the last twelve hours have been wall-to-wall mum. Everything is pointing me in this direction, Scar. I think it's some kind of sign." Scarlett wincing and Brett scoffing should have perhaps been a deterrent. They were not. "So, I thought we could move in together first, and then in the spring, we'll get married, and maybe begin making our own family together, just like you wanted. It'll be perfect."

My soon-to-be roomie stood frozen for a painfully long amount of time. The confusion on her face was not dissipating as she stepped back and out of my grasp.

"Finn, didn't you learn anything from Evie and Nate? Not to mention the whole house debacle? You can't decide all this on your own and just expect me to go along with it. And you most certainly can't ask me to be your wife just because Iris needs a mum."

"It's not *just* because she needs a mum. I love you, Red. And I know you want to get married. I've seen the Scarlett Austen signatures you scribble at work."

Hysterical laughter halted Scarlett's reply and made me jump six feet. "Please. Somebody bring me some popcorn. This is fucking gold."

With one hand on her hip and the other pointed toward the hall, Scarlett replied, "Brett, so help me God, if you don't leave right now, I'm going to...to...well, I don't know. But I need you out. Now!"

"Lette, come on. You can't seriously be choosing this clown over me."

"Brett, that's enough. Get out, and don't call me that. My name is Scarlett."

Still laughing, Brett climbed to his feet and grabbed his keys off the island counter. "She's all yours, Flim."

It took all my strength not to chase down and kick that guy's ass. But I had more important things to deal with. "You don't really want me to leave, do you, Red?"

"Honestly, I don't know, Finn. I don't know what's happening. I feel like I've been sucked into a black hole of stupid."

My hackles rose. "Stupid. Marrying me is stupid?"

"No, of course not. But Finn, we've only been together for a few months. The kids only just found out about us, and you want us to move in and get married without even talking about it first? We don't even have a key to each other's places."

"You do now. Look." I fished the key from my pocket and placed it on Scarlett's palm. "It's brass." Okay, even I knew that sounded stupid.

Scarlett's eyes darted between the key and me. Her eyes slowly pinched as she began to chew her lip. "This is the first time in my life I've been independent. I am just starting my career. I have my own home. I want you, Finn. I do. But I'm not ready to move in together yet, and I'm certainly not ready to get married."

"But the signatures."

"That's just playing around. A fantasy. Scarlett Austen, Jane Austen. It was just a game."

"Oh, so I'm a novelty to you?"

"No, no, that's not what I meant. Stop twisting my words. I love you, Finn. Surely you can see this has just come out of nowhere. For goodness' sake, until recently, I was convinced you were going to leave me and go back home."

A little dumbfounded, I clenched my fist and held it over my mouth. "What made you think that?"

She swallowed heavily. The elegant, long lines of her neck clenched and relaxed, and my fingers ached to touch her again, to soothe her. "I never told you this, but that day you went missing after your fight with Evie, Jan inadvertently let slip about your three-year plan. The one that had you going home in two and a half years and starting your own firm."

"Oh."

"Yeah, *oh*. I've waited for you to tell me about it. But you didn't, and I wasn't brave enough to ask. Just when I finally let go of the fear and began to feel secure, you throw this at me."

"Well, this should make you happy, then. I tossed that plan ages ago. I want to be with you. And if we shack up and get hitched, we're both getting what we want. Security for you, security for Iris."

"And what about love, Finn? What about wanting to spend the rest of your life with me because you love me and because we share the same goals and dreams? I'm not becoming someone's wife because they think I'm a good mum and have child-fuck-ing-bearing hips!"

Nothing she was saying was making sense. "Is this about Brett? 'Cause if it is—"

"Okay. You need to leave now."

"I'm offering you everything you wanted."

That cracked her. Silver lines of pain—the pain I caused—streamed down her face. All too late, I was hit with the clarity that fear and grief had stolen. "Finn, if you love me like you say you do, I am asking you to go away right now before one of us says something we are going to regret." I wanted to argue. To fight. But I knew she was right. "Please, Finn. Please just leave."

In hindsight, what I did next was the first right thing I'd done all day. I left, whispering, "I'm sorry, Scar," before heading out the door.

44

FInn

DRUNK ON MY OWN stupidity, I lay in my own putrid filth. The longer I marinated, the more idiotic I became, and the more the stench seeped from my pores. I reeked of it, and I knew I did, but I was too far gone to be able to do anything about it.

I'd had no intention of proposing to Scarlett. Moving in together? Absolutely. That was the plan, hence the key. The whole marriage thing was like an out-of-body, knee-jerk reaction to a mega-dick's massive ego being wounded.

With every grinding tick of the second hand, I replayed my words.

"I decided that, yeah, we should get married. Iris needs a mum, right?"

"But the signatures!"

"It's brass."

Nonsensical ramblings of a desperate man.

Watching that fuck knuckle, Brett, touch my Scarlett sent a spark of dumb ripping through me that sizzled all the way up my spine before exploding my brain.

My asinine decision left Scarlett in tears, fracturing what I was so desperate to hold together. It had Brett laughing at me and inspired him to say the only smart thing he'd ever said in my presence. I was a clown. To make it all worse, when I finally did the right thing—shut my mouth and left—Brett was waiting outside. He said nothing as I passed. We just shared a glare before he pushed off the wall, stomped out his cigarette, and stalked back toward Scarlett's door.

I had no idea if he went inside, and I wasn't sure if I would ever find out.

The thought of seeing her after what I did was simply too traumatic, so I did what I did when Mum, Dad, and Shelby died. I avoided it all and hid like a coward. Each call, door knock, and texted plea that was ignored only dug my hole deeper. The guilt joined with the pain of my past that I thought I had begun to release, to form a massive ball of shit that pinned me beneath it in the dark.

It was crippling, and it seemed contagious.

I wasn't sure how many days had already passed, but my melancholy isolation was on its last legs while listening to Evie and Nate fight with my ear pressed against the wall, and it was kaput by the time I drove him to the airport and backed up his decision to leave. Well, the isolation was kaput. The melancholy lingered.

"Nate, you and me. Me and you. We're better off batching it like we did in the old days. Women are trouble...love is trouble." Hoping to find some depressing grunge to back me up, I changed to a newly discovered radio station, *Smells Like the 90s*, and struck gold. "Something in the Way"—the most depressing Kurt Cobain warbling ever. Perfect. "If you look at it one way, Evie refusing to say she loves you is a good thing. Trust me, it's better to make the break now, because every day you spend together will only tighten the vise-like grip she has on your heart till you walk in on her kissing her ex, and she refuses to marry you, and then it all explodes in a shower of vibrant, sticky, bloody confetti."

That charming thought was finished off by another brilliant idea popping into my mind. An off-the-cuff comment that was enough to plant a seed. "Going home is the right thing to do...and maybe not just for you."

Sadly, my shenanigans with Scarlett and almost driving off the freeway from tear-induced blindness were not my lowest point of the week. That was still to come.

With Evie and I both moping around and turning on each other, Jocelyn swung into action. Iris was packed off to stay with her friend Cole for two nights, and she booked her favorite house in Tarrytown. This meant I could continue to cry like a baby, and Evie could drink like a fish without scarring Iris for life.

Book-ending me in the luxurious backseat of Jocie's town car, the women in my life turned on me when I finally caved and told them what I'd done *and* what I was considering doing. Well, I felt like they did anyway. Their reasoning may have been as true and solid as the gold decorating Jocie's fingers, but I was in no state to appreciate it.

"Maybe Scarlett refusing to marry me was a sign." I sighed. "I've lost sight of why I'm here. I'm supposed to be making life better for us and honoring Shelby as I promised. But all I'm doing is fucking everything up. Maybe it's better this way. For everyone."

Evie leaned in, I thought to give me a cuddle, but no. She slapped me in the back of the head and launched into a tirade. "You're a freaking idiot, Finn. Honestly, you're lucky she didn't knock you out. I would have. I'm tempted right now."

"Well if you're such a romantic genius who knows all the rules in love, why are you sitting here with us while your boyfriend is waiting for a flight to get away from you? Come on, let's hear it, Evie."

Punching me right in the face was what I expected Evie to do—and perhaps what I wanted. Watching her fall apart, making her sob and cry and almost panic chuck, was not.

I really was an asshole.

Things went from bad to worse. Within hours of arriving, Evie, who rightly refused to speak to me, lost her mind and left to chase Nate. Then, as I scoured the wine cellars for the good stuff I knew Jocie had hidden, the already shaky ground beneath my feet slipped or was dragged away.

"Listen to me, I know how my nephew thinks, and he is going to try and run. We had a deal, Jason—Finn's opportunity for my business and influence. Now, I don't care what you have to do, but if that boy leaves, my money goes with it."

"Jocie?"

The woman who had guided me through the roughest of seas dropped her phone on her lap. I watched the color drain from her face, and her fingers began to tap nervously. A family trait, it seemed—right along with interfering.

Without prompting, the excuses began. "Finny, I did what I had to do to save you. For years you shuffled between Sydney and Byron, never leaving your apartment or the farmhouse outside of work or Iris. You were miserable. Torn between two worlds but not living a day in either. All I did was help you get your foot in the door."

"Help me? Jocelyn, you bought my job. I think that's a little more than a foot in the door. You shoved your ass in and squatted."

"I did no such thing. It was a mere enticement to get you an interview. If you think the partners of a multimillion-dollar architectural firm would hire you just to get one woman from Australia's business, then you're not as smart as I thought you were. Yes, I threw a little influence in and did it again just now, but it was all blustering. They would never have hired you if I didn't see the potential bursting from your skin."

"I don't want to hear it. This whole thing, coming to New York, has been a mistake." Her pleas for me to stay and listen continued as I packed my things, but in my mind, I was already gone.

The next day, Bernstein and Wright confirmed Jocelyn's version of events. "We'd already seen your work in Sydney, Finn. We had been looking for young designers for almost two years at that point. That was how we got Grant and Digby. Your aunt's business was an added bonus."

"As happy as I am to hear that, I think it's time for Iris and me to move on."

We talked in circles for almost forty minutes, and eventually, Jason conceded and walked me out. "Just do me a favor, Finn. Sleep on it for a day or two, and then come back in for a chat. We don't want to lose you. And I don't think we're the only ones." Jason motioned to his left, and there she was.

Her eyes widened, her cheeks flushed red, and those flecks of hazel were quickly drowned out by tears. The plans she held in her hands hit the floor, as did my heart.

"Finn!"

That same whole-body tingle I felt when I first saw her was overpowering, and I damn near fell at her feet. But I didn't. My decision was made.

Two hours later, Scarlett stood before me, drenched and shivering from the rain and possibly nerves. She gasped and physically shrank within herself when I opened the door and sobbed my name with so much pain it splintered my bones. But no matter how the ground wobbled and quaked beneath me, I had to remain solid and upright. Determined and confident. I could do this. I could send her away...as long as she didn't touch me. Or I didn't breathe in her scent. Or look at her for more than a second.

"I'm swamped, Scarlett. What can I help you with?"

Her body jolted. My bitter coldness hurt. "Wow, that's...rather brutal." The nail-biting began, and I looked up, allowing the briefest glimpse of her soft lips chewing on her thumb before looking away. Just that nanosecond in time, that moment of weakness left me desperate to touch her. To feel the weight of her body against me.

"Finn! What the bloody hell happened? I know you saw me today. Why did you ignore me? Where have you been?" Her voice carried the tears I was too cowardly to see.

"I just came in to resign and didn't want to make a scene."

"You resigned? Finn, what the hell is going on?"

"Nothing's going on. As I said, I'm busy." I began to close the door, but she jammed her foot in front of it, pushed it open, and barged in. With a head full of steam, she marched into the kitchen and froze when she saw the boxes.

"What are you doing?" Her voice was deep. Raspy. Heartbroken.

Apart from dying on the inside? "Packing."

"Yes, I guessed that, but why? Where are you going?"

The vomit steadily rising in my throat was forced back down, and I looked up and took her in for the first time. Her once-glittering eyes were dull and heavy with tears and lined with dark black circles. The bouncy curls I was so desperate to touch sat wet, clinging lifelessly to her tear-dappled, rosy cheeks. Even red-faced and puffy, she was still the most beautiful thing I had ever seen.

"Home. Byron."

"What? You're going back to Australia? Wh...What... Why? When? When did this happen?"

"I've been thinking about it for a while, but after everything that's happened, I'm convinced it is the right thing to do for Iris and me."

"Finn! That's bullshit."

"You're right. It is. It's complete and utter bullshit. The whole me-in-New-York thing is, and that's why I'm going. I don't have the same luxury as you, Scarlett. I'm the only parent Iris has. I don't have a *Brett* lurking in the background, just waiting to make a happy family. It is my job to provide Iris with a future. One worthy of the promise I made her mum. I let you distract me from that."

She opened her mouth, but nothing but a huff of air came out. It took her three attempts to eke out, "You let me distract you?"

"That's what I said."

"Good God, Finn. You're so predictable. You're so shit scared of how you feel, you've been looking for an excuse to get out of this for weeks. and now you think you found it. And it's shit, by the way. I distracted you. Please."

"Yes. Yes, you did," I said, my voice rising with every word. "And I haven't been trying to get out of anything. I've had nothing but you on the brain from the moment I saw you. I went against my better judgment, discarded my plan, and fell for you. I wanted to move in with you, for fuck's sake. But it took your rejection and my aunt's betrayal for me to see just how wrong it had all been. Maybe I should thank you for humiliating me in front of my understudy—or wait, am I his?"

"Daddy! Who awe you yelling at?" Iris's sweet voice called out from upstairs, breaking the hostile stalemate.

"You blindsided me, Finn. I didn't reject you."

"Really? It sure felt that way. Now I think it's time you left, Scarlett."

"Is that it? No allowing me to explain or have a conversation about our future? No telling me what the hell you mean about Jocelyn? It's just moving back to bloody Australia. We're done?"

"Yep, it's done. If you don't mind, I need to look after my daughter. You should go back to Ben and do the same. I wish you well, Scarlett. You can see yourself out." With my eyes trained on my feet, I walked away, my heart turning to stone as I realized that was the last time I would ever see Scarlett Grant.

45

Scarlett

T HAT NIGHT, FINN CAME to me in my sleep, As beautiful as ever, his head turned to mine. Our eyes locked and lingered in a heated gaze that scorched my soul from across the room, but it was fueled by a different fire and left a different kind of burn. Gone was the kindness, love, and passion. There was no trace of the lust I had taken almost sadistic pleasure in so many times. The soft, heart-shaped lips I dreamed of that I cherished and kissed a million times were stiff and thin and had turned to a cold, unfamiliar snarl. It was anger. Betrayal. The closest thing to hate I ever wanted to see.

I woke awash in tears and wished it were only a dream, not my mind torturing me with the day's lowlight reel. Unable to get back to sleep, I slid on my robe, shoved my feet into my slippers, and padded my way to the kitchen. Tea was what I went for. Ice cream, cake, and vodka were what I ate. Now, I have shed a lot of tears in my life, but nothing compared to the torrential downpour that took place at that table. Then, after I dropped my spoon, I slipped in the funky monkey ice cream that I'd also dropped and fell, star-fished on the kitchen floor. Lying there with my heart racing, my lips tingling, my fingers numb, and my eyes fixating on the wasteland of coins, jellybeans, and hair ties beneath my oven, I lost the plot—if I ever owned one.

What have I done?

Why find your backbone now, you stupid, foolish cow?

Why is my floor so dusty?

I'm not sure how long I lay there or at what point I fell asleep, but a soft breeze sweeping across my skin forced my eyes open.

That damn dust swept before me like tumbleweeds, and a pair of polished Louboutins appeared out of nowhere.

"Don't get me wrong. You're so gorgeous you can totally pull this look off, but Scarlett, my darling, why are you sleeping on the floor?"

"This is where I live now. Down amongst the dust bunnies and a disturbing amount of long red hairs. I've ruined everything. It's where I belong."

After a heaving sigh and a surprisingly loud knee crack for such a young man, Teddy sat beside me.

"Hello." I sniffed.

"Hi, Lionel. Is it me you're looking for down there?"

"You do know most twenty-five-year-olds wouldn't get that reference, don't you?"

"Yes, but you're not most twenty-five-year-olds. You're Scarlett. My best friend, the bravest woman I know, and my adoring student in all things eighties pop."

"I do adore you. And your syncopated beats."

"Excellent. Now, tell me, where is Ben? And again, why are we lying on the floor?"

Rolling to my side just enough to pull out the packet of gummy candy wedged between my boobs, I shoved a handful in my mouth and then replied, "Ben's with Brett still. I'm lying here because I dropped my spoon and fell. Then I remembered that, in this very kitchen, I threw Brett out for asking me to ditch Finn, and laughing when Finn proposed while I rode his back—Finn's back, not Brett's. Oh, and I guess it was more of a proposition than a proposal. One I refused before asking Finn to leave, too. And then I remembered Finn disappeared, then reappeared, but will soon be disappearing again because I refused him."

"Okay. I'm beginning to understand the floor dwelling." Exhibiting why Theodore William Henry Digby III was the bestest best friend that ever existed, Teddy lay beside me, held my hand, and cried right along with me.

Still nursing his own tender heart, Teddy did his best to keep me, and possibly himself, busy. He got me off the floor, took me back to bed, and called in sick for work. The rest of the day was spent silently snuggled together in bed, weeping, rehashing, and sucking on a bottle of wine like babies at milk time.

"You know, some might say this is all your fault, Teddy. This is why I made my rules."

As though he had been expecting a tirade, he answered emotionlessly. "Thought they were ideologies, not rules."

"Whatever. If you hadn't pushed me, I would never have gotten involved with him. And I wouldn't have eaten my body weight in brownies, ice cream, and fudge."

Two seconds later, I apologized profusely and threw myself at his mercy.

"Fuck, I'm so sorry. You, my darling friend, have stuck with me through everything. Please forgive me."

"There is nothing to forgive. You're heartbroken, and it's okay. You need to yell, scream, recklessly and unfairly lay blame, and eat lots of shit. It's part of the process."

"Is it, though? Is it not too much? I've only been with him for a few months, but I've fallen so hard. Maybe I should have just said yes. Fuck. What was I thinking? He is everything I want, and I turned him down."

Teddy kissed my head as I lay on his shoulder. "I know. He is what you want, my darling. But I am so bloody proud of you. Scarlett, the doormat, is dead and buried. Finn is being totally unreasonable, and I would put money on the fact that a big, muscly part of him will soon realize that. The boy is licking his wounds. No one that gorgeous comes without a massive ego, Scar. Trust me. I know."

"I hope so. But you know what hit me as we finished that last bottle of rosé?"

"Oh, God. Did you fart? Geez, Scar. I told you to take it easy on the nachos. How many times must I talk about your body's reactions to cheese?"

I laughed despite myself and cracked a good, sharp slap across Teddy's thigh. "No, I didn't fart. I was going to say something wise and prophetic."

"Pathetic or prophetic?"

"Um, possibly both. I'll let you be the judge." To emphasize the seriousness of my epiphany, I sat up straight against the headboard, put down my wine, and cleared my throat. "Don't you think it's kind of cruel that the man who encouraged and empowered me to see my strength and find my voice is also the first to run when I use it? Its first victim, I guess you could say."

"Shit, you're right. That sucks some majorly big hairy balls. It's also the wrong *ic*. More ironic than pathetic or prophetic."

"Must you correct my grammar whilst I pour my guts out to you? Is that really the best use of your time right now?"

"Sorry. It's a habit I've picked up from Asher. He's big on word use. Well, he was. Also, I was critiquing your semantics, not your grammar."

"Oh, for fuck's sake. My point is, I can feel myself growing and I want to keep growing, but I want us to grow together. Guess that's not going to happen now."

"I think it will...as long as you stop eating cheese and brush your teeth. I think you will grow to become a big, bushy weed that no one can trample on, and I think Finn is going to be sprouting right alongside you...and in you...and maybe, if he's lucky, on your fabulous ti—"

"Teddy!" I squealed, whacking him with my pillow. He grabbed it from my hands and threw it to the floor.

"What?"

Resuming my prior horizontal position, I snuggled against Teddy's chest and pressed a soft kiss right above his heart. "Thank you."

46

Finn

"Bloody English," I muttered under my breath as Teddy pushed his way inside and surveyed the room with tired, sad eyes. As his gaze turned to me, I saw that his ever-present, cheeky glimmer was present, but dulled.

"You look like shit, Captain Koala."

"Wow, thanks, Theodore. Nice to see you too. Anything else before you fuck off?" Teddy didn't bat an eyelash at my grouchiness. In truth, I think it bothered me more. I hated being like this with him. He was a friend I truly valued and would miss. But he was also a friend who had this incredible way of having me confess all manner of sins before I'd even realized what I'd said, especially when it came to his bestie. I'd also had three shots of tequila before he arrived, which meant I was super vulnerable to his powers of persuasion. I couldn't afford for that to happen this time.

"So, the rumors are true. You're really leaving?"

"Looks that way."

He picked up a roll of tape and began twirling it on his finger. "What about Scar and work?"

"I tried to resign today, but Jason refused to accept it. He told me to think about it for a few days. I humored him, but my mind was already made up. I can't be there anymore."

"You omitted someone. Scarlett. What about her?"

I ignored him, snatched the tape from his hands, and kept packing. I was on the same box as I was when Scarlett was here. Her visit had resulted in quite a downturn in activity.

"Finn?"

"What about her?" I snapped, looking up from the bubble wrap to find an unfamiliar face. I'd never seen an angry Teddy, but I was seeing it now.

It was clear he was trying to play it cool, but he had a giant, throbbing vein running down his temple that looked as though it may burst any second, and his fists were tightly gripping onto the cuffs of his jacket.

Angry Teddy was intense. I felt like I should revert to calling him Theodore.

"Okay. So, it's like that, then, is it? No talk of Scarlett, the woman you love, my best friend, that you and your fucked-up, self-pitying attitude have absolutely shattered? She's right. You really are a coward." He studied my room again, taking extra time to look over my neatly organized packing system and the almost exact replica of my desk at work. "Even here, you have everything just so, don't you? All your boxes and pens are lined up in a row. All under control."

"Control? I have no control over one single shitty thing in my life. I most definitely can't control myself around her. That's why I need to leave. She makes me feel like being wild, and impulsive, and doing crazy shit like asking her to move in, proposing, and..." The power of Scarlett took hold and compelled me to do something unthinkable. My hands surged forward and grabbed a handful of red, blue, and black pens. There may even have been a pencil. I picked those bad boys up and then shoved them back into one ungodly mess of a container. Panting, I fell back into my chair, feeling free, almost feral.

The ridiculousness of my actions forced a laugh to burst from Teddy and even drew the smallest of smiles out of me. "Whoa, Finn. Calm down, big fella. Don't go blowing a gasket on me. Are you okay?"

"No, I'm not okay. And I haven't been for a long time. On the surface, I may appear calm, controlled, and organized, but inside, it's tears, guilt, and grief. And it's ripping me apart."

The pity in Teddy's brown eyes made me feel sick. I looked away, focusing instead on the mess I made on my desk. Then I saw it, Shelby's letter, trapped beneath those damn pens. I'd spent hours poring over and tormenting myself with the damn things and decided to share the pain.

I picked it up, threw it to Teddy, and tried to find a way to explain myself. "I thought if I made a go of things here for a while, I could take Iris home and really give her the happy life Shel wrote about. But then Scarlett happened. For a while, I felt like I was betraying Shelby by feeling the way I did for her. That I was somehow taking Iris away from her mum. But the harder I fell for Scar, the quieter that voice became. I thought I was moving on. But when she turned me down, I realized how much I strayed from my plans and promises. How at risk I was again. It was a slap to the face with a wet fish, but it was exactly what I needed. I don't think I could survive losing her if things got any more serious, Teddy. And it's selfish of me to put Iris in that position too. That's why it's just better to go now before I get us both in any deeper."

Teddy sighed, closed his eyes, and took a deep breath. "Look, Finn, I don't want to sound all preachy, but have you ever thought about getting some therapy? I found a great therapist here in The Village, and I can give you his name if you like?"

"You go to therapy? But you're, like, the happiest guy I know."

"Duh, because I go to therapy. I hate to tell you this, Finn, but you're not the only one with chaos running below the surface. Coming out at twelve to the British aristocracy that is my family pretty much scarred me for life. I've done therapy on and off since. No one can manage everything alone, Finn. By the sounds of it, you've got a lot to manage. Grief and loss of any kind bloody suck, and if you don't deal with it, you end up losing even more. Even people, like—"

"People like Scarlett?"

"Yes, people like Scarlett. Don't leave, Finn. She loves you as much as you love her. I have no doubt that she will and probably already does want a family with you, but you can't just ambush her with a proposal and expect her to fall at your feet." Teddy stepped closer and started to play with my hair. Oddly, it was very calming. "That thing you said to Scar about Brettles being your understudy was really shitty. She hasn't looked twice at

Brett since we've been here. I know you're hurt, but that was a cheap shot."

"I know."

"Good, that's a start." For some reason, he sniffed his fingers and screwed up his face. "You didn't even give her the chance to think or explain how she felt, and that's the bare minimum you owe her. Now, as for this letter…" he said, placing it in my hand, "reread it. Your grief has blinded you to the beauty of Shelby's words. You're not listening to what she's trying to say, either." He took two paces, hummed, and stopped. "Also, you need to wash your hair. That shit stinks." With a pat on the shoulder and a kiss on the top of my smelly head, he was gone.

Melancholy moodiness had me slump onto the floor, and there I remained for quite some time, looking at the mess I'd made of my room—and life. Shelby's letter, the constant reminder of my selfishness, sat beside me. Blinking through my tears, I picked it up and read it for the hundredth time.

Maybe it was the dim winter light, or the sound of the snow pounding against my window—something Shelby, who'd never traveled farther south than Sydney, had never experienced—or perhaps the simple freedom of a messy desk I didn't immediately clean. Or maybe it was the seed that Teddy planted taking root, forging new pathways and possibilities in my mind. I couldn't be sure, but somehow, everything looked different.

We will be happy.

I'd tortured myself with those four words for weeks.

Shelby wanted to be happy, and she wanted me and Iris to be happy. But she was gone, and I was here on the floor, a shell of a man who couldn't be further away from that very thing.

I read her words again and again, and with each reading, more of the weight, guilt, pain, and suffering that Scarlett's love had already begun lifting shifted even more.

Mum and Dad chose to go to Sydney to get my gift. I didn't pour whiskey down the throat of the truck driver who met them on that lonely stretch of road. That was all him.

Yes, I was lost and sad, but I did love Shelby. We *were both responsible for her pregnancy, but neither of us was responsible for her death.*

I wasn't responsible for Jocelyn giving up her business to live with us, nor was I for Evie choosing to care for Iris.

None of these actions had been my choice, my doing...my fault. And the things we had any choice in whatsoever were all done for love.

Like Scarlett loved me.

Like I loved her.

Like the kids loved each other.

I wasn't saving Iris by taking her away. I was hurting her.

I'd become so determined to live in honor of Shelby that I'd forgotten to live in honor of myself.

My epiphany struck with such force that all the air was expelled from my lungs, and I moaned and flopped on the floor like a whale freshly pierced with a harpoon.

I had to make this right, and I knew how to do it...kind of. First, I needed to consult Frances O'Connor and Jonny Lee Miller.

A bitter flurry of snow bit at my back as I waited at her door.

Her shadow remained deathly still on the other side of the frosted glass, possibly contemplating whether to let me in or kill me where I stood. I heard her mumbling, her signature, "Christ on a bike," and then, after what felt like an eternity, the door slowly opened.

My heart leapt to my mouth. *God, she's beautiful.* Wearing nothing but a baggy tee, shorts so tiny I could just see them, a two-sizes-too-big cardigan and a look of pain that pierced my soul, she was stunning. Before she could speak, maim, or slam the door on my face, my hand darted out and claimed her.

"This is going to sound corny as hell, but I'm just gonna say it, and you can't stop me, and here I go... Scarlett Grant. I love you as a man loves a woman. As a hero loves a heroine. As I have never loved anyone in my life. I was so anxious to do what was right that I forgot to do what is right. But if you choose me, after all my blundering and blindness, that would be a happiness that no description could reach."

The phrase "on tenterhooks" must have been devised by a bloke in this exact situation as me, because nothing else could perfectly describe the next few seconds. With a blank expression and unblinking eyes, she stood still. I watched her lips as she ferociously worked them between her teeth, and her tears began to fall. "Finn. You...memorized Edmund's monologue from *Mansfield Park*?"

"I did. I know I haven't been perfect—far from it. I also knew I would cock up or say something stupid if I used my own words, and I hoped if anyone could convince you, make you believe and forgive me, Edmund and Jane Austen could."

I expected—no, hoped for swooning, and I almost got it. There was a definite tilt or lean, maybe a slight weakening of a knee. I was so close to holding her in my arms I could taste it.

"Finn, I love you. You know I do."

"I love you too, Scar—"

"This was incredible, and I appreciate the effort you took to memorize that scene because you know how much it means to me. But..."

But...

"I've never asked for perfection. I've asked for promises to be kept and words to be sincere. If you think, for one second, that I can be swayed so easily into giving my heart back to you—the heart that you seem to think you can rip out and stomp on at will—then you've got another thing coming."

"Scar, I—"

"No, I'm sorry, Finn. You are a fantastic guy, the best I have known. I know how much and for how long you've been hurting, but that's no excuse. You're not the only one to have known loss, and you don't own the rights to heartbreak, grief, or trauma." Sniffling back her tears, she shifted on her feet and wrapped her cardigan tightly around her body. I wanted to replace it with my arms, to hold her and make her believe how sorry I was, but the anger in her eyes told me that wasn't going to happen. "You have no idea what disappearing and threatening to leave for good did to me...to us. It was one thing for you to turn your back on me, but you turned your back on my son, and I don't know how to forgive that."

"Scar—"

"NO! You know how much he loves Iris and you, but because of your embarrassment and self-indulgent paranoia, you refused to listen to me or believe in what we have. I've made a fool of myself for you, Finn. I've embarrassed and shamed myself at every turn, but I've also shown up and faced you each time. You've ignored me for days and threatened to leave the country when you didn't get your way! How do I know you won't do this again? How do I know you won't find another memory to reinforce your guilt or make another mistake you run from?"

"I won't! You have to trust me."

"Oh, like you trusted me?"

"Scar, let me come in, and we can talk." I took her hand and moved to step inside, but she blocked the door, then looked down at our joined hands. For a second, her face softened. I could see the love in her eyes, but then she blinked, then blinked again, and it was gone. All of it.

"No, you can't. Ben is sick, and he's asleep on the couch. You need to leave."

"Red."

"Stop calling me that." She sharply pulled her hand away, then looked me right in the eye. "You don't get to call me sweet names anymore. Goodbye, Finn."

The snow whipped into a deafening blizzard, and the door was shut in my face.

47

Scarlett

M Y HOUSE—TEDDY'S HOUSE—WAS A gorgeous 19th-century brownstone that was as much architectural art as it was a home. One of my favorite features was in the living room—a stunning stained-glass window added in the 1920s that overlooked my tree-lined sidewalk. When either sun or streetlight hit it at the right angle, an almost ombre rainbow was cast through the living room and hall. It was magical. I sat in its midst, in my favorite nook, with my back pressed against the arm of my couch. As my fingers reached for untouchable colors, I watched Finn walk from my life.

Framed in falling clouds of white, he stopped and looked over his shoulder every few steps. Maybe he was hoping to see me running, and most likely falling, as I chased after him, and I almost did just that several times. But my pride and that stupid bloody list stopped me. **Ideology #8 - I never have and never will be any man's fool, no matter how hot or sweet or fuckable he may be.** So instead, I counted the footsteps he left in the snow and the seconds he stood and waited. It was six for both. Six steps. Six seconds. *How like him to make a perfectly ordered pattern.*

Though absolutely, devastatingly heartbroken, I had little time to dwell. Ben lay before me with non-descript tummy pain, poo bum, pukey illness and was drifting in and out of fevered slumber. I'd placed his head on my lap when I resumed my sleep, his arms wrapped around his Bluey teddy he was too big for except when he felt poorly. I willed myself not to wake him with my crying. Instead, I let silent tears fall against my cheeks and trickle down onto my sweater.

"Was that Finn, Mum?" he asked, rousing again.

"No, darling, it was just the pizza man."

"We don't have any pizza."

"I know. He came to tell me they'd run out." Luckily, he was half delirious with a fever and didn't pick up on the stupidity of my answer. Nor did he seem to notice the heaving sobbing that had our bodies rocking back and forth.

"I'm cold, Mummy." His sweet little voice diverted my attention from my spiraling, Bridget-Jones-like visions of my lonely death and returned it to where it should be.

"I know, darling. It's because you have a fever."

"If I have a fever, why am I cold?"

"Well, because your brain is tricking your body into thinking it's cold so it will turn your thermostat up. When we are hot, we burn all the germs inside us. The fever is killing what's making you sick. Do you understand?"

"Not really."

"Hmm, me either. Would you like to watch something on the telly?"

"Yeah, maybe. But I really just want to feel better."

I pressed a kiss to his hot little forehead and the tip of his little freckled nose. "I know, bubs. What would you like to watch? Maybe if we distract ourselves, we will feel better."

"Beatrix, please."

After wiping my face dry, I gently slipped Ben from my lap and leaned to the coffee table for the remote. Beatrix Potter cartoons, like Bluey, were Ben's go-tos when he was sick, and if I was totally honest, I loved them too. Like Jane Austen, Beatrix was an inspiration to me, a woman before her time and another that had known true heartbreak. At least she didn't die alone like Jane did—and I probably would.

A neurosis-induced, guttural cry escaped me before I could stop it. At the same time, almost as though he felt it brewing in my lungs, Teddy burst through my front door.

"I just saw Fi—Shit, Benny! Bluey! Beatrix! Are you sick, little man?" He dropped to his knees before me and kissed Ben's forehead. "He's burning up, Scar." He then kissed me on my tear-soaked cheek. "Shit, you are too. Come on, you two, off to bed."

"No, I am fine, Teddy," I sobbed. "Our Ben wants to watch Beatrix, and I want to watch with him."

"You need to rest. Let me lie with Ben, and we will watch that saucy minx Jemima Puddle-Duck on his iPad. No, don't look at me like that, Scar, and don't argue. Please, please just listen to me and do as I ask for once."

Ben's head twisted up toward me. "Mummy, don't cry. The fever is making us better, remember?"

That was when I lost it. My considerate son broke what was left of my pitiful heart. Teddy could see I was fracturing in front of his eyes. He lifted Ben from my lap, hung him like a ragdoll over his shoulder, and helped me to my feet. "Please, my darling. Please go to bed. I will get Ben sorted and come to you as soon as I can. You're no good to anyone if you're sick too." He kissed my cheek again, then ushered me up the stairs and into my room, all with Ben balancing precariously around him like a cape.

My head hit the pillow that still smelled of him, and the tears rushed from me like water through a burst dam. All I had wanted this entire shit fuck of a week was to see and hold Finn. The man was finally standing before me, quoting my favorite lines from my favorite movie, and I sent him away. Simultaneously proud, horrified, and regretful, I cried myself to sleep while imagining Finn's warm body spooning behind me.

At five a.m., a hand gently tapping me on the shoulder rose me from a heartsick, restless slumber.

"Scar. Scar, wake up, darling. I think we need to take Ben to the ER."

Turned out there was nothing wrong with me. A severe case of heartbreak-induced female hysteria brought on my fever. Ben, however, had appendicitis and was rushed into surgery minutes after arriving at the hospital.

It was the first time Ben had been so sick, and I did not cope well. Thank God Teddy was with me. He answered every question the doctors and nurses asked, took care of the forms, and upheld my sanity during the surgery, all while keeping me safely tucked under his arm. But as grateful as I was to have him with me, all I wanted, all I needed was Finn. I tortured myself with the memory of his hand swamping mine before I sent him away. I stared at my palms, flexing them open and shut, swearing I could still feel his touch. Every man that walked by, every shadow that moved drew a hopeful gasp, "Finn, you came!" But of course, it was never him.

Waiting for Ben to wake in recovery, watching his little chest rise and fall, his body covered in leads, cords, and beeping machines, left me hollow. The surgeon had just finished explaining that laparoscopy wasn't a viable option as the appendix was too inflamed. This meant young Benny had a pretty sizable incision. He also had an infection, and the combination of the two meant his hospital stay would likely be five days at least. The poor little thing could hardly talk when he woke, but his eyes were full of concern as he drowsily smiled and wiped a tear from my cheek. "Don't cry, Mummy."

"It's okay for Mum to cry sometimes, Benny," I whispered. "These are happy tears because you are okay and smiling."

As he did with most things, Ben coped better than I did over the next twenty-four hours. He was up and out of bed—not for long, mind you—but his cheeky exuberance could not be tamed, even with IV antibiotics and a scar he couldn't wait to show all his friends. Turned out, he wouldn't have to wait long to show one particular and favorite friend.

Elegantly passed out in one of those hideous fold-out bed contraptions as Ben napped, I was woken by a featherlight tapping on my cheek.

"Scaw. It's me, Iwis." I jumped and squealed a little when I saw my reflection in the window. It was a sight to behold. My greasy hair was piled into a messy bun at the top of my head, with large chunks plastered to my forehead, somewhat masking my crimson, bloodshot eyes. Then, there were the pools of drool glistening on my chin.

"Iwis...I mean, Iris?"

Blue eyes and freckles smiled up at me. "Hello, Scaw," she whispered, brushing the hair from my eyes. "We came to see Bunny, but Daddy won't come in."

"Oh my gosh, hi, sweetheart." I swept her into my arms. Bubble-gum-scented curls tickled my nose. I kissed her so hard I must have almost knocked her pigtails right from her little head. "You are a sight for sore eyes. I've missed you so much."

"I missed you too, Scaw. Is Benny, okay?"

"Hi, Iris! I'm fine. Come and look at my guts! It got ripped open, and they took stuff out, and now I have a cord plugged into me like an iPad." I giggled at my adorable kid, and my heart swelled to see the care Iris took when gently cuddling him. Then I remembered.

"Iris, where is your dad?"

"Just outside on the couch, Scaw. He didn't want to come in and make you sad."

I had cried so much over the last forty-eight hours I was surprised I had any fluid left in my body, but apparently, I did, and *those words were the key* to set them free. I leapt from my chair and hit the floor like a cat ready to pounce.

"Benny, are you and Iris okay if I talk to her dad for a minute?" They didn't even answer. Ben was too busy telling Iris how much of his guts had been torn from his body.

I poked my head around the corner of his room and out into the hall. I didn't see him immediately but could hear him humming.

Three paces down and two to the left, I found him on a green plastic sofa a man his size had no right to sit on, absentmindedly gazing out the window. He made no move to indicate he heard or saw me coming, but the tinted glass showed a slight upturn of his lips before he turned my way. "Hi, Finn."

He may have wished he had remained focused on the rain, as I looked a dreadful fright. But he never let on. He stood, and the smile that covered his face was one of the most beautiful things I had ever seen, as were his tears.

"Hi, Red—sorry. I mean, Scarlett. Is Benny okay?"

He didn't call me Red. Just as I asked. I hated it.

"Yes, he is, especially now that Iris is here. How did you—?"

"Teddy called me this morning. We got over here as soon as we could. I'm so sorry, Scarlett. It must have been such a shock for you."

"It was. He got so sick so fast. The surgery went well, but he has a slight infection, so they plan to keep him here for a few days." I'd kept walking as I spoke, stopping when he was within arm's reach.

"Sorry I waited out here." He motioned to the sofa and slipped an inch closer. "I wasn't sure if you would want to see me after...well, you know. But I had to come and make sure he was okay, that you were okay."

"We're okay." I nodded, sucking my lips into my mouth and releasing them slowly. "How are things with you and Jocie?" His brow and chin rose as he studied me with suspicion. My question took him by surprise. "Evie told me. Seems between her and Theodore, we're up to date on each other's news."

"Seems so." A smile warmed his face, but his natural glow was missing. There was no dimple pop, no naughty eye sparkle. I hated that too. "Everything was fine with Jocie once I calmed down and took a good, hard look at myself. My decisions of late have tended to be rather hasty and underdeveloped, I guess you could say. I'm lucky to have her. She's given me lots of good advice."

"I would imagine Evie contributed to that department too.

"Please, she hasn't stopped."

Finn shifted uncomfortably on his feet, unease written all over his features. I could see the words sitting on the edge of his lips, but he seemed almost too frightened to say them. Similarly, I was too scared to hear them. After starting and stopping two or three times, a burst of laughter from Ben's room cut him off. "Bunny! Youw scaw is cool! I want one!"

A shared smile and eye roll seemed to give him some courage. Slowly, he reached for and caressed my cheek. Only lightly, and only for a second. "I probably shouldn't say this, but I miss you like crazy, Scar. I wish...I wish I could take everything back, that I could be who you needed me to be. I'm just so bloody sorry."

My heart demanded I console him, to hold and kiss and forgive him. But stubbornly, I refused. *I am no man's fool.* "I miss you too. And I hate this. But regardless of everything that's happened, you are and always have been exactly who I needed you to be." His breath caught on a sharp inhale. His blue eyes were so heavy with emotion they became an unrecognizable shade of gray. "But I also need to be who *I* need. You helped me find my voice, Finn, and with or without you, I'm going to use it. I've stood up to Victoria twice this week, and I even told everyone about Ben. His photos are on my desk now, and his science award is pinned on the family board in the staff room, just like all the other mums' and dads' useless crap. It's the best feeling. Something I wish I'd done a long time ago. HR Jan was thrilled and very proud of me."

"I'm sure she was. I am too. We both should have done that long ago. In fact"—his eyes shot to my lips, then back to my eyes—"I plan to do the same when I come back next week."

Come back? Next week? A million tiny bubbles of joy burst beneath my skin, and heat burned my cheeks. I tried to stay still and calm but could also feel myself bouncing on the balls of my feet. Finn noticed, and that dimple was back and popping.

"Oh, so Eves didn't share that little tidbit, eh?"

I ignored that and tried to remain indifferent. "So, you're coming back to work? That's great. Jan will be thrilled with that too."

A silent giggle shifted his body. "She is. She promised me cake."

"Excellent. So, just to clarify... That means you're not—"

"Not moving back home? No—I mean, yes, I'm staying. Iris and I are staying."

"Wow. That's big. What brought on the change of heart?"

Finn rubbed a strand of my hair between his fingers, then gave it an affectionate tug. "You did, Scarlett. You, and Ben, and Iris. But especially you. You stole my heart the first time I saw you. I wanted you, and it wasn't just physical. Something about you called to me. Calmed me. Then I saw your sweetness. Your kindness. Your strength. Your tripping, spilling your coffee down your dress, and giving me my first, 'Christ on a bike.'

You're everything I want, Red. And I'm glad I helped you find your voice, because you've helped me find my peace. I know I have been an ass, and I know I have put you through a lot. But if you will have Iris and me, I'm...we're yours."

Maybe I was a fool. But I was a fool for one equally foolish man.

In the blink of a tear-filled eye, **Ideology #9 — Left free to make on-the-spot, rash decisions justifiable**, became, **Ideology #9 - Always forgive Finn Austen.**

All it took was a nod, and the jagged fragments of two scared and lonely hearts shifted back into place. He seized my waist and pulled my body against his. He looked into my eyes, smiled, then kissed me. His tongue teased my bottom lip, and every single part of me felt safe, and protected, and whole. I was free. Free to let go of my body, and my fear, and just be. It was so easy to become lost in him again, because in him, I had found acceptance. For him, I was enough, and for the first time in my life, I was enough for me too.

"Scarlett." He rolled his hips into mine, then stilled. I could feel him shake with restraint, and after one last squeeze of my bum, he clenched his hands and inched his body away. Not his lips, though. His lingered, ghosting mine. "I never want to let you go, Scar. Not ever. But I have to stop kissing you now, or I'm going to be arrested."

Faint giggles coming from behind us broke us apart on a sigh. "You were wight, Bunny. They were kissing." Peeking around the corner of Ben's room was Iris. But with one stamp of Finn's foot, she was off, laughing and telling Benny everything would be alright.

"I love you, Finn Austen," I said, gasping for air after another thorough kissing, "but I will fucking end you if you pull this shit on me again."

"Always with the threats," he giggled, then kissed me again. "I love you too, Scarlett Grant."

Circumstances as they were, seven long, grueling days passed before we had any time alone. But you can bet your ass, as soon as I was sure Ben was okay, I left him at home in Teddy's trusty hands and arrived at Finn's in search of his. Taking a page from his list-making book, I arrived with a bottle of red, a wishlist of depraved acts I demanded he perform on me, *and* the spare key he had so painfully returned. The minute he opened the door, I grabbed him, kissed him, and rubbed my body against his. "This key belongs to you. You're my home, Finn. You're my family. Take it. Use it."

"I will, Red. I promise."

"Good, now shut up and hold onto your socks, Finny. An unreasonable amount of fucking is about to take place."

48

Scarlett

"Mum, Mum, Mum, Muuuummmmmm. Wake up. It's Christmas."

My head popped out from my blanket, and my eyes attempted to focus on my clock.

Christ on a bike.

"Ben! It's 6 a.m., for God's sake. Go back to bed."

"I can't, Mum. We can't. We want to open our presents. Pleaseee."

"Bed! Or I will call Santa and tell him to come and take the gifts back."

Smugly smiling, I looked down and spotted my present, the one waiting for me almost every morning when I woke. Finn's mess of curls laid across my stomach, his face still hidden between my legs, too occupied with his English breakfast to come to the surface. All was quiet outside, so I lay back and let the warm pleasures of Finn's mouth wash over me again.

"Please, Mum. We're desperate."

"Yeah, we aww despewate. Come on, guys. Let us innnn."

I ran my hands through Finn's curls and tapped his head. "Great, Iris is there, too, now. We better get up—ouch! Hey, no biting." He said nothing, just chuckled.

"Muummmmmm."

"Fuck!" I swore. "Fine, give us ten—what? Oh, give us twenty minutes, and we'll be down."

Footsteps faded. I pushed my hips off the bed, beckoned Finn higher, and flipped him onto his back. "Twenty minutes, eh? We better get busy, big fella." Straddling his thighs, I positioned his hardness at my entrance and slowly slid down. Inch by inch, I took him in, relishing the stretch, the feel of him filling me.

His fingers dug into my hips and pulled me hard against him. "Fuck, Red. I don't think I'll ever get tired of that." When he was fully sheathed, when I could take no more, I began to move and grind into him. "All those nights spent waiting and dreaming," he sighed, "of being naked in your room, and here I am."

"Umm, was I involved in these dreams, or was this a thing you have about being naked in other people's rooms?"

"Bit...oh, yes, Christ... Bit of both."

Squeals echoed from downstairs. "Shit, we have to be quick, Finn...ohhh, fuck. They're going to destroy the place."

"If you keep clenching around me like that, I don't think that'll be a problem." Finn's giant hand cradled my back. He sat beneath me, capturing, and sucking my nipple, licking up to my neck and back down again, repeating the delights to the other breast, and adding a bite for good measure. I rode him hard, our eyes locked, our hands clawing at each other, twisting through each other's hair.

He was so beautiful like this, so big, so strong, and lost in a passion that never seemed to fade, no matter how many times he had me. "You're so fucking gorgeous," I whispered, grabbing his face and kissing him blindly. "Lie down," I demanded before pushing him onto his back. My hands roamed his chest and abs wet with sweat, and I raised my knees to feel him slide even deeper.

"I can feel all of you like that," he almost cried.

We fell into a fast, frantic rhythm, my untamed morning curls bouncing wildly around my head as I looked down upon my best friend and lover. "I still...can't believe this...this is real," he panted, molding my ass in his hands. "Scarlett Grant and her tight little pussy are fucking me on Christmas Day!" His comical but oh-so-hot carnal excitement pushed me closer to the edge. "I can feel it, Red. I can feel you coming." Reaching between my legs, he circled my clit with precision. "That's my good girl. Come for me, baby." I exploded almost immediately, the whole world shaking as I fell apart on top of him.

"God, I love watching you come," he growled, his thighs quivering. He rolled me onto my back, the weight of his body crushing mine as he pumped harder and faster. Still recovering from my orgasm, I was desperate to see Finn find his. I pulled my body from the mattress, licked, and bit his nipple, and then watched his perfect face twist as he froze, shuddered, and came inside me.

After too many jokes about Santa's sack and coming in my chimney, Finn and I crawled from bed, neither particularly in control of our trembling legs. I thought we had a lot of sex when we first got together, but since our reconciliation, we must have broken all bonking records in existence.

Our first Christmas together was going perfectly.

We finally left my bed and came downstairs to find the kids sitting beneath the tree. Iris had the presents already organized and sorted into piles, making Finn beam with pride. "Look, they're even sorted by size."

Seconds after it began, the unwrapping was over, and the floor was littered with paper and boxes. The kids were thoroughly spoiled with new bikes, toys, books, and—much to their disappointment—clothes.

Finn was excited about his new surfboard, wetsuit, and a solid few months' supply of Caramello Koalas. And I didn't do too badly, either. The first gift I opened was the Austen books, which I screamed in delight over, especially the gilded *Pride and Prejudice*. Along with the books, he gave me a beautiful Australian opal necklace that I'm terrified to know the price of, and a collection of framed sketches of Iris and Ben. How he got those two to sit still and pose for any length of time was a miracle, but it was worth it.

The showstoppers arrived just before we sat down to eat. The kitten Mrs. Horowitz was bringing for Ben had become two kittens. One as planned for Ben, and one for Iris. Never in my life had I seen such joy or heard more happiness from two kids than what I saw when the wee babies were placed on their laps. Both received names on the spot. Both were...interesting. Iris christened her kitty Katy because she looked like Katy Perry. Yeah, we couldn't figure it out, either. And Ben's cat was christened Salem because she was black, like a witch. Perfect sense.

49

Finn

I SAT AT SCAR'S dining room table, a stupid paper crown on my head and an even stupider grin on my face. I tightly held one of Scarlett's hands beneath the tablecloth and kissed the other every time she looked at me, which was a lot. I couldn't have been more grateful. My heart was as full as my belly.

And what had we feasted on? What had filled us all to the point of explosion?

Like in many scenarios in life, the Aussies and the English were unable to choose between the two traditions, so we combined them. Scar and Jocelyn cooked a traditional English Christmas that, in all honesty, was enjoyed by many Australians. Turkey, ham, chicken, stuffing, gravy, the best roasted potatoes I had ever eaten, and of course, pudding.

Evie and I did the modern Aussie seafood version—prawns, lobster, and oysters. We were all disappointed that our favorite Moreton Bay bugs couldn't be sourced in time.

It was a delicious and emotional meal. Halfway through dessert—yes, she also made the bloody banoffee pie again—it hit me. Not the pie, although that would hit me later, too, no doubt.

What hit me with such soul-inspiring clarity was that everyone I loved and cared about in this world—some that I'd come so close to losing—were here. I had chosen many members of this family, but they were family. Even with my mind-boggling carelessness and stupidity, I had managed to surround myself with so much love and affection that I could barely contain my tears. Between mouthfuls of pudding and tender kisses, I shared my realization with Scar, who was equally moved and a little proud.

By four p.m., Jocelyn and Evie were deep into a food coma, as were the kids. Teddy had taken off to celebrate or drink away the rest of his Christmas alone. I was pacing the hall, my cock harder than the trunk of the Christmas tree and standing at much the same angle.

Scarlett was hidden in her room, apparently preparing one last surprise gift. The way she'd whispered "*gift*" into my ear, with her eyebrows wriggling and a particularly naughty twinkle in her eye, well and truly got the blood pumping, hence my state.

She just had to bloody hurry up so I could see it. There was no telling how long we had till the little people woke.

Another few minutes passed. I had my ear pressed to the door, and I could hear her swearing and cursing, which did nothing to help my state because there was nothing I loved more than Scarlett and her dirty mouth. Another minute passed, and I'd waited long enough. "Red, I'm coming in."

"Finn, no. I'm not ready!"

I burst through the door, and there she was, standing in the middle of the room, her back to me. Her hair was twisted into a long, loose braid over her shoulder, and she wore the long white robe Ben had given her hours before. It sat deliciously over the curves of her body and barely covered her perfect ass.

"I thought I asked you to wait. I'm not ready, Finn. I can't get the damn thing on." On the bed laid a sexy-looking Mrs. Claus negligee thingy that would have looked fucking amazing. But nothing, no lingerie in the world, could look better than a naked Scarlett. Luckily, that was what I was about to see. Scarlett turned to face me, and the robe fell open as she did. Rather than stop it, she shimmied and let the gown slip from her shoulders.

Standing before me, completely naked, was the most beautiful thing I had ever seen. Every time I saw her like this, she stole the air from my lungs all over again. Her breasts, the feminine curve of her stomach, and the swell of her hips were all beyond perfection. My eyes roamed every inch of her truly glorious skin but were drawn down to her bare center. I had to have it.

I almost ran to her, dropping to my knees and plunging my head between her legs. My hands grabbed hold of her ass and pulled her onto my mouth. She moaned and almost fell over my back as I sucked her lips and slipped my tongue between them.

"Finn!"

I circled her clit, tapping and stroking, edging closer and closer, feeling her body tense in anticipation, then slipping away. I did it again and again, drawing frustrated grunts and groans. When her nails began to dig into my scalp, I yielded. I forced her legs wider and began flicking her clit until she started shaking. When she was right on the edge, I slipped away again, dipping my tongue deep inside her pussy, fucking her over and over. "You taste so good."

She was so fucking wet, but I needed more. I refocused my energy back on her clit and tried to ignore the blinding ache of my own.

She grabbed my head, gently guiding me into the perfect position, and cried for me desperately. "Your fingers, Finn. Please, I need you to fill me."

A moan, deep from within my soul, was my only response. I took one hand from her ass and slowly slid it up her thigh, running my fingers through her wetness and then sliding a single finger inside.

"More, I need more."

A second finger slipped in and fucked her, and she clung to my back, digging her nails into my flesh as I worked them in and out while continuing to taste her. The first few thrusts were awkward. I wasn't sure I was doing it right as I'd never done this in an upright position. But the wild, hedonistic reactions, movements, and sounds escaping her told me I was probably doing okay.

"Fuck me, Finn," she breathed. "Harder!" I added a third finger and pumped hard and fast against her G-spot. My tongue became frenzied, and I quickly found a rhythm that had her begging for mercy. Releasing her grip off my back, her hands pulled on my curls, her whole body shook, and her pussy tightened around my fingers. Finally, she released, coming on my tongue as she screamed my name repeatedly.

She pushed my head deeper in, moving my lips against her entrance, desperate for the wave to continue, for the feeling to never end. I let her use and abuse me for as long as she desired. When she could take no more, she stepped back. I pulled my head out from between her legs, slid to the floor, and took several long, deep, lung-filling breaths.

The combination of sexual thrill and lack of oxygen hit me hard, and I began to feel a little dizzy. Scar soon joined me, slumping to the floor, just as breathless and giddy.

"For the love of fuck, Finn. I hope you're not too exhausted. That lingerie cost me a fortune, and I'm not leaving this room till I get it on and you've ripped it back off."

Our hands entwined, and we sat looking at each other, laughing, panting, and smiling.

"Have you...phew, I'm knackered...enjoyed our first Christmas together, Miss Grant?"

"Why, yes, I have. How about you? Has today lived up to your always-lofty expectations, Mr. Austen?"

"Bloody oath."

"Oh, God. Are you going to go full Aussie on me? Should I open the Urban Dictionary on my phone in preparation?"

I sat up and flashed my cheekiest grin. The one I knew melted her bones. "Maybe it's a good idea. You will have to practice your Aussie for when we go home next month."

"What?" Scarlett bolted upright so fast, her head smacked into my chin, and we both fell back against the floor.

"Shit, Scar. I thought you'd be excited, not try to knock me out."

"Sorry, but Australia? You want us to go to Australia next month? But...but..."

"But nothing. It's all sorted, all approved at work. Hey, don't look at me like that, Red. This has nothing to do with me controlling the situation and everything to do with spontaneity, and to make sure that was the case, Teddy gave me the all clear. I didn't want to book the flights if we both couldn't get the time off work, and even if, for some ridiculous reason, you didn't want to go, I made sure the flights could be changed, and the four of us could choose somewhere else."

"The four of us? So, the kids are coming too?"

"Of course, I want you and Ben to see where Iris and I come from. Part of sharing our life is sharing our past. You've helped me see that, Scar. Technically, it may be five of us. I'm trying to talk Evie into coming."

"Free babysitting!" we chanted in unison while high-fiving.

"It's gonna be great, Red. A whole month of summer days, sleeping in, and sex on the beach."

The look on her face was worth a hundred airfares. Her mouth was forming a perfect little O before, but it was so wide now I could comfortably park my Jeep inside. "A month!"

"Yeah," I laughed. "It's a bloody long way to fly, Red. There's no point sitting on a plane for twenty-three hours and only staying for a week. A month gives us heaps of time. I can show you Byron, but we can drive to Sydney and up north to Queensland too."

"Oh, my God. This is incredible. I would love nothing more than to go home with you and to travel wherever you want to take me, Finn. This is the sweetest, most generous thing anyone has ever done for Ben and me. I just can't believe it. I am definitely freaking out, but it's bloody brilliant, thank you."

After a thorough kissing, the cheesy grin returned. "Ahh, you're welcome. I'm just so damned relieved you're pleased and said yes."

"Did you honestly think I would say no? You must stop with the surprises, though. I'm going to bloody pass out!" She was genuinely blown away. And so was I. Not only with her response, but with what a difference a few weeks and a few dozen heartbreaking, tear-filled conversations can make. I felt free. Happy. In love.

Signs of life soon returned to the house. Noisy little footsteps could be heard up and down the stairs, and adorable, contagious laughter soon followed. "Looks like your little outfit will have to wait, Red. Never mind, though. I'll get the kids out on the bikes and wear them out. We can get them asleep again in no time." Knowing Scarlett's nakedness gave me an unfair advantage, I decided to give a bit of cheek. "And hey, if the bikes don't work, we can always feed them some of your banoffee pie. That will knock them out for sure." I took off, running out the door and down the hall, laughing as she yelled after me.

"Wait! What do you mean? I thought you loved my pie!"

Epilogue

Scarlett

TIME SLIPPED BY SO fast that the memories made along the way were sometimes hard to hold onto. It was both a blessing and a curse that some phases and points of my life were a jumbled blur. A mash of faces, places, and events that seemed further and further away each year. But every moment spent with Finn had been etched into my body and soul. With vivid clarity, I could pinpoint the moment he first touched, kissed me, made me laugh, and cry. True, these memories were not so old, but I believed they would linger forever.

On the twelve-month anniversary of our first kiss, something big, something I hadn't planned but hoped madly for, finally happened, instantly becoming another memory to be treasured.

Benjamin and I arrived to spend the weekend at Finn's. It would be our first weekend with only him and Iris at his house. Finally, the master of his own domain, Finn was repainting the house and had somehow suckered Benjamin and me into helping.

Iris answered the door and was adorable, covered head to toe in bright-pink paint. After inviting us in, stopping in the kitchen for a quick cookie-and-milk refueling, she then led us to one of the spare bedrooms at the rear of the house, giggling cheekily, almost evilly, the whole way.

Something was fishy. "What are you up to, missy?"

"Nothing Scaw, I pwomise."

Like a fox with heightened senses, I stood clear of the door and nobly pushed Ben in front of me for cover. I was ready. The door was flung open to reveal Finn, equally but somehow neatly, covered in paint, similarly adorable, down on one knee with a bunch of flowers in his hands. Iris ran to his side, knelt beside him, and took a small bag of Benjamin's favorite chips out of her pocket.

"Scawlett, Benjamin," she said, then looking at Finn.

"Oh, right, my turn. We, uh..." Iris nodded impatiently, and after giving her a quick kiss on her nose in appreciation, he battled on. "We love you with all our hearts. You two are the best things that have ever happened to us, and I"—Iris elbowed his side—"oh, sorry, *we* have two things to ask you."

I legitimately thought I would die and truly wished I wasn't wearing a Guns n' Roses t-shirt and sweatpants with holes in the crotch.

"Will you, Scarlett and Benjamin, please come and live with Iris and me here—not in this room obviously—God, I mean, here, in this house? We want it to be our house...home. We want you to be our family." He stopped to take a deep breath, Iris using the time to reach up and dry her dad's eyes and dab the sweat from his brow. I began to move toward him, my hands covering my mouth in shock.

"Wait, wait, there's more." I did as I was told and froze on the spot. "Scarlett Elizabeth Grant, I cannot envision a life without you. I need you by my side forever." Iris then pulled a black ring box from the other pocket of her denim overalls. She smiled and opened the lid to reveal the most perfect diamond I had ever seen.

"Will you marry me, Red?"

It was perfect. Unlike the first time I heard him say those words, he was as perfect as the most perfect Austen-esque dream.

Until I moved.

"Yes! Yes to both!" I cried as both Benjamin and I ran to him. Aiming to jump in his arms, I leapt joyfully into the air, but my combat-boot-wearing foot caught on the handle of a nearby paint can. My foot slipped inside, and I, and the can, went ass over tit, somersaulting through the air, spraying paint like a sprinkler, and landing in a most ungrateful pile before him.

Of course I received hearty applause worthy of my fine acrobatics display. "That was fantastic, Mum! Do it again!"

Finn pulled me onto his knee with one of his biggest, sexiest smiles, whispering as he kissed me, "See that. That is why you have to be mine."

"I'm a mess," I cried, burying my face into my pastel hands.

"Yes, you are, but you're my mess." He smiled and took my hand in his. "My hot mess. And I love you," he said as he slid the ring on my finger, and we kissed and kissed and kissed. Iris then piled on top of Ben, and it was the happiest, sloppiest, most tear-filled group hug that ever took place.

After several minutes of joy, and celebration, and screaming into the phone with Teddy, Finn and I were desperate to be alone. Iris and Benjamin were sent outside to play and eat the chips. The minute the back door closed, and we heard the distinct sounds of laughter coming from the trampoline, we ran to Finn's room, laughing, kissing, and disrobing the whole way.

"Lock the door, Finn. Lock the door!" Finn peeled off his shirt, pushed me onto the bed, and then did what he was told, locking the door and checking twice that it was secured before turning, growling, and hunting me down. It wasn't hard. I was lying naked, legs splayed, waiting. He hesitated for a second. I had gotten paint on his sheets and possibly on the headboard, but he shrugged his shoulders and boldly went with it.

"I'm gonna ask you to marry me every day 'till I get to call you my wife," he sighed as he dove between my legs and ghosted his lips over every inch of my trembling body. When he finally made it to my mouth, he kissed me hard and deep and smiled his cheekiest smile against my lips. "And when you move in, I'm gonna fuck you every day too."

He slipped his fingers through the mess he'd made of me, then dared to laugh at the almost-hiss his touch incited. "Red, what the hell was that?"

"Shut up, kiss me."

"Not until you make that noise again. It was very sexy. I don't think I've heard that one before."

"Christ on a bike, just fuck me."

"Well, okay then. But I must say, the fact that I can still elicit new noises from you after a year does wonders for my ego." Still chuckling, he drove hard inside me, forcing not a hiss but a toe-curling scream from my lungs that half the street must have heard. He clapped his hand over my mouth, laughing and shushing me while pounding into me at a fierce, ungodly pace.

"Soon, you're going to be mine, Scar. My Mrs. Austen," he cried. "This is your home. Here with me."

"Yes," I cried. "I am yours. I will be Mrs. Austen forever."

"Will you make that noise forever?"

"Will you make me make it?"

"Let me try."

His smug face shone brightly above me. His hips slammed into my ass, again and again, becoming erratic and wild as he watched an orgasm unlike any I'd experienced crash over me. His hand clamped down over my mouth again as my moans of ecstasy filled the room, and my long, shaking legs twisted around his body. I clung to him for dear life, and he raced to his peak, crying my name, his lips on mine.

Finn was so confident in our acceptance of his proposals that amongst the cans of paint lined up in order of size and shade was a variety of colors for Ben to choose from to decorate his new space. A deep gray was selected, and work began.

We were all so eager to start our new life that while Finn and the kids painted, I went home to collect the first of our things. In honesty, it was part excitement and part need to get out of painting, which I bloody hated.

The timing was perfect and undoubtedly intentional.

Hard times—the British tax man—had hit the Digby family, and the poor bastards had been forced to sell two of their multi-million-dollar townhouses. I know, tragedy.

As well as being karma for their less-than-supportive attitude toward their darling son's "lifestyle choice," as they called it, the sale meant I would soon be out on my ass. Since Teddy's house remained in the portfolio, the plan had been for Ben and me to move in with him. Packing of non-essentials had already commenced and would now be tackled with even greater gusto.

Mrs. Horowitz had already moved on. After a nasty fall a few months ago—which she fully recovered from—she and her sixty-five cats had moved in with her son just one block away.

Just as he always did, Teddy arrived right when I needed him most—as I was about to fall and break my neck as I attempted to balance my first load of boxes down my front stairs and onto the pavement. I was caught in mid-air and set down safely by his strong and capable arms.

After holding me in a lingering embrace, he released me and, as per tradition, provided my daily vitamin D via a soft kiss on the lips. "What am I going to do without you, Theodore William Henry Digby?"

"Have sex every day and be ridiculously happy?"

"Ughh, perish the thought."

In an occurrence so rare I couldn't recall another example, Teddy helped me load the car in complete silence. I had so many things to say but no words to express. How could I say thank you for all he had done?

When the last box was packed, he closed the trunk and began to cry. "I know you're not leaving yet, but this really fucking hurts. I'm so happy for you, but bloody hell, Scar. I am going to miss you so much. It physically hurts to breathe."

I threw myself at him, almost knocking him to the ground. "I know, me too." It wasn't a goodbye, but it really bloody felt like one. "Thank you for everything, Teddy. None of this would be happening if it wasn't for you. None of it. Not America, not the job, not Finn. It's all because of you. I can never, ever, ever repay you."

"As much as my giant head would love to take credit for your many successes, I think you're selling yourself incredibly short. All this happened because you are intelligent, talented, and loving. You are everything good in this world, and everyone who meets you sees that. They see you, Scar. You have done this all yourself." Blubbering beyond comprehension, he held me close to his heart and kissed the top of my head. "You don't need Jane Austen to write you one. You are your very own heroine, Miss Grant."

Complete adorableness greeted me on my return. All three of my loves were huddled in a pile beneath the warmth of Iris's favorite Bluey blanket, sound asleep, with Katy and Salem curled beside them. My heartfelt sigh woke Finn, who impressed me greatly with that stealth commando roll that every parent knows. Rising gracefully and kissing me soundly, we enjoyed several minutes alone before the smell of the pizzas I'd brought home woke the eternally hungry kids.

Team Finnlett became family that night as we sat on the floor, eating, talking, laughing, and making plans. I looked to the man sitting to my right, stealing pepperoni off my slice and laughing at the sauce on my face—Finn Austen. The future was ours for the taking, and even though I had no idea what it would look like, where we would end up, or what would happen along the way, I didn't need to. I had faith in us and wholeheartedly believed that he would be there wherever I was. Whatever came our way, we would always face it together, because he knew. He knew I couldn't take my eyes off him, that I dreamed of him, lived and breathed for him, just as he did for me. He was my heart and soul. His neatness, fussiness, and pepperoni stealing were a part of me, just as my foibles, messiness, and paint-covered boots were of him.

The last of my ideologies had been crossed off: **#7 - Like Lizzie Bennett, only the deepest of love will induce me into matrimony. Morally, the same goes for sex, but that's flexible.**

Luckily for me, I got the hottest sex, the fiercest love, and would soon have the forever marriage. I was blessed. I was finally enough. And like Teddy said, I was my own heroine, finding my voice, choosing my hero, and throwing my rules to the wind. Day by day, I was writing my very own story, and I knew, in my soul, it would most definitely have a happily ever after.

Acknowledgements

Thank you for reading my debut novel! I hope you loved Finn and Scar as much as I do. I can't wait for you to fall all over again for Evie and Nate in book two.

There are so many people I need to thank, I honestly don't know where to start, but here I go. To the fantastic book team, I have built. To Evyn Evans and Jen Lockwood for your editing prowess. Evyn, you gave me such great structural feedback and really helped shaped my story for the better. And Jen, you made her shine. And me newest team memberm Roxanna, thank you.

Now to the smooshy feels.

The foremost person I can think of is my dad, who always called me Bindi. Tears have begun falling as I write this, but I will soldier on. Dad, your humor, your imagination, and your heart are carried within me daily and have undoubtedly influenced the stories and characters I write. I miss you so much it hurts, but I am grateful for every day I had with you. None of us is perfect. You indeed weren't, but I love you with all my heart.

Mum, I don't even know if you'll read this. I know things are different between us now, and that's mostly on me. But I will always be amazed at the life you built for us and the strength you displayed to your four little girls. And I know you did the best you could. I love you.

I am blessed to have three sisters who are different but some-how the same. Thank you, girls, for always being there. I love you. And to my In-laws, the Dutchies, thank you for taking me in and making me part of your family. I know what I am. I know it's not easy. But you guys are incredible and always have our backs. Thank you.

To Mark and my girls, Molly, and Emma. Oh, and Charlie and Penny. My love for you cannot be expressed in words. You amaze, vex, inspire, wound, rescue, and love me. I adore you. Thank you for choosing me. And especially to my Markie, we have been through so much, but we are still here. Still together. I love you.

Now, on to trouble. As I write this, I realize how many amazing women are in my life.

I am not an easy person to be mates with. I am terrible at keeping in touch. I forget birthdays, middle names, and special occasions. But for a long time now, there has been a group of women around me when I needed them. Annette, Tori, Carolyn, Kelly. I love you guys and hope you know how much you mean to me.

To my OL, fanfic and Bookstagram family. I would not have been able to do this without you. I cannot name you all, but you know who you are. We are like a crazy moving puzzle. Each of you is a piece that has contributed something I will be eternally grateful for. Our mutual obsession ignited something in me and started my writing journey. Thank you for the laughs, the tears, the fangirling, and the support.

Alissa, my final beta, thank you for your patience, humor, and guidance. I love you so much it's weird.

Finally, Shan and Era. I still remember the VM. I still have it saved. I would never have done this if it weren't for you. Thank you for the original beta work, and for believing in me. I've never known anything like it. You have given me so much. Thank you for it all. I love you.

Writing this book has been one of the biggest challenges in my life. Finding the words had not been the problem. For me, they are the easy part. The mental side of things is the killer. The fear, the doubt. The imposter syndrome. The- omg, people will know I read about SEX. It has been crippling at times, and the people I mention below have all contributed to my being able to push through. I had a later in-life diagnosis of a form of dyslexia which added another layer of difficulty to my writing.

It's frustrating having the words in my mind and not being able to express them how I want. I do get here eventually, but it takes a LOT of time. I always enjoyed storytelling/writing but struggled with it at school as I lacked the support. I thought I was dumb and still carry those scars today. But writing this 130k-word beast has shown me what I can accomplish when I set my mind to something and have the right people around me. I hope that with time, I can learn to let those old beliefs go and let my confidence grow.

My final words go to anyone living with mental health issues, including me. You are so much more than your anxiety, your ED, your depression, your OCD, ADHD, and Bipolar. You can accomplish so much. Do not believe the prick that stalks your thoughts.

You are not a burden.

You are someone's light.

You are safe.

You are whole.

You are loved.

You are enough.

My final words go to anyone living with mental health issues, including me. You are so much more than your anxiety, your ED, your depression, your OCD, ADHD, and Bipolar. You can accomplish so much. Do not believe the prick that stalks your thoughts.

You are not a burden.

You are someone's light.

You are safe.

You are whole.

You are loved.

You are enough.

Before You Go!

Be sure to check out the rest of Bindi's works.

Now Available

Secrets in Love – Evie Austen & Nate Myers. Book 2 in the West Village series.
Lost in Love – Teddy Digby & Asher Kim. Book 3 in the West Village series.

Kisses Cuddles Christmas and You – A Christmas novella.

Coming August 2024
Trouble in Love – Polly Hart & Luca D'Cruz. Book 4 in the West Village series.

And, coming late 2024
The Green Line – A two book college hockey series set in Boston.

About the author

Bindi Kennedy lives in Melbourne, Australia with her husband, two eternally embarrassed daughters, and the true loves of her life, her fur babies. She loves potatoes, hates balloons, and has an unhealthy obsession with Scottish Highlanders in kilts.

When she's not adding a heartfelt twist to her fun, flirty and spicy romcoms, Bindi can be found reading romance, or listening to Taylor Swift...probably while crying..

Contacts.

Stay up to date with Bindi's work.
Instagram @bindikennedyauthor
TikTok @bindikauthor
Facebook @bindikauthor
bindikennedy.com

Printed in Great Britain
by Amazon

43391197R00239